THE OPS ROOM GIRLS

It is 1939 and working-class Evie Bishop has received a scholarship to study mathematics at Oxford when tragedy turns her life upside down. She must seek a new future for herself; inspired to contribute to the war effort, she joins the Women's Auxiliary Air Force as an Ops Room plotter.

Posted to a fighter station on the Sussex coast, Evie befriends two other WAAFs — shy, awkward May and flirty, glamorous Jess. Faced with earning the approval of strict officers and finding their way in a male-dominated world, the three girls band together to overcome challenges, navigate new romances and keep their pilots safe in the skies.

But the German bombers seem to know more than they should about the base's operations, and soon Evie, May and Jess are caught up in a world more dangerous than they ever imagined . . .

VICKI BEEBY

THE OPS ROOM GIRLS

Complete and Unabridged

MAGNA
Leicester

First published in Great Britain in 2020

First Ulverscroft Edition
published 2023

A catalogue record for this book is available
from the British Library.

ISBN 978–0–7505–5054–3

Published by
Ulverscroft Limited
Anstey, Leicestershire

Printed and bound in Great Britain by
TJ Books Ltd., Padstow, Cornwall

This book is printed on acid-free paper

To my mum, the original Cowley girl.

1

Oxford, December 1939

Evie Bishop glanced at the clock above the stock room door for what must have been the hundredth time. Half past four. She had never known time to move so slowly. She lowered her gaze to the Dorothy L. Sayers mystery propped on her knees but couldn't force her jittery mind to focus on the words. Discarding it, she went to rearrange the tinned vegetables on the high shelves behind the shop counter, carefully turning each one so the label faced outwards. What seemed like an age later, another look at the clock showed her only five minutes had passed. It felt like she would never reach the end of her shift and finally be able to visit her mentor, Cornelia Gould, to learn her fate.

The bell above the door jangled. She turned, and her heart gave a lurch of shock when she saw who had walked in: Julia Harris. Julia — tall, elegant, swathed in furs — strode up to the counter and looked down her aquiline nose at Evie. 'My word, it's Evie Bishop.' Julia's voice had the same drawling, bored tone that had tormented Evie throughout her days at Oxford High School. 'I thought you were set for a glittering career at Somerville.'

Evie opened her mouth then shut it again. It was pointless explaining to a spoilt girl like Julia that being offered a place at a prestigious Oxford college was one thing, being able to afford to go was quite

1

another. Her insides squirmed. Her visit to Cornelia Gould could change all that. For Cornelia would tell her if she had won the scholarship that would allow her to take her place. It had been her shining goal for years. Years when she'd worked into the night solving equations by dim lamplight and spent every weekend reading physics and Latin texts in between serving customers at Henderson's. The one thing that had kept her going was the hope of studying for a maths degree at Oxford.

Julia, unconcerned by Evie's silence, continued with her taunts. 'Fancy seeing the teachers' pet end up a grocer's assistant. Just goes to show — breeding will out.'

That's rich, coming from a girl who would never have got into Oxford High if her father hadn't paid for her place. Evie, painfully aware that Mr Henderson, working in the stock room next door, would be able to hear every word, bit back the tart retort and forced a smile. 'What a surprise to see you here, Ju —' She caught the narrowing of Julia's eyes and hastily amended the name. 'Miss Harris. You don't usually shop at Henderson's.'

'I should think not. We'd never buy our groceries from Cowley.' The way she pronounced the name made it synonymous with *pigsty.*

Evie fought to keep the smile from fading. For a brief moment she was the poor scholarship girl at her grammar school again, blinking back the tears as Julia sneered: 'We don't want to sit with her. Who knows what we might catch?' It was only the beacon-like hope of her place at Somerville that enabled Evie to keep her chin up. 'How can I help you?'

'Well, I just happened to be passing, when I remembered I'm running out of soap.'

Just passing? Likely story. Evie turned to the shelves to inspect the depleted stock of scented soap. 'We have Palmolive at four pence.'

'I'll take a dozen.'

Evie was tempted to hurl the lot into Julia's face. So that was her game — stockpiling goods rumoured to be rationed before long. No doubt Julia had paid similar visits to shops all around Oxford. Others may suffer deprivation as the war shortages bit, but not the likes of Julia Harris. Evie gritted her teeth as she wrapped the soap in brown paper then rang up the amount on the till. 'Four shillings, please.'

Julia drew a leather purse from her handbag and counted out the coins, handing over enough money to feed Evie's family for a week. Then she looked Evie up and down with a contemptuous curl of her lip. Evie burned with mortification, painfully aware of her hand-me-down clothes and every darned hole and patch. Before Evie knew what she was about, Julia pulled an extra sixpence from her purse and pressed it into Evie's hand. 'A little something for your trouble.' Then, with a toss of her perfectly waved blonde hair, she left.

Evie shoved the four shillings in the till and slammed the drawer shut with a force that made the tins rattle on their shelves. She clenched her fist around the sixpence until it dug painfully into her palm. She wished she could afford to fling it after Julia, but, if added to the amount she already had saved, it would be enough to buy the book on vector geometry she'd seen in a second-hand bookshop last week. It was one of the required texts for her degree course. Her stomach gave another twinge of anticipation. If she had won the scholarship, she would reward herself with it.

She tucked the coin into her pocket then hesitated. Last night, she had been woken several times by her father's hacking coughs reverberating through the thin walls. Stan Bishop had never fully recovered from the mustard gas attack that had ended his active service in the Great War, and the sudden cold snap had made him worse than ever. The money would buy cough mixture. For a moment she fought an inward battle but really, there was no choice. She'd visit the chemist on the way to Cornelia's.

The stockroom door opened, and Mr Henderson emerged, holding a couple of battered tin cans. He paused in the doorway, shuffling his feet. From the look of pure pity he shot her, Evie was certain he'd heard every one of Julia's poisonous words. 'Don't pay any attention to Miss High-and-Mighty there,' he said. 'You're worth a thousand of her.'

Some of the tension eased from Evie's shoulders. 'Thanks, Mr Henderson.'

'Look, I'll manage alone for the rest of the afternoon. You can leave early for a change.' Mr Henderson glanced down at the cans in his hands as though he'd forgotten he was holding them. 'The keys fell off these tins of corned beef. I can't sell them, and my wife can't stand the stuff. You might as well take them.' Damage to Mr Henderson's stock was a regular occurrence, especially at times when Stan Bishop was too sick to work.

Twenty minutes later, Evie raced up Hollow Way on her bike, the bottle of cough syrup rattling against the corned beef tins in her basket. The icy air blasting against her face dispersed the last of her anger, leaving just one thought hammering at her consciousness: had she won the scholarship? If she had, she could

4

forget about all the humiliations Julia and her ilk had piled upon her over the years. It would all have been worth it. She allowed her thoughts to drift to what life might be like at Somerville. She saw visions of herself strolling through Oxford in a scholar's gown, laughing and talking with a group of friends. More images flooded her mind: a library full of books she could freely choose from; sitting in a sunny quad, studying with other young women. Funny how friendship featured in her dreams as much as study, but Julia had seen to it that Evie's school years had been friendless, and she'd felt the lack keenly.

Trying not to dwell on her loneliness, she turned her thoughts to what she could do if she got her maths degree. Be like Cornelia, maybe, and follow an academic career. If she got work at Oxford, she'd be able to take care of her parents, make up for all the sacrifices they had made to allow her to stay on at school past the age of fourteen. She would even be able to take them on holidays by the sea. Her mother had often spoken wistfully of how good the sea air would be for Stan. Their wish for his recovery was the one thing they agreed upon.

Evie tightened her grip on the handlebars. Her mother had made her feelings plain ever since Evie had passed her Higher School Certificate with Distinction last summer, and Evie knew the arguments off by heart. *With your head for numbers you could get a good job in a bank, especially now the young men are getting called up.* This was usually followed by: *You're a Cowley girl, Evie, and Cowley girls don't go to university. I rue the day Miss Gould took an interest in you, filling your head with nonsense.* And the knockout blow: *Your father and I made huge sacrifices to keep*

5

you in school. It's time you paid your way. In vain had she argued that an Oxford degree would set her up for a far better career, that she would be able to support her parents if only they could wait a few more years. In her heart she knew it wasn't the money that bothered Dora but the feeling that in mixing with men and women from a higher class, Evie would be doomed to rejection and disappointment. She acted like it was 1840 instead of nearly 1940 and refused to accept that in this day and age a good education would help Evie break through the class barrier. Her father had supported her, though, encouraged her to follow her dreams. 'God knows we had dreams of our own, Dora,' he would say. 'Let's not be the ones to destroy Evie's.'

But what if she hadn't got the scholarship? Evie tried to shut out the thought as she sped through the dim twilight, the frost nipping her gloveless fingers. She turned right into Barracks Lane and the rows of terraced houses gave way to fields. Without it she couldn't afford to take her place at Somerville. All her sacrifices — all her parents' sacrifices — would be for nothing. She had a horrible vision of sitting in a dreary office, surrounded by ranks of other women, heads bowed over soulless, repetitive tasks. Suddenly she didn't want to see Cornelia, didn't want to learn her dream had died, but already the silhouette of Magdalen Tower loomed ahead. Magdalen Bridge then the High Street passed in a blur, and before she could work out how to slow time, she was outside Cornelia's house on Charles Street. She propped her bike against the wall and walked to the back door on trembling legs.

The cook opened the door, enveloping Evie with

6

the aroma of baking bread. 'Miss Gould says you're to go straight to the library.'

Evie's throat was so tight she couldn't force out any words of greeting. Instead she gave the cook a tremulous smile and walked through the passageway, her footsteps clicking on the polished wood floor in time with the tick-tock of the grandfather clock beside the front door. She rapped on the library door and walked in.

It was Evie's ambition to possess a room exactly like this one day. Bookshelves bulging with leather-bound books lined the room from floor to ceiling. Blackout curtains covered the large window, but the bright lamps and glow from the blazing fire gave the room a cheerful feeling. As always, Evie was struck by the mingled scent of beeswax and lily of the valley. Cornelia Gould sat behind a gleaming walnut desk, peering through her wire-rimmed spectacles at a book. A few tendrils of steel-grey hair had escaped from her bun, softening her sharp features.

The moment Evie stepped through the door, her mentor sprang to her feet, her face creasing in a broad smile. 'Oh, my dear. I'm so thrilled for you.'

Evie could hardly hear Cornelia through the pounding in her ears, but then her brain registered the words she'd been longing to hear ever since the elderly lady had offered to help her study for the Oxford entrance exam. 'You've got the scholarship.'

Evie could hardly take it in. 'Are you sure?'

Cornelia nodded, her blue eyes bright. 'Absolutely. I had the news from the Dean herself. They were most impressed with your application. You'll get the official letter and forms to complete in a few days, but that's just a formality.'

Evie felt light-headed and breathless. 'I can't believe it's actually happening.'

'Believe it, my dear. You've earned this. I knew from the first moment I saw you, poring over a maths book when your mother came to clean my house, that you had the ability to go far.'

Evie bathed in the encouragement she never got from her mother. Images flooded her mind of herself walking purposefully over Magdalen Bridge, a book of advanced mathematics under her arm, her scholar's gown fluttering in her wake. 'Thank you.' She gave a half gasp as tears sprang to her eyes. Her next words were forced out between sobs of joy. 'Thank you! I could never have done it without you.' She gave Cornelia a smile that was so wide she thought her cheeks might split. 'I'm going to be a Somerville bluestocking!'

* * *

Her smile remained glued to her face throughout her shift the next day. After she'd shut the door on the last customer and switched the sign to 'Closed', she picked up a duster and vigorously polished the shelves, humming *Ding Dong Merrily on High*. She was standing on a stool, stretching to reach around the tins of bicarbonate of soda on the top shelf, when the telephone shrilled in the stock room. The ringing stopped, followed by the gruff rumble of Mr Henderson's voice. She couldn't hear the words, but something about his tone burst the bubble of her happiness. She paused and stepped down from the stool, straining to hear.

She heard the clatter of the receiver being replaced and the heavy tread of Mr Henderson's footsteps.

Evie hastily resumed her dusting.

'You're needed at home,' Mr Henderson said.

Evie looked up, startled, to see Mr Henderson leaning in the doorway, a look of sorrow in his eyes.

Her mouth went dry. 'What's happened?' But she already knew the answer.

'It's your father. He's been taken ill.'

★ ★ ★

Evie dropped her bicycle down in the front yard and dashed through the door. The house was in darkness and so cold the back room fire must be out. She knocked her knee against the bannister as she groped for the hall light switch.

'Mum? Dad?' she called, rubbing her throbbing knee.

A murmur of voices drifted from upstairs, and Evie would have gone up, but the kitchen door swung open, silhouetting a stout, squat figure against the sudden light.

'Evie, dear, is that you?'

Evie's seeking hand finally found the light switch and she turned it on to see their neighbour, Mrs Wilkins, in the doorway.

'Oh, Evie, thank goodness. Your mother asked me to wait here for you.'

Evie clung to Mrs Wilkins' hand. 'How is he?'

Mrs Wilkins shook her head, her jowls wobbling. 'He was sweating and coughing fit to burst when I saw him. Looks like pneumonia to me.'

Evie made to climb the stairs, but Mrs Wilkins held her back. 'The doctor's with him. Wait until he's finished.'

They retreated to the tiny kitchen. Evie, straining to hear what was happening upstairs, hardly took in what Mrs Wilkins was saying. Mrs Wilkins made her a cup of tea, and Evie gulped it down, wincing as it scalded the back of her throat.

'How did he get home?' She had to say something just to pass the time before the doctor finished.

'Foreman brought him. Would have taken him to the hospital, but your father refused point blank. You know what he's like.'

Evie nodded and took another sip. Then came the creak and groan of floorboards above her head and the heavy thud of feet upon the stairs. She clattered her cup and saucer upon the counter, slopping tea in the saucer in her hurry, and flung open the kitchen door in time to see Dr Beale on his way to the door.

'I'm sorry.' Dr Beale looked at Evie with compassion. 'There's nothing more I can do. It's just a matter of time.'

2

'No!' Evie pushed past the doctor and ran up the stairs. When she reached the front bedroom, she put her hand to the doorknob, but suddenly hesitated, afraid of the deathly silence within.

Then she heard her father break into a fit of coughing and she pushed open the door.

Her mother was there, bending over the bed, murmuring soothing words to ease her father through the paroxysm. When Evie trod on the loose floorboard just inside the door, her mother spun around, her mouth working.

'You,' she spat. 'I hope you're satisfied. He wouldn't be in this state if he hadn't felt the need to work day and night to fund your schooling.'

Stan's coughing eased, and he drew a gasping breath. Evie's mother immediately bent over the bed. Evie, her heart in her mouth, stepped closer.

It was as though she saw her father's true appearance for the first time. Yellowing skin stretched over jutting cheekbones and jaw. A sheen of perspiration glistened on her father's brow, and the hollows beneath his eyes and cheeks were shaded with an ominous grey blue.

'Oh, Dad,' she whispered.

Her mother turned on her, mouth a thin, quivering line, but Stan reached up and grasped her hand.

'Leave us, Dora. I —' He broke off for another fit of coughing. 'Go on, love,' he whispered when he

11

regained his breath. 'I'm dying for a cuppa.'

Dying. Tears pricked at Evie's eyelids. Dora also flinched and their gazes locked, united in a moment of pain.

Then Dora straightened. 'Don't you dare tire him out.' She stalked from the room.

Stan groped for his daughter's hand. Evie caught it, fresh tears spilling down her cheeks at the feeble grip. Her father had always been her strength. His steadfast belief in her had been her mainstay. Had kept her going at those times when the rest of the world had seemed against a girl from Cowley ever making it as an Oxford scholar.

'Promise me you won't give up, my girl.' Stan's voice was thready but held the same conviction it always had when he spoke of his hopes for his daughter's future.

'Please, Dad. Don't tire yourself.' Her throat ached, making it difficult to force any words out.

The grip tightened briefly. 'I mean it. Promise!'

Evie sniffed, wiping away tears with her free hand. 'That doesn't matter now. Just concentrate on getting better.'

'No!' Even though his voice was scarcely more than a breath, the fierceness made Evie's own breath catch in her throat. 'You've worked so hard.' He held her gaze, and Evie couldn't have looked away even had she wanted to. Her father's strength was fading from one heartbeat to the next, but what little reserves he had left he used to imbue his words with authority. 'Don't let the sacrifices be for nothing.'

She choked. 'I . . . I won't.'

Stan's grip relaxed, and he closed his eyes. For a moment, Evie thought he'd drifted into sleep. But

12

then his eyes opened, and the death mask cracked into a smile. The sun seemed to flood the room, and her father was back with her. 'My girl. I'm so proud of you, Evie.'

Evie swallowed back the lump in her throat. Her father's face sparkled and blurred through her tears, but she forced a smile. 'I'll do you proud, Dad. I'll do it for you.'

Stan's eyes fluttered closed, his features relaxed in a smile. By the time her mother nudged open the door, a cup and saucer in one hand, he was asleep. Dora set the teacup down upon the dressing table, then she smoothed the candlewick bedspread. Evie glanced at her face and was shocked to see her mouth drawn tight as though in pain, her chin trembling.

She rose and gripped Dora's hand, ushering her into the chair she'd just vacated. 'Sit here, Mum.' She had to swallow against the tightness in her throat. 'I can fetch another chair.'

Throughout the long night that followed, Stan didn't once open his eyes. Evie and Dora sat beside the bed, hardly daring to move, listening to each laboured breath. As the hours wore on, his breathing became gradually shallower, the pause between inhalations increasing.

Evie clung to his hand, as though she could will her life force and warmth through the connection. *Stay with us, Dad. Please don't go.* But she knew in her heart he was fading. All her senses were focused on Stan, watching for each rise and fall of his chest, listening for the rasp as he dragged more air into his lungs, jumping each time his fingers twitched in hers. Even though her eyes were heavy and gritty from lack of sleep, she didn't dare tear away her gaze. Outside, the wind rattled at the windows and its shrill banshee wail tore down the chimney.

Finally, about an hour before dawn, Stan gave a long, slow, rattling exhalation. Evie waited a long time for his next breath, but it never came.

* * *

'Goodbye, Evie dear.' Mrs Wilkins, always the last to leave any gathering, stood beside the front door and smiled as Evie helped her on with her coat. 'Do let me know if there's anything I can do for you or your mother.' She paused. 'I suppose you've given up with that whole Somerville business now.'

Evie, her throat aching from the effort of holding back the tears all morning, forced a smile. 'Oh no. I'll still be going to Somerville in the autumn. But I'll pass your kind message on to my mother.'

Mrs Wilkins said nothing but pursed her mouth in obvious disapproval. Then she stepped over the threshold and waddled down the path, turning up her collar against the damp air.

Evie shut the door and sagged against it, relieved that the last guest had finally left. She allowed herself ten precious seconds of quiet before returning to the front room to help her mother clear up. It was the morning after New Year's Day, the day of Stan's funeral. Dora had insisted upon inviting the mourners to the house after the dismal service at the cemetery under skies as grey and heavy as Evie's heart. The neighbours had all brought plates of sandwiches and cakes to supplement the food Evie and Dora had provided. Evie had been touched at their generosity at a time when people were stocking their larders in preparation for the

14

introduction of rationing in just six days.

In honour of the occasion they had used the best room in the house, but it felt wrong to Evie to commemorate her father in here. He had never liked the front room, complaining it had a soulless feel, and Evie had to agree. There was no denying Dora took great care of its appearance: lace antimacassars draped the back and arms of the sofa and armchair with mathematical precision; the convex mirror hanging from the picture rail gleamed from regular polishing; a vase filled with dried pink rosebuds, matching those on the wallpaper, stood in the precise centre of the console table beneath the window. Maybe it was the sterile cleanliness or maybe it was the slight mustiness in the air, the inevitable result of leaving the room unused most of the time, but Evie always felt uncomfortable in here. She preferred to think of her father in the cheerful, if scruffy, back room.

'If you think you're swanning off to college when I need you here, you've got another think coming.' Dora Bishop turned on Evie almost as soon as she entered the room.

Evie swallowed, her throat raw from days of weeping. Not this argument again, today of all days. 'But Mum, I promised Dad —'

'Well, he's not here, is he.' Dora picked up the empty plates that were scattered around the front room, weaving around the dining chairs that had been brought in from the back room to supplement the seating. She stacked them with swift, jerky movements, the crashing of crockery setting Evie's teeth on edge. 'And now I'm all alone, you want to go off and leave me.' Her voice wobbled, and Evie's heart twisted.

15

Several times in the ten days since her father's death, Evie had considered giving up her dream of a degree to look after Dora. However, each time the thought crossed her mind she was back beside her father's death bed, and she could hear the urgency in his voice despite the struggle to speak. *'Promise me you won't give up, my girl.'* The memory always strengthened her resolve.

'But it's not until October. Surely by then—?'

'No. It's time you did your bit. I'll admit it was a good idea to get your Higher Certificate. You can get yourself a good job with that — with all the men joining up, the banks are crying out for educated girls to fill the vacancies. I've spent years working my fingers to the bone to put you through the High. It's time you paid your way.'

Dora seemed to imply Evie hadn't lifted a finger to help, but she'd taken the job at Henderson's and several tutoring jobs to help support her parents, taking an extra year after leaving school so she could start to repay them for everything they'd given up. It hadn't been easy finding the time for her own studies. Evie counted to ten before answering, doing her best to keep the irritation out of her voice. 'I could get a much better job with a degree. And it's not as if I'll be far away.' Evie was grateful her father had made her promise to go. It would have been hard to hold out against her mother otherwise. She felt guilty enough as it was, but she wouldn't be leaving for months. Surely her mother would have had a change of heart by then. And Mrs Wilkins was a good neighbour. With Evie coming home every weekend, her mother would be well looked after. No. When the official letter came through from Somerville, she'd accept the scholarship without a qualm.

The letter. She paused in the act of stacking plates. Come to think of it, she would have expected to have heard from Somerville by now. It had been almost two weeks.

Drawing a shaky breath, she went to the kitchen. There was a pile of letters on the shelf just inside the door. Her scholarship offer must be buried underneath all the messages of condolence from friends and family. She put the plates in the sink, wiped her hands on her apron and turned to the papers. To her dismay, Dora followed. She couldn't deal with this now.

'Mum, please, let's talk about this tomorrow.' She shuffled through the correspondence: handwritten letters from uncles, aunts, cousins, neighbours and colleagues. All brief, given the increasing paper shortage, but heartfelt, nonetheless. She shuffled through the stack three times, sure she must have missed it, but there was no typed letter. Nothing bearing the Somerville crest. 'Have you seen a letter from Somerville?'

Dora shot her a sidelong glance, then picked up a tea towel and used it to pick up the kettle from the stove. She poured hot water into the sink, sending steam billowing into the cramped kitchen. She seemed to take a painfully long time to empty the water out of the kettle.

'I've already told you you're not going to Somerville.' Dora stuck out her chin, but she wouldn't meet Evie's gaze.

A cold trickle of unease ran down Evie's spine. But no. The emotion of the day was playing havoc with her imagination. 'I promise we'll talk about it properly

17

later, Mum. I won't leave you in the lurch. It's just —'
Her voice wobbled as she caught sight of her father's
coffee mug standing upon the draining board, sparkling clean, the only unused cup in the house. Her
next words, forced through her tight throat, came out
in a husky whisper. 'Not today. Please.'

'There's nothing to discuss.' Dora's voice held an
odd tone of defiance and triumph that set alarm bells
ringing in Evie's head.

She licked dry lips. 'What do you mean, Mum?
What have you done?'

A long silence filled the kitchen, broken only by the
drip of the tap. Then: 'The letter came the day after
your father died. I answered it in your name. I turned
down the scholarship.'

★ ★ ★

Evie felt nothing. No anger, no surprise, just leaden
numbness. It was as though she'd known something
like this would happen. Suddenly she couldn't face
her mother. She had to get out, away from this suf-
focating kitchen, out of the house. She stumbled into
the hall, grabbed her coat and strode outside, slam-
ming the door behind her so hard, the door knocker
rattled. For some time, she walked without paying
attention to where she was going, blinking away the
drizzle that stung her eyes. Then she saw she was on
the Cowley Road. A bus heading into Oxford pulled
into a bus stop a few paces away.

An idea struck, and she hurried to climb aboard.
She would go to Cornelia, explain what had happened and ask her to intervene. Cornelia would sort
everything out.

She got off the bus on the High Street and strode towards Charles Street. But with each step her feet grew heavier as bitter certainty overtook her. Her mother had turned the scholarship down over a week ago. Another girl would have been offered the scholarship by now. Another girl who had dreamed of being an Oxford scholar for years. Cornelia would be powerless to do anything. Besides, it wasn't fair to ask her to take on Evie's problems. Evie was used to solving her own problems.

She wandered aimlessly, scarcely noticing where she was going, aware only of the rain beading on her eyelashes, blurring her vision, and a heavy ache in her chest. The last thing she'd said to her father was a promise not to give up her dream of Somerville. How dare her mother dash all of Evie's hopes, force her to break her promise?

It was as though the icy shell that had formed around her heart ever since her father's death suddenly cracked, letting in all the feelings she'd been shielded from. A sob of rage burst from her, causing several passers-by to turn curious gazes upon her. She hastily dived into an empty side road, away from the bustle of the main thoroughfares. Golden sandstone walls towered above the cobbled lane on both sides, shutting out the world. The hum of voices, the tap and scrape of many feet upon the gritty pavements and the chiming of bicycle bells faded the farther she walked. She drew several deep breaths, forcing herself to calm down and think. There had to be a solution, some way she could fund her degree. She still had a place at Somerville, after all; it was just the scholarship Dora had turned down. Maybe she could defer her place and apply for a scholarship again next year?

Yet everything in her rebelled at spending another year working in Henderson's or shuffling paper in a bank when she wanted to be learning new things.

She reached the end of the narrow lane and found herself on busy Broad Street, near the Clarendon Building. The imposing Palladian-style building had been taken over as a recruitment office after the outbreak of war, and now Evie found herself gazing at posters of men and women in uniform, all doing their part to fight the Nazi threat. Her eyes fell on a poster for the Women's Auxiliary Air Force. It showed a young woman in air force blue, gazing keenly into the distance. There was an air of purpose about her, determination. She wasn't whiling away her time in a job her heart wasn't in. She was using her God-given talents in the service of her country and she wouldn't let anyone hold her back.

For a wild moment, Evie was struck by the urge to volunteer as a WAAF and leave her disappointment and dreams behind. What with her studies and her father's illness and death, she hadn't paid a great deal of attention to the progress of the war; beyond the blackout and the fuss surrounding the introduction of rationing, it hadn't affected her personally. Even so, she'd been aware of the rumours that Hitler intended to invade France and the Low Countries in the spring. If she couldn't go to Somerville, perhaps the WAAF would provide the purpose and comradeship she craved.

She hesitated. Why not go in? It wouldn't do any harm to at least find out more.

Her limbs trembling, she approached the building. She'd just climbed the first stone step to the porticoed entrance when an image of her mother, bowed with grief, came to mind. She stopped and leaned against a column, feeling the scrape of the chilly sandstone beneath her fingernails. It was one thing to move to Somerville, less than four miles from home, but it was quite another to join the WAAF and have no say over where she was sent. For all she knew she could end up in the Hebrides. Angry as she was, could she really do that to her mother? She closed her eyes, willing herself to think rationally and decide upon a course of action.

Her stomach rumbled. A glance at her watch gave her a shock when she saw it was five past three. No wonder she was hungry — she hadn't eaten a thing all day, having been unable to force a morsel past her lips either before the funeral or during the reception afterwards. She could almost hear Cornelia Gould telling her sternly not to make hasty decisions upon an empty stomach. She drew her purse from her pocket and counted her money; she had just enough for a bowl of soup and still leave change for the bus fare home. She trudged back down the steps and headed down Broad Street towards her favourite café. Maybe she'd be able to think straight once she got some food inside her.

She never made it to the café. As she drew level with the entrance to Boswells, the department store doors opened, and three young women strode out surrounded by a cloud of perfume. At the centre of the trio, tall, confident, dressed in furs, was none other than Julia Harris. Evie's stomach gave an unpleasant lurch, and she turned abruptly, desperately trying to keep out of sight behind a group of elderly women sheltering beneath umbrellas. But ill fortune made Julia glance up before she reached safety.

21

'Why, if it isn't Evie Bishop.' Julia's sneering voice rang out above the babble of voices in the street. 'You remember Evie, girls. Would you believe the teachers' pet is now nothing more than a common shop girl?'

The three girls giggled, and it was just like being back at school, Julia and her cronies circling like a pack of hyenas. Evie felt her face burn, and something inside her snapped. Scarcely knowing what possessed her, she found herself marching towards her tormentor, fists balled at her sides. Julia gave a little yelp and took a hasty step back, as though fearing Evie would hit her. Evie saw Julia's immaculately made-up face through a red mist. She took another step forward, backing Julia against the stone pillar beside the shop doorway. Julia's friends sidled away, looking alarmed.

'There's nothing wrong with earning a living,' she spat. 'It beats living off your daddy.' She felt as though she was standing outside herself, watching someone else. She could no more control the words pouring from her mouth than stop the drizzle falling from the leaden clouds. 'Anyway, I'm not a shop girl any more — I've joined the WAAF. I'm going to do something useful with my life. Something I can be proud of. Not like you, who has nothing better to do with her time than stockpile soap.'

Her final salvo fired, she marched back up Broad Street, without so much as a glance over her shoulder. In a daze, she went straight up the steps of the Clarendon Building and into the recruitment office. As luck would have it, there was no queue, and she found herself sitting in front of the recruiting sergeant before the mist had fully cleared from her head. 'I want to join the WAAF,' she said.

'Can you drive or cook?' the sergeant asked. He

barely glanced at Evie but studied the paper on the desk in front of him, pen poised.

'I can't drive,' Evie replied.

'Cook, then.' The man went to write a note on the form.

Evie felt like she'd swallowed a lead weight. The last of the haze dissolved. What was she doing? She'd rather work in a bank than spend the duration cooking. It was only the thought of bumping into Julia Harris again and having to explain that she hadn't joined the WAAF after all that made her keep going. 'I can't really cook, either. Well, nothing more than eggs and toast,' she stammered when the man glared at her. 'I mean, I'm better at maths.'

The man looked at her in sudden interest. 'How good?'

'I won a scholarship to Somerville to read mathematics.' Suddenly her brain clicked back into gear, and she could see her way forward. By signing up to the armed forces, she could defer her place at Somerville until the end of the war. In the meantime, she could put money aside from her pay to fund her degree if she wasn't able to get a scholarship.

The man looked impressed. 'In that case, I'll put you down for clerk, special duties.'

And that was that. Before she knew it, she'd given her details to the sergeant and she was told to await her calling-up papers by post. She had no idea what 'clerk, special duties' meant, but it was too late to ask now. Anyway, it had to be better than cooking.

She left the Clarendon building on shaky legs. She was joining the WAAF. There was no going back, and nothing her mother could do to stop her.

23

3

'Excuse me, is there room for me in this carriage?'

Evie glanced up at the tall, gangly girl in the door-way, clutching a long, white canvas bag. Then she looked around the empty compartment. She smiled back at the girl. 'It'll be a squash, but I'm sure we can make room.'

The girl blushed. 'Oh, thank you. I mean, I can see it's empty, but I didn't know if —'

Evie's heart went out to her. 'I'm sorry. It was a feeble joke. Do sit down.'

The girl took off her coat and put it with her bag on the overhead rack; she was so tall she had no trouble reaching that high, unlike Evie, who had been forced to stand on tiptoe. It suddenly struck Evie that her bag looked remarkably similar to her own kit bag.

'Are you a WAAF?' she asked.

The girl's face lit up. 'Yes. I'm on my way to my first posting.' She had an accent Evie couldn't place, placing heavy emphasis of the 'ing' of 'posting'.

'Me too!' Evie held out her hand. 'I'm Evie. I mean, Aircraftwoman Bishop, second class. On my way to RAF Amberton in Sussex.'

The girl gave a delighted squeak. 'The same as me!' Her smile transformed her face and now she didn't look so plain. She clutched Evie's hand and shook it enthusiastically. 'I'm May Lidford. Oh, I was so worried about going to my first posting all alone. I am glad I've met you.'

Relief washed over Evie. 'That's wonderful. I'll be glad of the company.' She'd had a hectic early-morning train journey from Leighton Buzzard to London, in a train packed with servicemen, followed by a bewildering series of bus journeys across the city to Victoria Station, worrying all the while that she would miss her train. It was good to know she didn't have to face the rest of the journey alone. 'Where did you do your training?'

'West Drayton to start with — I was there at the beginning of February.'

'Me too! But I was there in March, then clerk S.D. training at Leighton Buzzard.' Evie still felt a thrill at the sense of excitement she'd had when she'd had to sign the Official Secrets Act before starting her training as an Operations Room plotter, which was one of the roles that came under the heading of 'clerk, special duties'. It had given her a sense that she was about to become part of something important. 'What did you train as?'

'Driver. I've just finished the course in Liverpool.'

Although Evie wasn't shy, she hadn't made any friends at her initial training in West Drayton or Leighton Buzzard. She'd looked rather longingly at the girls who had naturally formed groups and wondered how they managed to make friends so easily. She hadn't had time to be lonely, though; the instructors had taken them through a rigorous schedule of drills, inspections, classes and assessments that filled their waking hours. Now she was on her way to a long-term posting, she was glad to meet another new girl. Maybe making friends wouldn't be so hard after all.

'I see you didn't get a uniform either.' Evie indicated the plain navy-blue skirt, white blouse and knitted jumper she had left home in. It seemed the authorities had been taken aback by the number of recruits the WAAF had attracted, and there weren't enough uniforms to go round. The only uniform items she'd received were her gas mask, steel helmet, shoes, a kit bag and her identity tags — a red circular disc and a grey lozenge-shaped one, both with her name and service number stamped into them.

'No. In the reception depot, they took one look at me and said they hadn't expected to kit out a giraffe.' May laughed and Evie joined in, glad to see her shy new friend was able to laugh at herself.

Out on the platform, the guard blew his whistle, and the train jolted forward. Evie hastily closed the window to keep out the steam, then leaned forward to look out, as though the airfield in West Sussex would already be in view.

'I've never been to Sussex before,' May said, echoing Evie's thoughts. 'I've never been outside Birmingham. I wonder what it will be like.'

'This is my first time outside Oxford,' Evie replied. 'I just know we won't be far from the sea.'

'It's exciting isn't it?' May's face was alight as she watched the houses of London fly past. 'I mean, I know I should be sorry there's a war on, but I'd never have had the chance to leave Birmingham if I hadn't joined up.'

'What did you do before you joined?'

May's face clouded. 'Stayed home, keeping house for my father and four brothers.' She pressed her lips together and glanced down, fidgeting with the buttons on her dark grey cardigan. One of the buttons was dark blue instead of black like the others, and when May moved her arm, Evie could see the left elbow had been darned.

Evie's heart went out to her, knowing all too well how it felt to wear clothes that seemed to have more patches than original cloth. 'I've always wished I had a brother.'

'You wouldn't have wanted mine.'

Evie instantly regretted what was merely meant as a conversational observation. She felt uncomfortable, not knowing if she should ask for more details, or if May would prefer not to talk about it. 'Is that why you joined up — to get away from home?'

May nodded. 'What about you?'

'The same, I suppose.' Evie, too, was reluctant to explain the whole sorry tale to someone she scarcely knew. 'My mother thinks I should be happy with my lot in life,' she said in the end. 'Wanted me to be content with a humdrum job, get married and live a life identical to hers. The WAAF was my only way out.'

'Yes! Freedom from men.' May's mouth set in a stubborn line. 'I'm never going back. After the war I'm going to make a life for myself. Get a job. Move to London.'

After the war. As the train puffed south, Evie watched as the suburbs of London gave way to fields and hedgerows. Spring had arrived in the weeks since she had impulsively joined up, and now the first signs of April greenery tinged the countryside. How many more months and seasons would pass before the war was over? What would happen to her in the meantime?

It was nearly midday when the train arrived in Chichester, the nearest mainline station to Amberton. Evie and May wrestled their bags off the luggage rack and climbed down onto the platform. A young man in RAF uniform with a corporal's stripe on his sleeve stood by the entrance, leaning against the wall, a cigarette in his hand. Guessing he was here to collect them, they hurried up to him and gave their names.

'Hop in,' he replied, indicating the truck parked nearby. 'We've still got one more to collect.'

Evie climbed into the truck after May and looked around for the other person they were here to meet. From her seat she could see the passengers who had alighted leave the station and drift away. Then she heard a great hiss of steam and the chug of the engine as the train pulled away. There didn't seem to be anyone left. The corporal sighed, looked at his watch and dropped his cigarette on the pavement, grinding it beneath his toe. He turned to climb into the truck.

The station door swung open and a glamorous blonde woman in RAF blue strode out, swinging her gas mask case as if it were a Chanel handbag. Her hair was waved in a style more usually seen on a Hollywood actress than a passenger on the Southern Railway. For a moment, unlikely as it seemed, Evie wondered if Ginger Rogers had turned up.

'Get a move on, Halloway,' the corporal barked.

'Sorry I'm late, Corp,' she said, batting her sweeping eyelashes at him. 'Nearly missed the stop.'

'Don't tell me you were chatting up some poor unfortunate young man.' The corporal scowled and swung into his seat.

Halloway flashed him a smile, her teeth sparkling white against scarlet lips. 'Jealous, Corp?'

She climbed in and took her place next to Evie. 'What 'ave we 'ere? New recruits?' She stuck out her hand. 'Jess Halloway. Been here a month already. Stick with me and I'll see you right.'

28

Evie gazed out with interest as the truck left the town and followed winding roads into the countryside. After the busy streets of Cowley and Oxford, the wide open spaces of the South Downs made her feel as though they were on their way to a picnic rather than her first WAAF posting. A pale green haze hung over the hedgerows, and daffodils nodded their heads as the truck sped past. Occasionally they went through a village, some with half-timbered cottages, others a mixture of flint and red brick. Evie was charmed to see many had thatched roofs. These huddled dwellings, often clustered around village greens, were very different from the rows of identical terraces and semi-detached houses she was used to in Cowley, or the imposing, many-spired college buildings of the city centre.

They had just crossed a humpbacked bridge with a bump that nearly flung Evie out of her seat when a roar overhead made her flinch. Two fighter planes blotted out the sun, propellers whirling, so low she cowered down upon the bench, positive they would hit the trees fringing the road and come crashing down upon their heads. The RAF roundels were clear on the underside of the wings. May squeaked and covered her ears, but Jess's only reaction was to smooth her hair once the aircraft had safely flown past.

'Hurricanes,' she announced.

'From Amberton?' Evie gazed after the Hurricanes, which were now disappearing behind a large house in the distance. A thrill rippled down her spine.

Jess nodded. 'We've got three Hurricane squadrons at the moment, but there's a rumour we're getting a

29

new one soon.'

May seemed to have recovered from her shock and was gazing at the point they had last seen the Hurricanes with wide eyes. 'Do you think they've been in combat?'

'Nah. That's all happening over in France. Hurricanes and Spitfires don't have the range. They'll have been on a training flight.' She leaned closer to the other two. She shot a glance at the corporal and lowered her voice. 'There's a new officer just arrived in Ops, though, come from France. They say his squadron was shot to bits. He's got a bit of a sharp tongue, but that doesn't stop half the girls swooning over him. Squadron Leader Kincaith is going to break some hearts, you mark my words.'

Evie's heart sank at the thought of working with a sharp-tongued officer. Not that she had any intention of vying for anyone's affections, no matter how good looking he was. 'I'm being posted to the Operations Room. I hope he's not too bad.'

Jess grinned. 'He's not so bad really. I work in Ops, too, by the way. Go on, don't look so surprised. I can put on a posh speaking voice.' She straightened up her shoulders, stuck out her chin, and recited with perfect diction, 'The rain in Spain falls mainly on the plain. How now, brown cow?'

All of a sudden, Evie wasn't looking at a working-class Cockney girl, but a fragile upper-class English rose who looked as though she spent her days taking tea on the vicarage lawn.

'Gosh, how did you do that?' May asked, gazing at Jess with admiration.

'I was an actress before I joined up. You don't get very far in that profession unless you can talk posh.'

30

'Can you teach me?' May asked. 'They said I showed aptitude for clerk, special duties, but my speaking voice wasn't clear enough.'

'I can try. What are you posted as, then?'

'Driver.'

'Go on! That's the best job. You get to drive pilots.' Jess said 'pilots' like most people would have said 'film stars'. 'When did you learn to drive?'

'My dad's a . . .' May's gaze shifted from Jess's face before meeting her eyes again. 'Well, he's a sort of delivery man. He taught me to drive so I could help out.'

'Of all the luck! You'll be out, driving the top brass while I'm stuck down The Hole, under the nose of Flight Officer Hellerby.' Jess grimaced at Evie. 'It's Ellerby really, but all the girls in Ops call her Hellerby. You'll understand why soon enough.'

Evie's heart sank. 'Is she really awful?'

'I'll say. Only last week she bawled me out in front of everyone for putting the wrong number of fighters on a plot. 'Umiliated, I was. Wasn't my fault, neither. It was that bugger Stanley Nixon who didn't get it right when he rang the number through. But Hellerby always comes down hard on us girls when we make a mistake. Plenty of the men think girls shouldn't be allowed in Ops, and Hellerby 'ates it when we do anything that gives them an excuse to complain.'

While in Leighton Buzzard, Evie had heard that some male officers weren't happy with allowing WAAFs any job that wasn't typing or cooking. 'Are all the men like that? Against women taking over the men's jobs, I mean?'

'Some of them were at first, but most of them have seen we're just as good as the men, if not better. The

31

senior controller, Peter Travis — he's an absolute dear. He's always saying us girls do a better job than the men. You'll like him. You and me together, we'll win round the likes of Hellerby and Kincaith.'

The truck jolted to a stop. Evie had been so absorbed by Jess's information, she'd neglected to look where they were going but now she saw they had stopped in front of a barrier. A man in air force uniform, a rifle slung over his shoulder, hurried out of a hut and, giving the driver a wave, raised the barrier to let them through. Evie's heart sped up. They were here! She looked around with interest as the truck drove through the gateway and passed several red-brick buildings and, further away, a group of Nissen huts. Many of the huts had sandbags stacked around them, and several men were hauling more down from a truck and adding them to the stacks. A large field lay beyond the buildings, with an orange windsock flapping at the far end. Wooden huts were dotted around the edge of the field with fighter aircraft standing nearby. Evie could see men, tiny as ants from this distance, crawling over the wings of some of the aeroplanes or working on the engines.

A thunderous roar split the air behind her. Evie jumped; next to her, May give a startled yelp. Three more Hurricanes swooped so low Evie could swear her hair ruffled when they passed overhead. The vibrations of the engines thrummed deep in her chest. She followed their path as they banked into a steep turn, following the edge of the airfield.

Jess tapped Evie's arm and pointed to a grassy hump in the ground with a descending ramp leading down. There were more sandbags protecting the ramp, and a guard stood at the entrance. 'That's The Hole,' she said, raising her voice over the growl of the

Hurricanes. 'Where you'll be working.'

Evie eyed the dark entrance with trepidation. It looked for all the world like the entrance to an underground tomb.

The truck jerked to a halt outside a red-brick building.

'Come on.' Jess jumped down. 'The pair of you need to report to the Squadron Officer and get your arrival chits signed. I'll show you where to find her. Meet me out here when you're through and I'll show you around.'

Before Evie followed, she couldn't resist watching the Hurricanes as they completed their circuit and glided down to land. She shivered from a mixture of nerves and anticipation. Maybe she wasn't in Somerville College, but this place, and the other airfields like it all over Britain, was where the action was going to be, and she was going to be a part of it.

★ ★ ★

Jess met Evie and May on the steps of the Admin block once they'd reported to the Squadron Officer. She took their arms. 'Come on, I'll show you around. I'll take you to the Waafery first, so you can drop off your kit.' She pointed to a large house which stood just beyond the bounds of the station. Only a high hedge separated it from the airfield. 'There it is. As you can see, we get a grandstand view.'

'Gosh, you could fit about twenty houses the size of my dad's in there,' breathed May.

Evie, too, looked at the house in wonder. Even at this distance, she could see it looked more like a small manor house. 'I'd get lost in a house that size. I

33

thought we'd be sleeping in Nissen huts.'

'It's even better inside. Mind you, it's a tidy step, but a thousand times better than a Nissen hut.'

They hefted their kit bags onto their shoulders and Jess led them back to the station entrance. 'It'd be quicker if we could get to the house from the airfield, but there's no way through the hedge.' Jess glanced at May. 'You'll be all right. Most of the WAAFs get ferried in and out of the Waafery by truck, but those of us in Ops have to fend for ourselves. It's about a twenty-minute walk. I usually cycle, though.'

They turned right out of the gates and strolled down the tree-lined lane that hugged the perimeter of the airfield. Evie could see that although it was a pleasant walk in the sunshine, it would be miserable in the rain or dark. 'I suppose I could send for my bike,' she said. It would mean writing to her mother. Her insides knotted at the memory of Dora's look of shocked pain and betrayal when Evie had returned from Oxford and announced what she'd done. Ever since, Dora had treated her with icy politeness, placing a barrier between them that Evie had been unable to break down.

Not that she'd tried too hard. Even now, thoughts of her mother had her clenching her fists into tight balls. She forced herself to focus on the present, let the birdsong and views of rolling downland wash away the anger. It was pointless dwelling on what couldn't be changed. Pointless, but oh, so easy.

As they turned into a narrower lane, she plucked a random topic of conversation from the air. 'Why did you join up, Jess?' she asked. 'Being an actress sounds so glamorous.'

'Not as glamorous as you might think.' Jess's pretty

face clouded briefly, but then she gave an over-bright smile. 'Anyway, when I saw a poster of a WAAF in blue, I 'ad to join up. The colour suits me, don't you think?'

Evie smiled, as she was supposed to, and decided not to press Jess on her true reason for joining the WAAF. They walked on in companionable silence, Evie enjoying the birdsong and the musical sigh of the wind in the trees.

Beside her, May was gazing around, her eyes wide. 'It's so . . . empty,' she said. 'Nothing like Birmingham.' She smiled. 'I think I'm going to like it here.'

Finally Jess announced, 'Here we are.'

They had arrived at a white gate flanked by two stone lions. The sign on the gate had 'High Chalk House' painted in flowing gold script. A smaller gate was set into the wall a little way to the left of the imposing entrance, and Jess led them through it.

Beyond the gate a driveway wound through a clump of larches, the first tinges of green dotted on the fringed branches. On the other side was the remains of a sweeping lawn now dug into vegetable plots, recalling happy Sunday afternoons in Cowley, working in the back garden with her father. Stan would have loved this garden. Maybe it was the strangeness of her surroundings, but Evie was struck afresh by the realisation she would never see him again, never work beside him in the garden, getting dirt in her fingernails, chatting about the latest fascinating fact she had learned at school. A wave of desolation swept over her and she blinked away the tears, praying the others wouldn't notice.

May put a timid hand on her arm. 'Is something wrong?'

She shook her head. 'Just missing home.' She forced a smile. 'Come on. I'm dying to see inside.'

High Chalk House stood on rising ground on the other side of the erstwhile lawn. Seen up close, it was even larger than it had appeared from the airfield.

'We don't have to go through there, do we?' May pointed to the imposing main entrance at the top of the drive. Steps led up to a towering pillared portico and a huge set of double doors. May looked as intimidated as Evie felt. They were the kind of doors opened by footmen for women in furs and sparkling jewels. She could almost hear her mother's voice telling her it was too grand for the likes of her.

Much to Evie's mingled relief and disappointment, Jess shook her head. 'They're bolted. This way.' She led them down a path that skirted the side of the building and round the back into a yard. There were various outhouses, for storing wood, vegetables and gardening equipment, Jess told them. Now Evie could see that the imposing front was little more than a facade, hiding a more homely looking half-timbered building.

'There are two wings,' Jess said, leading them to a door with peeling black paint and a stained-glass panel of a peacock. 'We get this one, officers the smarter one.'

The door opened into a large kitchen. A huge old-fashioned range occupied one wall and a sturdy scrubbed oak table dominated the rest of the room. 'Pantry and scullery are through there.' Jess pointed to a door in the shadows to the right. 'The main rooms are this way.'

She led them down a flagstoned passage to a small sitting room. Its polished floorboards were covered with a large rug patterned with scattered rosebuds, and the rosebud theme carried over to the wallpaper. A tiled fireplace dominated one wall, flanked with bookcases on either side. Several ancient, sagging sofas and armchairs were ranged around the room. A couple of WAAFs were curled up in armchairs, knitting or darning stockings, and they greeted Evie and May with smiles when Jess introduced them.

'I'll show you to your rooms. We're right at the top.' Jess led them back out into the passage, then up two flights of narrow, creaky stairs. Evie guessed this must have been the servants' staircase in former times. Once at the top, they went along a long corridor. Just as Evie was starting to wonder if she'd ever have the energy to make it back to her room after a late watch, the corridor ended in a large square room with three doors leading off. There were three armchairs, even more decrepit than the ones in the Rose Room, and a large window with a cushioned window seat. She looked out and saw it had a view across the airfield to a patchwork of fields beyond.

'Best view in the house,' remarked Jess. 'This used to be the schoolroom. I'm sharing the nursemaid's old room with one of the WAAFs you met downstairs, but you two have the old nursery.' She opened the door and Evie and May walked in.

Evie gasped at the size of the room. It was far bigger than the cramped room she'd had in Cowley. Two beds with iron frames stood on each side. Like the beds she'd had during training, they were stacked with three separate 'biscuits' — square cushions that had to be placed end to end to end to form a mattress — blankets, sheets and pillows. A corner room, there were large windows on two of the walls and Evie was delighted to see it had the same view of the airfield that she'd seen from the schoolroom. The curtains were a faded pale green, with blackout curtains fitted behind. A frieze of rabbits, mice and ducklings decorated the walls.

'I'll leave you to unpack,' Jess said. 'Give me a shout when you're ready and we'll head back to the station. I'll show you where to report tomorrow, then we can grab a bite at the NAAFI.'

* * *

An hour later, Evie doubted she'd ever find her way around the station unaided. She'd seen the Admin block, the locations of the air raid shelters, the entrance to the Operations Room, the equipment and transport sections and, finally, the squadrons' dispersal huts. The dispersal huts were where the pilots waited before being sent on training flights or missions, and Evie couldn't imagine needing to go there in the normal course of her duties. She decided Jess had wanted an excuse to flirt with the pilots. Finally, her head spinning, she was relieved to go into the NAAFI, which was situated in an ugly wooden building next to the Admin block. They queued at the counter and received bowls of lentil and barley stew, chunks of bread and butter and steaming mugs of strong tea.

'So tell me,' Jess said when they were sitting at a table, mopping up the last of the stew with their bread, 'what made the pair of you join up?'

May raised her chin. 'I wanted a career, but my father and brothers thought I should stay at home to wait on them hand and foot.' She gave a small smile. 'I knew if I signed up they wouldn't be able to stop me, so I gave them the slip one day and did the deed. It was agony, waiting for my call-up papers. When they came, I thought Dad would have a stroke, he was that angry. But he couldn't stop me leaving once it was official.' She swallowed her last mouthful of stew. 'I can't tell you how good it feels to eat a meal I didn't have to buy all the ingredients for, cook and clear up afterwards.'

Evie stared at May in surprise. She'd dismissed the girl as nothing more than a mouse, albeit a tall, gangly one. 'That was brave of you. It's hard to go against family.' She swallowed, remembering her mother's grim face when Evie had received her call-up papers after an agonising six-week wait.

'I can't tell you how free I feel, being here,' May said. 'I'm never going back. They're bullies. They worked my mother into an early grave, and I would have gone the same way if I hadn't escaped.'

'Good for you.' Evie raised her mug in a salute. 'We all seem to be looking for a better life in the WAAF.' She explained what had led her to join up.

'Was your mother angry?' May leaned forward.

Evie nodded. 'Still is. She hasn't answered any of my letters yet.'

Jess patted her arm. 'She'll come round.'

'I hope so, or my first leave is going to be a bundle of fun.'

Once they'd returned their empty dishes to the kitchen and cleaned their eating irons, they trooped outside.

'Halloway!' Jess sprang to attention. A WAAF officer was advancing on Jess, her expression grim. Her auburn hair was scraped back into a bun with not a single strand out of place; her uniform looked

39

as though she had spent hours pressing every seam. 'You're not in some tawdry revue now. Straighten your collar.'

'Yes, ma'am.' Jess hastened to comply.

The officer turned her icy gaze on Evie and May, and it was all Evie could do not to take a step backwards. 'Who are these? New girls?'

'Yes, ma'am.' Jess introduced them.

'Ah, so you'll be joining us in Ops.' The officer looked Evie up and down when Jess said her name, and it struck Evie that this must be the dreaded Flight Officer Ellerby. 'I wasn't pleased to be sent a girl straight from training. I requested an experienced plotter. Are you any good?'

'I . . . I think so, ma'am.'

Ellerby didn't look convinced. 'Well, I'll be watching you. Any mistakes and I'll have you transferred to the Orderly Room. There's no place in Ops for a girl who doesn't know what she's doing.'

Evie watched Ellerby's departing back with a sinking heart. She'd been looking forward to the excitement of Ops — the hub of an RAF station's activities — but if she ended up operating a filing cabinet in the Orderly Room, she'd go mad with boredom. No matter that she'd excelled in training, she was bound to make blunders with Ellerby's gaze boring between her shoulder blades.

'Blimey, I'm glad I'm not in Ops,' May said, regarding Evie with shocked sympathy. 'Thank God I learnt to drive.'

Evie wished she could drive. Right now, she'd rather steer through a hail of bullets than do her first watch under Ellerby's baleful stare.

4

By the next morning, Evie's stomach was a writhing knot. Her hand shook as she showed her pass at the entrance to The Hole where the Operations Room was located. It didn't matter that she had excelled at all the exercises and tests during training, she just knew she was going to make a terrible blunder and end up being ordered out by an irate Flight Officer Ellerby. She could only pray that Ellerby wasn't on duty this morning. If she could get through her first watch without Ellerby assessing her every move, she could probably cope with future watches under Ellerby's eye.

She descended the steep flight of concrete steps into a gloomy tunnel lined with exposed pipework and cabling. At the foot of the steps was a large steel door. Evie opened it and peered through, half expecting to see a dungeon with damp stone walls and water dripping from the ceiling. Instead she saw a large, brightly lit room, set up in a very similar fashion to the mock-up room she had trained in. It was dominated by the large plotting table that held a map of the south-east corner of England and the Channel. There were blackboards on the whitewashed walls, with information on squadron readiness, status reports and weather, and there was also a wall-mounted clock that had each five-minute interval coloured alternately in a red, blue or yellow triangle. A wooden platform stood at one end of the room

41

supporting a row of desks equipped with lamps and telephones. Her heart gave an unpleasant lurch when she saw Ellerby occupied the middle desk.

Evie's legs shook as she walked up to the senior controller and saluted, trying to avoid looking at Ellerby.

The senior controller, a red-haired man in his late twenties or early thirties, greeted her with a jovial smile. To Evie's mind, he looked like a vicar in his pulpit. 'Ah, the new girl,' he said after returning the salute. 'You've picked a good day to start — should be quiet with just a few training exercises. As you can see, the table is a hive of activity.' He pointed at the other plotters around the table, most of whom were sitting in silence, knitting, crochet or darning in their hands. 'I'm Squadron Leader Peter Travis, by the way.' He turned to introduce his Ops 'A' and Ops 'B'.

He turned to the Ops 'A'. 'This is George Parry.' The man indicated gave her a cheerful wave. 'And this' — Travis pointed to a tousle-haired man in his mid-twenties — 'is Alex Kincaith, Scourge of Ops. Not long arrived himself and here until his squadron is back up to strength.'

Evie smiled at him, but Kincaith merely scowled without so much as a glance at her. A shame, as he'd be good looking without the permanent frown. Something about the curve of his mouth and the laughter lines winging his eyes gave the impression he wasn't always ill-tempered. In fact, Alex Kincaith wouldn't look out of place on the screen of a Hollywood picture.

'Bishop!' Evie jumped at Ellerby's voice. 'What are you waiting for? Take your place.' Ellerby pointed to a chair. 'I can't see the table through your head.'

42

Cheeks burning, Evie sat in the place indicated. She took some comfort in seeing she was next to Jess.

'The cheek of her,' hissed Jess, when Ellerby consulted her clipboard. 'It's not as if there's anything on the table to see yet.'

The other girls around the table shot her sympathetic smiles. Heartened, Evie checked the box of pieces beside her place to make sure she had all the necessary arrows, blocks and numbers and noted the clock's current colour. It changed every five minutes, and woe betide the plotter who placed an arrow that failed to match the clock's colour. She picked up her headset, but at that moment Jean Ellerby looked up from her notes and frowned at her. Evie fumbled the headset and it fell to the floor.

'Careful!' Ellerby snapped. 'Do you know how much one of those costs? Well?' she demanded, when Evie didn't answer.

'No, ma'am.' Evie wished the Germans would come right now and drop all their bombs upon the Ops Room.

'I don't, either,' the senior controller said in a mild voice.

There was a soft twitter of laughter from the plotters, and Evie shot him a grateful glance. She picked up the headset and put it on, taking great care not to drop it this time. Flight Officer Ellerby subsided and sat back in her chair, seeming to be making a detailed study of whatever was written on her clipboard.

Evie took advantage of the inactivity to study the numbers and call signs of the squadrons at Amberton. These were written on a blackboard at the back of the room followed by a long list at the various possible states of readiness. There were three squadrons:

Wagtail, Popcorn and Catseye. At present, none were in the air, but Wagtail was at readiness.

For a while there was no sound but the clicking needles of the girls who were knitting. Then the controller turned to Kincaith. 'Right, let's get Wagtail into the air.'

Kincaith picked up his phone and gave the order. He spoke in a soft Scottish accent, Evie noticed. A short while later the report came through from the observation tower, informing them that twelve Hurricanes had taken off.

Travis picked up his receiver. 'Wagtail leader, this is Belfry. Vector one niner zero at Angels two zero.'

'Wagtail leader, received and understood. Climbing to Angels two zero.'

A plotter standing on the other side of the table picked up a wooden block, labelled it with the squadron number, number of Hurricanes and altitude and placed it upon the table, pushing it into position with a long wooden rake.

Evie watched, glad that she was on the 'hostile' side of the table, so would be unlikely to have to place any plots today. Seeing the plotter at work reminded her that she did know what she was doing. Her nerves eased. As reports from various observation stations filtered through, Evie watched the plot approach the coast, where the squadron would go through its training exercise.

Time flew by and before she knew it, she was released for a short break. She climbed the steps and emerged, blinking, into bright sunshine and headed for the NAAFI. She was delighted to see May just settling at a table, spreading out a map. Evie joined her.

'How's your first day going?'

'I haven't done much, just finding out where all the tools are stored. But I'm driving an officer to the railway station this afternoon, and I'm terrified I'm going to get lost. With all the signposts being removed, I've got to memorise the route.' May indicated the map.

'At least you haven't been dressed down by an officer in front of the entire Ops Room.'

May's eyes filled with sympathy. 'Oh no! What happened?'

Evie described her encounter with Flight Officer Jean Ellerby. 'She's everything Jess said she was,' Evie concluded. 'I know why she calls her 'Hellerby' now. My only hope is that she'll be transferred. Preferably to the north of Scotland.'

'I'm sure the rest of your watch will be better.'

'Ask me again when I've survived it.' Evie drained her tea and stood. 'Well, I'd better get back. Good luck with your first trip. I'm sure it will be fine.'

May grimaced. 'Ask me again when I've found the station without going via Edinburgh.'

The girls laughed and went their separate ways. Evie descended the stairs into The Hole with a lighter heart. She'd never known before how sharing a problem, being able to laugh about it with someone else, made it weigh less heavily. So what if she'd been reprimanded by Hellerby? By all accounts she wasn't the only one, and she'd certainly earned the sympathy of the other plotters in the process.

She took her seat at the plotting table and settled in for the remainder of her watch. She envied the girls who'd had the foresight to bring knitting or books with them. Tomorrow she'd bring something to do.

She was so absorbed in deciding whether she could get away with bringing a text book that she almost didn't register the information that suddenly came through on her headset. But the stir around the table brought her back to the task at hand. Oh heavens, it was on her section of the plot. Of all the ways to start her job properly! With trembling fingers, she picked up a wooden block and quickly slotted the numbers H01 onto the top row: the first hostile plot of the day. Then came the estimated number of aircraft: one. Using the rod, she pushed it into position.

The senior controller leaned over his desk and frowned down at the table. 'Where did that come from?' He turned to Evie. 'It was definitely reported as a hostile?'

'Yes, sir.'

The other plotters confirmed she'd plotted it correctly, even, mercifully, Jean Ellerby, although judging from her pursed lips, she'd make mincemeat of Evie if she made a mistake.

Peter Travis rose and walked along the platform, frowning down at the table as though trying to view it from all angles. He had an odd, lurching gait. He studied the table a moment longer then returned to his desk. 'I'll check with Group.'

Another update crackled through her headset. While Travis spoke on the phone, she moved the marker to its new position, then placed an arrow on the table indicating the direction the plot had moved from its previous position. Thank goodness she'd kept a close watch on the sector clock, so she'd immediately known to select a blue arrow to match the colour indicated by the minute hand. She was all too aware of Jean Ellerby's critical gaze.

'No,' said Travis, replacing the receiver, 'it's definitely not one of ours. Group has all our flights accounted for.'

'It's heading our way,' Kincaith said.

Following the direction of the arrows, Evie's chest tightened as she saw the unknown aircraft was, indeed, heading for Amberton. But the plane — wherever it was from — was still out to sea. Plenty of time for it to change course.

'Right.' Travis glanced at the squadron readiness board. 'Scramble Catseye Red and Blue flights, Alex.'

Kincaith picked up the phone and gave the orders.

Evie was getting used to the procedure now. She waited with bated breath until the observer reported six Hurricanes had taken off, then watched a plotter place a marker representing them. Then Travis called Red Leader and vectored the Hurricanes on an intercept course with the unknown plane. Another update came through on the mystery flight, and she swiftly moved the marker. Noting the clock's minute hand had moved from blue to red, she placed a red arrow.

By now, all pretence at other work had ceased. The unoccupied plotters had put down their knitting and were on their feet, all eyes pinned on the marker which moved ever closer to the English coast and Amberton. On the other side of the table, the plot with the jaunty yellow flag proclaiming it to be Catseye squadron, closed the gap.

Evie was painfully aware that Travis was using her plot to direct Catseye squadron. If she made a mistake, the Hurricanes wouldn't be able to find the unknown aircraft — until it was spotted by an observer, the readings from the Home Chain stations could only be an estimate. When she received the next update, she took especial care to check she had used the correct colour arrow and placed the marker as accurately as possible. Of course, they'd been told in training how important accuracy was, but it was only now, with a possible hostile flight heading for her location and only six brave pilots and their Hurricanes between Amberton and danger, that the full responsibility of her task sank in.

Breathlessly, she watched as the gap between friendly and hostile plots narrowed, her own plot unwavering in its course. Surreptitiously she wiped her damp palms on her skirt. She hoped Ellerby hadn't noticed, or she'd probably think she was too nervous to be useful and should be removed from the Ops Room. When the two plots met, she found herself cringing, as though the planes would actually crash. She had to remind herself they were unlikely to be at the same altitude.

Travis spoke into his receiver again. 'Belfry to Red Leader, you should be right above it. Report.'

There was silence, then a crackle over the speakers. 'Red Leader to Belfry, I see it. A Blériot. French. It's seen us, but not moving away or attacking.'

Travis frowned. 'French? What the blazes?' He spoke in the receiver again. 'Belfry to Red Leader, understood. Escort the Blériot to Belfry. Repeat, escort Blériot to Belfry.'

'Red Leader to Belfry, received and understood.' Then a short while later, 'Red Leader to Belfry, we're on our way in.'

There was a release of breath all around the room. Evie was suddenly aware that her legs trembled beneath her, and she sank onto her chair. A moment later there was a touch on her elbow, and she saw it was the WAAF who was to relieve her. She glanced at the clock, amazed at how quickly the watch had sped by.

Peter Travis stopped her as she headed for the stairs. 'Good work, Bishop. I bet that's a first day you won't forget in a hurry.'

'Thank you, sir. You're quite right, I won't.'

'I'm off to meet our mysterious French pilot. Do you fancy tagging along, to see the result of your hard work?'

Evie had to admit she was burning with curiosity to see who had given them all a scare. 'Thank you, sir.'

Travis moved towards the stairs and reached them from his side of the platform at the same time as Evie got there. Evie stumbled and trod on his left foot by accident.

'I'm sorry, sir.'

'What?' Travis looked at her blankly for a moment, then followed her gaze to his shoe, no longer gleaming but scuffed where Evie had stood on it. His face cleared. 'Oh, nothing to worry about.' He rapped his leg just below the knee, and Evie was startled to hear a hollow *clunk*. Seeing Evie's confusion, he grinned. 'You can stamp on that foot as hard as you like. I won't feel a thing. Bit of a prang a couple of years ago. Now I just tell our pilots where to go.'

'Oh. Sorry, sir.' Evie felt her cheeks burn. With an effort she dragged her gaze from Travis's left leg.

'What about you, Alex? Coming?' Travis asked.

Only now did Evie see that Alex Kincaith stood just behind her.

'Try stopping me.'

Evie's stomach performed that odd swoop again. Feeling her cheeks blazing even hotter, she climbed the stairs out into the sunlight. A car was waiting by the entrance. The moment Peter reached the top of the steps, the driver got out and opened the passenger door. To Evie's delight, she saw it was May.

'Slight change of plan,' Travis told May as he climbed into the front seat. 'Take us to Catseye dispersal first. There's a plane we need to meet before we carry on to the station.

Evie took her place in the back beside Alex Kincaith. She swallowed, forcing herself to look ahead and not glance at Kincaith. She was angry with herself for the frisson of excitement at finding herself so close to him. She was here to work, not flirt with men.

The car pulled away smoothly. Evie was glad for May's sake that Jess had dragged them round all the dispersal huts the previous day, so May knew where to go and didn't have to embarrass herself in front of the officers by asking for directions.

'I owe you an apology, Bishop.'

Evie was so surprised she could hardly take in what Kincaith had said to her at first. 'What? Why?' Then she remembered she was addressing an officer and a wave of horror crashed over her. 'Sorry, sir. I mean . . .' She trailed off, unsure how to dig herself out of the hole.

Kincaith smiled which, if anything, made her even more flustered. 'I wasn't very welcoming earlier. I was in a bad mood, but that's no excuse.' His accent really was rather attractive.

'Oh. That's . . . It doesn't matter, sir.'

She sat back and gazed straight ahead, unable to meet his gaze.

* * *

Alex was charmed to see a faint blush steal up Evie Bishop's cheeks. She really was an attractive girl. It had been a pleasure to watch her at work, her brow puckered in concentration. It had helped him forget his frustration over Group's inexplicable delay with reforming his squadron.

'Anyway, welcome to Amberton,' he said. 'And the Ops Room. I should have said it earlier, but I was trying to do five things at once, as usual.' None of them flying, which was the only thing he wanted to do.

He had no idea why these words were spouting from his mouth. He was an officer, for heaven's sake. There was no need to explain himself to a mere aircraftwoman. Closing his mouth, he gazed out at the airfield as the car sped towards Catseye's dispersal hut. Funny. He'd never noticed before how long it took to get out to the airfield.

At last, after the silence between Alex and Evie Bishop had stretched to uncomfortable proportions, the gawky young WAAF driver pulled up outside the dispersal hut and they all climbed out.

Peter glanced at his watch. 'They should be back any minute by my reckoning.' He turned to the armed men who were approaching at a run and directed them to surround the Blériot as soon as it had landed. 'I'm not taking any chances,' he said to Alex in an undertone. 'I smell a rat. If the French Air Force were sending a plane over, they'd have told us.'

Alex glanced up as the tell-tale drone of Merlin engines reached his ears. Six Hurricanes came into view surrounding a biplane. 'We'll find out who it is soon enough.'

5

Peter snatched a pair of binoculars from one of the pilots who'd come dashing out of the hut at the sound. He peered through them, twiddling with the focus. 'Got them!'

Soon the fighters were rolling to a halt over the field and the Hurricanes taxied towards their dispersal pens where the ground crew jumped onto the wings and helped the pilots out of the cockpits. The armed guards who had been waiting ran up to the Blériot and surrounded it.

The man who climbed out was dressed in a tatty civilian suit. No parachute or Mae West, just an ancient flying cap and goggles. He jumped to the ground and was immediately seized by two guards, who led him over to Peter and Alex. He talked all the while, but Alex couldn't catch the words. He fell silent when he was finally standing in front of them.

'He keeps saying, 'chess key', sir,' one of the guards said. 'Foreign accent, too. Think he's a Jerry.'

The man shook his head. 'No, no. Not Jerry. Jiří. Chess key.'

Something about his accent clicked and brought to mind memories of sitting beside his grandmother's fireside. Alex could almost smell the peat fire and hear his *babi*'s soft voice as she told the story of The Twelve Months. He coughed to clear his throat, which had suddenly become tight. 'I think I know what he's saying.' He turned to the pilot. '*Jste Čech?*'

The man nodded vigorously. '*Ano, ano!*' Before the guards could stop him, he'd broken free and seized Alex in a bear hug.

Alex managed to extricate himself and turned to Peter, doing his best to ignore the muffled giggles of the two WAAFs. 'He's Czech.'

Peter raised his eyebrows. 'You speak Czech, Alex?'

'Aye, I do, thanks to my Czech grandmother. I'm a bit rusty now, but I think I can manage.' He hadn't spoken the language since his maternal grandparents had dragged him away from the loving home of his grandpa and *babi*, to be brought up in the austere home in the Isle of Skye, away from what they had regarded as the bad influence of his Catholic grandmother. But he'd continued to speak it to himself in secret. He was shocked by the sense of longing hearing those few words of Czech brought back.

'Ask him his name and what he's doing here.'

Alex conveyed the question. The reply was a torrent of words that Alex was forced to ask the man to repeat more slowly several times before he finally got the whole of it.

'His name is Jiří Stepanek. He was a pilot in the Czechoslovak Air Force. When the Czechs were forced to surrender, he went to fight in Poland. After Poland fell, he travelled across Europe, trying to get to England. In the end he stole this Blériot from the French Air Force and ended up here. He says he wants to fly for us.'

Jiří must have caught the meaning of Alex's final words. 'Fly, yes. Fly Spitfires.'

'Steady on,' said Peter. 'Spitfires are high-performance machines. Very different from the biplanes you've been flying.'

Alex didn't have time to translate, for Jiří seemed to pick up the tone of Peter's words if not the full meaning. With a scowl, he reached into his inside pocket and pulled out a dog-eared book, which he thrust into Alex's hands with a stream of Czech too fast for Alex to catch.

Alex opened the book and saw each page was divided into columns, with handwritten notes and numbers in each. Although he'd never learnt to read and write Czech, he could see it was a pilot's log book. He flicked through it and whistled. Jiří had logged several thousand hours, well over a hundred being combat hours.

'See,' Jiří said in Czech. 'I bet I've got more experience than most of these fresh-faced pansies combined.'

Alex bit back a laugh and decided not to translate that part. 'He does have a lot of experience,' he said to Peter.

Peter shrugged. 'It's not my decision to make. We'll send him to the station commander, but I expect he'll have to go to Group. He can't fly until he's learnt English, anyway. He's got to understand the directions coming across the radio.'

Alex translated for Jiří's sake while Peter instructed the guards to take Jiří to Bob Law, the station commander. He felt a twinge of regret as he watched the Czech pilot being escorted away. It had felt strange speaking Czech again, bringing back a rare happy memory from his childhood. He had also felt useful again. It didn't matter how many times the station commander told him how valuable it was to have an experienced pilot in Ops, he wouldn't feel he was pulling his weight until he was back in the air.

He strolled back to the car, where Evie Bishop

54

stood with the driver, both gazing at the Czech pilot with wide eyes. 'How did you enjoy your first watch?' he asked her.

A faint blush coloured her cheeks, and she gave a breathy laugh. 'It was more exciting than I'd expected.'

Alex caught himself staring at her fingers, which fiddled with the collar of her blouse. He dragged his gaze back to her eyes. 'Well, you've proved you can cope with the work. You should be proud of yourself.'

Evie's smile broadened, displaying a set of white, even teeth. 'Thank you.'

What was he thinking? He gave an abrupt nod and turned, waving away Peter's offer of a lift. The walk would clear his head, and if he spent any more time in Evie Bishop's company, he'd do something stupid like invite her for a drink. He headed for the Admin block. He was going straight to the station commander to say he should be in charge of a squadron, not wasting his time in the Operations Room. He firmly squashed the thought that working in Ops held more appeal now Evie Bishop had arrived.

★ ★ ★

The next weeks passed swiftly for Evie. As dramatic as her first watch had been, it had reassured her that she could handle her job, and her confidence increased with each day. The thing that made her happiest was her growing friendship with May and Jess. It was a thrill to have someone to spend time with when she was off duty. They often spent their free evenings curled up in armchairs in the schoolroom, sharing the latest gossip. Now the weather was improving, they had started taking walks together, exploring the woods and winding lanes around Amberton.

'Have you noticed how Hellerby's accent gets posher the angrier she gets?' Jess remarked one day. The three girls had a rare afternoon of leisure together. Instead of spending it in the smoky NAAFI, they had packed a picnic and taken their bikes up into the Downs. Now, replete with jam sandwiches and slices of fruitcake, they lay on their backs on a grassy hillside while tiny blue butterflies flitted around them and skylarks flung their songs into the air. The May sunshine was so warm all three girls had rolled up their shirtsleeves and removed their stockings. Up here, the sound of aero engines was a background rumble rather than the ear-splitting roar it was on the station. More akin to the drone of the bumblebees browsing through the clover.

Evie laughed, curling her toes into the prickly grass. 'It does at that, but I'm beginning to get used to her. I think her bark is worse than her bite.'

Jess turned on her side and regarded Evie with wide eyes. 'Seriously? No, you're 'aving us on.'

'I mean it. She's not so bad.'

'You're only saying that because you've never made any mistakes. You'd think differently if you'd been on the receiving end of one of her tongue-lashings. Unless . . .' Jess's eyes narrowed. 'This is nothing to do with Hellerby, is it? More to do with the golden glow that surrounds you whenever a certain young squadron leader is in the room.'

May sat up. 'Squadron Leader Travis?'

Jess didn't shift her gaze from Evie, making Evie squirm. 'Course not. Alex Kincaith.'

'I don't know what you're talking about.' Evie looked down and started to rip up clumps of grass.

She firmly squashed the memory of sitting beside Kincaith in the back of the car and how flustered she felt when he was near.

'Really?' Jess arched an elegantly pencilled brow. 'How about the way you watch him when you think no one's looking? Or the way you hang on his every word.'

'I don't!'

'Or the way he walks up and down the gallery to get the best view of you.'

'He does?' Evie froze, her hand full of torn grass. Then an ant crawled across her fingers, tickling her back to awareness. She shook it off, dropped the grass then brushed her hands to rid them of the last strands sticking to her palms. 'Don't be silly. He's looking at the plots, not me.' She fanned her face. The sun was much hotter than she'd expected. If she didn't take care, she'd get sunburnt. 'I think he likes to walk around because he hates sitting still for a long time.'

'Oh, so you *have* been thinking about him?' The knowing curl of Jess's lip made Evie's insides squirm.

'I'm glad I don't work in the Ops Room.' May's comment saved Evie from having to answer Jess's accusation. 'I'd hate to have my every move watched like that.'

'I thought you wanted a transfer to Ops?' Evie gazed at May in surprise.

'Why 'ave I been slaving to 'elp you speak the King's English, then?'

Evie had to bite back a laugh, always amused at how Jess could switch from a cut-glass BBC accent to her native East End at the drop of a hat.

'Oh, well, that was before I started,' May stammered. 'You spend all your time in that dark hole while I get to spend my days out in the open air. I didn't think I'd enjoy it, but I do.' She picked a buttercup and twirled it between her fingers. 'I am grateful for your help, Jess. I think the officers prefer it when their driver doesn't speak in a broad Brummie accent.' She laughed but looked down at the patch of clover by her feet, as though suddenly fascinated by the fluffy pink flowers.

'And is it one officer in particular you enjoy talking to?' Jess asked in an arch voice.

'No! You know I'm not interested in men. I mean, some are nicer than others, like . . . like Peter and . . . and others. But —'

'Ah, so it's *Peter*, is it now? Not Squadron Leader Travis?' Jess gave a delighted grin. 'I'd have thought he was a bit old for you. He must be at least thirty. I suppose he's not bad looking, though. I wonder what it would be like to be with a man with only one leg?'

May gasped. 'You mustn't speak about him like that. He's been kind to me, that's all. You know I don't want anything to do with men. Being in the WAAF is a chance to get away from men, not to get mixed up with any others.'

May's cheeks were pink, and her mouth had started to tremble, making Evie wonder just how bad May's home life had been. It was clear to her that May had developed a fondness for Peter, but that had been a long speech for shy May. Evie decided it was time she stepped in to rescue her friend.

'I think that's wise, May. I agree. This is our first taste of independence. I'm not in a hurry to give it up either.'

May flashed her a grateful smile.

'Anyway,' Evie continued, 'I have more news. Jess

— our twenty-four-hour passes have been approved. We've got the whole day off next Thursday, same as May.'

Jess sat up, eyes blazing. 'We can go into Brighton — do some shopping, go to the pictures. What do you say? Let's get off this station for a day and spend some of our hard-earned cash.'

'Sounds wonderful,' Evie said. 'I've always wanted to go to the seaside.' But it wasn't the anticipation of seeing the sea that made warmth swell in her chest, or the prospect of a shopping and cinema trip. It was the realisation that after years of loneliness, of wistfully listening to the other girls at school planning weekend visits, she finally had friends who wanted to spend time with her. They could have been planning a day out to a grim industrial slum together and she'd have still been excited. She turned to May and saw the same delighted smile lighting May's face that she could feel on hers. 'What do you think?'

'I'm game. I'll see if I can get one of the other drivers to take us to the station.'

'Oh, May, you're a star.' Jess enveloped May in an enthusiastic hug. 'Girls, we're going to have a wonderful day, and forget all about the war.'

Evie felt a twinge of guilt. She sat up, wrapping her arms around her knees, and gazed across the land to the patchwork of fields until they merged into a blue smudge that must be the sea. She shivered. 'I heard our soldiers are completely cut off on the beach at Dunkirk. There's nothing between us and the Germans now apart from the sea. Are we fools to ignore what's happening just a few miles away?'

To her surprise, it was May, not Jess, who answered. 'If the Germans come, we'll all be plunged into the dark. One day of sunshine and happiness out of a lifetime of misery — surely we can have that.' She gazed out in the same direction as Evie. 'I won't let them take that away from me.'

'Well said, May.' Jess patted her shoulder. 'Come on, I'm dying of thirst. Let's open this ginger beer.'

They lay back on the grass, chatting, drinking ginger beer straight from the bottle, but Evie couldn't quite recapture her earlier carefree mood. She cursed herself for bringing up the subject of the doomed British Expeditionary Force. Gazing up at the sky, she watched the clouds scud past, brilliant white against the cornflower blue sky. How long before German bombers were diving out of those clouds and the twitter of birdsong was drowned by the drone of their engines?

★ ★ ★

Alex was just finishing another tedious, pointless watch in the Ops Room when the phone rang. Peter picked it up.

'Very good, sir,' he said. 'I'll tell him.'

He replaced the receiver and turned to Alex. 'Station commander wants to see you. What have you done now?'

'Nothing, as far as I'm aware.' He picked up his cap and rose. 'Better go and see what he wants.'

Nothing was the perfect description of how he was spending his time. Despite the station commander's frequent assurances that Alex would get his squadron back soon, there was still no sign of it happening. It was humiliating to be flying a desk instead of being out there with the other pilots who were struggling to protect the BEF from the Germans. When he'd been posted to Amberton he'd been assured he wasn't to look on the transfer as a punishment. But now Alex was less sure. Maybe the powers that be had decided he wasn't to be trusted to command his squadron. And always there was the niggling thought that he *was* to blame. That he should have known the Germans had set a trap for his patrol.

He climbed the steps from The Hole and emerged blinking into the sunlight. It always came as a shock to find it was daylight outside, after hours by electric light. Tugging his tunic so it sat straight on his shoulders, he strode to the Admin block and knocked on the station commander's door. He entered when bid and saluted.

'Come in, Alex. Sit down.' Bob Law opened a desk drawer, pulled out a silver cigarette case and offered it to Alex.

Alex declined, but some of the tension eased from his shoulders. It seemed he wasn't here for a dressing down. He sat down opposite Bob at the large oak desk that dominated the office. Neatly laid out on the desktop was a maroon leather blotter, a fountain pen, an ash tray and an Art Deco wooden photo frame containing a photo of Bob's wife. A buff folder lay on top of the blotter; Bob tapped it with his fingers as he spoke.

'I've got good news for you. You're getting your squadron back.'

'At last! I mean, thank you, sir. Where?'

'Right here. Group assures me we have space for an additional squadron. I've yet to be convinced, but needs must and all that.' Bob took a silver lighter from his pocket and took a maddeningly long time

61

to light his cigarette. Alex curbed his impulse to grab
him by the collar and demand he answer all his questions right now. Would he be flying Spitfires? Which
new pilots would he be getting? Were all his original
pilots remaining with the squadron? The ones that
had survived, anyway.

'Is anyone I know joining us?' he prompted, after
Bob had taken a few puffs.

'You should recognise one.' Bob tapped ash into
the ashtray. 'You know, it was quite an eye-opener
to discover you spoke Czech. I don't know why you
never mentioned it before.'

'It's not something I really think about.' Where
was Bob going with this? 'I haven't spoken Czech
since . . . well, since I was a child. About the squadron, what—?'

'Ah, yes. Well, Group were mighty relieved to
learn we have a squadron leader able to speak the
language. You see, we've had quite a few Czech pilots
arrive recently, all insisting they can fly fighters and
continue their war against the Germans. Fighter
Command have decided to make up the numbers in
your squadron with some of them.'

'Have you seen any reports on them? What are they
like?' Although he didn't care who he had to command as long as it meant he could get back into the
air at last.

Bob looked shifty. 'There have been a few teething
problems with the pilots filtered into other squadrons. Nothing you won't be able to handle.'

'Like what?'

'Ah, mostly to do with not following protocol.'

'Can you be more specific?'

Bob scratched his chin then appeared to come to

a decision. 'Very well.' He picked up the folder from his desk, flipped it open with a sigh and read from a sheet inside. 'Insubordination, rowdiness, drunkenness.' Bob looked up at Alex over the top of the sheet of paper. 'And those are just the good reports. But this is where you come in. You've got the advantage of speaking the same language, which means you won't have the same problems with communication that we've had with them so far. You'll soon knock them into shape. They won't be ready for operational flying to start with. For a start they need to improve their English so they can understand orders over the radio, and they won't be used to flying high-performance fighters, either.'

'What will we be flying?'

'Hurricanes.'

Alex felt a pang of disappointment. He'd longed to get his hands on a Spitfire. Still, Hurricanes were great fighters, too. Given the choice between piloting a telephone in The Hole and being up in the clouds in a Hurricane, he'd pick the Hurricane any day.

'When do the men arrive?'

'Two weeks. In the meantime, I've got to sort out billets, hangar space, ground crew and a dispersal hut. Your first Hurricanes are arriving tomorrow.' Bob tossed the file on the desk in front of Alex. 'There you go. These are the men you'll be dealing with.'

Alex retired to the anteroom in the officers' mess, ordered tea at the bar then sank into a leather armchair to read up on all the pilots of the soon-to-be-reformed Brimstone squadron. After he'd read the first page, he drained his tea and ordered a whisky. There were only six pilots remaining from the time Alex had commanded them in France; the other ten were Czechs. Bob hadn't exaggerated when he'd listed the complaints that had already built up against them. It seemed their single-minded desire to take revenge on the Germans led them to regard standard RAF protocols as irrelevant. There had also been several unfortunate run-ins with the civilians near where they'd been billeted. Apparently, the locals had been suspicious of the foreign-sounding men who had suddenly started frequenting their pubs. It had resulted in more than one fight. Alex made a mental note to inform the villagers about the Czech pilots. With the newspapers full of warnings about German parachutists, he didn't want the farmers to start taking pot shots at the 'foreigners' with their shot guns.

He flicked through the list of names and the details of each pilot. All had experienced combat flying, he was relieved to see. That would make his job easier. He paused when he saw the name 'Jiří Stepanek'. Wasn't that the pilot who had arrived in the Blériot? He read further and saw that it was. He could only hope the other pilots had a better grasp of English. But it looked like he'd have to ask Bob to employ an English teacher as well.

Still, the prospect of command and action put a spring in his step as he left the anteroom. He was in the mood to celebrate. The only trouble was, he had no one close to share his news with.

He would go to the pub. Maybe Peter would be there. He hurried outside, only to collide with Evie Bishop as she pushed an ancient rusty bike towards the gates. He dropped the file and papers slithered out onto the path.

'I'm sorry, sir,' Evie gasped. She gave a hasty salute, then propped her bike against the fence and stooped to help him collect his papers. He couldn't help noticing her face now sported a charming stripe of freckles across her nose, as though she'd seen the sun recently. She'd obviously put her free afternoon to good use yesterday. Although how he remembered Evie had had the afternoon off yesterday, he couldn't say. He didn't usually pay much attention to the WAAFs' comings and goings.

He waved away her apology. 'I wasna looking where I was going.' He checked himself. His maternal grandparents had insisted he speak standard English, punishing him if he slipped into the broader Scots he had spoken in Glasgow. Although he had hated it at the time, he had to admit it had helped his career. It usually came naturally, but it must be the excitement of getting his squadron back that had made him forget himself. A sudden image hit him of sharing his news with Evie, seeing her face light up with happiness for him. It was so powerful he found himself saying, 'I've just had some good news, actually. I was off to the pub to celebrate. Care to join me?'

'Oh!' A becoming blush tinged her cheeks. 'I don't ... I mean ... I'd arranged to go there with some friends. But I might see you there.'

'I'll look out for you.'

Alex watched her departing back, admiring her long legs and slender waist. Then he caught himself. She clearly hadn't wanted to go with him, and it was for the best. Something about Evie Bishop fascinated him, and he couldn't afford a distraction. Not now when his whole attention needed to be on getting his men safely through the war. He didn't want a repeat of what had happened in France.

6

'He did what?' Jess turned sharply away from the mirror to look at Evie. 'Oh, now look what you've made me do.' She grabbed a tissue and peered into the mirror hanging above the fireplace, dabbing at the line of crimson lipstick that trailed from the corner of her mouth to a point halfway up her right cheek.

'He asked if I'd go with him to the pub.'

May poked her head out from round the bedroom door. Her dark hair hung in glossy waves past her shoulders, and she was brushing it out. 'A man asked you out? Who?'

'Alex Kincaith. But he —'

'Squadron Leader Kincaith?' May froze, eyes wide, her hairbrush halfway down a lock of hair. 'What did you say?'

'Look, it's not as if he asked me to walk out with him. He just said he was going to the pub to celebrate good news and asked if I wanted to join him.' Evie had run over the incident in her head all the way back to High Chalk House. She'd been so surprised by his abrupt question she'd hardly known what to say. She still didn't know what to make of it. 'I'm sure if he'd met a different WAAF he'd have asked her instead.'

Jess, her make-up now flawless, closed her lipstick with a snap and leaned back against the mantelpiece, arms folded. 'What did you say?'

'I told him I'd already promised to go out to the pub with you two.' She'd been relieved when she'd remembered the arrangement they'd made over breakfast.

'You said no to an officer?' May pulled the brush from her hair and clutched the doorpost as though it was the only thing holding her up. 'I'd never have dared.'

'I can't believe you'd turn down an officer for us.' Jess looked uncharacteristically uncertain. All of a sudden, she looked younger; less like a Hollywood actress, more like the English girl of twenty that she actually was.

'We're friends, aren't we? I mean, I've never really had friends before, and I don't want to lose you now.'

Jess gave her a beaming smile. 'You're a true pal, Evie. That's what you are. None of my so-called friends in London would have said no to an 'andsome man to spend a night with the girls instead.'

'My father never let me go out in the evenings, so I've never had friends before,' said May. 'But that's what you both are to me. Friends.'

Evie smiled at them both, feeling a surge of affection for the two girls. When she'd dreamed of the friends she would make at Somerville, she'd imagined bookish academics just like her, but she was glad she'd met May, with her artless affection, and Jess, with her daring and sense of fun. They both showed Evie what had been missing in her life. Even though she had only known them for a few weeks, she couldn't imagine life without them.

'Now, are you both ready for a friends' night out?' Jess asked.

Evie returned from her musings with a bump. 'Oh no,' she said, her stomach lurching in dismay. 'I mean, Kincaith will be there.'

67

'You told him you would. You can't back out now.'

'But what would I say?'

'You don't have to say anything if you don't want to.' Jess patted Evie's arm. 'You'll be with us. Anyway, aren't you a bit curious to know what he wanted to celebrate? It must be good news if it made Kincaith want to go out for a pint with a pretty girl instead of glare at her across the Ops Room.'

'I suppose . . .'

'Besides, we're celebrating an' all. You two look cracking in your new uniforms, and if that's not a cause for celebrating, I don't know what is.'

Evie couldn't resist looking down at her smart new air force blue tunic and skirt, and smoothing them down. For a new batch of uniforms had finally arrived, and both Evie and May were now fully kitted out, down to the huge 'blackouts' — the most unflattering knickers Evie had ever seen. Designed to repel all invaders, as Jess had put it. But while the other WAAFs complained how the wide belts bunched their tunics around their hips and rear end, Evie couldn't get over the thrill of having clothes that were brand new. Not a patch or frayed hem in sight. A glance at May's shining eyes told her May felt the same. 'I do feel as though I'm finally a proper WAAF. All right, then, the Horse and Groom it is. What do you say, May?'

May beamed. 'A night out at the pub with my friends. Who'd have thought I'd ever say that?'

'Are we ready then?' Jess glanced at the mirror and smoothed a stray blonde lock into place.

'No wait, I have to do my hair first,' said May.

'You've got beautiful hair. Why do you want to go scraping it back from your face? You look like Katharine Hepburn with it down.'

May flushed. 'Don't say that. You know I don't.'

'You look gorgeous,' Evie said firmly. 'Jess is right — with those cheekbones and eyebrows, you're the spitting image of Katharine Hepburn.'

'No. You're just saying that.' May scraped her hair back from her face and darted back into the bedroom.

Jess shook her head with an exasperated sigh. 'Whoever told her she was ugly should be shot. She's a real looker.'

Evie agreed. Personally, she thought May's father and brothers had a lot to answer for. She could only guess what poison they'd dripped into the poor girl's heart. She thanked her lucky stars she'd had a father and mother who'd loved her. Maybe she and her mother hadn't seen eye to eye over how she should live her life, but she couldn't deny Dora loved her.

May reappeared with her hair now fastened in a severe bun.

Jess put an arm around her shoulders and marched her to the mirror. 'Now look at that face. You've got natural beauty, you 'ave. The kind you grow into. Not like me, who needs to pile on the lipstick and powder.'

May looked into the mirror, but her gaze slid from her face to Jess's. 'You're just saying that to make me feel better.'

'I'd never do that.' Jess reached up to touch May's hair but dropped her hand when May flinched. 'I won't take it down if it makes you uncomfortable but let me do this at least.'

May held still, and Jess teased a few tendrils loose at her temples. It softened the look considerably.

'There you go.' Jess stepped back to admire her handiwork. 'With that new uniform and all, you look gorgeous.'

Evie linked arms with the pair of them. 'What with Katharine Hepburn on one side and Jean Harlow on the other, Alex Kincaith won't look at me anyway.'

Jess laughed. 'Don't you believe it. He hasn't been able to take his eyes off you ever since you arrived.'

Those words were still ringing in Evie's ears when they walked into the Horse and Groom twenty minutes later. The Horse and Groom had long since been taken over by the inhabitants of RAF Amberton, and the more retiring locals had deserted it for the Stag, some two miles away. The public bar was full of rowdy airmen. Even though some WAAFs had daringly joined them, Evie, May and Jess didn't go in there. Instead they entered the snug and looked for a free table. As soon as they walked through the door, Evie was aware of Kincaith, sitting with Peter Travis and Bob Law. His eyes met hers and she felt a jolt in the pit of her stomach. He raised his pint in a silent greeting, and Evie felt the heat rise in her cheeks. She would have walked past to take a seat at another table, but Travis happened to glance up.

'Come and join us, ladies. What will you all have?'

Evie opened her mouth to murmur an excuse, but Jess got there before her. 'Thank you, sir,' she said, taking a seat next to the station commander. 'A port and lemon for me, please.'

There was nothing for it but to sit down. She took the nearest seat, which happened to be between the station commander and Kincaith. The next moment she sprang to her feet and gave a hasty salute. 'I'm sorry, sir,' she said, 'I forgot.'

Bob Law gave a negligent wave. 'We don't bother with all those formalities when we're off duty.'

70

Evie swallowed and nodded. 'Thank you, sir.'

'What will you have, Evie?' Travis asked, rising.

There was no way she was drinking alcohol in front of such senior officers. Her head was already swimming from finding herself sitting beside Alex Kincaith. 'A lemonade, please, sir.'

'No need for all the 'sirs' while we're here. And how about you?' Travis turned to May. It seemed to Evie that he saw her for the first time, for his gaze lingered on her face. 'It's Lidford, isn't it? I'm sorry, I don't know your first name.' There was a softness to his tone Evie hadn't heard before.

'May, sir.'

'Call me Peter.'

'Peter.' May lifted her gaze to his face and gave a tremulous smile.

Watching them, Evie had the curious feeling she was intruding upon a private moment.

'Right,' said Peter, turning to the rest of the group with what Evie felt was great reluctance, 'I'll get the drinks, but I'll need help carrying them.'

Alex Kincaith leapt to his feet, clearly relieved for an excuse to get away from Evie for a while. He must be regretting his spur-of-the-moment invitation already.

But as the evening progressed, and they toasted Alex and his new squadron, Evie's attention kept drifting back to Peter and May. May said very little, which wasn't unusual, and Peter addressed all his remarks to the group, but there was something about their posture that set Evie thinking. Maybe it was the way Peter's head seemed to tilt towards May while he told the group he would enjoy seeing Alex vent his spleen upon the Germans instead of the Ops Room staff, or perhaps it was how May's body angled towards him even when she turned to say something to Jess. Whatever it was, Evie's suspicions were raised. She could only hope May wouldn't get hurt. If anyone was vulnerable, it was May. She resolved to speak to her about it at the earliest opportunity.

★ ★ ★

Evie's irregular hours meant the opportunity didn't come until a couple of days later, when the three friends took their trip to Brighton. May was allowed to take a car for the day, on condition that she drive one of the Ops Room officers to the station for an early train, as he was transferring to another station for operational flight training.

They parked by the station and, after saying goodbye to the officer, caught a trolleybus to take them down to the seafront. Climbing on board, Evie wrinkled her nose at the smell of stale cigarette smoke.

The moment they had taken their seats, Evie twisted round, propped her elbows on the back rest and fixed her gaze on May, who had taken the seat behind. 'What's up between you and Squadron Leader Travis?'

'Nothing.' A faint blush coloured May's cheeks.

'No, Evie's right,' Jess said. 'When I saw you together at the pub the other night, I had the definite feeling he was soft on you. Just how many times have you been his driver?'

'It's not like that. I mean, I've had to drive him places, and he's been friendly, but that's all it is.'

Evie was about to argue when the trolleybus turned a corner and suddenly they were on the seafront.

'We're here!' Her voice was shrill with excitement. She craned her neck and gazed, all worries gone at the sight of the sparkling blue expanse, the view framed on both sides by the two piers snaking out into the sea.

They jumped down from the bus, and Evie ran to the iron railings, leaning over them as she drank in the view. She took off her cap to allow the warm breeze to ruffle her hair. Drawing a deep breath of tangy, salty air mingled with the aroma of fish and chips, she tilted back her head to let the sunshine warm her face. The rhythmic surge of breaking waves was a constant presence, like the wind rustling the leaves in a wood on a stormy day; gulls glided above the waves, their shrill cries filling the air. 'If I close my eyes, I can almost believe there's no war on, and we're here for our summer holiday.' A pang of sorrow struck as she remembered how she had dreamt of bringing her father to the coast. He would have loved it here. The sea shimmered and blurred as tears welled in her eyes. She hadn't had much time to miss Stan since joining the WAAF, but now she was struck afresh by the realisation that every day out from now on, no matter how enjoyable, would be one without her father.

But Jess wouldn't allow her to wallow for long. She grasped Evie's arm in one hand and May's in the other and tugged them towards the steps. 'Come on, let's go down to the beach.'

Evie blinked away her tears and shook off her melancholy as she galloped down the steps onto the pebbles. They crunched underfoot, and Evie had to cling to Jess's arm to keep her balance as the stones shifted with each step. They removed their shoes and stockings and left them bundled up in their tunics by the steps. Then they hobbled down to the water's edge, wincing whenever sharp pebbles dug into their bare feet.

'Careful you don't splash your skirts,' Jess said. 'Sea water stains are a bugger to remove.'

There was no way Evie was going to spoil her pristine uniform. Copying Jess, she raised her hem above her knees before wading into the water. She gasped as the chill water lapped her toes. Beside her, May yelped as a wave washed up to her ankles. They stood there for some time, squealing and giggling with the shock of each cold wave. Eventually, unwilling to risk spoiling their uniforms, they left the water and returned to their pile of clothes. They spread their tunics and sat upon them, stretching out their legs to catch the sun and dry them.

'You should have seen this place before the war,' Jess said after a while, her eyes alight with memory. 'My Auntie Vera brought me here once for a day out. We walked out on the Palace Pier, ate sticks of rock and had fish and chips on the sea front. The perfect day. It's a shame the piers are closed.'

Jess spoke so little about her life before the war it was something of a surprise to see her in a reminiscent mood. She usually lived firmly in the present. Evie hesitated, wondering if she should ask her more about her life in London, but then Jess gave a little laugh, and the moment was gone. 'Time to explore.'

She led them along the seafront to the Palace Pier, then after regretfully noting that the decking had been pulled up, they turned their back on it and went to see the Royal Pavilion. Evie and May gasped when they caught their first glimpse of its many domes, pinnacles and delicate tracery around the windows.

'I feel as though we've wandered into India,' May breathed. After walking all the way around to view it from every angle, they gave in to Jess's urging and spent the rest of the morning exploring the quaint shops, giggling over humorous postcards, admiring paintings of seascapes and investigating crammed antique shops. Eventually, Jess complained of sore feet, so they bought fish and chips for lunch and found a bench on the sea front to eat them straight out of the newspaper. As Evie unwrapped her chips, a headline jumped out at her: 'Our Brave Men at the Flanders Coast'. Below ran a report of the desperate attempts to rescue the troops from the beaches. The sunshine seemed to dim. What with that and the closure of the piers, she felt vaguely resentful at the war for intruding upon the day out she'd eagerly anticipated for so long. She made an effort to shake off the thought of soldiers huddled on beaches. Gradually the haunting images faded, and she became aware of the sun warming her face again.

The girls lingered on the bench, throwing their leftover chips to the seagulls. 'Come on,' said Jess finally, crumpling up her newspaper and throwing it into a bin. 'I refuse to leave until you two have bought something.'

'We bought fish and chips,' May said, licking the last of the grease from her fingers with relish.

'Doesn't count. It has to be something to keep. I know!' Jess clapped her hands. 'Lipstick and scent. No self-respecting girl should be without them. When we were in the pub, I heard someone talking about a midsummer dance at the village hall. You'll need something for that. No arguing,' she said, when both

Evie and May protested. 'There's nothing like a bit of lipstick and a splash of scent to perk a girl up. Come with me.' She picked up her brown-paper packages from their earlier foray and marched off.

She led them through the streets to Hannington's Department Store. Evie gawked up at the impressive Georgian-style façade, wondering if they would be allowed in. Jess, however, walked in as if she was royalty, bestowing a gracious nod upon the doorman. Soon they were examining lipsticks under the eagle eye of the shop assistant. Evie, who had never worn make-up in her life, reached for the cheapest brand, but Jess slapped her wrist. 'No. If you're going to buy just one lipstick, you need quality and the perfect colour. And that goes for you, too, May. Let me choose for you. It's not as if you have much to spend your pay on.'

Evie sent a fair bit to her mother every month and was saving as much as possible towards her degree, but she bit back the argument that sprang to her unpainted lips. There was no harm in spending a little on herself.

'Go on, then,' she said. 'What colour should I choose?'

Jess studied her. 'With your red hair and pale skin, you should get a plum. Or maybe a burgundy.'

The assistant showed her all the lipsticks in those shades, and Jess picked up a rich burgundy. 'This one. Try it.'

Evie applied it carefully, mimicking the way she'd seen Jess apply her lipstick, then looked in the mirror. She was shocked and pleased at the transformation. The burgundy shade didn't drain her pale face as so many bright colours seemed to do, and it brought out the blue flecks in her grey eyes.

'What did I tell you?' Jess said, triumphant. 'Perfect! Now for May.'

'I've never bought anything for myself before.' May gazed at the array of colourful lipsticks. 'I wouldn't know where to start.'

Even the assistant's face softened at that, and Jess squeezed her arm. 'That's why I'm here. Now, with your colouring, you'd look stunning in anything.' Her hand hovered over a bright scarlet, but at May's horrified gasp she conceded, 'Perhaps you're not ready for that.' She picked out a deeper red and read the label. 'Garnet Dusk. You'll look gorgeous in this.'

May applied it. Yet again, Evie had to admire Jess's keen eye. The subtle shade seemed to bring out the warm glow of her skin. Peter Travis would be knocked off his feet when he saw her wearing it. She opened her mouth to say it, but changed her mind, not wanting to embarrass May. She handed over the money for her lipstick and felt absurdly excited to take charge of the tiny package. Although she didn't regret a single day of her hard studies, it meant she'd missed out on the simple pleasures of life, such as a day out with friends and buying little luxuries like lipstick. When she'd joined the WAAF, she'd never thought it would give her the chance to do such things. So she didn't protest when Jess marched them to the perfume counter.

The perfume stocks were sadly depleted; the artful display couldn't disguise the lack of variety. But with Jess's help they both managed to find a scent they liked. May opted for a light floral scent and Evie picked a delicate perfume with citrus tones. They both chose the smallest bottle available, but Evie felt quite daring and grown up as she walked out onto the street carrying her new purchases. With her smart new uniform, new lipstick and a dab of scent on her wrists, she felt like a glamorous character in a film. She couldn't help imagining the admiring glances she'd get at the village dance when she appeared wearing her new purchases. What would Alex think?

She hurriedly squashed that train of thought. What Alex Kincaith thought was of no consequence to her.

At the end of the afternoon they returned to the car with dragging feet. It had been the perfect day, and Evie wished they could stay longer. She turned to the sparkling sea for one last look, then followed her friends up the road to the station. But when they got back to their car, they found the road blocked by army ambulances. A group of men and women in army uniform stood by the side of the road, talking in low, tense voices.

'What's going on?' Jess asked a corporal who stood beside the nearest ambulance, smoking a cigarette. 'We need to get out.'

'You'll 'ave to wait, love,' the corporal replied. 'Train's due in with evacuees from Dunkirk. We're driving a load of 'em to the 'ospital.'

No sooner had he spoken than they heard a heavy rumble and the squeal of brakes. Dirty smoke drifted onto the road from the station. The corporal threw down his cigarette, ground it under his heel and went to join the others who were hurrying towards the platform.

'I suppose we'll have to get out of the way and wait,' Evie said. She bit her lip, hoping this wouldn't make them late.

They stood by the car, not wanting to climb into the baking interior until they were able to leave. Presently a procession of soldiers hobbled out of the station. Some were carried on stretchers, some supported by nurses, others could walk unaided or on crutches. All were caked in dirt and blood, with stained bandages and dressings. Their uniforms were torn; many of them were missing tunics and shirts.

Then the stench reached Evie's nose: the sour smell of unwashed bodies; the metallic tang of blood; the putrid reek of infected wounds. She gagged and hated herself for her weakness when she couldn't imagine what these men had endured for the sake of their country. But in their dull eyes she saw their nightmare reflected. They were downcast, in an attitude of pain, defeat and despair.

She had to do something; she couldn't just stand there, gawking at these suffering men without doing something to help. But what? All she could think was that the men looked half-starved. Remembering a precious bar of chocolate that she'd stowed in the car for the return journey, she grabbed it. The chocolate was soft, but better than nothing.

Her gaze fell on a lad who must have lied about his age to get into the army. He looked no more than fifteen. Wincing, he limped towards one of the trucks. A fifteen-year-old should be playing football with his friends, not watching them getting shot up on a godforsaken beach. Fighting nausea, she went to him and pressed the chocolate into his hands.

He looked in her direction, but his eyes were unfocused. Or perhaps they gazed at some horror only he could see. 'Thanks, miss,' he croaked.

You shouldn't be thanking me, she wanted to cry. *It should be me thanking you.* But her throat closed, strangling the words.

The lad swayed, biting back a groan. She grabbed his arm. 'Here. Lean on me. It's not far.' Murmuring encouragement, she took his weight and guided him to the ambulance. Tears sprang to her eyes, but she blinked them away. It took all her self-control not to gag at his stench. When they reached the ambulance, hands reached out to help him on board. He slumped onto one of the stretchers and gazed upwards. Evie hated to think what scenes of horror were playing out in front of those blank eyes.

She turned to see May and Jess also helping the wounded into the trucks. Noticing another soldier stumble, she dashed to take his arm. Back and forth they went, offering support and kind words. It was precious little, but it was all she could do. Doing nothing was unthinkable.

Finally, the doors slammed on the last ambulance and the trucks drove away.

The three friends sat in the car, unmoving. Evie wished she could cry, vent her emotions in some way, but every time the feelings inside swelled and threatened to burst free, it was as though a fist reached inside and squeezed tight, denying any release.

'This is real,' was all she could say at first. The others nodded.

'I had no idea.' Jess's voice was scarcely more than a tight whisper.

Gradually Evie's scattered thoughts and emotions coalesced into a coherent idea. She knelt on her seat so she could look at both May and Jess and gripped the seat-back so tightly her knuckles turned white. 'This is serious, girls,' she said. 'I can't speak for you, but until now, I think I was just playing at being a WAAF.'

80

May frowned and Jess looked down, studying her nails.

'I mean, I took my job seriously,' Evie clarified, 'but I wasn't doing it for England or our pilots, I was doing it for me. I was doing it to escape home.'

'Me too,' muttered May.

'And me.' Jess met Evie's gaze. 'But we're going to change, aren't we?'

'I am. I'm not doing it for me any more.' Evie pointed out to sea. 'The Germans are only a few miles on the other side of that, and there's nothing but the sea between them and us.'

'The sea and our pilots,' May said.

'Yes. And that's important. If we do our jobs properly, then they can do theirs. Unless we do our part, then everyone in Britain could end up like those poor boys. From now on, I'm doing my job for our pilots and for Britain. Are you with me?'

'Count me in,' said May.

'What are you waiting for, then?' Jess said. 'Drive us back home. Me and Evie are on early watch tomorrow.'

7

In the days following their trip to Brighton, Evie and her friends went about their duties with fresh determination. They weren't the only ones — a hum of expectancy hung over the station. More sandbags arrived and were added to the stacks around buildings, gun emplacements and observation posts. There were increased drills at different times of day, so everyone knew what to do in the event of a raid, and the orders to carry a gas mask and helmet at all times were enforced more strictly. When Evie was on duty, she was aware of everyone watching the plotting table like hawks, waiting for the hostile plots to appear from the Channel. Everyone knew it was only a matter of time. The Germans were moving their squadrons into position and when they were ready, they would strike.

'It's the waiting that gets to me,' said Jess a week after their return from Brighton. The three girls had all got a break at the same time and were eating their lunch in the NAAFI. 'I almost wish they would come so we could get it over with.'

Tin mugs and eating irons rattled on tables as a group of Hurricanes roared overhead. As well as the intensified preparations on the ground, all squadrons had increased their training flights and were also patrolling the coast, watching for signs of attack.

'I know what you mean,' Evie said, when the noise level had dropped. 'But I can't help thinking that when we do start, we'll be looking back on days like today with nostalgia.'

'Have you heard anything, May? You've been driving Peter Travis and Bob Law all round the country it seems. Surely they've let something slip.'

'Even if they had, you know I couldn't tell you. Loose lips, and all that.'

Evie nodded, pleased to see May gaining in confidence and able to assert herself. 'Sorry. I shouldn't have asked.'

'As a matter of fact, there is something I can tell you. Peter heard that the villagers were thinking of cancelling the midsummer dance.'

'They can't do that!' Jess couldn't have looked more upset if she'd heard Christmas had been cancelled. She half rose, and Evie wouldn't have been surprised if she'd marched into the village, demanding they change their minds.

May waved her down. 'It's all right. It's going ahead. They were worried about the blackout, but in the end, they boarded up the windows.'

Jess subsided. 'You could have started with that. Nearly gave me a heart attack. It's all very well putting my duties first, but a girl needs to let her hair down.'

'Oh, I nearly forgot. The new pilots arrive tomorrow.'

Evie grinned at Jess. 'That should make you happy.'

Jess scowled at her. 'I meant what I said when I told you I was being serious from now on.' Then her expression lightened. 'Although it would be rude to ignore them. I mean, they're a long way from home. It's our duty to make them feel welcome.'

★ ★ ★

Alex stood outside the Admin block, watching the ten new pilots of Brimstone squadron climb out of the truck. The six pilots who had been with the squadron in France were arriving tomorrow, but Alex had asked for the Czechs to arrive a day early. He eyed them with a sinking heart. *Bloody hell.* If their flying matched their appearance, they were doomed. Even though they'd been issued with RAF uniforms, they still managed to look tatty. Top buttons were undone, ties loose, and instead of standing to attention when they lined up in front of Alex, they slouched.

Still, their job wasn't to look good on the parade ground, but to fight Germans. Alex picked out Jiří Stepanek from the group, recalling his insistence he wanted to carry on the fight he'd started in Poland.

'Welcome to Amberton,' he said. 'I'm Squadron Leader Alex Kincaith. Once you've been through the formalities in Admin and found your billets, I'll take you to dispersal to discuss training.'

Blank faces. The men shuffled their feet and glanced at one another, eyebrows raised.

Damn. If they couldn't understand him on the ground, what hope did they have when they were in the air, a flight of Bf 109s zooming down on their tails?

He repeated his greeting in Czech, and immediately there was a ripple of interest and the Czechs leaned in to listen. Thank goodness he'd brushed up on the language in the past couple of weeks.

Once he'd sent the pilots off to find their billets, Alex went to find the station commander. As luck would have it, Bob Law walked out of the door just as he reached the Admin block.

'Did you get anywhere finding an English teacher

for the Czechs?' he asked Bob Law after they'd exchanged pleasantries.

Bob shook his head. 'Not for want of trying, but there wasn't anyone available. I've decided to make other arrangements and get a couple of our WAAFs to do it.'

'Who?'

'All in good time. I need to tell the girls in question first.'

A couple of hours later, formalities complete and the pilots' meagre possessions stowed in their sleeping quarters, Brimstone squadron assembled in the new dispersal hut. Alex was impressed at how quickly it had been constructed, together with the dispersal pens for their Hurricanes, latrines and even a bunk room. The best feature as far as Alex was concerned was his office, in a separate room at the back of the hut. He had a feeling he was going to need to get away from the men from time to time.

He glanced around the hut at the pilots, all lounging in wicker chairs. Some had their feet upon the tables; some were slouched so low Alex couldn't tell if they were awake or asleep. He addressed them in Czech. Later he would insist upon English, but he needed to be certain everyone understood. 'My job over the next few weeks is to get you ready for operational flying. We will focus on three things: familiarisation with Hurricanes; tactical exercises and learning English. Until you've achieved the grade in all three areas you won't be passed ready for operational flying. I can't stress how important it is to get you operational as soon as possible. The Germans are only a few miles away, and unless we have enough pilots in the air, there will be nothing to stop them. I can't begin to imagine what will happen if our fighters don't stop them.'

'We don't have to imagine. We've already seen it.'

Alex paused, aware of his blunder. All these men had fled Czechoslovakia for Poland when the Germans had taken over their country. He'd read the reports on them. They'd all flown in combat over Poland, then escaped across Europe. The details had been sketchy, but he knew they must have slept rough and pilfered whatever food they could find on the way. Jiří Stepanek's ragged appearance upon arrival bore testament to the tough conditions they'd endured while he'd been living in comfort here at Amberton. Worst of all, they had family and friends living under Nazi rule.

He frowned at the young man who had spoken — a man with black hair and intense blue eyes. The two rings on his sleeve showed he'd been awarded the rank of Flying Officer. 'Milan Mašek, is that right?' When the man nodded, Alex continued. 'You're right, of course, and I know you're impatient to continue the fight. Well, so am I. But you won't be allowed on operational flights until you know enough English to understand orders. Starting tomorrow, we'll spend the mornings on training flights and afternoons on English and radio protocols.'

And God help the poor WAAF who was seconded to try drumming English into this rabble. He resolved to sit in on the first few lessons to ensure the men understood their importance.

* * *

86

Evie rotated her shoulders with a groan at the end of another tiring watch and tried stretching the kinks out of her spine. 'I could murder a cuppa,' she muttered to Jess, who had come off watch at the same time.

Before they could troop up the steps, one of the girls who had just arrived stopped them. 'Flight Officer Hell— Ellerby wants to see you both right away.'

Evie glanced at Jess. 'What about?'

'No idea.' The WAAF gave them a sympathetic smile. 'Good luck.'

'What have we done now?' Jess wailed as they climbed the steps out of The Hole.

Evie shrugged, trying to look unconcerned, but her insides were churning. 'We'll find out soon enough.' Try as she might, she couldn't think of anything she'd done wrong.

'What if she wants to transfer us? We could end up anywhere.' By the time they'd paused outside Ellerby's office, straightening their uniforms and smoothing their hair, Jess had convinced them both they were about to be shipped off to some isolated station in the far north of Scotland.

They entered and saluted when summoned. Ellerby looked up at them, her mouth turned down, lips pressed in a tight line. Although there were chairs by the desk, she didn't invite them to sit.

'Think you're too good for the Operations Room?' was her opening salvo.

Evie's heart lurched. She opened her mouth, but Jess got there first.

'I beg your pardon, ma'am?' Jess stood to attention, staring straight ahead. 'Have we done something wrong?'

Ellerby waved a sheaf of paper in the air. 'This.

I've seen you in the village pub, consorting with the officers. I've had a request for your services, and I can only think that you both used your wiles to make sure you were chosen.'

Was there any point in saying she didn't have the first idea how to use her wiles? Evie wasn't even sure she had any. 'S-sorry, ma'am,' she said, 'what services?'

'I'm talking about teaching English to the Czech pilots. Decided you were bored spending all day in Ops, did you? Thought you'd found an easy way to get out of your duties?'

'Teach the Czechs?' Evie's voice came out in a strangled squeak. She didn't know the first thing about teaching English, let alone to a group of pilots whose reputation for rowdiness preceded them. She exchanged glances with Jess and saw her confusion mirrored in her friend's expression together with a gleam of excitement. Well, Jess could teach them on her own. She'd far rather stay in the Ops Room, where she was dealing with numbers. Numbers made sense. They weren't frightening and never did anything unexpected.

In the end, she decided their best course was honesty. Clasping her hands tightly behind her back, she said, 'I don't want to get out of my duties, ma'am. I know how important they are.' She held Ellerby's gaze, willing her to believe them.

'Honest, ma'am,' Jess said, 'we didn't know a thing about it until now.'

Jess's accent had slipped; oddly enough, it seemed to tip the scales in their favour. Ellerby's shoulders relaxed. 'Be that as it may, the matter is out of my hands. The orders come from higher up.' She placed the papers upon the desk and folded her hands on top of them, regarding the girls steadily. 'The station commander will explain your duties himself, but before you go through, I want to impress upon you the seriousness of the task.' Her eyes flicked briefly to Jess. 'If I hear of any inappropriate behaviour, I'll have you back permanently in Ops, even if the Air Chief Marshall himself should ask for you. Understood?'

'Yes, ma'am,' they both said. Evie's stomach performed loop-the-loops. Now Ellerby would be waiting for them to make mistakes, looking for an excuse to remove them from a duty Evie didn't even want. Still, if the order had come from the station commander, there was nothing to be done but accept the duty and do her best. While praying she didn't earn Ellerby's disapproval.

Ellerby held their gaze for a moment longer, then sighed. 'Very well. You'll still be expected to perform your usual duties, so I'll be keeping an eye on you.' She rose. 'Come with me.'

She led them out to the station commander's office, where she saluted smartly. 'Bishop and Halloway to see you, sir.' Then she left.

Trembling, Evie stepped forward and saluted, seeing Jess do the same at her side.

Bob Law greeted them with a smile. 'Come in and sit down,' he said. 'Did Flight Officer Ellerby explain why I wanted to see you?'

Evie sagged upon the nearest chair. To her relief, Jess answered. Evie doubted her voice would work. 'She mentioned something about teaching English to the Czechs, sir, but that's all.'

Bob Law gave a wry smile. 'Let me explain. At present, their English is rudimentary at best. Until they can obey orders in English and be understood over the radio, they would be more of a danger than a help in the air.' He leaned forward over the desk. 'I needn't tell you the Germans are building up their forces on the other side of the Channel. We need Brimstone squadron ready for operational flying as soon as possible, and that means they have to learn English.'

'But why us, sir?' Jess asked, echoing Evie's thoughts.

'I've been trying to get hold of an English teacher for some time, but there are none available. That's forced me to look to the staff already on the station to expedite the matter.' He turned to Evie. 'You have the most impressive academic record of the WAAFs on the station, and I gather you've done some tutoring.'

'Well, yes, sir, but that was maths.' And she'd been coaching shy girls for the Oxford High entrance exam or their school certificate, not a bunch of Czech pilots.

'It's still teaching experience.' He addressed Jess. 'Now, I know you have no teaching experience, but as an actress, you must be capable of commanding the room. And, of course, it requires a good understanding of language. Between the two of you, I have every confidence you can do a creditable job.'

Evie gazed at him in dismay but kept quiet. She quailed at the idea of teaching a roomful of men. Her only shred of comfort was that she wouldn't be alone but have Jess's company.

'When do we start?'

'Tomorrow afternoon.' Bob handed her a file. 'As you work in Ops, you're familiar with radio communications. Here's a list of the words the pilots need to use and understand, in addition to everyday English.

The first lesson will be at fifteen hundred hours in the briefing room. You'll find a list of lesson times in the file. I can't release you from all your Ops Room duties, but I've worked lessons around your watches and arranged to release you from nights.'

As they were on their way out, Bob stopped them at the door. 'By the way, Squadron Leader Kincaith will be sitting in on the lessons.'

Evie walked out of the Admin block, her head in a spin.

'I don't believe it,' Jess hissed the moment they were out of earshot.

'I know,' Evie sighed. 'How does teaching long division to girls qualify me to teach English to a bunch of pilots?'

'No, that's not what I meant.' Jess's eyes shone. 'We'll be with pilots. And no more night watches. We won't have to leave the midsummer party early!'

Despite herself, Evie couldn't help laughing at her friend. 'You're incorrigible. What happened to taking our duties seriously?'

'What could be more serious than preparing pilots for operational flying?' Jess gave a cheeky grin. 'And if it involves spending an hour a day with pilots, all the better.' Then she pulled a face. 'Pity we'll have Kincaith sitting in on lessons, though. It won't be so much fun with him watching our every move.'

Evie didn't like to admit the thought of seeing Alex was the only crumb of comfort she had. 'He speaks Czech, though. We're going to need him to translate at first.'

'I suppose,' Jess said, looking doubtful. 'Come on. Let's grab some food in the NAAFI and plan our first lesson. I aim to dazzle.'

8

Alex paced outside Brimstone's dispersal hut. Laughter drifted from within, followed by a crash that sounded like breaking furniture. He ignored it; he would deal with the Czechs later. All his attention was on the sky. The remaining six members of Brimstone squadron were on their way. Only a few minutes before he had to look them in the eye again, see their accusation. In his impatience to get back into the air he'd been able to ignore the burden of guilt for the most part but now he could feel his back bowing beneath its weight.

Soon the throb of Merlin engines reached his ears, and then he could see them: six specks against the blue sky. He wished time would slow down, putting off the moment when he had to face the surviving pilots from his former command, but before he knew it, the Hurricanes were swooping low over the airfield. All five made a perfect landing and, directed by the waiting Erks, taxied towards their dispersal pens. Alex became aware of his nails digging into his palms; he had to make an effort to unclench his fists before striding towards the newcomers with what he hoped was a convincing smile.

The canopy of the lead aircraft slid back, revealing the grinning face and bright red hair of Alex's second, Flight Lieutenant John Harper. 'Good to see you again, sir,' he cried as he clambered to the ground. He disentangled himself from his parachute and handed it to one of the ground crew before jogging over to join Alex.

'Welcome to Amberton.' Alex swept a glance from Harper to the other pilots who had all now climbed from their Hurricanes and were gathering round. He couldn't bring himself to look anyone in the face, dreading to see the glares of accusation.

Harper clapped Alex on the shoulder. 'Wouldn't want to be anywhere else, sir. I've been pestering Group for weeks to return me to Brimstone. There was talk of being permanently assigned as instructors, but I wasn't having any of it, and I know the lads here felt the same.'

There was a general murmur of agreement, and Alex finally dared to look his comrades in the face. He saw nothing but gladness and eagerness. These were the only ones who had survived their last mission in one piece. Where were the dark looks, the mutterings he had braced himself for? It was a shock to find acceptance when he was responsible for leading them into disaster. They were watching him expectantly, so he said a few words of greeting to each one, he hardly knew what.

Another crash from the dispersal hut made him flinch. 'I'd better show you the dispersal hut while it's still there.' This was met with chuckles, and gradually the dread lifted. Beyond belief, it seemed as though all his former pilots were happy to have him back as their CO. He gave his first genuine smile of the day. 'It's good to have you all back. Brimstone squadron wouldn't be the same without you.'

He led the way to the dispersal hut. 'I'll introduce you to the new lads, but then we'll have to leave you to it for a while. They've got their first English lesson.' More bursts of laughter escaped from the hut. 'God help the poor WAAFs who are supposed to be teaching them.'

* * *

The English lessons would be held in Briefing Room 2, located in one of the wooden huts behind the Admin block. When Evie and Jess arrived, they found that the sun, pouring through the windows, had heated the room to a stifling degree. They flung open the windows to let in some air, then arranged the room for the lesson. Evie, her heart pounding, eyed the large map covering one wall right up to the rafters.

'That'll be useful when we cover bearings, but we won't need it today,' said Evie. She found it oddly difficult to draw breath. Why couldn't the station commander have asked them to do something easier? Parachute into Germany and single-handedly take Hitler prisoner, for instance.

Jess didn't seem to be suffering from nerves at all. She looked around the room, hands on hips, then pointed at a blackboard propped in a corner. 'We can use that, though.'

Evie blew out a shaky breath and nodded. Between them, they picked up the board, but Evie's hands were trembling so hard she lost her grip and it crashed back to the floor. By the time they'd placed the blackboard and arranged ten rickety wooden chairs in an arc facing the board, she felt as though she had hundreds of butterflies fluttering in her stomach.

Then the door banged open, and the Czechs walked in on a wave of laughter and cigarette smoke. They nudged each other when they noticed the girls

94

and muttered to one another, grinning. Their walks became swaggers; they made a show of straightening their tunics and smoothing back their hair. Heat seared Evie's cheeks, and it took all her strength not to flee the room. The only thing that kept her in place was the thought of the tongue-lashing she would receive from Flight Officer Ellerby if she failed in her duty.

Jess edged closer. 'Chin up. Don't let them see you're scared,' she murmured so that only Evie could hear. It was easy for Jess to say; she was used to facing a crowd. Still, she endeavoured to imitate Jess. She straightened her shoulders, raised her chin and set her face in what she hoped was a confident expression. As confident as anyone could look with cheeks the colour of beetroot. Oddly, though, faking unconcern did make her feel better. Even when the men sat, arms folded, and raked the girls with bold gazes, she managed to swallow her nerves and pretend she was doing nothing more terrifying than teaching fractions to a group of ten-year-olds.

She'd expected to feel self-conscious in Alex's presence, but when he swept in, she felt a surge of relief. He rapped an order in Czech and the men sat up and fell silent. Then Alex approached the girls. 'I'll keep them in order. Just give me a nod if you need me to translate anything.' He took a seat in a corner at the back, and some of Evie's tension eased.

Before the lesson, Evie and Jess had decided to cover simple introductions, and move on to numbers if there was time. Jess had volunteered to start, leaving Evie to teach the numbers.

Jess stepped up on the dais, squared her shoulders and clasped her hands behind her back. From where

95

Evie was standing, she could see Jess's fingers were tightly knotted, but that was her only sign of nerves. She gave the group a wide smile and spoke in her best BBC accent. 'Good afternoon. My name is Jess Halloway, and this' — she gestured towards Evie — 'is Evie Bishop.'

There was a mumbled greeting that sounded more like cattle lowing than any actual words. To Evie's admiration, Jess's smile didn't waver. Instead, by drawing a clock on the blackboard and setting the hands to different times, she explained the differences between 'good morning', 'good afternoon' and 'good evening'. Then she went around the group and got everyone to introduce themselves. She repeated their names, stumbling a little over unfamiliar pronunciation, and that seemed to break the ice with most of the group. They laughed at her mistakes but not unkindly.

One man, however, slouched against the wall, watching the proceedings with his black brows pulled together. He had jutting cheekbones, dark hair and piercing blue eyes. Evie braced herself when it was his turn to speak, but he simply said, 'Good afternoon. My name is Milan Mašek.' From the easy way he spoke, albeit with a strong accent, she guessed his English was far more advanced than the other pilots'. She had the sense he was biding his time, waiting to make some kind of point, although what that was, she couldn't guess.

When Jess moved on to pointing at one of the men and asking another, 'Who is he?' one of the men — a sergeant pilot called Josef Kaspar — laughed and replied, '*Je to úplný blázen.*'

Judging from Alex's glare, it wasn't complimentary.

Alex half rose, but a pilot officer — Karol Šimek if Evie remembered correctly — stood up and let loose a stream of angry Czech. Eventually he turned and said to Jess in broken English, 'I tell him to be sensible.'

Jess smiled and thanked him, then continued the lesson. Evie glanced at Alex again; Karol must have translated correctly, because Alex made no further move to interfere.

By the time it was her turn, Evie's mouth was so dry she feared she would be unable to speak. She picked up the chalk to write the numbers from zero to twelve on the board. Her hands trembled violently; her number three was distinctly wobbly. Halfway through number five the chalk snapped and fell to the floor. There was no way she was bending down to pick it up with all those men watching. Face flaming, she grabbed the other stick from the ledge. Then that piece broke. Now she was left trying to write with only the stub of chalk that she'd thankfully managed to hold on to. If only someone would speak or even laugh, she would feel better, but the silence stretched out to eternity. The only sound was the scratch of the chalk and the thundering of her heart. She'd never realised before how long it took to write thirteen numbers. The butterflies in her stomach performed spectacular aerobatics, and she was profoundly aware of the scorch of nine pairs of eyes upon her back. Oh, God, she was going to throw up or faint. She'd never live down the disgrace.

Then an image hovered in front of her, an image that had never been far from her thoughts since the day in Brighton. Yet again, she saw the crowd of wounded soldiers, the horror of what they had suffered etched upon their faces. She drew a steadying breath. *Evie Bishop, if those men can endure spending days under fire, trapped on a beach, you can cope with teaching a few men to count in English. Surely it's not too much to ask.*

She swallowed and opened her mouth, but the sullen man, Milan Mašek, raised a hand. 'A question, please?'

Oh no. Why now? 'Of course.' By some miracle she managed to force out the words. She gave him what she hoped was the kind of confident smile Jess had used, but it felt more like a strained grimace.

'You ken fly?' She presumed 'ken' was his way of pronouncing 'can'.

Where was he going with this? 'No.'

He folded his arms and slouched even lower. 'Then you have nothing to teach me. I am here to kill Germans. That is all.'

Alex sprang to his feet, but somehow Evie knew what she had to say. If she let Alex answer for her now, she would never gain the respect of the class. She flung out her hand to stop Alex intervening. 'Just translate for me, so everyone is absolutely clear,' she said to him. She had no doubt Flying Officer Mašek would understand without a translation, but she needed everyone to hear this, so they all knew neither she nor Jess were to be treated with contempt. 'I may not be able to fly, but I won a scholarship to Oxford University to read maths, so I think I'm just about qualified to teach you to count to twelve. You want to fight the Germans, well, believe me, I want you to be up there fighting them too. The station commander has made it clear to me that you won't be allowed in the air until you can all speak English well enough to communicate over the radio, and it's up to me and

98

Miss Halloway to make sure you can do so. If you're not prepared to learn, I'm sure you can find a bomber crew only too willing to throw you out over Germany, where you can fight Nazis to your heart's content.'

Quite where all the words came from, she didn't know. Something that had been building up inside her ever since Brighton, she supposed. She bit back a smile when Alex's eyebrows rose at her comment about the bomber crew, but he translated anyway. She knew when he'd got to that part, because a ripple of laughter broke out. She glanced at Milan, expecting more hostility, but he gave her a grudging nod and sat up straighter. She couldn't resist glancing at Alex. His mouth curved in a slow smile, and he gave her the thumbs-up. Her heart leapt. She couldn't have felt more proud if she'd been awarded first class honours at Oxford.

After that the lesson passed without incident. Evie's confidence increased, and she even managed to explain, with a little help from Alex in the translation, that over the radio, they should pronounce five as 'fife' and nine as 'niner'.

By the end of the lesson, she was pleased with how it had gone, but she felt like she could sleep for a year. She opened her mouth to dismiss the class, but Milan put up his hand again.

God, give her strength. What now? 'Yes?'

'One more question. Will you both come to the pub with us tonight?'

She relaxed and allowed herself the first genuine smile of the lesson. 'We'd be delighted.' She said a sad mental goodbye to the idea of a quiet night in the schoolroom of High Chalk House, drinking cocoa with Jess and May. They would find it much easier to teach Brimstone squadron if they could make friends with them.

★ ★ ★

The snug at the Horse and Groom was Brimstone squadron's undisputed territory that evening. It was a warm evening, so all the windows were wide open, and Alex feared the raucous Czech folk songs drifting up the lane would put off Evie and Jess from joining them.

'How did their first training flights go this morning?' Peter Travis had to shout to make himself heard above a particularly rousing chorus. In the middle of the group of pilots, Jiří Stepanek was sitting on Josef Kaspar's shoulders and, arms outstretched like wings, they raced around the room in time to the music, dodging between the tables. Alex winced as Jiří struck his head on a particularly large horse brass dangling from one of the roof beams. If Evie had any sense, she'd turn round and go straight back to the Waafery.

He tried to ignore the twinge of regret that thought caused while he answered Peter. 'No one died and no one crashed. They even remembered to lower their undercarriages before landing.' It had been a close-run thing in a couple of cases, though. Alex had stood helplessly on the ground, yelling and waving frantically at planes as they made their final approach with the undercarriages still up. Alex was surprised his hair hadn't turned white. Not for the first time, he wished there was such a thing as a dual-control Hurricane. Watching his pilots take off in a high-performance fighter with no prior experience of one was the most

100

helpless feeling in the world. Still, near-misses with the undercarriage aside, they'd all performed well, putting their Hurricanes into rolls and dives with ease. 'We'll start on interception exercises tomorrow. See how well they've learnt their numbers.'

Peter raised his eyebrows. 'What's that smile for?'

Alex had been unaware he was smiling. 'Oh, I was just thinking of the way a certain red-headed WAAF managed to face down a roomful of rowdy Czech pilots.'

As though summoned by his thoughts, Evie walked into the snug, followed by Jess and the shy, gawky driver. Although judging from the way Peter's face softened, he didn't seem to consider her at all gawky.

Alex rose, intending to get the girls a drink and move the men away from the corner table so they could all sit down. But a cheer went up from the pilots and they milled around the girls, making it impossible for Alex to get close. Each pilot bowed to the girls and bade them 'Good evening' in an exaggerated English accent. Then they took delight in counting how many pints each had drunk.

'Poor May,' Peter muttered. 'I don't think she'll be enjoying this. I'll see if she wants to sit outside.' He'd scarcely finished speaking before he was forcing his way to May's side. He spoke in the girl's ear, and then guided her out of the door. Alex had to admire how quickly he'd taken advantage of the situation. He tried to force his way through the crush to Evie and Jess, but could only watch as Karol Šimek — the man who'd rebuked Josef for not taking the lesson seriously — did what Alex had intended to do, and moved men away from the corner table so Evie and Jess could sit down.

At least it meant Evie was sitting next to him, but his hackles rose when Karol fetched the girls their drinks and sat beside Evie, placing himself between her and Alex. Couldn't she see his charm was fake? He was only acting that way to get what he wanted. He'd thought Evie was more intelligent than to fall for a line like the one Karol was now spinning. He was forced to simmer in silence while Karol described to the girls how he had stolen a German officer's car and used it to escape into Poland. A likely story. The Nazis would have shot him before he'd so much as started the engine.

When Karol went to the bar to get another drink, Alex took the opportunity to move next to Evie. 'I didn't get the chance earlier, but I wanted to tell you both how impressed I was with your lesson and the way you handled the men.'

Evie smiled, but it was Jess who answered. 'I was gobsmacked when Evie tore into that Milan bloke.' Alex had to smile at the way her BBC English slipped when she was excited.

At that moment, Milan himself pushed through the crowd to stand at Jess's elbow. Jess glanced up at him and scowled. 'You should be ashamed of yourself, speaking to Evie like that. It's obvious you speak English well, so you should be helping us, not making our jobs more difficult.'

Milan gave her a half bow. 'You are right, of course. That is why I am here — to apologise and buy you both a drink. And you, of course, sir,' he added with a nod to Alex.

They gave their orders, and Milan elbowed his way to the bar, Jess going with him to help carry the drinks. Suddenly it was just Alex and Evie alone at

102

the table. It seemed to Alex that the noise receded. The haze of cigarette smoke seemed to blot out all the other people in the room, and he could only see Evie's sweet face before him.

'You've made an impression on Milan,' he said. She'd made an impression on Alex, too, but he wasn't going to let her know that. 'You'll have no trouble with him any more.'

The smile she gave punched him in the gut. 'I wonder what happened to him to make him so . . .'

'Pig-headed? Annoying?' he suggested with a smile.

She laughed. 'Something like that.'

He shrugged. 'We can't know what they've been through. They've had to leave behind their families and friends to the tender mercies of the Nazis. They arrived here with little more than the clothes on their backs. All they want to do is lash out at the Germans, and what they see as our petty rules are preventing them from doing that.'

Her brow puckered. 'Do you have family in Czechoslovakia?'

He shook his head. 'Well, not any I've met. I must have distant cousins, I suppose, but I don't know anything about them.'

He glanced at the bar, but Milan was still waiting to be served. That gave him a few more minutes alone with Evie. Nothing could come of it, but he was starting to look forward to these brief moments with her. At times like this he could forget there was a war on, pretend he was free to pursue a relationship with a woman. 'What about your family? Where are you from?'

'Oxford. My mum still lives there, but my dad . . .' She pressed her lips tightly together, but she couldn't quite hide their quivering.

'I'm sorry.' Alex felt an impulse to take her hand, but he resisted, doubting she would welcome it. He racked his brains for a change of subject. Then he remembered one of the things she'd said in her spirited tirade. 'Did you really win a scholarship to Oxford?'

'Yes. Why — don't you think girls belong there?' She was obviously too upset to filter her speech. Alex bit back a smile when her face turned scarlet and a look of horror formed on her face at the realisation she'd snapped at an officer. 'I'm sorry, I —'

'Don't apologise. And you're right, in a way. A few years ago, I'd have been very surprised to hear of a girl reading maths at university, but seeing how well you and the other WAAFs cope I've been forced to rethink my opinion.'

'I'm glad to hear it.' Evie smiled at him, and his heart swooped.

'I think you've changed more minds than mine. What made you give up your scholarship?'

Evie's pretty face clouded. 'I didn't give it up. My mother turned it down for me. It's not just men who think women belong at home.'

'Maybe she'll change her mind when she learns about the difference you and all the WAAFs are making to the war effort. What would she think if you became an officer?'

Evie gave an incredulous laugh. 'Me? She'd definitely think I'd got too high and mighty for my own good.'

'I'm serious. You displayed definite officer material, the way you handled Milan. You should think about it.'

But Evie just shook her head. 'A girl from Cowley, an officer? It'll never happen.'

The others returned with their drinks at that moment, so there was no chance to pursue the conversation.

But all through the rest of the evening, he couldn't tear his gaze from Evie, admiring the way her hair shone a deep coppery red when it caught the light and how her face seemed to glow each time she smiled. The voice in the back of his mind reminding him he had no right to get involved with a woman was growing quieter, drowned out by another voice. The new one asked, why not? Why not snatch a little happiness while he still could?

105

9

'No,' Jess said, scowling at May. 'I'm not stepping a foot out of this house until you do as I say.'

'But —'

'I said no. It's bad enough having to wear our uniforms, but you're not going to the dance with your hair scraped back like an ancient schoolmistress. Hand me your brush.'

Amused, Evie watched resignation chase reluctance across May's face. May handed over the brush, and Jess unpinned May's hair and brushed it out until it fell in a lustrous mahogany sheet over her shoulders. With deft fingers, Jess coaxed it into waves and pinned it in the front.

'There,' she said, stepping back to admire her handiwork. 'All the pilots will be wondering what Katharine Hepburn is doing at the Amberton village dance.' She turned May round to face the schoolroom fireplace, where the mirror hung upon the chimney breast. 'Take a look, if you don't believe me.'

May peered into the mirror. 'I look so different,' she breathed.

Jess's face softened. 'You're the same beautiful May, but with better hair. Now do you believe what we've been telling you all along?'

May didn't look convinced, but she didn't attempt to change her hair.

Jess turned on Evie. 'I don't know why you're smiling like that. It's your turn.'

Evie submitted to Jess's ministrations. 'You can't make me look like Katharine Hepburn.'

'More like Greer Garson.'

Evie had no idea how she did it, but under Jess's skilled fingers, her straight red hair was soon falling in Hollywood waves.

'Now for the finishing touch.' Jess handed Evie her lipstick.

Evie hesitated. The burgundy lipstick, that had made her feel so daring when she'd bought it in Brighton, was now forever associated in her mind with the distressing sight of the beaten soldiers returning from Dunkirk.

Jess must have read her mind, for suddenly her expression was serious. 'Listen to me, Evie Bishop. Today all our pilots are safe, but you must have heard the mutterings of the senior officers. We only have a short time, a few weeks at most, before the Germans try and do to us what they've done to the rest of Europe, and our boys will be on the front line.'

Evie did know. Only that morning, in the Operations Room, she'd overheard Peter Travis muttering to the Ops 'A' about the latest intelligence of German squadrons building up near the French coast. It wouldn't be long before all that air power was unleashed in the skies above England.

'I don't see what that has to do with me wearing lipstick.'

'We don't know how many of our boys will still be here next month or next year, but tonight they're coming to dance with pretty girls and have fun. We owe it to them to look our best, not like we're about to go on duty. So put on your lipstick and scent — and you, May — then let's show them some Hollywood glamour, and help them forget the war for a few hours.'

Evie couldn't argue with that, so she applied the lipstick and gave herself a spritz of perfume. She had no more time for doubts, for Jess glanced at her watch and squealed, 'Hurry! The transport will be at the door any minute.'

They grabbed their gas masks and dashed down the stairs.

The transport dropped them beside the green in Amberton, opposite the village hall. It was a pretty brick and flint building, with a steeply pitched tiled roof. There was a little garden at the front. It had probably been a mass of flowers before the war, but now ranks of greens and vegetables filled the beds. When the driver cut the engine, the cheerful strains of *Little Brown Jug*' drifted out from the open doors. As it was Midsummer's Eve, the sun was still up but it hung low over the trees, painting the sky a deep gold. Evie had no doubt there would be plenty of revellers still up to see the sun rise, but as she was on an early watch the next day, she'd be sure to take the first transport back to High Chalk House.

Several of the Czech pilots greeted them with enthusiastic good evenings as the three girls walked arm-in-arm into the hall, through the door and then the heavy blackout curtain. Evie had a quiet smile when Peter Travis gazed open-mouthed at May and looked in danger of dropping his drink. Although she'd been wary of the obvious attraction between the two at first, worried the inexperienced May would get hurt, now she'd got to know Peter better, Evie was convinced he would be good for May and she wished the two would admit their feelings for each other.

108

His kindness and encouragement had done much to bring May out of her shell, and Evie knew he could be depended upon not to let her down. There wasn't even the worry that Peter might be killed or captured. Being based in Ops, he was about as safe as it was possible to be with a war on.

Evie looked around the hall. There was a real band, she was pleased to see, set up on the stage at the end of the long room. Light flooded down from spotlights high up on the rafters, illuminating round tables set around the edges of the hall. The centre was filled with couples dancing, feet tapping on the polished floorboards. Most were in uniform; the RAF and WAAF personnel far outnumbered the villagers. The civilian suits and dresses stood out among the air force blue.

The girls hurried to place their gas masks upon an empty chair. Jess whipped her compact out of her case and gave her face a quick inspection before replacing it. They were about to cross to the bar, when a tall pilot approached. There was no mistaking the dark hair and ice-blue gaze of Milan.

'Good evening, ladies,' he said, then turned to Jess. 'Would you like to dance?'

Evie watched them whirl into the dance, feeling a twinge of envy at the ease with which Jess glided across the dance floor. Evie had learned the foxtrot and waltz at school — apparently dancing was a necessary skill for young ladies — but she'd never been to a real dance before. She didn't know if she had the nerve to dance even if she was asked. Still, it was fun to watch, and she had May for company.

No sooner had that thought struck than Peter Travis approached and asked May to dance.

May blushed a becoming pink and glanced at Evie. 'Go on,' Evie said. 'I don't mind.'

May accepted, still blushing, and placed her hand on Peter's arm, allowing him to lead her onto the dance floor. Evie watched them with a smile. Neither of them seemed to know any dance steps, but they held on to each other and shuffled from side to side in time to the music, laughing each time one or the other tripped.

'What's so funny?'

Evie jumped at the sound of Alex's voice. She turned to find him standing beside her. 'Oh,' she said, pressing a hand to her chest in a vain attempt to slow her rapid heartbeat. 'I didn't see you there. I was just smiling at May trying to dance with Squadron Leader Travis.' Suddenly remembering Alex's rank, she wondered if she should salute, but a glance around the hangar showed her other WAAFs talking and dancing with officers and not a salute in sight. The formalities seemed to have been suspended for the dance.

Alex followed her gaze and smiled. 'I hesitated to ask you to dance because I don't know how, but that doesn't seem to have stopped those two.' He offered her his hand. 'Will you dance with me? Or, to be more accurate, will you stand patiently while I trip over your feet?'

Evie took his hand with a smile, then faltered at the surge of warmth that flowed up her arm from their joined hands. 'I . . . I do know how to dance, you know. I can teach you.' She was gabbling to cover her confusion. 'We can try a foxtrot.'

'Go on, then. You'll find it more of a challenge than teaching English to a bunch of rowdy Czechs.'

110

Before she could reply, his right hand was on her back, and she stood facing him, her right hand still clasped in his left. She dared to place her right hand on his arm and shivered at the feel of firm muscle through the cloth of his sleeve. Painfully aware of the heat of his hand upon her back, she demonstrated the basic step of a foxtrot.

'Start with your left foot forward,' she said, moving her right foot back to match. 'Now step forward with your right. Good. Now sidestep two quick steps to the left.'

Soon they were dancing in time with the music. It was more of a gallop than a foxtrot, but Evie didn't care. Her senses were overwhelmed with the music, Alex's nearness; even the faint scent of coal tar soap that clung to him seemed exotic because it was part of Alex.

She leant back so she could smile up at him. 'See, I knew you could do it. How come you can't dance, anyway? I thought it was practically an essential accomplishment for a dashing English pilot.'

'Ah, but I'm not English. I'm Scottish, and I was brought up by my very austere grandparents.' The soft roll of each 'r' emphasised the assertion.

'Oh.' She wanted to ask what had happened to his parents but hesitated in case it was a painful subject.

Alex must have understood her dilemma for he waved away her concerns and explained. 'I was orphaned a long time ago, when I was too young to really understand what was happening. My father was killed in the last war, and my mother died of Spanish Flu just after.'

'I'm sorry.' She had the feeling this wasn't something he shared with many people, and felt she wanted to return the confidence. 'The last war destroyed so many lives. My father was gassed. He survived but never fully recovered. He died last year.'

'That must have been tough. Is that why your mother turned down your scholarship?'

'Probably. I never asked. I couldn't stay in Oxford after that, seeing others enjoying student life while I slaved at some menial job, so I joined the WAAF.'

'That was brave of you.'

It was as if all the other dancing couples faded out of existence. All that was left was the music, and Alex holding her in his arms.

Then the band segued into *Cheek to Cheek*. Neither of them said a word. Whether Alex pulled her closer, or if she leaned in herself, she didn't know, but now she was pressed tightly to his body, and she melted into his arms. Alex was too tall for them to actually dance cheek to cheek, but they swayed in time to the music, not following any particular dance. Evie was pressed so close she could feel the rapid beat of his heart. Or was it hers? It was impossible to tell. If he dipped his head just a little, their faces would be close enough to kiss.

Flustered, suddenly unsure, Evie looked over Alex's shoulder; her gaze fell on all the uniformed men grouped around the bar. Then her mind seemed to play tricks on her, because she wasn't seeing the strong, healthy men of RAF Amberton, but the bent, broken bodies of the soldiers she had seen in Brighton. Then the image shifted to her father coughing his lungs out and her mother's drawn, anxious face. She shivered and pulled away slightly, overcome with a sense of dread. The war was closing in and when it arrived, Alex would be on the front line. As much as she shied away from the thought, she had to face facts: there was a high chance that Alex would be killed.

'Are you all right?' The concern in Alex's eyes nearly undid her. More than anything she wanted to forget the war and be held by Alex all night, but the longer she stayed with him, the greater the risk of falling in love.

'I . . . The heat's making me a bit dizzy.' Who was she trying to fool? Alex was making her head spin, not the heat. She should walk away, leave while her heart was still her own. Because if she fell in love with Alex and then lost him, her heart would shatter.

'Let me get you a drink.'

A rapid drumbeat sounded the opening bars of 'Sing, Sing, Sing', pounding in time with Evie's heart. When the rest of the band took up the tune, Evie saw Peter Travis lead May back to her seat. This was her opportunity to murmur an excuse and return to her friends, but the words wouldn't come. She allowed Alex to guide her to a quiet corner seat and sat tapping her feet in time to the music while he went to fetch drinks. Surely another few minutes in Alex's company wouldn't hurt. But when he returned, he handed her a glass of punch then sat beside her in silence, scowling into his beer mug. She shot him several slantwise gazes. Maybe he was just being kind, and didn't really want to be with her. She tried to ignore the lurch of disappointment. That was what she wanted, wasn't it? She should leave.

She was braced to rise, racking her brains for an excuse, when Alex cleared his throat. 'Evie, I . . . Oh, dash it, it was easier when I rehearsed this in my head.'

113

Her mouth went dry. The frenetic tune urged her to run, but her legs wouldn't move. All she could do was wait, throat tight, while he tried again.

'What I mean is, if this was any other time, I'd be asking if I could court you, but this war . . .'

She seized on it. 'Yes, the war.' Her voice shook, and she swallowed, cross with herself. This was what she wanted, wasn't it? She should be relieved Alex was offering her an escape. 'It's the wrong time.'

'Aye. Chances are I won't make it. At the moment there's no one who would mourn my death, and I want to keep it that way.'

I would mourn. But she couldn't say it. She felt winded by his casual acceptance of death. Her head spinning, struggling to comprehend how anyone could endure that burden, she forced a smile. 'Anyway, I have to focus on my duty. I can't afford any distractions.'

Evie ignored the tiny voice in the back of her mind that told her it was too late. She already found Alex Kincaith a powerful distraction.

★ ★ ★

Well, this wasn't awkward at all. Alex sipped his beer, unsure what to say next. Maybe he'd misread the dreamy expression on Evie's face when they'd been dancing, but he'd been sure when she'd tilted her face up to his, she'd wanted him to kiss her. He'd wanted to. If they hadn't been in a crowded room, he would have done, but he wasn't going to share their first kiss with the entire village.

Fool! Despite silently rehearsing what he wanted to say to her while they danced, it had come out all

114

wrong. He'd been trying to ask if she'd wait for him, but the only thing to come out of his mouth had been a list of all the reasons they couldn't be together.

She needn't have agreed quite so quickly, though. It looked like he'd misread the looks she'd given him. She obviously hadn't felt the same spark of electricity when their hands had met. It was a good thing he *had* got his words wrong. Imagine if he'd told her of his growing feelings, asked her to wait for him so he could court her when all this was over, only for her to declare that she didn't feel the same way. He shuddered to think of the pity in her eyes every time they met after that.

A figure in uniform approached. Karol Šimek. Alex tensed. He smiled a greeting, trying to hide his dislike of the man. It was unfair to take such an immediate dislike to someone. It could only be because Evie liked him and was taken in by his charm.

Karol stopped in front of Evie's chair. 'I was going to ask you to dance, but if you're too tired . . .'

Evie rose. 'Oh, no. I'd be delighted.' She shot a sideways glance at Alex, but then turned a bright smile upon Karol and took his arm.

Alex watched them go. Clearly Karol had mixed in the circle of society expected in an officer, for he was an accomplished dancer. He didn't need to look at his feet and he certainly wouldn't trip. Instead he whirled Evie around the dance floor, weaving expertly around other couples. Other couples turned to watch them. Not surprising when they looked so right together — the elegant, sophisticated young pilot partnering the fiery redhead who shone with an inner radiance that made Alex's breath catch. Karol guided Evie around the corner in perfect time with the music, then dipped her right in front of Alex. When she rose, her face was flushed, and she gazed into Karol's eyes, her beautiful face alight with laughter.

He couldn't take any more of this. He strode out of the hall and found himself walking up the road towards the station. His shadow stretched long and thin ahead of him as though straining to escape from the idiot it was attached to. Eventually he came to the fence separating the RAF station from the village. He leaned against a huge copper beech that towered over the fence and watched the sun sink low over the treetops.

After a while, calm acceptance washed over him. What did it matter if Evie danced with Karol Šimek, or every member of Brimstone squadron, come to that? She'd declared her intention to focus on her duty, and he believed her. It was the right thing to do. If he was going to get his squadron through the war, he needed to do the same. And in the end, whether Evie had feelings for him was irrelevant. He was aware of an ominous heaviness in the air. Thunder clouds were gathering, would soon unleash their fury in the skies above Britain. It was no time for personal considerations. Each had their own small but important role to play, and Britain's only hope of survival was if everyone did their appointed tasks to the best of their ability.

Halting footsteps sounded behind him, and he spun around to see Peter Travis approach.

'Not disturbing you, am I?' Travis asked.

Alex shook his head. 'Why aren't you dancing with that driver of yours? I thought she was rather smitten with you.'

'Best that she's not.' Peter pointed at his leg. 'Not exactly every girl's dream.'

'What does she think — have you asked her?' Alex didn't know the girl in question very well, but from what he'd seen, she wouldn't have cared if Peter had a false leg, hooks instead of hands and an eye patch.

'What's the point? She deserves better than this.'

Alex wondered what had brought this on. The last he'd seen of Peter, he'd been dancing with the striking driver — May, that was her name — looking as though he hadn't a care in the world. 'I don't know what you mean,' he said, uncomfortable with the turn the conversation had taken. 'You're one of the finest officers on the station.' He hesitated. Talking about his feelings was totally alien to him, but he couldn't let Peter — whom he was fast coming to regard as his closest friend — believe he didn't deserve love. 'No one who matters will think any worse of you for having a leg missing.'

'Only me.'

Peter muttered the words so quietly, Alex wondered if he'd heard correctly. He fumbled for the right words, but this was so far outside his experience he could find nothing. 'You —'

But he was saved from having to finish his sentence when Peter burst out with, 'Maybe I'd feel differently if I'd got this fighting Germans, but it was a stupid accident. Meaningless.'

'I doubt the pilot you saved would look at it that way. Or his family.' Alex hadn't known Peter then, but he'd heard the story from others who had. Peter had been working as an RAF instructor, training fighter pilots in Harvard planes. The trainee pilot had crashed on landing, and the Harvard had burst

117

into flames. Peter had pulled the injured pilot from the cockpit but his leg had been burned so badly in the process it had needed to be amputated.

Peter grunted but didn't look convinced. 'I'm thinking of retraining, you know. Applying to fly fighters.'

'But we need you here.' Alex gazed at Peter in astonishment. 'What's brought this on, all of a sudden?'

'It's not sudden. I've been thinking about it for a while.' Peter gazed across the airfield. 'I thought losing my leg had put an end to my career as a pilot, but then I heard about Douglas Bader. If he can fly with no legs, I can do it with one.'

'But you're needed in Ops.' Alex couldn't imagine anyone other than Peter, so unflappable in an emergency, controlling the action.

'There are plenty of men who could do my job, but not so many who can fly fighters. And I'd be up in the air again, Alex. I can't tell you how much I've missed it.'

'I suppose I can understand that.' Alex tried to imagine how he'd feel if he was permanently grounded. There was a feeling of freedom, of release when he was swooping through the clouds that nothing on the ground could compete with. He had a fleeting thought of spinning round the dance floor with Evie in his arms, but quickly pushed the thought away.

'Look, promise you won't say a word about this to anyone,' Peter said. 'I haven't thought it through yet and it might come to nothing.'

'I won't say a thing, on the condition you talk to me before making any decisions you can't back out of.'

'Done. Well, I suppose I'd better show my face back at the dance.'

About to follow Peter, Alex looked down when his eye was caught by the glint of the setting sun reflecting on something half buried in the grass on the other side of the fence. He crouched down and reached through the fence to pick it up. It was a small glass tube. 'Strange. What do you think this is?' He handed it to Peter. It looked a little like a tiny light bulb.

Peter held it up to the dying light and squinted at it. 'Looks like one of those valves you find in a radio.'

Alex took it back and slipped it in his pocket. 'Probably dropped by one of the Erks.' If a member of his own ground crew turned out to be responsible, he'd have them on a charge for wasting precious resources. 'I'll show it to our R/T fitter in the morning.'

They strolled back to the hall. On the way, Alex caught sight of a couple in the distance, walking arm in arm. He got an impression of a tall, dark-haired man and a glamorous blonde. As he watched, the man stooped over the woman as though about to kiss her. Alex looked away with a wry grin. It seemed Milan was getting some extra-curricular English lessons from Jess Halloway. Well, at least someone was having a better evening than him and Peter. He could only hope Milan didn't get his head turned over Jess. She struck him as someone whose heart was not easily touched.

* * *

Much later that night, the three girls were curled up in their armchairs in the schoolroom, sipping cocoa. All three had changed into their pyjamas — they had long ago eschewed nightgowns in favour of more

119

practical nightwear, in case they had to leave the house in a hurry due to an air raid — and were snuggled in blankets they had brought through from their rooms. Evie knew she should go to bed; she had to get up in only five hours to be ready for the early watch. She was too fired up for sleep, though, and she relished this chance to talk through the gossip from the dance. And, more than anything, she wanted to tell them about her conversation with Alex. She still couldn't work out what it had meant. At first, she had thought he'd been making excuses because he thought she'd developed feelings for him which he didn't return. But looking back over the way he had looked at her when they were dancing, the way he had confided in her about his family when she knew he was intensely private about his feelings, she wasn't so sure.

She laughed while Jess entertained them by describing the antics of one of the Czech pilots, but Evie's mind was still focused on Alex.

'He didn't see Kincaith standing right behind him until it was too late.' Jess wiped her eyes. 'What I wouldn't give to be a fly on the wall tomorrow when Kincaith tears a strip off him for cheek.'

'I don't think Alex will be too hard on him.' Evie couldn't resist speaking up in his defence.

Jess arched an eyebrow. 'Oh, so it's Alex now, is it? I couldn't help noticing how cosy the two of you looked dancing together. Is there something we should know?'

'Course not!' Evie felt her cheeks burning. But then she relented. Jess had so much more experience than her; if anyone could tell her what Alex had meant, it was her. 'But . . . well . . . he took me aside later and started saying stuff about how things would be different if there wasn't a war on.' She related the conversation. 'What do you think?'

Jess chewed her lower lip. 'If it was anyone else, I might think they were trying a line on you — making you feel sorry for the heroic pilot who was putting his life on the line for king and country so he could have his way with you.'

Evie's cheeks burned hotter. Partly at Jess's frank words, but also from a thrill about what letting Alex 'have his way' with her might involve. She hurriedly slammed the door on those thoughts. She had to remind herself that she hardly knew Alex. This was infatuation, nothing more.

'Not Kincaith, though,' Jess went on. 'I'll give him this much: he's tough, but he's not cruel, and he says what he means. What's more, from the way he looked at you tonight, any fool could have seen that he cares for you. Play your cards right, my girl, and you could land yourself a pilot. And a squadron leader, at that!'

'I meant it when I said I was serious about my duty,' Evie said. 'This isn't a time for chasing officers — we've all got jobs to do. Or didn't you mean it when we pledged to focus on our work?' It was easier to deflect the conversation to Jess than examine her feelings about Alex. And she couldn't put her dread of losing him into words in the superstitious fear that saying it would somehow make it come true.

'I did mean it. I'll never forget those poor lads in Brighton. But that doesn't mean I can't have fun in my free time.' Jess waved away Evie's protests. 'Oh, don't worry — I won't let my head get turned. Nothing's going to distract me from my work.'

'You looked like you were letting Milan distract you.' Evie had meant to sound light-hearted, but the words came out sounding far more accusing than she'd intended. She'd noticed Jess's smudged lipstick and Milan's ruffled hair when they'd returned to the dance after disappearing for some time. She'd attended enough squirm-inducing lectures during her initial training to know what kind of trouble a girl could find herself in, and she hated to think of anything like that happening to Jess.

Thankfully, Jess didn't take offence. 'Oh, don't worry about Milan. I promise I won't go losing my head over him. He's a good-looking bloke, but there's no danger of me falling for a Czech. He'll be back off to Czechoslovakia when all this is over, so this can never be more than a bit of harmless fun.'

'Promise me you'll be careful? You don't want to end up being kicked out of the WAAF.'

Jess put down her mug on the little table by the arm of her chair and gazed at Evie, her eyes wide. 'Oh, Evie, that ain't going to 'appen. I'm not like that any —' She bit her lip. 'I mean, I would never do anything like that. Me an' Milan had a bit of a kiss and a cuddle, nothing more. And nothing more will happen. All I meant when I said I would have a bit of fun is that I'd go on a few dates with anyone I liked. But there's no danger of me falling in love.'

Evie leaned forward and placed her hand over Jess's. 'Sorry. I shouldn't jump to conclusions. I was worried for you, that's all.'

'Don't be. I promise I won't do anything that will land me in trouble and I'm not going to fall in love.'

'I think I'm in love.'

Evie gaped at May. She'd almost forgotten she was there, she'd been so quiet. 'In love? With Squadron Leader Travis?'

May nodded. She picked at a loose thread in her blanket.

'Well, go on!' Jess urged. 'You can't drop a piece of news like that and then go silent. Have you told him? Does he love you?'

'Course I haven't told him. How — why would I do that? This is the last thing I need.' May looked so miserable that Evie's heart went out to her.

'May, just because I've said I'm not interested in getting involved with a man, it doesn't mean I expect you or anyone else to avoid them.' Evie hoped May's present unhappiness wasn't anything to do with what she'd said. From what she'd seen, Peter Travis had genuine feelings for May, and he was a good man. If anyone needed love and affection in their life it was May, who seemed to have experienced precious little of either from her own family.

Jess chimed in. 'You'd be mad to turn him down. He's a squadron leader. And you'll hardly notice the leg after a while.'

May rounded on Jess. 'It's nothing to do with his leg. I'd love him if he had both legs missing.' She turned to Evie. 'And I'm not turning him down because of anything you said, Evie. It's my poor mum.' May paused and drained her cup.

This was a long speech for May, and Evie thought she'd leave it there, but after she'd put down her mug, May continued in a voice that shook. 'I watched my dad, and later my brothers, too, wear Mum down. She worked long hours in the house, harder than my ungrateful dad ever did, yet at the end of the day, Dad would put his feet up and not lift a finger while Mum and me cooked, cleaned and did laundry. He treated her no better than a slave, and it killed her

123

in the end.' May's voice wobbled, but she shot such a defiant glare at Evie when Evie rose, intending to put her arm round her friend that Evie sank back into her chair. 'Before she died, Mum warned me not to fall into the same trap. She told me Dad had been all sweetness and soft words right until he got the wedding ring on her finger. He only showed his true colours after that. The WAAF has helped me get away from Dad and my brothers, and I'm not going to give up my freedom by marrying any man, no matter how much I might think I love him.' Having said her piece, May looked away, pressing her hand to her mouth.

There was a short silence while Evie and Jess stared at May. A wave of pity washed over Evie, and she groped for the right words to comfort her friend. 'Not all men are like that. My dad was always kind to me and Mum.' A sudden longing struck her to hear her father's voice again. He would know exactly what to say.

May shook her head. 'I'm not saying all men are like that, but it's impossible to know you've married a dud until it's too late. I'm happy now, for the first time in my life. I'm not going to give that up for any man, no matter how much I . . . however kind and charming he behaves.'

Evie was sure Peter could never be unkind, and she thought May knew that, deep down. She hoped May would be able to accept Peter's love one day. There was no danger he could lose his life in the skies. Not like Alex.

Evie shivered. Now the dance was over, life at Amberton would be focused wholly on preparation for the threatened German invasion. Whether it would happen in a few days or weeks, no one knew. But everyone knew that when it came, Amberton's pilots would be on the front line.

10

Alex gazed morosely as Wagtail squadron's 'A' flight zoomed low over the airfield, ruffling the boundary hedge before coming in to land. No more training flights for them. As the Hurricanes taxied to their dispersal pens, Alex could see lines of bullet holes in the fuselage of one machine and another sported a hole in the tail. He breathed a sigh of relief when all pilots emerged unhurt and ambled towards their dispersal hut. One, however, looked up. On seeing Alex, he waved and jogged over to meet him.

'Come to see how it's done?' It was Brian Sinclair, Wagtail's CO. He was accompanied by a strong smell of glycol.

'How *not* to do it, I'd say,' Alex replied, pointing to Brian's Hurricane. It was his tail that had a hole punched through it.

Brian winced. 'I got caught on the hop. Too busy shooting down a Dornier to spot the 109 hiding in the sun.'

Alex shuddered. The Germans' favourite tactic was to place themselves between the British aircraft and the sun, rendering themselves all but invisible. He remembered only too well the feeling of dry-mouthed horror at seeing a swarm of 109s appear from nowhere. That was how his own squadron had been ambushed. Suddenly the warmth leached from the air and he was back in the thick of the fight, watching dry-mouthed as the Hurricane that had been flying alongside only moments before now spun towards the ground in a spiral of flames and black smoke. He fought the urge to close his eyes and block out the images. Nothing could ever make him forget what had happened, forget he had led his own pilots to a needless death. Brian was giving him an odd look, so Alex hastily groped for something to say. 'What was it like out there?'

'Hotting up, but nothing we can't handle. They're still biding their time, testing out tactics.'

'With a bit of luck, they'll wait until Brimstone is operational.'

'How long, do you think?'

'We'd be ready now, if the lads didn't keep forgetting to speak English over the radio. Their English is good enough now when they remember to use it. I was on my way to plead my case with Bob when I saw you come in.' The sooner he got back in the air, the easier it would be to force his guilt to the back of his mind.

'Good luck with that. We could do with you lot out there.' Brian clapped him on the shoulder. 'Better dash. Must write my report before someone else claims my Dornier.'

As Brian strolled off, Alex stood for a while, drawing several deep breaths, waiting for the last of the nightmare images to fade. The pilots who had survived might have forgiven him, but he never could. Finally regaining control, he was about to find Bob when he happened to glance across at his own machine and noticed the R/T fitter at work on it.

He changed course and went to speak to him. 'Did you find the problem?' On his last flight, his radio had kept cutting out. It was bad enough trying to keep his pilots organised when they could hear him; it was chaos when they couldn't.

The fitter nodded. 'Nothing serious, sir. Just a loose connection. It's as good as new now.'

Alex thanked him and was about to move away when he remembered the mysterious glass bulb he'd found after the dance. 'Did you find out about that radio component I showed you?'

'Yes, it was definitely from our stores. If I find out which careless sod left that lying around, I'll kick him into next week.' The fitter paused. 'Unless it was one of those German parachutists. I read in the paper the Jerries are parachuting in and working with fifth columnists.'

'I think it's more likely one of your lads was in a hurry to get down to the pub and dropped it. We'd notice if there was a stranger roaming the station.'

Unless it was someone stationed here. The thought flitted through Alex's mind as he resumed his walk to the Admin block. The he shook his head and laughed at himself. He was getting as bad as the paranoid reporter who had written the article, warning locals to watch out for parachutists. The team at Amberton were a family, all looking out for each other. No one here was an imposter. The enemy was lurking on the other side of the Channel, poised to strike. There was no need to make up any more.

★ ★ ★

It didn't take long for the midsummer dance to become no more than a gilded memory — a fond reminiscence of how good life had been in the distant past. Judging from the grim expressions of the senior officers, attack was imminent. There were increased raids upon shipping, and in the Operations Room, Evie plotted the progress of German fighters as they carried out lightning raids upon convoys in the Channel. Amberton's squadrons had been ordered to intercept a few of these attacks. She would never forget the heavy silence in the room when the news filtered through that a young pilot from Popcorn squadron had been shot down in flames over the sea. No parachute had been seen. Evie had never spoken to the pilot, but she'd seen him at the dance and had a clear picture of his youthful face as he'd stood with his friends, laughing as though he didn't have a care in the world.

More than ever, she was grateful that Brimstone squadron had still not been passed for operational flying. She could only pray that she would be able to keep a clear head and concentrate on her work when the wooden blocks on the plotting table represented pilots she'd come to know and like. As for how she would feel when Alex was with them . . . She tried not to think too hard about that.

As June passed into July, bombing raids began. These were mostly concentrated on Kent and the east coast, but on the fifteenth of July she was saddened to hear that part of Brighton had been bombed. She couldn't bear to think of damage to the cheerful seaside town that had given her such a happy day. According to Peter Travis, the Germans were still testing out strategies; the main battle was yet to begin. Although their sleep had been interrupted by air raid warnings, no bombs had yet fallen on them, and Evie began to resent having her sleep interrupted, huddling in the shelter in the grounds of High Chalk House while knowing she had a full watch to carry out the next day and another English lesson to deliver.

By the time August arrived, Evie's nerves were stretched to the limit. She almost wished that the threatened invasion would start, and put an end to the awful waiting. Just when it seemed that the Germans were ready to unleash their full force, the weather broke, and they were given a reprieve. At least it gave her and Jess more time to drill the required English into the Czech pilots. Their English was now much improved, so to practise their radio skills, they were given bikes and radio sets and sent over the grounds of High Chalk House, with Alex giving them orders over the radio. She could tell from the black looks and mutterings of the Czech pilots that they regarded this as childish and beneath them. They were all impatient to join the other operational squadrons and start fighting Nazis.

In the second week of August, the weather cleared to cloudless skies and sunshine. Evie, on early watch, was aware of high tension in the Operations Room. Popcorn squadron was already assembled at readiness in their dispersal hut, awaiting the order to scramble. As she took her place at the plotting table, the Ops 'B' officer relayed orders to Wagtail squadron warning them to be at readiness in fifteen minutes. She cast a quick glance over the map to catch up with the situation. At the moment it was clear of hostile plots, but she had no doubt that would change. The sun had risen, and the weather was fine. A year ago, she would have rejoiced at the prospect of a perfect summer's day. Now it meant ideal weather for raids.

She had scarcely taken her seat when the chatter came through on her headset, giving the position and

130

approximate numbers of a hostile plot. With trembling fingers, she slid the correct details into a wooden block and pushed it into place on the map. Around her other plotters were also moving more hostile plots into place. Evie's stomach tightened. There had been the odd raid in previous days, but nothing like this.

Above her, she was aware of Peter Travis frowning down at the map.

'Scramble 'A' flight, and put 'B' flight on standby,' Peter ordered. 'And I want Catseye at readiness now.'

A hush fell over the room. It was as though everyone held their breath. All eyes were on the table, gazing at the plots, which were frozen in time. It was hard to imagine they represented dozens of hostile aircraft, all intent on wreaking destruction upon England's shores. But exactly what part of England they were aiming for wasn't yet clear.

An update came through her headset and she moved the block to its new position and placed a yellow arrow showing the direction it had moved. The other plotters were doing similar, and when Evie sat back and looked at all the hostile plots, she felt a wave of nausea. If they continued along the same path, they would converge over Amberton.

Peter broke the silence. 'Looks like we're in for a bumpy ride.' The understatement made Evie smile, and the ripple of laughter eased the tension. Just as Peter had intended, she supposed. 'Stay calm and concentrate on your own tasks, and we'll be fine.'

Then Evie was too busy to think. It was all she could do to manage her plots accurately. The past few weeks had been busy, but this was another level altogether, and instead of targeting shipping convoys, it was clear German strategy had changed and they were aiming for the RAF stations.

Those manning the desks were also more busy than usual. There was a flurry of activity as reports came in from observer stations, communications came in from the airborne squadrons and Peter got on the phone to Group.

'It's the same everywhere,' Peter reported when he finished. 'Group can't send any reinforcements because there aren't any to spare. We're on our own.'

By this time the station commander had joined them. 'If we send all our operational squadrons out to intercept, we'll have nothing left to protect the station from the hostiles that get through,' he said.

Peter pointed at the table. 'If we don't throw all available aircraft at that lot, they'll all get through.' Even Evie, inexperienced as she was with the tactics of air battles, understood the dilemma. The numbers on the block she was currently moving read 30+: that plot alone represented at least thirty hostile aircraft heading for Amberton, and there were two other hostile plots on the table, one showing 25+ and the other 10+. Their three operational squadrons consisted of twelve Hurricanes each. Thirty-six against sixty-five, possibly more. Every one of their Hurricanes would be needed to be sent out if they were to have a hope of stopping the enemy wave from reaching Amberton, but that would leave the station undefended from any bombers that broke through.

Bob Law glanced at the board summarising the readiness state of each squadron. 'What about Brimstone?'

The blue arrow Evie was about to place dropped from suddenly uncooperative fingers and clattered on the floor tiles. She picked it up, praying no one had noticed. Brimstone had been placed at readiness, waiting for permission to go out on a training flight. While she nudged the arrow into position, she strained to hear Peter's reply.

'It's your call, sir. Their flying isn't a problem, but they still start gabbling Czech over the R/T when they get excited. Which is most of the time.'

'Get them in the air now.'

Evie's stomach twisted as she heard the Ops 'B' give the scramble order. Scarcely two minutes had passed before the observer's report crackled through the speakers: 'Twelve Hurricanes taking off. Initial M for Mother.'

This was the moment Evie had dreaded. The plots on the table had changed from just a series of numbers to friends. The voices that filtered through the R/T might be the very last time she heard some of them speak.

And Alex was up there with them.

The room became a blur, and a strange buzzing filled her ears. She was vaguely aware of a voice giving the order for all non-essential station personnel to take shelter. Then another voice — Peter's — ordering Brimstone to climb to Angels two-zero and patrol.

A sharp voice sliced through her daze: 'Three colours on the table! Bishop, concentrate!'

Evie jumped. Her vision cleared, and she saw that she had, indeed, forgotten to remove the outdated information that threatened to create confusion. Her cheeks burning with mortification, she hurriedly swept the yellow arrows from the map. It was a mistake only an inexperienced plotter should make. Just because Alex was going into action, it didn't mean she had an excuse to neglect her duty. If anything, she should be more focused than ever. Alex's safety and that of everyone on the base depended upon her accuracy. Her only comfort was that Section Officer Ellerby wasn't present; she'd have never heard the last of it from acid-tongued Hellerby.

As soon as another update came through her headset, she was ready. She moved the block showing the hostile aircraft were now nearly at the coast. From now on, the Chain Home stations would be unable to track them, as they looked out to sea. Ops would rely solely on observer posts reporting what they could see in the skies.

Evie's heart hammered against her ribs. This was it. The war had finally reached Amberton.

Peter's calm voice broke the tense silence. 'Focus on your work, everyone, and we'll be fine.' He addressed the plotters. 'Remember, whatever you hear, you're safe down here.'

But Evie couldn't help thinking of May — was she on the station or out driving? And what about Jess? She had gone off duty only half an hour ago. As she watched the plots converge upon Amberton, she breathed a soft prayer for her friends.

★ ★ ★

Jess strolled towards the NAAFI, rolling her neck and shoulders to relieve her aching muscles. With the change in Ops Room watches to four hours on, two hours off, it wasn't worth returning to High Chalk House. She'd had a bit of a walk around the base to stretch her legs, now she needed breakfast. She closed her eyes, dreaming of the cups of steaming coffee she'd drunk when living in London. If she kept that

134

rich aroma, that taste in her mind, maybe she could make herself believe the NAAFI was serving up delicious coffee like that instead of what she could only imagine was mud mixed with hot water.

She had her hand on the door handle, her stomach rumbling with the anticipation of food, when the wail of a siren started up. A voice came over the tannoy, telling everyone to take cover.

'Helmets on!' a voice snapped behind her.

Her gut twisted as she fumbled to put on her helmet and fasten the strap under her chin. It was starting. They'd had a few air raid warnings at night, but nothing had attacked the base. This time Jess's instincts told her they would be in the line of fire. This was what the senior staff had been muttering dire warnings about for the past few weeks. Her knees feeling weak, she was about to turn right to make a dash for the nearest shelter when she happened to glance left and see May running towards a different shelter. Poor May would be terrified. Jess wasn't aware of making any decision, but her feet moved of their own accord, and she was sprinting after May.

She had the airfield in view and now she could see the pilots of Brimstone squadron climbing into their Hurricanes, bright yellow Mae Wests flapping on their chests and parachutes strapped on behind. Dear God, no! She stopped dead and stared, her gaze instinctively seeking out Milan's Hurricane. There he was, standing beside the machine while an Erk helped him put on his parachute. The propeller was already spinning. As she watched, Milan climbed into the cockpit. It was too far to see what he was doing, but she knew he'd be running through the cockpit drill she and Evie had included in their lessons. The words marched through her brain now, meaningless but persistent: hydraulics, trim, mixture, pneumatics, fuel, flaps, trim and switches.

Someone grabbed her arm — Flight Officer Ellerby. 'Get a move on, Halloway. You're in the way.'

'Sorry, ma'am.' Somehow, Jess managed to get her frozen limbs to move. The last thing she saw before she ducked into the shelter was Milan giving the 'chocks away' signal.

'Jess!'

It was May's voice, but it took a moment for her eyes to adjust to the dim light of the single lantern swinging from the apex of the curved corrugated iron ceiling. Then she made out figures sitting on wooden benches lining the walls, and she saw May, huddled near the rear of the shelter, beckoning to her. The other WAAFs around her obligingly shuffled up, so Jess could sit next to her friend.

'You can squeeze in next to me, love.' It was a corporal driver who spoke. When Jess had first arrived at Amberton, she'd enjoyed flirting with him. Now she couldn't imagine what she'd seen in him. He was good looking, but it was Milan's intense blue gaze, the cheekbones that could slice through steel, that filled her thoughts.

She forced a grin, not at all in the mood for flirting. 'In your dreams, Corp.' A ripple of laughter ran around the shelter as she sat next to May instead. 'You all right, May?'

May sucked in a deep breath. 'Do you think they're going to bomb us?'

Jess hesitated. She couldn't repeat any of the talk she'd heard in Ops, and anyway, she didn't want to frighten the poor girl more than she was already.

'They can try, but our boys will stop them.'

That earned her a cheer from all in the cramped shelter.

'That's the spirit, Halloway.' It was Jean Ellerby who spoke. Jess was so shocked to receive praise from Hellerby she nearly slipped off the bench.

'Where's Evie?' May asked, looking around as though expecting to see her there.

'On duty. She'll be fine. Ops must be the safest place on the whole station.' Then, guessing who else May would be worried for, she lowered her voice so no one else would overhear. 'Peter's there, too.'

She gave May's hand a squeeze and was rewarded by a tremulous smile.

'I think I'd rather be out there, doing something,' May said. 'I wouldn't be so nervous if I had something to occupy my mind.'

'Same here,' muttered Jess. She envied Evie. If Jess was on duty now, she wouldn't have time to worry about Milan or any of the other pilots she'd come to regard as friends.

Or maybe not. In Ops, they would hear the R/T communications with the pilots. She thought of Evie, listening to Alex while he was up there, fighting for his life. No, maybe it was better not to hear.

'What's the matter?' May was gazing at Jess with concern.

'Brimstone squadron is up there.'

She didn't need to say any more. May would understand her worries, just as she understood May's concern for Peter. Both had declared they wouldn't act on their feelings, but it didn't stop them having the feelings in the first place.

A deep, ominous throb of multiple engines that

137

Jess felt rather than heard came from outside. Not the growling Merlin engines of a Spitfire or Hurricane.

'Here they come,' muttered one of the men.

Jess squeezed May's hand and could only pray that Milan and his squadron had been able to climb to a great enough altitude before the Germans arrived. She'd listened in on enough attacks to know that having the advantage of height was key to a successful attack. Around her she was aware of people crossing themselves and muttering prayers. She could feel the rapid beat of May's pulse through their clasped palms. Or was it her own?

Then there was no more time for thinking. There was a high-pitched whistle followed by a loud crash that made the ground quake beneath them. Several people cried out or screamed. Jess opened her mouth and choked as gritty dust rasped in the back of her throat. Then another crash, and another. Jess and May clung on to each other, flinching with each bang. The lantern dangling from the ceiling swung drunkenly, making the shadows shrink and expand in a nightmarish fashion.

For some reason the cockpit drill ran through her head over and over: *hydraulics, trim, mixture, pneumatics, fuel, flaps, trim and switches*. Another whistle. Jess ducked her head instinctively. May's fingernails dug into the back of her hand. Another crash. The whole shelter shook. *Hydraulics, trim, mixture, pneumatics, fuel, flaps, trim and switches*. Oh, God. She was going to go mad if this kept up. If only there was something she could do to occupy her mind.

Then Jess remembered her training as an actress, how performing always swept away her stage fright. She drew a deep breath and tried to pretend she was on stage. 'Come on, we can't let the Germans frighten us,' she called out. 'Who knows *'Roll Out the Barrel'?*' She sang the first line in a quavering voice too feeble to compete with the blasts and machine gun fire coming from outside. She cleared her throat and tried again, her voice stronger now. Then May and two others picked up the next line. 'That's right, join in, everyone.' A few more joined in and the singers' voices swelled in volume. Finally, everyone was singing.

Jess flung the words as loud and clear as she could, each one a defiance of the Germans and their attempt to batter Britain into submission. She smiled at everyone as she sang, encouraging them to put their whole heart into it, to refuse to let the Germans win.

When the song ended, Jess didn't waver, but plunged into *'Down at the Old Bull and Bush'*. If she closed her eyes she could almost believe she was in the pub, singing along to the piano, instead of stuck in a cramped shelter, surrounded by the smell of stale beer and cigarette smoke rather than the musty tang of damp earth combined with sweat and fear.

Then a shrieking whistle sounded directly overhead. Jess carried on singing, but others faltered and clamped hands to their ears. Jess didn't hear an explosion, but the force of it knocked her back against the wall. The lights blinked out, and everything went black.

139

11

Alex's nerves thrilled as he put his Hurricane into a climbing turn. Looking out on either side, he could see the other members of his squadron doing the same.

Only yesterday evening he'd demanded to know when Brimstone would be sent on operational flights, and Bob Law had told him it would be when his pilots had learned not to fill the airwaves with 'that damned Czech chatter'. Well, his pilots hadn't improved overnight, so it could only mean they were being sent to intercept a threat that was too great for Amberton's other three squadrons to handle alone. The fact that they'd been scrambled with no warning could only mean the threat was nearly here.

He checked his altimeter. Still too low. Would they have time to climb higher than any hostiles before they arrived? A brief flash of memory struck — Bf 109s screaming down upon his squadron from the sun.

The R/T crackled, and Peter's voice came through his headset. 'Red Leader, this is Belfry. We have hostiles approaching at zero-niner-fife. Do you see them?'

Momentarily disoriented by his spiralling climb, Alex needed to check his compass to pinpoint the bearing. He checked his altitude again: nearly fifteen thousand feet.

Then he saw them — a black cloud casting a

fast-moving shadow over the patchwork of fields and woods. Heinkels. And they were heading straight for the base. His instincts screamed to dive after them, but remembering France, he glanced around the sky before giving the order. There they were — four Bf 109s about a thousand feet above the Heinkels.

'Belfry, this is Red Leader. I see them. Heinkels heading right for you.' He relayed orders to Blue, Yellow and Green sections to take the Heinkels, but the 109s were his. 'Red two, Red three, this is Red Leader. 109s at two o'clock. Tally ho!' He repeated the order in Czech for good measure, then aimed for the 109s and dived. This was for the men he had lost in France.

Checking to see that his wingmen were following, he braced himself for the moment when the 109s would see them. He became aware that his fingers were clenched so tight around the control column that his knuckles were white. He forced himself to relax, but kept his thumb poised over the firing button, ready to send his chosen target plummeting from the sky. Another quick glance around showed him his wingmen diving to intercept two of the other 109s. Good. They weren't firing too early. Wasting ammunition was not an option; if the station was under attack it would make landing to rearm difficult to say the least. The remainder of his squadron was swooping down to meet the Heinkels. Even as he watched, the first wave of German bombers reached the station and unleashed their cargo. Bastards! Evie was down there!

Then he was upon the 109s and there was no time to think. He lined up his target in his sights and fired, sending a stream of bullets into the fuselage of the

109. He caught a brief glimpse of the pilot's white face and then he was past. He instantly put his Hurricane into a series of tight turns designed to shake off any pursuit from his own tail, then sought out his prey again. There it was, black smoke billowing. As he watched, the canopy opened and a figure as tiny as a toy soldier climbed out and leapt clear, then the 109 spiralled into a dive. A streak of white unfurled, then blossomed into a parachute canopy. Alex made a mental note of the location where the German pilot would land so he could be caught. Then he turned his attention back to the fight. He was just in time to see the remaining three 109s haring towards the coast, a Hurricane in pursuit. His number two was not far away, so that could only mean the idiot heading out to sea after three 109s had to be Karol. Damn him — he knew the man was trouble.

'Red three, this is Red Leader. Do not pursue, repeat, do not pursue.' He relayed it in Czech as well. Whether Karol heard him or not was doubtful. By this time the R/T was a cacophony of excited shouts as his pilots shouted warnings and instructions to each other. In Czech, of course. Well, he couldn't do anything more for Karol now. He signalled to his remaining wingman to follow and dived into the melee of Hurricanes and Heinkels.

He was lower now and could see the station. Fountains of earth sprayed up as bomb after bomb struck the ground. In a matter of seconds, flames engulfed a hangar. His mouth went dry.

Another Heinkel swooped low, preparing to drop its bombs. Alex snarled at it and set an intercept course. He'd downed his 109 for the boys of his old squadron, but now all he could think was that Evie was down there, and if he didn't stop this Heinkel, she might be underneath the bombs it released. It took all his will-power to hold back from firing until he was sure he would score a hit. The relief when he finally pressed the button was immense. From the way the Heinkel's nose suddenly jolted up, he knew he had hit the pilot. Just before Alex turned away, the plane dropped into a dive. From that height, there could be no recovery. He banked, seeking out his next target.

* * *

A blast shook the Ops Room. The floor heaved beneath Evie's feet, making her stagger. She clutched the edge of the table to keep her balance. A trickle of plaster dust pattered onto the plotting table; Evie reached across to brush it away. The fragments were sharp; they scratched her palms and knuckles, drawing blood. She glanced up at the ceiling, half expecting to see it sagging, but although several cracks now zig-zagged through the white plaster, the structure still looked solid. Copying the other girls, she climbed up onto the table on her hands and knees to brush away more dust, ignoring her stinging hands. Most of the plots lay scattered across the table or the floor; she picked them up and replaced them as accurately as she could. Not that accuracy was a problem when they could hear all too clearly where the action was taking place. She dreaded to think what the situation was like up on the ground. For once, those on duty in the Ops Room probably knew less of the raid than the others on the station. By the sounds of things, the fight was going on above their heads, but the only information filtering through to them was from

Brimstone's R/T and, inevitably, the pilots had reverted to Czech in their excitement. Only the occasional orders from Alex gave her the momentary comfort of knowing he was still alive and well. The observers were too busy operating the guns to report anything of use.

All the while, the pilots of Popcorn, Wagtail and Catseye squadrons were conducting their fight over the Channel, doing their best to ensure no further bombers got through. Evie could only pray there would still be an airfield for them to land on when they returned.

Another explosion shook the room, throwing Evie to the floor. Her knee struck something hard, sending a flare of jagged pain up her leg. She picked herself up, shaking.

The station commander managed to get through to one of the ground staff on his telephone. When he replaced the receiver, his face was grave. 'One of the shelters took a hit.'

Peter swore. It was the first time Evie had seen his composure crack. 'Casualties?'

Bob shook his head. 'No idea until the crew on the ground manage to reach them. It wasn't a direct hit, so there's hope, but the entrance has caved in.'

Evie immediately thought of Jess and May. Both were up there, in the thick of the attack. They must be in one of the shelters. Dear God, please don't let them be in the one that had been hit.

She listened in to the reports filtering through in a fever of anxiety. The noise from above eased, and observers reported the survivors of the raid were now departing. Evie still had a job to do, so she adjusted the numbers on her plots and calculated their route from the approximate direction given by the observers. It gave her a great deal of satisfaction to see the numbers reduced from the amount that had arrived.

Then a hand touched her arm. She was surprised to see the WAAF who was supposed to relieve her. Glancing at the clock, she saw it was, indeed, the end of her watch. 'You look as though you could use a break,' the girl said with a crooked smile.

Evie stammered a reply then snatched up her tunic and dashed outside. When she stepped out, she stopped, coughing from the clouds of dust filling the air, unable to take in the scene of devastation that met her eyes.

When she had gone down the steps four hours earlier, the station had been pristine, with neat buildings and verges, everyone going about their duty in an orderly fashion. Now, barely a window was intact. Shattered glass glistened on the grass and tarmac. Most of the buildings were still standing, but one of the hangars was now a twisted pile of iron. Smoke billowed from the blazing wreckage of three Hurricanes. Her stomach wrenched and she thought she would be sick until the calm realisation dawned that these were not aircraft that had crashed but were parked in their dispersal pens. Wagtail's dispersal hut was also a smoking ruin, and Evie was thankful that the entire squadron had been in the air when the bomb had struck.

Crowds of men and women scurried down the roads, weaving around the smoking bomb craters. Evie raised herself on tiptoes, seeking out Jess and May. A few times a wave of relief struck when she spotted a blonde or brunette hairstyle, but the crushing weight of worry returned when she saw it wasn't either of her friends. Her stomach tightened when she saw the crowds working around one of the shelters near to the NAAFI. Jess had been going to the NAAFI.

She forced her leaden feet to move and dashed for the shelter.

When she saw the devastation, her vision went grey. The bomb had struck close to the entrance, bringing down the front portion of the shelter. The blast had piled a vast bank of rubble where the door had stood, and the rescuers were frantically digging through it.

She picked out a WAAF corporal who she recognised. She had been helping shift the rubble, but now stood, mopping her brow, pausing for a rest. 'Excuse me, Corp. Do you know who's inside?'

'Looking for anyone in particular?'

'May Lidford and Jess Halloway.'

The corporal's eyes grew grave. 'Lidford's definitely in there. I saw her go in. No idea about Halloway, though.'

A young airman paused in the act of shovelling and turned to face Evie, perspiration making streaks on his dust-smeared face. 'Jess Halloway? Yeah, I saw her go in this one.'

Evie choked back the sob that threatened to escape and went to help digging, but the airman held her back. 'Careful. The whole roof could collapse. Best leave it to us.'

All Evie could do was stand beside the remnants of the shelter and pray May and Jess were alive and unhurt.

* * *

146

Alex banked, and watched as the Heinkel he'd just shot down plummeted into a field. Thank God it was clear of houses. He didn't think he could forgive himself if he'd sent a plane crashing into an occupied building.

He banked sharply, twisting his neck to search the air. To his amazement, the sky was empty. He'd never get used to this. One moment it would be a seething mass of battling aircraft, diving and turning, weaving a tangled knot of white contrails and black smoke. The next there would be nothing but the clouds. He'd flown some way from the airfield by this time and for a moment he couldn't work out where he was. He peered down at the ground, seeking out a familiar landmark. Finally, he spotted a railway line, a slash of steel through the landscape. Unrolling his chart on his knees, he was able to match it with the main London to Southampton line. That was all he needed to plot a bearing back to Amberton.

When he drew near to the station again, he saw the last of the Heinkels heading for the coast. He didn't chase them, knowing at that distance he would be unlikely to intercept them while he still had enough fuel to return to safety. He flew a pass over the airfield, going cold at the destruction the bombers had wrought in such a short time. Craters pocked the airfield, and all that remained of one of the hangars was a tangled mess of corrugated iron. The main buildings seemed to be intact, but judging from the churned-up earth, there had been some near misses. The last thing he noticed before he banked was a huddle of people at the entrance to one of the bomb shelters. Then he flew a circuit and landed in the strip that had been marked out as clear.

Most of the other pilots had already landed and were milling around the dispersal huts. Alex left his Hurricane in the able hands of his fitters for refuelling and rearming and quickly reported the parachutist from the 109 he had shot down. Then he went to find his pilots. *Dear God, let them all be here.*

The only one missing was Karol; no one had seen him after he'd flown off in pursuit of the Messerschmitts. With a heavy heart, Alex was about to add his name to the 'Missing' list, when the drone of Merlin engines approached.

It was Karol's Hurricane, looking as pristine as it had on take-off. Alex marched out to watch him make a perfect landing. He waited while Karol stepped out of his parachute harness and hung it over his wing, but as soon as the pilot was out of earshot of the Erks who were now working on the Hurricane, Alex went to meet him.

'I got a 109,' Karol greeted him, showing no signs of reading the anger in Alex's expression. 'Went down over the sea.'

'Put it in your report. But you won't be able to claim it, because no one else saw it happen.'

'Oh, I —'

'You chased after those 109s when I'd given you a direct order not to. In case you hadn't noticed, they were leaving the fight, and the station was under attack.' The tirade was pouring from Alex's mouth, and he could do nothing to stop it. It was as though all the anger and tension of the attack were being unleashed after he'd suppressed them during the battle.

Karol, clearly only now realising his error, stood to attention and made no attempt to excuse his mistake.

'We needed you here, Karol, and you were off on your own futile chase. I don't care what personal feud you have with the Nazis — God knows, every other pilot in the squadron has a reason to hate them, but they were following orders and fighting the bombers that were attacking the station.'

'I'm sorry, sir. I'll pay attention next time.'

'I haven't decided if there'll be a next time.'

Karol's eyes widened. Good. Let him stew for a while. It would do him good to spend some time pondering his error. 'I can't afford to have anyone up there chasing after their own personal vendettas. If you can't follow orders, there's no place for you in the squadron.'

'Yes, sir.'

'Now, go and make your report. I'll let you know what I've decided after you've submitted it.'

Alex returned to his office feeling drained. His anger had given him the strength to carry him this far, but now it was gone, his energy had seeped away with it. He slumped in his chair and picked up his pen, trying to ignore the babble of voices in the rest of the hut.

A shadow loomed in the doorway, and he looked up to see the station commander. He hastily rose and saluted.

Bob returned the salute, then waved Alex back into his seat. 'I just wanted to commend you for putting on a good show,' Bob said. 'Consider Brimstone operational from now on. No more English lessons.'

A wide smile threatened to split his face. 'Thank you, sir. That means a lot.'

'You will try and get the Czechs to speak English over the R/T, though, won't you. Poor Ops Room

149

crowd can't make head nor tail of it.'

'I'll do my best, sir. What's the damage down here?'

'Not as bad as it could have been. Thanks to your boys, we got most of our aircraft up in the air. Three of Catseye's Hurricanes were grounded for repairs, and they were smashed up. A couple of the ground crew were hit by shrapnel, but nothing serious. One of the shelters took a hit, though. The entrance is blocked so we can't tell how bad. I thought you'd want to know, because it seems one of the WAAFs who was teaching your lads is in there.'

Icy hands squeezed his heart. 'Who?' It was the only word he could force out through suddenly dry lips.

'Halloway.'

Alex hated himself for the wash of relief. He had no wish for harm to come to Jess. 'What about Evie Bishop?'

'In Ops. They got a bit shaken up, but nothing major.'

It was a good thing he was already sitting; he doubted his legs would support him, he felt so wobbly with relief.

'Do you need a hand digging out the shelter? My lads would want to help, I'm sure.'

'They need all the help they can get.'

Alex saw Evie the moment they got to the huge bank of churned earth where the entrance to the shelter had been. It took all his strength not to sweep her into his arms in front of everyone. Her hair was no longer red, but was matted with a white powder, and there were smudges of dust on her face.

'Alex,' she choked, when she saw him. 'Evie and May are down there.'

'We'll get them out. What happened to you?' He brushed some of the powder out of her hair, revealing the gleam of red beneath.

'Oh.' Evie looked at the dust on Alex's hand and reached up to brush more from her hair. 'I hadn't noticed. It must be plaster dust. Bits of the ceiling came down over the plotting table. I must look a fright.'

'You look fine.' More than fine. Beautiful. But he didn't want to burden her with his feelings when she clearly didn't feel the same. For now, he would be satisfied Evie was safe and do what he could to help free their friends trapped inside the shelter.

12

May blinked, her ears ringing. She was lying on something soft, and there was another object across her legs, but she couldn't see a thing. Blackness pressed upon her eyes. She raised her hand to her face and waved it, but although she felt the air fan her face, she saw nothing. Panic clutched her throat.

'Jess?' Her voice was little more than a croak. She cleared her throat and tried again. This time her voice was clearer but sounded strangely deadened. 'Jess, can you hear me?'

There was a groan, and the object on her legs moved. 'May? What happened?' There was a scrabbling noise and then May felt a hand pat her leg.

She grabbed the hand. 'Is that you, Jess?'

'I certainly 'ope so. Otherwise I'm 'olding 'ands with a stranger.'

A ripple of laughter sounded around the shelter, and relief blossomed in May's chest as it became clear she wasn't alone in the dark. Belatedly realising she must be lying on top of the WAAF who'd been sitting to her left, she raised herself to a sitting position, and she felt the girl next to her do likewise.

The girl gave a low groan.

'You all right, love?' May asked, feeling for the girl's arm with her free hand and giving it a squeeze.

'Don't know. Think I banged my head.'

'Here.' May removed her tunic and wrapped it around the girl. Picturing the seating arrangement,

May recalled that the girl had been sitting at the back of the shelter. She must have hit her head on the wall. 'You'd better lie down. It's Walker, isn't it?' May recalled recognising the girl when she'd scrambled into the shelter. Walker had only arrived at the station yesterday and also worked in the transport section. Hell of an introduction to life at Amberton.

'Yes.'

'Well, just lie still, and help will be here soon.'

'At least the bombing's stopped.' Jess's voice sounded close to her ear, making her jump.

'Thank God for that.' The ringing in her ears had hidden the fact that the bombardment had stopped, but now she noticed it, the silence from outside was a welcome relief.

That, together with having Walker to look after, made May less afraid. Her daze gone, she could think clearly. 'Is anyone else hurt? Everyone check the people on either side of them.'

The shelter filled with the murmur of voices, all oddly muffled. Then a man's voice spoke up. 'Girl next to me is out cold, but I've found a pulse.'

'That you, Charlie?' It was Jess who spoke.

'S'right.'

'You were next to Flight Officer Ellerby, weren't you?'

'Yeah. Think so.'

'How bad is she?' Jean Ellerby was the only officer in the shelter. May hadn't thought she'd ever welcome hearing the flight officer's sharp voice, but right now, she would have loved to have someone in authority take over.

'Can't tell. Can't see a bloody thing in this dark.'

'Has anyone got a torch?'

'Wait, I think there are some stored under the benches.' There were further scrabbling sounds, then, 'Found one!'

A click, then suddenly May was blinking in the amber light. She looked round at the pale, strained faces. There seemed to be fewer than she remembered. Then she shifted her gaze to the entrance or, rather, where the entrance had been and gasped with horror as it filtered through to her brain what she was seeing. Everything beyond Jean Ellerby's still form lay beneath a pile of earth and twisted corrugated iron. A masculine hand protruded from the rubble.

'Jesus Christ Almighty,' Charlie said, but it sounded more like a prayer than blasphemy. 'Must be Jack Johnson under there.' The young corporal who had invited Jess to sit with him. May swallowed at the reminder of how quickly things could change in the war. One moment a man was laughing and joking, without a care in the world, the next he was buried alive.

He had to be alive. May couldn't bear to think of the cheery corporal having his life ripped from him in such a cruel fashion.

Meanwhile, Jess had crawled forward and was now examining Jean Ellerby. 'Doesn't look too bad. Just a bump to the head.' She glanced up at the ceiling. The corrugated iron beside the collapsed section was sagging badly. 'Better move her to the back, in case more of the roof comes down. Give me a hand, will you, Charlie?'

Between the two of them, they managed to get Ellerby to the back, being as gentle as circumstances allowed. May shuffled closer to the front to make room for them. They found the first aid kit under the bench and Jess tended to Ellerby and Walker.

Worryingly, everyone else seemed to be looking to May for guidance. That would teach her to speak up. She couldn't help a fleeting thought of Peter. He would know what to do. He had a calm, reassuring presence and exuded a natural air of authority that enabled him to take charge in any situation without the need to bark orders like so many officers. She couldn't help a glance back at Jean Ellerby.

But someone needed to do something, and everyone seemed to expect it to be her. Maybe some of Peter's leadership skills had rubbed off onto her, for suddenly she knew what had to be done.

'We need to clear as much of this rubble off Jack as possible.' She looked round the group. 'Is it just Jack under there? I thought there were more of us.'

A girl that May recognised as being one of the cooks in the canteen spoke up. She had been huddled on her bench, weeping, but now she gulped and said, 'There were two girls between me and the entrance.'

'Oh, God.' May gazed at the pile of rubble to the girl's left. She couldn't imagine anyone was alive under there.

'They could be in a pocket of air,' another girl said.

May nodded. She doubted any of the corrugated iron roofing had survived the blast, but if it had, it could still be protecting those beneath the rubble.

She looked at the cook, who had started sobbing again. A short while ago that would have been her, but with the help of Evie, Jess and Peter, she was now realising she'd developed some courage. Without them, she knew she could all too easily have been like the girl, so she didn't want to be too hard on her. She spoke to the cook. 'Help must be on its way by now — the raid's over. We need to let them know we're alive under here.' She pointed to an intact section of ceiling. 'Find something to make a noise and bash on there for all you're worth.'

The girl nodded and pulled out her eating irons. She banged her spoon on the roof with a force May wouldn't have believed possible from so slight a girl. The din did nothing to help the ringing in May's ears, but at least it gave the girl a task she could usefully do.

'Right.' May addressed the others, raising her voice. 'We need to clear the rubble off Jack and try to find the others.'

It was heart-breaking work. The moment they scooped back one handful of earth and chalky rubble, more trickled in to take its place. Soon May's nails were torn and bleeding and she had a large bruise on her shoulder where it had been struck by a lump of flint. Part of her wanted to retreat to a corner and cry, but a larger part, the part that had blossomed under Evie, Jess and Peter's friendship, found the strength to carry on.

After what felt like years of digging, they uncovered Jack's face. Charlie, who had moved forward to help, bent down and felt for a pulse. But May knew what he'd find, even before he shook his head.

'He's gone.' Charlie took off his jacket and covered the battered face that they'd worked so hard to free. 'Poor blighter. At least it would have been quick.'

There was still no sign of the missing girls, and May knew in her heart that they must also be dead.

They all remained in silent contemplation for a moment, with no sound but their breathing, heavy from their exertions. The cook stopped bashing her spoon on the iron roof. No doubt all thinking, as May was, how easily it could have been them lying dead. Then May heard it: a dull thump coming from the other side of the rubble; muffled voices.

No one needed telling. As one, they drew breath and yelled, and the cook resumed bashing her spoon. After a moment May hushed them, and she held her breath, waiting. Then came a voice, sounding clearer now. 'Hang in there. We're nearly through.'

They cheered again. May was startled by a touch on her arm. It was Jean Ellerby. Judging from the lines radiating from the corners of her eyes, she was in pain, but she now had a large dressing over her head wound, and at least she was conscious. 'You did well there, Lidford. It's not everyone who can keep their head in a situation like this. You and Halloway did the WAAF proud. I'll be putting you both in for a commendation.'

The next moment, May was engulfed in Jess's arms. 'You were wonderful, May. I'm so proud of you.'

May hugged her back. 'I couldn't have done it without you. I was so scared at first. If you hadn't started us singing, I'd have been a quivering bundle of nerves even before the bombing started.'

Then there was another tumble of falling rubble, and daylight poured into the shelter. Those inside cheered as, one by one, they half scrambled and were half dragged from the hole. May found herself standing in warm sunshine, a blanket wrapped around her. Then she was engulfed in an enthusiastic hug.

'Oh, May, thank God! I've been so worried. Are you hurt?' It was Evie.

May hugged her back, relief making her knees tremble. 'I'm fine. But —' She swallowed. 'Oh, Evie. The

157

ones by the door . . .' She stepped back and wiped her eyes, forgetting how grimy her fingers were until she felt the cakey mud smear across her cheeks.

'Here.' Evie produced a large, clean handkerchief and handed it to her. Then, as May wiped her face, she asked, 'What about Jess? How is she?'

'She's fine. She was right behind me.' May turned and pointed at Jess, who was that moment being helped out of the burrowed entrance. Evie dashed over to lend a hand.

That was when May's gaze fell on two still forms laid out beside the crater, covered by blankets. Two more rescuers moved towards them, carrying Jack Johnson. The airman's head lolled, and his arms dangled, knocking against the legs of those bearing him. The men placed him reverently beside the other two and draped a blanket over him.

May started to shake, and her teeth chattered. She tried to stop it, but they only clacked harder.

A strong arm wrapped around her shoulder. 'Good God, May! Were you down there?' Peter's voice rumbled in her ear.

She didn't trust herself to speak, knew she'd disgrace herself by sobbing if she tried. She simply nodded and then dabbed at her cheeks with the borrowed handkerchief to blot away the tears that she couldn't control.

'Come and sit down.' May allowed Peter to guide her to the steps outside the officers' mess. She went to sink down on them, but Peter hoisted her up and marched her inside.

'What are you doing?' she gasped. 'I can't go in there.'

'I can bring any guest I choose, and I choose you.'

His last three words made May's stomach swoop. *Don't be ridiculous, May, he doesn't mean anything by it. He's being kind, that's all.*

Ignoring May's protests over her filthy state, Peter guided her into a large yet cosy room, filled with luxurious armchairs and sofas. There was a bar in the corner, where two airmen were busy with brooms. From the clink of broken glass, May guessed most of the glassware hadn't survived the raid.

'Sit here,' Peter said. 'What would you like to drink?'

May became aware that she was parched. 'A cup of tea, please.'

While Peter went to fetch it, she perched on the edge of the nearest armchair. Its high back, padded arms and soft cushions invited her to sink into it, but she was terrified of ruining the plush maroon upholstery. She'd thought the chairs in the schoolroom at High Chalk House were the last word in luxury, but this chair belonged to a whole other world, as far removed from the schoolroom as the schoolroom was from the poky back room of her father's house in Birmingham.

She shivered again, only now noticing that the blanket she'd been given upon emerging from the shelter was still draped around her shoulders. She huddled in it and shuffled closer to the edge of the seat, wishing she was out in the sunshine with Evie and Jess.

Peter returned with a cup and saucer. She took it, marvelling at the delicate china which was so fine as to be translucent. She wished her tea had arrived in a battered enamel mug. She wouldn't be afraid of dropping that.

Peter sank into the opposite chair with a sigh. 'I'm

159

sorry. I thought you'd be more comfortable in here after all you've been through, but I've got it all wrong.'

'Oh no, you've been so kind, and I'm grateful. I just . . .' She made a gesture that took in the sumptuous furniture, the oak panelling and the fine china, willing him to understand. 'I don't belong here.'

A faint smile curved his lips. 'You know, there are still days when I look around this room and feel I don't belong here, either.'

'You?' May took a sip of tea to hide her confusion. To her surprise it was strong and sweet, not the tasteless, pale, slightly flavoured hot water she'd expected to find in a place like this. It was an honest, working-class brew. She drank it gratefully. 'Ah, that's good.'

Peter laughed. 'I asked for the kind of tea my mum would make. 'Drink up,' she'd say. 'It'll put hairs on your chest'.' He looked around the room with a sad smile. 'She sacrificed so much to let me stay on at school. And when I joined the RAF, it was as a sergeant pilot. We weren't all from Eton and Harrow, you know. So I should have realised how uncomfortable a place like this can make you feel.'

He rose. 'Shall we finish our tea outside?'

May nodded, relieved, and sprang up so fast her cup rattled on the saucer. As she followed him outside, she longed to ask him more about his background, but didn't know how to begin. But she couldn't deny something had changed between them. Not that the news that his background might not be so different from hers made her like him more — Peter had never made her feel uncomfortable about her own humble beginnings. No, it was the way he had looked after her. If her dad and brothers had witnessed her being dragged out of a collapsed shelter, they wouldn't have

160

asked how she was or made her a drink. They would have complained their supper was late. But Peter's care cracked the brittle shell she'd erected around her heart as protection against her family's indifference. Maybe not all men were like her father. Peter had gone out of his way to be kind to her yet seemed to expect nothing in return.

A blossom of warmth flowered in her chest.

★ ★ ★

Evie eyed her two friends with concern as she passed them steaming mugs of cocoa. 'Are you sure you're both well enough to go back on duty tomorrow?' They had both been sent back to High Chalk House and told to take it easy for the rest of the day. Evie had worked extra watches to make up for the WAAFs who had been too shaken to go back on duty, but then had been given the whole night off to make up for it. She'd returned to find Jess and May much recovered, but still looking pale. Jess had a large bruise on her forehead, and May's shoulder was still painful. She also sported a raw-looking graze on her chin.

'I can't speak for May, but I'm fine,' said Jess, wrapping her hands around her mug. 'Besides, I'd never be able to look our pilots in the eye again, if I cried off sick after just being trapped in a shelter for a short while.'

'What about you, May?'

May didn't seem to hear. She gazed into the distance, blowing the steam off her cocoa.

'May?'

Jess laughed. 'She can't hear you. Too busy dreaming about Peter Travis.'

'What?' May's eyes snapped into focus, and she blushed. 'I wasn't!'

'Admit it. I can't believe he took you into the officers' mess. What was it like?'

'I've already told you about a thousand times.'

'I know, but I'm trying to imagine it, so I can dream of being entertained there by a handsome pilot.'

The conversation looked like going round in circles for some time yet. Evie yawned and rose. 'Well, I might have been given the night off, but I've got to get up early. I'm off to bed.'

May reached up and took her hand. 'Are you all right, Evie? You look a bit pale.'

Evie forced a smile, although she did, in fact, have a slight headache. 'I'm fine. Just tired from focusing so hard all day. It's getting so that I still see plots when I close my eyes. I hope we have a quieter day tomorrow.'

Jess scowled. 'I doubt it. I think today's raid was just the start.'

Evie had a horrible feeling Jess was right.

13

If anything, the action was more intense the next day, although, thankfully, no raids got through to Amberton. Reports filtered through of heavy damage to other stations, and the Chain Home station on Ventnor had been damaged. Plots still came through thick and fast, and all four squadrons only had the briefest time to refuel and rearm between patrols before being scrambled again.

Evie did her best not to think too hard of Alex. Tried not to wonder, each time Brimstone squadron took off, if this would be his last flight. Instead she concentrated on her task, back and shoulders aching from bending over the table and pushing the plots with the long rakes. After all, she wasn't the only plotter with a friend in one of the squadrons, and everyone else managed to go about their duty calmly.

Then, just before she was due her first two-hour break, a report from Milan Mašek crackled over the R/T. 'Belfry, Brimstone Green Two. Green Leader has crashed in the sea.'

There was a brief silence. From the corner of her eye, Evie was aware of one of the plotters — Harriet Digby — standing upright, the plot she'd been about to place still in her hand.

'Brimstone Green Two, Belfry. Did you see a parachute?' It was the assistant controller who spoke, Peter being off duty.

A hiss of static filled the room for an agonising

163

stretch of time. No one spoke, and Harriet Digby remained frozen until Milan's voice came through the R/T. 'Belfry, Brimstone Green Two. No parachute.'

The assistant controller gave the order for the coast guard to be contacted. 'Although I doubt he'll have survived.'

Harriet gave a little gasp and sank into her chair. One of the WAAF officers hurried across to her, and Evie recalled seeing Harriet dancing with Alex's second-in-command, Flight Lieutenant Harper. She'd even heard rumours the pair had become engaged despite the short time they'd known each other.

Harriet stood up and drew a shaky breath. 'I'll be all right, ma'am,' she said, and turned back to the table.

But Evie was close enough to see the tears splashing upon the table after the officer had returned to her post.

She couldn't shake off the memory of Harriet's grief, or the thought of the pilot who'd crashed into the sea. Her thoughts inevitably turned to Alex. How would he react to losing a member of his squadron? She also couldn't forget that he was still out on patrol. Just because he hadn't been shot down yet, it didn't mean it wouldn't happen. If she felt this way now, how would she feel if she was walking out with him? She shot a sidelong glance at Harriet. No, she'd made the right decision to remain friends.

But the tension as she strained for updates on Brimstone squadron's whereabouts, mingled with the concentration, only served to worsen the headache that had plagued her all day. Therefore, when she was released for her two-hour break, she grabbed a hasty cup of tea from the canteen then ambled out of the station and into the cool of the woods. Maybe an hour or so strolling along the shady paths would be enough to soothe her head and her spirits before it was time to return to The Hole.

She deliberately chose a path that wound around the hillside and led to the opposite side, away from the incessant roar of aircraft. She could still hear them from this path, but the sounds were muffled, and she could push them to the back of her consciousness. It was torture, not knowing if each Hurricane coming in to land was Alex's.

Making a huge effort, she tried to enjoy the moment, breathe in the air, tinged with its scent of leaf loam, and let the birdsong drift over her. The wind in the leaves sighed like breaking waves, and every now and again there was a rustle and a flash of russet as a squirrel leapt from branch to branch. She paused by a tangle of brambles, surprised to see deep purple blackberries. She'd been so focused on her duties the past few weeks, she'd forgotten it was now late summer. Back in Cowley, she'd always eagerly watched for the signs of the passing seasons, so it was a shock to realise she'd let these first hints of autumn's approach pass her by. With death haunting the lives of the men and women on the station, she'd lived day-to-day, not daring to look too far ahead. But here they were, only a few weeks from autumn. She knew from snatches of conversation overheard in Ops that if the RAF could hold out against the Luftwaffe until the autumn storms arrived, the Germans would have to delay their planned invasion. No wonder they were throwing their full might against the air force now. The Germans had to break the air force before they could attempt a full invasion.

'But they won't break us,' Evie vowed. She felt an awed sense of privilege that she was part of the fight, part of the reason why the Germans were not finding it as easy to break them as they'd predicted.

That was when she heard a soft, metallic tapping. Although the noise was quieter than the other woodland sounds, it was so out of place, Evie noticed it immediately. It seemed to be coming from behind the bole of an enormous beech.

Curious, she went to investigate. She was a few strides from the tree when she stepped on a twig; a nearby magpie shot from its perch, chattering in alarm.

Immediately, the tapping noise stopped, and there came a scrabbling noise. Then a familiar face peered around the trunk, and Evie relaxed.

'Karol! What are you doing up here? I thought Brimstone was out on patrol.'

Karol scrambled to his feet, brushing dried leaves from his trousers. He held a battered brown leather satchel that he hugged to his chest. 'The CO, he ground me,' Karol said in his heavily accented English. 'He is angry because I chase Messerschmitts.' He mimed lining up his gun sights and firing. 'I shoot one down, but he is still angry.'

'Oh, I'm sorry.' Although she could understand why Alex wouldn't want to risk flying with a squadron member who didn't follow orders. 'How long for?'

Karol shrugged. 'Until I learn to obey orders.' Then he grinned. 'Until then, I can walk with pretty WAAF?'

Evie glanced at her watch. 'I've still got an hour or so before I need to go back.' Maybe some company would help her forget her nagging headache, and she

166

couldn't deny the Czech pilots were entertaining company.

'*Dobrý.*' Karol slung the satchel around his neck and then offered her his arm.

Evie took it, wondering why she could feel so at ease with Karol, yet never knowing what to say or how to behave when with Alex.

They strolled further around the path, until they came to a view point where they could see fields stretching out below them and, in the distance, the glint of the sun on the sea.

Karol stopped and gazed across the landscape. 'The sea is *krásné.*' He appeared to grope for a word. 'Beautiful.'

Evie glanced at him. 'Is this the first time you've been near the sea?'

Karol nodded. 'We have no sea in Czechoslovakia. Only lakes.'

'Are there lakes where you come from?' Evie was picturing a fairy-tale land of forests, mountains and lakes.

'No. I am from Praha . . . Prague.'

'What's that like?' Evie breathed, marvelling that the men of Brimstone squadron hailed from such exotic places.

'Old and beautiful. I hope you can go one day. I think you would love the castle and the squares. The city is built upon seven hills.'

'Just like Rome.'

'Yes, only better.' Karol laughed. 'But tell me about England. Do you come from near here?'

'No. I'm from Oxford.'

'Oxford! I've heard of it. Oxford University. Very famous.'

Evie shook her head with a smile. 'I come from a less famous part of the town. No famous universities, just factories.'

'Ah, factories. What do they make?'

'Mostly —' She stopped, suddenly remembering all the posters plastered in the NAAFI, with warnings to 'Keep Mum' and 'Loose Lips Sink Ships'. Not that she suspected Karol of sinister behaviour — he was an RAF pilot. But if she started trying to judge who to disclose information to, and who to keep in the dark, she would spend her life trying to decide on people's motivations. Far better to be safe and not give out that kind of information. She gave a careless laugh. 'Oh, but I never took an interest in anything like that.' She groped for a change of subject. 'Anyway, tell me more about yourself. What were you doing up here in the woods, all alone?' She pointed at the satchel.

Karol clamped it closer to his body. 'You won't laugh?'

'I won't. I promise.'

'I draw.'

She frowned, then her brow cleared. 'Oh, you mean sketching? Drawing the view, that sort of thing?' When Karol nodded, she reached out towards the bag. 'Can I see?'

He clutched the satchel tighter and shook his head. 'No, no. It's not very good. Just for me.'

She relented and let her arm drop to her side. It was on the tip of her tongue to ask what had made the tapping noise, but then she realised it was probably something simple like his pencil tapping against his teeth. They walked on a little further, then she glanced at her watch. 'Goodness! I must go back, or I'll be late for my next watch. Are you coming?'

Karol shook his head. 'I will stay here and draw some more.'

Evie didn't press the matter. He'd looked so forlorn when he said he'd been grounded, he probably wanted to stay away from the reminder that he couldn't fly with the rest of his squadron. Either that, or he was avoiding Alex.

She waved goodbye and dashed down the path.

* * *

Evie's hopes that a walk would clear her headache proved futile. It must be the same for all the plotters, so she said nothing. The relentlessness of working four hours on, followed by only a two-hour break before being back on duty for another four hours was grinding them all down. But yesterday's raid had shown her how vital her job was if they were to prevent any more bombers getting through. And the image of the three lifeless bundles beside the bomb crater continued to haunt her. As did each report of a pilot lost.

She'd allowed time for a drink and quick meal before returning to duty, but although she gulped down her tea, thirsty after her walk, she could only manage a few mouthfuls of the unappetising corned beef sandwich. The prospect of returning to the hot, stuffy Ops Room killed any desire to eat.

Jess was already on duty when Evie entered the Ops Room. She flashed Evie a quick smile when Evie took her place beside her, then she studied Evie's face and frowned. 'Are you feeling all right? You're ever so pale.'

'I'm fine. Just a bit tired.'

But she found it harder than usual to grasp the

current state of all the raids and the flights sent out to intercept them. The blocks and arrows danced on the table, making it impossible to focus. The harsh overhead lights burned her eyes, and each time she got a new position through her headset, the voice jarred her headache. She struggled to keep up with the plots, several times dropping the blocks.

'Pay attention, Bishop,' the WAAF officer snapped in her ear suddenly, making her jump. 'You've just placed your numbers upside down.'

'Sorry, ma'am.' She picked up the block.

'Not that one!' The officer snatched it out of her hands. 'What's wrong with you, Bishop?'

'I don't think she's very well, ma'am.' That was Jess's voice, swirling into the mix of bright lights and disembodied voices.

Then there came a cool hand pressing upon her brow followed by a sharp intake of breath. 'You're burning up, girl. What on earth possessed you to stand watch in this state? Come and sit down.'

Without knowing how she got there, Evie found herself sitting on one of the beds in a side room where WAAFs snatched sleep between watches at night. Something cool pressed against her palms, and she saw she'd been handed a glass of water. She raised it to her lips, grateful for the trickle of water across her parched tongue.

'We've sent for the MO. Just lie there until he comes.'

The officer turned to leave, but Evie called her back. 'I can't stay here. I'm needed on duty.'

'We need plotters who are well enough not to confuse one of our squadrons for a hostile plot,' the officer replied.

170

'I did?' Evie buried her aching head in her hands. 'I'm sorry.'

The officer patted her on the back. 'Don't worry about it. You're one of our best plotters. I know it's not a mistake you'd ever make when you're yourself. The best thing you can do for the station now is to get yourself well as soon as possible so you can return to your duties.'

Much to her disgust, the Medical Officer told her it looked like a dose of flu. He had her taken to the infirmary, where she was dosed with aspirin and put straight to bed. She must have dozed off, for the next thing she knew the soft golden light of early evening was streaming through the window, and Jess and May were standing beside her bed, holding a bunch of six crimson roses.

'We took them from a bush at High Chalk House,' Jess explained as she arranged them in a vase. 'And we pinched this from the house.' She tapped the fine china vase, decorated with a bold pattern of leaves and tulips. 'May's getting positively daring.'

'What if an officer had caught you?'

'As a matter of fact, one did.'

'Oh no. Please tell me you didn't get into trouble.' The last thing Evie wanted was for her friends to end up on a charge on her account.

Jess grinned. 'It was Hellerby. When we told her what it was for, she promised not to tell anyone as long as we returned it after you were better.'

'Ellerby?' Evie put her hand to her aching head. She must be worse than she'd thought. 'I thought she was looking for any excuse to tear a strip off you.'

'That was true until Jess showed how brave she was during the raid,' May said. 'And then she helped

171

Ellerby after she got knocked out, so now Jess is her favourite WAAF. She's even talking about Jess being officer material.'

Jess looked pleased. 'I should add that May was far more of a hero. She took charge after we got trapped.'

Evie was pleased for her friends that they had done so well. She yawned, a wave of exhaustion sweeping over her.

'We should go,' Jess said. 'Leave you to rest.'

They turned to leave, but Evie called them back. 'Wait. Brimstone squadron. Did they all get back safely? Apart from Flight Lieutenant Harper, I mean.'

'All down without a scratch. They're in the pub as we speak.'

Evie lay back and let sleep drift over her, able to relax now she knew Alex was safe.

* * *

After three days, Evie was feeling much better. As exhausting as she found her watches in The Hole, she'd missed it, and hated not knowing exactly what was happening in the air in their sector. Lying in bed, listening to the roar of aircraft taking off and landing, she continually fretted over the safety of the pilots. It was horrible not knowing if her friends had landed safely, not knowing if Alex was safe. Every day she eagerly awaited visits from Jess and May, and was only able to relax when she knew all the pilots had returned. She learned with dismay that two young pilots from Popcorn squadron had been shot down over the sea and were presumed dead. They'd only arrived in the squadron two weeks earlier, and she hadn't met them, but she mourned their loss all the same. One of the Czech pilots from Brimstone had been shot down over Kent, but had bailed out and returned unharmed that night.

Now she was feeling better, she looked forward to her return to Ops, where she could get all the news first-hand.

'Absolutely not,' the MO said, when Evie mentioned it to him. 'You've only just recovered from a high fever. If you go back down into that stuffy hole before you're fully fit, you'll make yourself ill all over again. No. I'm putting you on sick leave for a week. Go home. Spend some time with your family.'

Evie's heart sank. Somehow, she doubted a week in her mother's company would provide the rest the MO intended. She'd written to her mother every fortnight and sent postal orders every month for as much money as she could spare. Dora had always replied, but her letters had been stiff, revealing only the barest details of life in Cowley. It seemed Dora hadn't forgiven her daughter for leaving. With the distance between them, Evie had been able to ignore her own feelings of betrayal towards Dora but now she was returning home, the reckoning between them loomed large. Her visit to Cowley was going to be awkward, to say the least.

14

The next day, Evie was issued with travel warrants and ration coupons, and packed off back to Oxford for a week. May drove her to the station, and Jess managed to wangle a change in her hours so she could come along for the ride.

'I'm going to miss you both while I'm away,' Evie told them, as the car sped along the country lanes. 'I don't know what I'm going to do without being able to talk things through with you in the evenings.'

'You'll be too busy catching up with old friends to miss us,' Jess said with a laugh.

'I never really had friends until I met you,' Evie replied sadly. 'I was too busy studying to make friends. Promise you'll write?' *And tell me how Alex is.* But she kept that thought to herself. Time away from Alex with no word of him would be good for her. A chance to shake off her infatuation for a man she barely knew.

'We promise,' May said. 'But you know we won't be able to tell you much.'

Evie nodded gloomily. The censor would remove even the slightest hint of information on RAF activities. They weren't even allowed to write about the weather. On top of that, the knowledge that their letters were being read by others was inhibiting. 'Any news is better than none.'

All too soon, she was on the train, leaning out of the window, waving to Jess and May as the train puffed out of the station. But as she sat back in her seat she thought again about the effect of censorship on letters. Maybe her mother wasn't as cold as her letters made her appear. Maybe she just hadn't wanted the censor to know their business. She took comfort in the thought as the train carried her away from her friends and back to the home she'd left in bitterness and disappointment.

★ ★ ★

Alex sat at his desk, frowning over his latest combat report. It was bad enough they had to fly four or five missions a day with barely a chance to visit the latrine between flights, let alone eat or drink. Having to write everything up afterwards was the last straw. He glanced out of the window, to where his pilots were lounging in deck chairs, soaking up the late afternoon sun. With luck, the next time the phone rang it would be to stand them down for the day. The relentless cycle of dawn-till-dusk patrols was wearing even the most happy-go-lucky pilots down. An evening at the pub would do them all good.

The telephone shrilled, and every muscle in Alex's body tensed. Karol went to answer it. Karol had followed orders to the letter since he'd begun his punishment. He hadn't even complained about being grounded. Alex supposed he ought to release him to fly soon.

Karol replaced the receiver. "A' flight, scramble,' he cried and rang the bell to alert the pilots.

Alex flung down his pen and dashed out to his Hurricane. 'I knew I shouldn't have allowed myself to start planning a trip to the pub,' he said to Milan, as the dark-haired pilot staggered out of his deck

175

chair, rubbing sleep from his eyes. After his rocky start, Milan had proved a great support to Alex, helping keep his compatriots in check. For that reason, Alex had chosen him to be second-in-command after Harper's death.

His stomach tightened as the reality of Harper's death intruded on his thoughts again. For the most part, he'd been able to shut out his feelings regarding the loss of another squadron member. He had to, or he thought he might never claw his way out of despair.

Milan wrinkled his nose. 'I'd rather be shooting at Germans than drinking the dishwater you British call beer.'

Alex grinned and clapped Milan on the back, forcing all thoughts of death out of his mind. He pulled on his parachute, hauled himself onto the wing of his Hurricane and into the cockpit. The fitter had already started the engine, so he ran through the cockpit drill, then signalled for the chocks to be pulled away. Within moments, he was taxiing across the field, gathering speed.

As ever when he flew, all tension drained away the moment the wheels lifted off the ground. It was as though he left all his worries on the station and he was floating as light as the clouds. Time enough to pick them up when he landed.

'Brimstone Red Leader, this is Belfry.' The controller's voice crackled through his headset. 'Climb to Angels two-zero then vector one-seven-niner.'

'Belfry, Brimstone Red Leader. Understood.'

He climbed in the opposite direction to the vector he'd been given, having quickly learned the danger of not gaining enough height before encountering the hostiles they'd been sent to intercept. He glanced

176

to either side to check his pilots were in formation, satisfied when he saw the other two Hurricanes of Red section on each wingtip, and Blue section slightly below and behind them. Soon they were up among the puffs of cloud, which gleamed brilliant white in the sunshine. Above them the sky was a clear blue expanse. He always found the contrast between the serenity of flying above the clouds and the frantic tangle of dogfights hard to fathom. It seemed an obscenity to mar the peaceful skies with gunfire and killing.

Once they had reached twenty thousand feet, Alex steered on the vector they'd been given, and kept an eye out for raiders.

'Brimstone Red Leader, Belfry. You should be right on top of them.'

Alex scanned the skies. He just caught a glint of sunlight on glass when Milan's voice cut across the R/T: 'Bandits two o'clock.'

Alex glanced ahead and to the right and saw them. Nine Dorniers. He called them in, then gave the order to attack. 'Red two, Red three, break and attack. Blue Leader, maintain your position.' It was a routine they were used to: half the flight would attack the bombers while the rest circled overhead, watching for enemy fighters that were inevitably waiting up in the sun, intending to 'bounce' unwary attackers.

Sure enough, as soon as they commenced their dive, he heard Milan call out: '109s at six o'clock. Look out, Red Leader, there's one on your tail.'

Alex instinctively threw his Hurricane into a barrel roll, but he wasn't fast enough: he felt the thud of bullets hitting the fuselage. He shot a glance over his shoulder and saw a 109 swooping down on his tail.

Another Hurricane — Milan's, he thought — was gaining on it. It bought him time to fire at his Dornier. He waited until the last possible moment, then fired.

Nothing. He pressed the firing button again. No response.

His mouth went dry. By this time, he'd overshot the Dornier. Another glance over his shoulder showed him that Milan had hit his mark. Black smoke plumed from the 109's engine, and flames licked around the engine cowling. One 109 down, but he had no idea how many were left. Even as the thought crossed his mind, he spotted two more Messerschmitts swooping down from above.

He pulled the joystick back into his right thigh, putting the Hurricane into a tight climbing turn. God help him — what was he supposed to do? He hammered on the button, in the vain hope that it would somehow unstick whatever was jamming his guns. All the while he kept his Hurricane twisting and turning, doing his best not to present an easy shot to the 109s. Without weapons, he needed to get out of the fight, but that was impossible when he could see nothing but hostile aircraft, all seemingly intent on shooting him out of the sky.

'This is Red Leader,' he yelled into the R/T. 'My guns have jammed. For God's sake, someone get these bloody Jerries off my tail.' His lips twitched at the thought that if he survived, he would have to put himself on a charge for breaking radio protocol. Funny how such absurd thoughts could strike at moments of extreme stress.

He heaved the Hurricane into another turn, diving to pick up speed, and caught a glimpse of two

Hurricanes plunging into the fray. Another Bf 109 appeared to starboard, bursts of flame spewing from its machine guns. His canopy smashed, and there was the tinkle of glass as his compass exploded in minute shards. Then came a sharp sting in his upper arm.

He pulled up into a twisting turn. Below him, two Messerschmitts collided and disappeared in a ball of flame. He glanced frantically around the sky and exhaled a shaky breath to see his machine was clear of hostile aircraft. He climbed out of the fight, feeling weak now the immediate danger was over. The other Hurricanes were all still in the fight, their vapour trails weaving with those of the enemy, forming a giant cat's cradle in the sky. He hated to leave but there was nothing he could do to help. His guns weren't working, and half his instrument panel had been shot out. He would only put the entire squadron in danger if he hung around, forcing the other pilots to protect him. He tried to signal to them that he was leaving, but his radio was dead. All he could do was turn in what he prayed was the direction of Amberton and leave the fight.

A strange tiredness swept over him. At first, he put it down to a reaction to his narrow escape, but then he felt something warm trickle down his left arm. Glancing at his sleeve, he was shocked to see a red stain blooming upon the fabric. Now he remembered the stinging sensation in his arm when the 109 had attacked. He must have been shot! Strange he hadn't noticed before.

His head was starting to swim. The instrument panel blurred in and out of focus, the dials dancing before his eyes. Suddenly his oxygen mask seemed to be smothering him. He tore it off and drew gulping breaths. Grey dots obscured his vision. Hell, he was going to faint. Looking down all he could see was sea, and he realised he had no idea where he was. God help him, if he didn't land now, he was going to pass out and crash.

Bail out. He had to bail out. He pulled at the canopy release, but it was stuck. Either that or he didn't have the strength to open it in his weakened state. Whatever the reason, it didn't matter. If he didn't find land and somewhere to put down his Hurricane, he was going to crash.

He looked at his oxygen mask, dangling on his chest. When had he taken that off? That was a damn fool thing to do at this height. He fastened it around his face with trembling fingers and drew gulping breaths. His vision cleared and with it came calmer thinking.

Right. He couldn't bail out, so he was going to have to find the coast and search for a landing site. If he could avoid running into enemy patrols, all the better. Light clouds obscured his view, so he lost a little height until he was below the cloud base, then scanned the horizon, desperate for the sight of the coastline. Nothing. This was impossible. The Channel wasn't that wide, and they hadn't flown far out to sea before they'd met the Dorniers. He felt like he was trapped in some kind of nightmare, doomed to an endless search for land until he ran out of fuel and crashed.

Evie. He wished he'd kissed her now. He couldn't make sense of the tangled thought processes that had made him hold back from kissing her at the dance. Now it just looked like he'd been afraid. Afraid she would reject him. He was going to plunge into a watery grave, and he didn't even have the memory of a kiss from the woman he loved to take with him.

No. That wasn't going to happen. He must be flying in the wrong direction. He performed a wide, banking turn, and peered out, praying the coastline would come into view. Then he saw it — a faint line on the horizon to starboard. He went cold with the realisation that he'd been flying parallel to the coast all this time. If he'd continued in that direction, he'd have ended up in the Atlantic if his tanks hadn't run dry first. He gave a grim smile. If he made it back in one piece, he would be sure to tell Evie it was the thought of her that had helped him find land.

Now he had a landmark to steer by, he set a course, then examined his arm. If he was going to make it to land, he had to stop the bleeding, or no amount of oxygen would keep him from losing consciousness. There was no room in the cramped cockpit to remove his jacket, even if he could have done so without getting hopelessly tangled with his oxygen feed, Mae West and parachute. He would just have to do what he could. Judging from the tears in his upper sleeve, the bullet had passed straight through the flesh of his upper arm. He could move his arm, so didn't think the bone was broken. Doing his best to hold the control column steady with his knees, he pulled off his scarf and combined it with his handkerchief for a makeshift pad and bandage.

By the time he'd finished, the coast was almost below him. He gazed down to see a strange spit of land with water on either side. He followed the line to the right, to see it led to an island. Of course — it must be Portland Island. He fumbled to shake out his chart across his knees and peered down at it. Yes!

181

He blessed whatever guardian angel had led him to cross the coast at such a distinctive location. Now all he had to do was follow the coast to Chichester Harbour, and he could find his way back to Amberton from there. He glanced at his fuel gauge — thankfully one of the few instruments still working –and breathed a sigh of relief when he saw he had enough fuel to get him back. The first thing he was going to do when he landed was find Evie and kiss her.

It was only when his wheels touched down that he remembered Evie was home on sick leave.

★ ★ ★

'Sir!'

Alex, returning to dispersal after being patched up by the MO, glanced around to see who was calling. To his dismay, the MO had grounded him for at least a week. He'd threatened to order him to bed in the infirmary, but Alex had refused point blank. It had done no good to tell the MO he'd had no trouble flying after he'd been hit; the MO wouldn't let him return to combat flying until he was fully fit. That left him stuck behind a desk for at least a week.

Chief Technician Rawlins caught Alex up just as he reached the dispersal hut. He saluted then glanced to his right and left before saying, 'I checked your guns as you asked, sir.'

'And?'

'I couldn't find anything wrong until —'

'Impossible! They wouldn't fire at all.'

'I know, sir. The patches were all intact.' Rawlins was referring to fabric patches taped over the gun ports after rearming to keep out moisture. They

182

would be blown off the first time the guns were fired. 'That's why I looked more closely. I found these.' Rawlins held out an oil-stained hand with a few slivers of wood resting on his palm.

Alex frowned down at them. 'Matchsticks?'

'They'd been rammed into the air feeds. A bloody pain in the arse to prise them free, sir.'

Icy cold fingers stroked the nape of his neck. 'Is there any way they could have got there accidentally?' Although he already knew the answer.

'No, sir. This was sabotage.'

It was as though the heat was sucked out of the air. Alex was prepared for death at the hands of the Germans, but to know he'd nearly been killed by the malicious actions of someone on the station made him feel sick.

Thoughts whirled through his head. His first impulse was to order all the fitters to examine each Hurricane for signs of tampering, but that would surely alert the saboteur.

'Don't mention this to anyone else,' he said in the end. 'I need to report this to the station commander before we take any action.' Then it occurred to him that the saboteur would be on the alert now that Alex had managed to return his Hurricane in one piece, or near enough. He would be waiting for the alert to be raised now it was certain the sabotage would be discovered. 'No, wait. Say you think I must be losing it. You checked the guns and they're in perfect working order. Let the saboteur think the matchsticks must have worked free in the flight. I don't want him to know we're after him.'

Alex turned to go and find Bob Law, when another thought occurred. 'And for God's sake, go over all

183

the Hurricanes with a fine-toothed comb when they return. I don't know how you're going to do it without raising suspicion, and I don't care. Say it's a random inspection, or something. Just make sure they're safe to fly before they're scrambled again.' Right now, Rawlins was the only man he could trust.

'Then you haven't heard?' There was no mistaking the bad news in the sergeant's ominous tone.

Alex clenched his fists. 'Who?'

'Sergeant Pilot Josef Kaspar, sir.' Rawlins' voice seemed to come from a great distance. Kaspar was a member of 'B' flight. They must have been scrambled shortly after 'A' flight. 'They were sent to intercept a hostile flight shortly after you left. The other pilots say he was shot down in the first attack. None of them saw him fire a shot.' Through a roaring in the ears, Alex heard Rawlins' final words. 'He didn't bail out, and his kite burned up before it crashed.'

Josef's ghost hovered by his shoulder all the way to the station commander's office. *Find the bastard who did this to me*, he seemed to be saying. Alex had no idea if it was his own imagination or if Josef really had come back to haunt him. Either way, it made little difference. Alex had every intention of seeing the traitor hang. Rawlins' words beat through his head with each step. Josef had died in the worst possible way. He had an image of burning hands clawing at the canopy of a blazing Hurricane. It was every pilot's nightmare, and thanks to the saboteur, it had come true for Josef.

Alex was shaking with anger and horror by the time he reached the Admin block. He stormed through the station commander's ante room.

'Wait. You can't go in there,' the adjutant cried

184

when Alex strode to the station commander's door without pausing. 'He's in a —'

Alex ignored him and flung open the door. The MO was inside, his back to the door. For a split second, Alex hesitated. No doubt the MO was here to make his report on Alex's injury. But his rage carried him through. 'Leave,' he said to the MO. 'I have to speak to Bob. Now.'

'If this is about your —'

'It's nothing to do with it. Go.'

The MO rose and, after a significant look at Bob, he left.

'Now, listen, Alex,' Bob began, 'the MO said to expect you to protest, but I really can't allow you to —'

'This is nothing to do with my arm.' Alex marched up to the desk and dropped the matchsticks in front of Bob. 'Rawlins fished these out of my guns' air feeds.'

Bob stared at the tiny pieces of wood then back at Alex's face. 'You mean —'

'Sabotage.' Then he added a belated, 'Sir.'

Bob's mouth set in a grim line. 'Any suspects?'

Alex went to rake his fingers through his hair, only to drop his arm with a wince. 'It'd be quicker to list who I don't suspect.' He paced in front of the desk. 'Rawlins is in the clear — he found the matchsticks and showed them to me. If he'd been the saboteur, he could have chucked them away, and nobody would be any the wiser.'

'Anyone else? Oh, for God's sake, sit down before you pass out.'

Alex dropped into the chair. The fight seemed to drain out of him, and only now he realised he was shivering and felt sick. 'There's only one other I know for sure can't have done it, and that's poor Josef. But any of the Erks could have done it.'

'Or a pilot.'

Alex gazed at Bob, dry mouthed. 'I can't believe a pilot would knowingly do that to a fellow pilot.'

Yet you shoot down German pilots without a thought. He swore he could see the retort forming on Bob's lips. Or was it his own conscience? In his mind he saw a flash of wide eyes in a pale face: the German he had shot down yesterday. Or was it the day before? He'd made so many flights in the past weeks, his memories were merging.

Bob seemed to understand his conflict, for he said nothing for a while, just picked up one of the match-sticks and studied it, twisting it between thumb and forefinger. 'I don't want to suspect a pilot any more than you do,' he said finally in a heavy voice. 'But we can't afford to rule anyone out. This is too serious a crime. It's bad enough I have to write letters to wives and mothers of pilots shot down by Germans' — he jabbed with the match towards a half-written letter on his desk — 'without wondering if they were shot down as a result of sabotage.'

Alex looked at the letter. In the normal course of things, he should write to Josef 's family. But they were in Nazi-occupied Czechoslovakia; no letter would get through.

Bob's voice interrupted his thoughts. 'I'll start by interviewing Rawlins.'

'You? Oh no. It was my kite that was sabotaged, a pilot in my squadron killed. This is my investigation.'

'Which is precisely why I'm sending you on a week's leave.'

'What? You can't —' Alex half-rose, but his legs

186

shook so hard he quickly dropped back into the seat.

'Listen to me, Alex. For a start you've been injured; you need time to recover.'

'I don't.'

'Yes, you do. Look at you — you're as white as a sheet. You'll be lucky if you've got the strength to drag yourself up to your bed, let alone chase round the station looking for a saboteur.'

'I'll manage.'

'I'm sure you would. You're a stubborn fool when you've got a bee in your bonnet. But you're missing the point.'

'Which is?' It was a good thing Bob wasn't a stickler for formalities, or he'd be up on a charge for addressing a superior officer in such a belligerent tone.

'If you go blundering around the station in your state, asking questions, when you should be on sick leave, everyone will realise you suspect foul play. Everyone, including the saboteur. Our only hope of flushing him out is if he doesn't suspect we're on to him. By rights, I should leave it to the RAF Police, but that would send the saboteur to ground, and we'd never know who it was.'

Alex subsided. He could see the sense in what Bob was saying, much as he burned to expose the traitor and wring his neck with his own hands.

Bob continued. 'If I haven't made any progress by the time you get back, you can take over, but until then I want you out of it.'

'Wait. Get back?' While some officers counted down the days until they could see their families again, Alex had no wish to see his grandparents, and all his friends were serving in various locations. Or dead.

Bob gazed levelly at Alex. 'I've had a report that your Hurricane is too damaged to fix on the station, but it's flyable. Tomorrow morning, you're to fly it to No 1 CRU. I don't want to see you back for a week.'

'But . . .' Alex paused. The Civilian Repair Unit was in Oxford. Evie was in Oxford.

He rose and saluted. 'Yes, sir.'

If he couldn't join the hunt for the saboteur, he would find Evie and fulfil the promise he'd made to himself when he'd thought he was going to die. He wouldn't return to Amberton until he'd told Evie he loved her.

15

Evie had hoped the train journey to Oxford would give her the space to work out what to say to her mother. However, the train was so crowded and noisy, she hadn't been able to think at all. By the time she climbed off the bus on Hollow Way, her stomach was tied in knots. Her feet dragged as she turned into George Street and saw the familiar green gate halfway up the street. She didn't have a key to the front door, so she squeezed through the narrow side passage and into the back garden.

Her mother was standing outside the back door, running clothes through the ancient mangle. She had her back to Evie, and as the handle of the mangle made an ear-splitting shriek, she obviously hadn't heard her shut the gate.

Evie stood and watched her in silence for a moment. Dora seemed to have shrunk in the intervening months. She was hunched over the mangle, wearing a faded pinny, her salt-and-pepper hair scraped into a straggly bun. She looked tired and old. A wave of sorrow swept over Evie at the sight of her brisk, active mother so reduced.

She slung her kit bag down and took off her tunic. 'Here, let me do that, Mum. You look all in.'

Dora had been about to wring a tattered pillowcase. She dropped it onto the paving slabs and straightened with a gasp. 'Evie!' She looked her daughter up and down, her mouth working. 'Oh, look at you, all grown up.'

She seized Evie in a hug. Evie returned it, swallowing back the tightness in her throat. Dora's damp hands left clammy patches on the back of Evie's shirt, but Evie didn't care. For now she could forget her anger and simply enjoy the comfort of being held by her mother again. 'It's good to be back.'

Dora eventually released Evie and stepped back, subjecting her daughter to an assessing gaze. 'You're too thin. What have they been doing to you?'

'Nothing.' Evie was immediately on the defensive. 'I had flu.'

'In August? They can't be treating you right.' Dora fed another pillow case into the mangle; the bearings screeched with every turn of the handle. 'If you'd only got a bank job —'

Evie didn't wait to hear more. Muttering something about finding oil, she darted into the shed but soon realised her mistake. The mingled scent of linseed oil, wood shavings and pipe smoke evoked her father's presence so strongly, she could almost believe he was there beside her. A wave of loss threatened to overwhelm her, the last thing she wanted when she needed unclouded wits to face her mother.

She closed her eyes. *Oh, Dad. You always used to keep the peace between me and Mum. How am I going to get through the week without you?*

She hadn't seriously expected any reply, but a sudden deep sense of calm washed over her, and the scent of pipe tobacco grew stronger. In that moment Evie could almost imagine her dad was beside her, his arm around her shoulders, telling her everything would work out for the best.

She breathed deeply, drinking in the peace and

the feeling of reassurance. She was unwilling to leave this feeling of her father's presence — she'd missed him so much — but she couldn't put off a proper talk with Dora for ever. Brushing tears from her cheeks, she picked up the dusty oil can and returned to her mother, braced for more criticisms. However, Dora remained silent while Evie oiled the mangle.

Evie stepped back. 'There. Try that.'

The handle turned with ease. Dora picked up a sheet and put her hand to the handle. Then she glanced at Evie and gave a tight smile. 'Thank you, Evie. You're a good girl.'

That was far more than Evie had expected. Offering silent thanks to her father, she started to peg the washing on the line. She looked around the garden as she worked. In the months before her dad had died, he hadn't been strong enough to keep the garden under control. It had fallen to Evie and Dora to do the weeding and planting and kneeling side by side, pulling up weeds and planting seeds for the following year's harvest gave them their rare times of companionship. Now, nettles and thistles grew strong and tall in all the vegetable beds and choked the entrance to the Anderson shelter by the back fence. Carrot, beetroot and onion stalks peeped through in places, but it was clear her mother hadn't touched the garden since Evie had left.

Dora finished wringing the last of the laundry then helped Evie peg it out. 'I'll make tea,' she said when it was done.

Evie had to swallow back the tears again when she came downstairs from a quick wash and change and walked into the back room. She half expected to see her father in his chair; it was a punch to the gut to remember he would never again be there. She sat in her usual seat and took the cup and saucer from Dora with a weak smile, trying not to look at the space where her father should have been.

'I'll never get used to not seeing your dad in here,' Dora said, sinking into her chair with her own cup of tea. It was as though she had read Evie's mind. 'I miss him so, Evie.' She paused, her cup halfway to her mouth. 'I . . . I've missed *you*.'

Still no apology. No admitting that her actions had sent Evie away. But even as the thought crossed her mind, Evie could almost hear her father's voice. *One step at a time, Evie, my girl. Give her time.* Some of her resentment drained away. 'I've missed you, too, Mum. And I'm sorry for leaving you alone with all this.' Evie made a gesture that took in the empty chair and through the window to the jungle of a garden.

Dora leaned forward and squeezed Evie's hand. 'I'm glad you're home.'

Evie didn't press for more. Tomorrow was time enough to air their differences. Today she'd be grateful for the fragile peace.

* * *

The next morning, Evie woke to the slam of the front door. A glance at her watch told her it must be Dora leaving for work. She stretched, enjoying the luxury of a whole day to herself. She could do what she liked, wear a cool cotton dress instead of her uniform and, best of all, she had a few hours' grace before she had to face her mother again.

Her happiness lasted until she went to look in the pantry for breakfast. Dora had always kept it well

192

stocked, even if with plain, simple food. Now the large marble slab under the stairs had more space than produce, and what it held didn't look appetising. There was a saucer holding a sweaty piece of cheddar, a few tins of pilchards and corned beef and a small loaf. The jar of oats was nearly full, though, and there was milk, so Evie made a bowl of porridge and sweetened it with a teaspoon of honey. She gazed out thoughtfully at the garden while she ate it and sipped her tea. Rationing had only just begun when she'd joined the WAAF, so she hadn't experienced its full effect. Nevertheless, she was sure she would have heard if rationing was making food this scarce.

A lump of lead settled in her chest, and the porridge turned to ashes in her mouth. She had joined the WAAF in a fit of anger without considering how it would affect her mother, and this was the result. Dora had aged beyond her years and she wasn't looking after herself properly. Well, she had a week to put it right. To start with, she needed to arrange some nourishing meals. She could also sort out the garden. There were good vegetables growing there, if only they could be rescued from the weeds.

She drained her cup, scraped up the last of the porridge from the bowl and went into the galley kitchen to wash up. Once everything was dried and put away, she picked up her gas mask case which, following Jess's example, she now used as a handbag, and went to the local shops.

She returned an hour later with a string of sausages, two pounds of potatoes, runner beans, onions and a punnet of cherries. She unloaded the goods in the pantry, unable to resist popping one of the cherries into her mouth and relishing the explosion of tart sweetness. Fresh fruit had been in short supply at Amberton — it was always stewed beyond recognition by the time it reached the plate. Then she donned an old skirt and blouse and set to work in the garden. She would have loved to visit Cornelia, but that would have to wait. She had neglected her mother, and the least she could do was get the garden into some kind of order.

There was something therapeutic about pulling up weeds, the sun warming her back and the scent of turned earth and bruised leaves filling her nostrils. It recalled happier times, connecting her with her father, who had first laid out the vegetable patch, and also her mother, who had taken over work on the garden when Stan had become too ill. A sense of peace stole over Evie, like the feeling she'd had in the shed the previous day. A feeling that her dad was nearby, telling her everything would sort itself out. A blackbird trilled its liquid song from its perch on the fence, bringing a lump to her throat. Stan had loved to listen to the birds and even when he was too ill to go out, he would sit by the open window so he could hear the birdsong.

She lost all track of time, only stopping when the slam of a door dragged her back from her thoughts. She straightened and turned, wincing as her back and shoulder muscles protested. Dora stood beside the back door, mouth agape as she took in the cleared vegetable beds, the orderly rows of vegetable stems that could now be clearly seen, and the basket heaped with carrots, beetroot and onions, the soil still clinging to them.

'I see you've been hard at work,' Dora said. This was in the same sharp tone Evie had become

194

accustomed to over recent years. Evie braced herself for the criticism that inevitably came when her mother used that tone with her. But Dora's voice softened, and she said, 'Are you sure you're well enough?'

Evie grasped at the offered olive branch and smiled. 'I'm sure. The MO ordered me to get plenty of fresh air.' She gathered an armful of weeds from the pile she'd created and carried them across to the compost heap behind the shed.

She jumped when an aircraft roared overhead. Her heart calmed when, glancing up, she caught sight of the RAF roundels on the underside of each wing.

Dora had clapped a hand to her chest. 'Bless my heart, these Spitfires make a terrible racket. I don't know how you can live by an airfield.'

'It's a Hurricane,' Evie corrected. 'And you get used to it.' She smiled. 'My friends and I have decided we can't sleep now when the airfield is quiet. The noise is kind of comforting.'

Dora narrowed her eyes. 'You sound like you actually enjoy the WAAF.'

Evie brushed the earth from her hands and joined her mother by the back door. 'I love it,' she said. 'It's hard work, but I'm doing something useful. Making a difference.' Hesitantly she placed a hand on Dora's arm. 'I would never have been happy, shut up in an office, moving piles of paper from one side of the desk to another.' She had a sudden flash of understanding of Alex's frustration while serving in Ops. Much as she feared for him, he needed to be active, feel he was doing his part.

Dora patted her hand. 'I know, dear.' Then, as though she'd shown enough gentleness for one day, she said, 'Now get a move on and take that veg to the pantry. Then go and get changed while I make lunch. Although what I'm supposed to do with those sorry excuses for sausages you've gone and bought, I don't know. More bread than meat, if you ask me.'

When Evie came downstairs, dressed again in the cotton frock she'd worn to the shops, she was greeted with the appetising aroma of frying sausages and onions and the sound of Dora's voice raised in song. It struck her then that she hadn't heard her mother sing in years. When Evie was a child, Dora had sung constantly as she went about her work but gradually, as Stan had become sicker and she'd had to make up for his loss in income by taking on more cleaning jobs, the songs had stopped. But Dora had a beautiful voice, high and pure, and hearing her sing '*Early One Morning*' brought a lump to Evie's throat.

'Do you have to work this afternoon?' Evie asked as they sat at the dining table and tucked into a hearty lunch of sausages and onions accompanied by potatoes and runner beans. She couldn't remember the last time she'd enjoyed a meal so much.

Dora shook her head as she swallowed a mouthful of potatoes. Evie was relieved to see her eat with more relish than she had as she'd picked at last night's meal. 'This is the afternoon that I usually clean for Miss Gould, but she's away, so won't be needing me.'

'Cornelia's away?' Evie felt a rush of disappointment. 'I wanted to visit her.'

'I think she comes back this weekend.' Dora gave her a soft smile. 'She's always thrilled to get your letters. She's so proud of what you're doing.' Then she added so quietly that Evie wasn't sure she'd heard correctly, 'As am I.'

'Oh, Mum.' Evie could hardly force out the words,

her throat was so tight. 'I'm so sorry I —'

'No. Never be sorry. I'm the one who should be sorry. I . . . I was just so scared for you.'

'Scared? Why?' Evie gazed at Dora in astonishment. Dora had always been so sure of her opinions, so forceful. She couldn't imagine her ever being scared.

'Because you reminded me so much of your father.' Dora gripped Evie's hand, squeezing tight. 'You have to understand — your father and I had such high hopes when we married. He was an apprentice mechanic, with a bright future ahead of him. And then all it took was' — her face crumpled — 'was one bloody gas attack.'

Evie struggled for words but failed. In all her years, she'd never known her mother to utter more than an irritated 'oh dear' when things went wrong. She'd become accustomed to coarse language at Amberton but it was something of a shock to hear it from her mother.

'When you did well at school, I was proud. So very proud,' Dora continued. 'But then when you won your scholarship to Oxford High and set your sights on Somerville . . . I was haunted by your father's high hopes, and his disappointment when his health didn't let him fulfil them. I didn't want the same to happen to you.' Her last words ended on a wail, and tears spilled down her cheeks.

'Oh, Mum!' Evie reached blindly for her mother, unable to see through shimmering tears. She clutched her in a hug, unable to hold back the sobs when Dora squeezed her tight in return.

'Can you forgive me?' Dora choked. 'I've written to Somerville, you know, explained what I did. The dean wrote me a lovely letter in return, said there would be a place for you after the war.'

'Oh, Mum, you didn't have to do that. Of course I forgive you.' It was as though a huge pressure lifted from her chest. In the dark days following the funeral and her mother's confession, she'd longed for a sign of contrition from her mother. Only now did she realise her anger and resentment were long gone, and she didn't need an apology. 'It's all worked out for the best. I'm happy in the WAAF. It wouldn't have felt right, being at Oxford while others were sacrificing so much.' And that was the truth, although it hadn't struck her until now.

Dora stepped back, wiping her eyes. 'It's done you good. There's a confidence about you now that you didn't have before. You're obviously doing well there.'

'I love it. And Alex — he's one of the squadron leaders — he even thinks I could make an officer.'

Dora gave her a sharp glance at the mention of Alex, and Evie felt her cheeks burn. It was as though his name had been poised on her lips, waiting for the slightest excuse to be spoken. But she couldn't think of Amberton without thinking about Alex. She braced herself for an acerbic comment, but all Dora said was, 'Well, you can tell me all about it while we finish the weeding this afternoon. It's high time I got back in the garden.'

Evie didn't know when she'd last enjoyed her mother's company so much. She chatted about her life in Amberton, telling her all about May and Jess, while trying not to mention Alex again. Dora surprised her by confessing she was considering taking a job at the Morris works.

'They're crying out for women to work in the

Civilian Repair Unit now most of the men have been called up. It pays well, and they give full training. It would be my way of doing my bit. What do you think? Maybe I'd end up repairing planes from Amberton.'

'I think it's a wonderful idea.' The last of her guilt fell away. Her mother was going to be fine.

At the end of the afternoon, Evie was covered in earth with burrs snarling her hair and scratches up both arms, but she was smiling broadly as she carried yet another basket of produce into the pantry. She'd just placed everything into cardboard boxes on the floor when she heard a knock on the door.

'I'll get it,' she called to her mother, who was making tea.

She wiped her hands down her skirt as she strode down the narrow passage, trying to brush away bits of dried leaves, but she only succeeded in smearing more dirt into the cloth.

She opened the door and nearly slammed it shut in shock.

Alex smiled at her and took off his cap. 'You're a hard lass to track down, Evie Bishop.'

16

Alex had never seen a woman as beautiful as Evie looked right now. A shaft of sunlight lit her from an open door behind her, lighting the coppery tendrils of hair that had come loose and framed her face with a halo. Instead of the uniform he was used to seeing her wearing, she had on a light cotton dress, sprigged with delicate green leaves. It emphasised her narrow waist and revealed more of her shapely legs than her heavy uniform skirt.

Her hand had flown to her mouth when she'd opened the door, but now she let it fall. 'Alex. What are you doing here?'

Before he could answer, a woman's voice called from the room at the end of the narrow passage. 'Is it Mrs Forester, Evie? Don't keep her standing on the doorstep. Invite her in. The kettle's on for tea.'

'It's not Mrs Forester,' Evie called over her shoulder. Alex was intrigued to see a dried leaf snarled in a lock of hair at the nape of her neck. 'It's . . . Oh.' She faced Alex again. 'You'd better come in.'

He followed her down the passage in silence, his footsteps ringing on the quarry tiles. He caught a glimpse of a woman — Evie's mother, he supposed — through the open door, placing teacups on a tray, then Evie opened a door on the left and led him into a shabby but cosy room, lit by the bright sunshine pouring through the open windows. There was a small round dining table beside the windows,

200

covered in a yellowing lace cloth, with four Windsor chairs arranged around it, their dark wood scratched in places but gleaming. The main feature of the room was the fireplace, with its plain wooden mantelpiece. Two armchairs with worn upholstery stood on either side of it. The only other furniture was a small table to the left of the fireplace, holding an ancient wireless.

The ponderous ticking of the clock on the mantelpiece punctuated the silence. Alex had rehearsed what he would say to Evie on the flight to Oxford and polished his speech while searching the streets of Cowley, but now his mind was as empty as the sky had been on his flight here.

'What are you doing here, Alex? How did you find out where I lived?'

He didn't know how to answer the first question, so he grasped the second one gratefully. 'I remember you saying you'd worked at a grocer's in Cowley, so I did a tour of grocery stores until I found the right one. The man there gave me directions.'

'But why — ?'

'Wait.' It was as though his body took over while his mind still refused to work. He reached out and tugged the withered leaf free from the tangled lock of hair. Standing this close, he could breathe in the scent of soap that lingered on her skin, see the quiver of her pulse point at her throat. His fingers brushed the nape of her neck, and she shivered.

Quite what would have happened next, Alex didn't know, but the woman he'd seen in the tiny kitchen walked in, cups and saucers rattling on the tea tray she held. 'Tea, Mrs — ? Oh.'

Evie sprang back, her hand going to the back of

201

her neck. 'Mum, this is Al — Squadron Leader Alex Kincaith. He's . . .' She turned to him, a delightful pucker forming between her brows. 'Why are you here?' Her cheeks glowed crimson.

Now the words sprang to his mind. *I came to tell you I love you. That life is too precious, too fragile to waste a single moment.* But with Evie's mother in the room, he had to fall back on another answer. 'I've brought my kite to the CRU for repairs. It got shot up yesterday.'

The blood drained from Evie's face. 'With you inside?'

He cursed himself for not choosing his words more carefully. It was automatic to fall back on the flippant way the pilots spoke: a way of keeping the perpetual fear at bay. He tried to wave her concerns aside. 'It was nothing.'

'Were you hurt?' she asked. Although he hadn't wanted to worry her, the concern in her voice made his heart swell.

'No. Well, nothing more than a scratch.'

Evie raised her eyebrows, so Alex pre-empted her next question with, 'Bob wouldn't have let me fly up to Oxford if I wasn't fit, would he?'

'I suppose not.' But Evie didn't look convinced.

'Do sit down, Squadron Leader Kincaith. Would you like some tea?'

Alex hid his start of surprise with a smile and wrenched his gaze from Evie. He'd forgotten Evie's mother was there. 'Tea would be lovely, Mrs Bishop. And please call me Alex.' Seeing Evie about to carry one of the dining chairs to the fireside, he took it from her and placed it between the armchairs before sitting in it himself.

Mrs Bishop poured the tea, added a dash of milk

and handed him his cup with a smile. 'Alex. Then you must call me Dora.'

Evie's round-eyed stare at her mother told him this was an honour Mrs Bishop didn't confer lightly.

Dora twisted her hands in her pinny. 'I'm afraid there's no sugar, but there's honey if you'd like to stir in a teaspoon of that. And would you like something to eat? There's no cake, but I could make some sandwiches.'

He caught Evie's doubtful glance, and it struck him how rationing was making its mark on this tiny household. He cursed himself for not bringing something with him. He'd visited enough grocers to have put together a hamper fit for a lord. He hurried to put the poor woman at her ease. 'Just tea is fine. I'm not hungry.' But the thought of food reminded him that he hadn't eaten since breakfast and his stomach rumbled.

He sipped his tea while Dora poured cups for Evie and herself, then both women sat in the armchairs. Evie sat on the edge of hers, as though planning to leap up at any moment.

For what seemed like an eternity, the only sound was the ticking of the clock and a flock of starlings squabbling outside the open window. Alex took another sip and studied the pattern of pale pink rose buds on his saucer.

Then Evie spoke in a rush. 'We saw a Hurricane fly over earlier. Was that you?'

Alex seized the subject gratefully. 'I suppose it must have been.'

Evie gave a soft laugh. 'I got so used to watching out for your Hurricane at Amberton, it's funny to think you flew over this house without me realising it was you.'

Her words enveloped him like a warm blanket on a cold day. She watched out for him? If Dora hadn't been in the room, sipping her tea, back poker-straight, he would have spoken the words he'd come here to say. Instead he placed his cup on its saucer with careful precision before replying. 'Funny to think I flew over this house without knowing it was yours.' Although it was probably a good thing he hadn't known. He'd have been so busy straining for a glimpse of her he'd have probably flown into a chimney.

He glanced up from his cup at the same time as she looked at him. Their eyes met with a jolt to the stomach. She was sitting in a pool of sunlight that warmed her cheeks to a pink glow. He felt he would burst if he didn't release the words in his heart, but Dora's presence meant he couldn't say anything other than the polite, conventional words the British were supposed to say when drinking tea.

'How long are you staying in Oxford?' It was Dora who spoke, and it cost Alex physical pain to tear his gaze from Evie to address her mother.

'A few days. It depends how long it takes to get my plane fixed.' And whether Evie wanted to see him again. If she did, he wouldn't leave a second before he was due back with his squadron.

'Have you been to Oxford before?' Dora asked.

He shook his head.

'Well, then, you should take the time to explore. It's a beautiful place. Evie could show you around, couldn't you, Evie?'

'I'd like that.' He gazed at Evie, willing her to agree. 'That is, if you're well enough?' He cursed himself for not remembering she'd been sent home to convalesce.

'Don't feel you have to if you need your rest.'

'Oh no. I mean, I'd love to.'

'Then that's settled. I'll come and fetch you tomorrow morning at ten, and you can show me the sights.'

Her glowing smile was all the answer he needed.

* * *

Evie spent longer than usual in front of the mirror the next morning. Yesterday she'd simply twisted her hair into a knot at the back of her head, and she'd spent the whole of Alex's visit acutely conscious of her drab appearance. She brushed her hair until it gleamed, then pinned it into the style Jess had told her suited her face, sweeping it up into rolls at her temples, letting it fall loose behind. She hesitated, then applied the lipstick she'd bought in Brighton. She smiled as she did so, wondering how Jess and May were getting on at Amberton. She would write them a long letter this evening.

She gazed at her reflection, a flutter of anticipation in her chest. What news would she have to tell them by the end of the day?

The roar of a motor engine split the air, making Evie jump. No one around here owned a motor car, but the engine sounded far more powerful than one belonging to a tradesman's van. Curious, she slipped into the front room and peered out of the window. She could hardly believe the sight that met her eyes. A sleek, green sports car was parked right outside the house. The top was rolled down to make the most of the warm sunshine, and the man climbing out of the driving seat was none other than Alex.

He glanced at the house. Evie straightened with a

jerk and stepped back from the window, her cheeks heating at the thought that Alex might have seen her watching him.

She tensed, listening to the creak of the gate then the even tread of his footsteps up the short path. Even though she was expecting it, she still jumped when the rap of the door knocker echoed through the house. She blew out a steadying breath and smoothed the front of her skirt. She'd spent ages searching for a cotton dress that wasn't frayed or moth-eaten, but in the end had resorted to putting on her uniform. There was no way she was going to embarrass Alex by obliging him to be seen with a girl in tatty clothes.

'Alex,' she greeted him as she swung open the door. Even speaking that one short name seemed to use up all the breath in her lungs.

'I thought we'd see Oxford in style,' Alex said after greeting her. He indicated the car.

'I thought you flew up,' Evie said, still struggling to draw breath into her tight chest.

'I did. This isn't mine. I bumped into a pilot friend of mine in the bar of the Randolph last night, home on sick leave. He offered to lend me his car while I'm here, and there's enough petrol as long as we don't go too far afield. It's a Lagonda V12. What do you think?'

He waited while she collected her gas mask then escorted her down the path. She gazed at the car in awe. It was so highly polished she could see their reflection in it. She hardly recognised the elegant WAAF walking beside the tall, handsome man in his pilot's uniform. She gave a shaky laugh as she saw curtains twitching in the windows of more than one house on the street. She could just imagine Mrs Wilkins, the

206

street busybody, pursing her lips and saying to her husband, 'I always said that Evie Bishop was getting too big for her boots.'

'I don't know what the neighbours must think,' she said, 'but I think it's wonderful.'

He opened the passenger door and took her hand to steady her as she lowered herself onto the leather upholstery. Even with the roof down, she was immediately surrounded by the scent of leather and polish.

'I can't imagine what my grandparents would say if they could see me now,' replied Alex. 'This is a far cry from the Austin 7 my grandfather owned.'

It occurred to Evie then that she knew very little of Alex's family background. It was one of the consequences of the war: it flung people together who would otherwise have never met or had anything in common. But somehow the old way of doing things, the importance of learning about a person's background, didn't seem relevant any more. The only thing that mattered was the here and now. She would enjoy today, for who knew how many days of sunshine and freedom were left to them?

'Where shall we go?' Alex asked, shutting her door.

She knew exactly what she wanted to do. She wanted to live the dream she'd cherished for so long. 'Let's start with Christ Church Meadow.'

She directed Alex towards the city centre, across Magdalen Bridge. They parked on the High Street, opposite Magdalen College's impressive tower. She fiddled with the door latch, unable to get it open.

Alex climbed out of the car and walked around to her side. 'Allow me.' He opened her door and took her hand. She was hardly aware of climbing out from the car. All she knew was the spark between their joined palms, the delicious tingle that flowed from fingertips all the way down her spine. She straightened up and lifted her gaze to his face. He was gazing down at her with an intensity in his eyes that set her stomach aflutter.

'A man should take care of his date.'

She swallowed. 'Is that what this is — a date?'

'Aye.' He faltered, looking younger, all of a sudden. 'If that's what you want, of course.'

She couldn't stop the beaming smile. She was sure Jess would lecture her about retaining an air of mystery, keeping a man on his toes. But there was no hiding the way she felt. 'Yes. It is.'

Alex's answering smile must have matched hers. He tucked her arm into his, and they set off at a slow amble down the street. It was a good thing she had his arm to support her, as her legs were trembling so hard, she doubted she could have walked unaided. She led them down Rose Lane, where the trill of birdsong drifted over the high wall of the Botanic Gardens, competing with the chatter of thoughts jumbled in her head. How was this going to work? He was an officer, while she was a mere aircraftwoman. She was working class, he was . . . Well, she wasn't sure exactly what he was, but there was something about his soft Scottish burr that gave an impression of refinement. Of class.

And she could never forget Harriet Digby's tears when she'd heard the news of her fiancé's death. Was she setting herself up for more grief if she opened her heart to Alex?

Alex must have read something of her inner debate, for he stopped and placed his hands on both her shoulders. His gaze bored into hers. 'I can't offer you much, Evie. You know what I do, and I won't let my feelings for you stop me from doing my duty. I can't promise you a tomorrow. I don't know how many tomorrows I have. All I know is we have today, and I want to spend it with you.'

'Yes.' Relief and happiness bubbled through her. 'That's how I feel, too.'

They resumed their walk, and the walls and hedgerows opened out upon the wide green space of Merton Field. Evie led them around the edge until they entered the broad expanse of Christ Church Meadow. The upper end of the meadow was busy with schoolchildren making the most of the last few days of the long holiday, kicking footballs, playing tag and flying kites. It was soothing to walk in silence, listening to the children's shrill laughter with the soft whisper of the trees in the background. Evie's heart was too full for words, and she was glad that Alex didn't feel the need to talk about what they'd just said. It was enough to know they wanted to be in each other's company. She wouldn't let herself worry about what a relationship with Alex would mean. She would simply enjoy being with him today.

'My *babi* — my Czech grandmother — would have loved it here,' Alex said after a while as they strolled on the tree-shaded path along the River Cherwell. 'She often used to take me to Kelvingrove Park in Glasgow. Said it reminded her of the parks in Prague.'

'Glasgow? I thought you lived on Skye?'

'It was my maternal grandparents who lived on Skye,' he replied. 'My mother volunteered as a nurse in Glasgow at the start of the last war, and that's where she met my father. I lived with my *babi* and grandpa after she died, and they lived in Glasgow too.'

'How did they meet?' She'd often wondered how a Czech woman had ended up living in Scotland.

'My grandfather was a concert pianist. He travelled all over Europe in his day, back in the last century. He met and married my *babi* in Prague.'

'And that's why you can speak Czech,' Evie said. Then she frowned. 'How did you end up on Skye?'

A shadow passed over Alex's face, and he looked so sad Evie regretted asking. 'My grandpa and *babi* were Catholic. My mother's parents are Presbyterian. They never forgave my mother for marrying a Catholic, and broke off all contact with her. But when they heard my mother had died, leaving me an orphan, they were determined I should be brought up by them. My grandpa and *babi* fought to keep me, but when I was seven, my grandpa was taken ill with TB. Grandfather MacLeod said I should be taken away from the risk of contagion.' Alex's brows drew together as though from sudden pain, and he swallowed. 'I never saw them again. My grandpa died a month after I left, and Babi followed only a fortnight later.'

Evie could only squeeze his arm, her heart too full to speak for a moment. After a silence broken only by the splashing of ducks in the river, she said, 'How awful. You must miss them.'

'All the time,' he replied. 'But I don't want you to think my MacLeod grandparents were unloving. They were strict, but only did what they believed best for me.'

Evie wasn't fooled, though. She could read in his bleak expression how it must have felt to be taken from the grandparents he loved to live with people he hardly knew.

210

'Anyway,' Alex said in a lighter tone, clearly signalling the end of the subject, 'now I can remember my *babi* by practising Czech on our new pilots.' He quickened his pace, for they had slowed almost to a standstill while he spoke of his grandparents. 'Come on. I thought you were going to show me Oxford.'

It was a glorious morning, made all the better by Evie's feeling of closeness to Alex now he had shared something so personal. They followed the path along the tree-lined banks of the Cherwell, and Evie pointed out the college buildings that could be glimpsed through the branches. All the while she was acutely aware of Alex's strong arm beneath her hand, and the way her heart stuttered whenever their eyes met. She felt as though her feet were floating a few inches above the path. Before she knew it, they'd passed the point where the Cherwell met the Isis and were now approaching Folly Bridge. From there they turned up St Aldate's and back into the town. At that point, recollecting her promise to act as Alex's guide, Evie showed him Christ Church Cathedral, Carfax Tower, and led him around the narrow lanes between the colleges.

'I can see where the phrase 'dreaming spires of Oxford' comes from now,' said Alex, gazing up at the honey-coloured pinnacled buildings surrounding Catte Street. His gaze drifted to the sky, where a few white clouds scudded across the blue. A pucker formed between his brows and Evie tensed, knowing he must be thinking of his friends who might be fighting a desperate battle at this very moment.

'What's it like, up there?' she asked.

When he lowered his gaze, his eyes were as opaque as the clouds. He gave a tight smile. 'It's all over so

211

fast, there's not really time to think.' He took her arm. 'Now I'd like to buy you lunch. Where shall we go?'

It was clear he didn't want to talk about his experiences, and Evie regretted her question. Nevertheless, she could sense he was deeply troubled about something and wished he would confide in her. And it wasn't as if she was unaware of the dangers fighter pilots went through — she witnessed them at every watch, albeit from the safety of the Ops Room.

'Evie?' Alex prompted.

'Oh!' Evie felt her face colour and she had to rack her brains to remember what he'd asked. 'I . . . ah, I don't usually eat out in Oxford.' And when she did it was in the kind of cheap café she didn't think Alex would want to visit.

'Not to worry,' Alex said easily. 'I'm staying at the Randolph. They serve lunch, I noticed, so we'll eat there.'

The Randolph! He might as well have suggested eating at Buckingham Palace. Evie could only nod mutely and allow Alex to lead her there. She could hardly believe that she, plain Evie Bishop from Cowley, could be walking through the famous Gothic doorway, into the plush interior of the most exclusive hotel in Oxford. She tried not to look too awed as they followed the waiter to their table, but she couldn't resist looking around at the impressive oil paintings lining the walls and craning her neck to see all the college shields encircling the walls near the coffered ceiling.

She only came back down to earth when, after taking their seats beneath a portrait of a Cavalier, a man at the next table gave an abrupt exclamation. Evie glanced at him and saw him throw a silver cigarette lighter upon the table. 'Dashed thing won't work.' The man leaned across the gap between his chair and Alex's. 'I say, you don't have a light, do you?'

Alex patted his pockets and produced a book of matches which he handed to the man. The man lit his cigarette and returned the matches with a murmur of thanks. It was all over in a moment, but instead of putting the matches back in his pocket, Alex turned them over and over in his hands, seemingly transfixed.

'What's wrong?' she asked. She was starting to worry that something had happened to him. Was there more behind Alex's leave than his Hurricane needing repairs? She had been so surprised and flustered at his sudden visit yesterday that she hadn't questioned it.

Alex gave a small start and slipped the matches back into his pocket. 'Nothing.'

But she suddenly remembered his evasive reply when she'd asked him if he'd been wounded when his plane had been damaged. Nothing more than a scratch, he'd said. Come to think of it, he did look pale. She felt a twinge of guilt at the long walk she'd led him on.

She leant forward. 'Something is wrong. You said you weren't hurt much, but that means you were wounded. Are you here on sick leave?'

Alex fiddled with his spoon. When he looked at her, he wouldn't quite meet her eyes. 'Do you think the MO would let me fly if I'd been badly wounded?'

'No. But he would if he thought you needed a rest and it was the only way to get you off the station.' A muscle in his cheek flinched, and she knew she'd hit home. 'I'm right, aren't I? What happened to you?'

Alex sighed. 'Honestly, it's not bad, but I took

a bullet in my left arm. Just a flesh wound. But I can't — Bob Law thought it best if I stayed off the station until I'm passed fit for active duty.'

Evie eyed him doubtfully. He still seemed to be paying more attention to his spoon than her. He was hiding something, she was sure. Something even worse than a bullet to the arm. She studied his face. Now she was looking, she could see the traces of strain in the lines around his mouth and eyes. She could almost say he appeared haunted. If only he would confide in her, but she had no idea how to make him talk. It brought home to her that in some ways she didn't know him at all.

17

A waitress came to take their order, and by the time she had gone, the moment had passed. Evie couldn't help fretting about it for a while, but then something else happened that drove it from her mind.

A stir at an adjacent table caught her attention, and she glanced up to see none other than Julia Harris sitting down opposite a horse-faced woman who must be her mother.

'Oh, Lord,' she muttered before she could stop herself.

Alex looked up in surprise. 'What's the matter?'

Evie answered in an undertone. 'Don't look now, but the girl who made my school life a misery has just sat down at the next table.' It seemed she was doomed to bump into Julia whenever she came into Oxford. When Alex made a move to look, Evie clutched his arm. 'I said don't look!' Alex opened his mouth, but Evie cut off any questions. 'Not here. I'll tell you all about it when we leave.'

The waitress arrived with their food at that point, so it wasn't difficult to distract Alex by asking about his meal. However, Julia was positioned in Evie's line of sight, so she couldn't help noticing her nemesis, and what she saw filled her with glee. Julia shot Alex several looks and, judging from the way she let her gaze linger, found Alex very attractive. Evie had to agree. Alex was breathtakingly good looking, with his strong brows, tousled hair and athletic build. But with the additional glamour that clung to all RAF pilots, it made for an irresistible mix. Best of all, Julia's glance had flicked in Evie's direction once or twice, and it was clear she didn't recognise her.

At the end of the meal, Evie excused herself to visit the powder room. As she walked past Julia's table, Julia glanced up, looked away, then did a double-take, eyes wide. 'Evie? Evie *Bishop*?'

Evie paused, and felt the same palpitations and clammy hands that always afflicted her when she bore the brunt of Julia's attention. But then she seemed to hear Jess, whispering, *'Chin up, Evie. You've proved you're worth twenty of her, and you look wonderful.'* In her other ear, May was saying, *'You're the truest friend anyone could hope for. If she doesn't like you, it's because she's jealous.'* And suddenly she didn't care what Julia thought of her. She had two of the best friends in the world. Julia's opinion was nothing compared to theirs.

She straightened her back and gave Julia a cool smile. 'Oh, hello, Julia. Fancy meeting you here.'

With a brief nod to Julia's mother, she made to leave, but a touch on her arm stopped her. It was Alex. 'You're looking tired, darling,' he said. He turned so his face was hidden from the Harrises and gave her a flicker of a wink. 'I've arranged for you to have a coffee in the lounge while I fetch the Lagonda.'

Evie wanted to squeal with laughter as she strode to the powder room, chin in the air, aware of Julia's eyes boring into her back. To cap it all, Alex returned and was helping her into the Lagonda just when Julia walked out of the door. The look on Julia's face was one she'd treasure for the rest of her life. Her habitual haughty expression had been replaced by one of pure, purse-lipped envy.

Evie gave Julia a cheery wave as the luxury car pulled away from the kerb. 'Lovely to see you, Julia.'

She and Alex were still laughing as they sped over Magdalen Bridge and headed towards Cowley. She knew she would never again feel inferior in the presence of Julia or any other bully, and she had Jess, May and Alex to thank for it.

★ ★ ★

The next morning was as warm and clear as the last. Perfect for flying. Alex did his best to push that thought from his mind as he followed Evie's directions and drove up the narrow lane to the top of Shotover Hill. After the bustle of the city the day before, they'd both wanted to go somewhere quieter today. But reminders of the war followed them even to this tranquil part of England. A Hurricane bearing lines of bullet holes along its fuselage was limping into the CRU at the Cowley Works when they drove past, and a strong military presence at Shotover House revealed that it was now being used as a prisoner of war camp. Evie's mother had warned them that they might not be allowed up Shotover Hill, as sometimes there were military exercises up there, but to his relief, all was quiet when he parked in a layby at the top of the hill and turned off the engine. The only noise was the cooing of wood pigeons and the gentle hiss of the breeze through the trees.

Evie had brought along a picnic blanket and had offered to make sandwiches, but Alex had come prepared. Remembering Mrs Bishop's embarrassment over her lack of food, he had managed to get a hamper made up at the hotel. He lifted the basket out of the boot and followed Evie out onto the hillside where she spread the blanket in the shade of the hedgerow. It was too early to eat, but neither wanted to walk. They lay back on the blanket and let the peace wash over them. Evie wasn't wearing her uniform today, but a light short-sleeved dress in green cotton with white polka dots. It was slightly frayed at the hem, but she would have been beautiful even dressed in rags. Evie radiated an aura of calm, and, after yesterday's triumph over that despicable school bully, she seemed to have grown in confidence.

Although he knew he needed to talk, he felt no sense of urgency. Instead he lay back and watched the clouds scud overhead, listening to the birdsong, watching the sway of wheat and barley in the patchwork of fields stretching out below them. The occasional roar of a motor engine only served to make him aware of the peace of this particular spot, away from the bustle of the city at the bottom of the hill.

A lark flung its exultant song into the air above his head. He squinted against the sun's glare. Finally, he found it, a tiny fluttering speck against the sky's expanse. He followed it with his eyes as it swooped and trilled.

'That's how I feel when I'm flying.' The words came unbidden. He kept his eyes on the lark, but he was speaking to Evie, willing her to understand. 'Everything else falls away. There's just the feeling of lightness, of being removed from the troubles of the world.' This was what he had tried and failed to say yesterday. Surrounded by the noise of the city, he hadn't been able to find the words.

He heard Evie catch her breath, knew without looking that her attention was fixed upon him. It was easier to speak his heart without looking at her, so he kept his gaze upon the lark. 'Of course, in combat it's different. There's the knowledge that I could die.' He paused, unsure how to express what he knew deep down but had never put into words before. 'I don't hate the men I'm fighting, but they've been sent to destroy us and break down our defences, and I can't allow that to happen.'

He hadn't come here with the intention of sharing his innermost thoughts with Evie. He'd meant to tell her he loved her. But now he understood that before he told her she had his heart, it was vital she understood and accepted all the feelings it harboured.

His voice sank to little more than a whisper, and he studied his hands, unable to look at Evie. 'But when I'm back on the ground it's different. They follow me, the men I've killed. I don't know if I'll ever be free of them.'

Evie gave a choked sob, and he twisted to look at her. He'd half-expected to see an expression of revulsion, that she wouldn't be able to be friends with a man who had so much blood on his hands. Instead, her eyes brimmed with tears. Her mouth was pulled tight, but that couldn't conceal the way her lips trembled. 'It isn't fair.' Her voice quivered with suppressed emotion.

'I . . . Why?' Of all the responses he'd expected, this hadn't crossed his mind.

'That you should be the one to shoulder all the guilt. You and all the other pilots fighting to save us. But we all play our part.'

'You don't bear any guilt.'

'Why not?' She laid a gentle hand over his, making him draw a sharp breath at the surge of heat that flowed up his arm. 'We're told enough times that we all play a vital part in Britain's defence. Everyone. The top brass who decide which station should deal with incoming enemy aircraft; the controllers who send out the squadrons; even me.' She dashed the tears from her eyes and gave him a level stare. 'I plot the positions of the incoming German flights. If it wasn't for me, and all the WAAFs and servicemen along the chain, you wouldn't be in the right place to intercept them. You might be the one who shoots a plane out of the sky, but *we* put you there. If you feel guilty, so should we.'

'*Do* you feel guilty?' It had never occurred to him that anyone other than the pilots who fired their guns or dropped bombs should feel tainted by the deaths.

Her eyes focused on a point far in the distance. 'No. I mean, I've thought about it, but no. I'm always relieved and grateful when one of our squadrons stops enemy aircraft from getting through.' Her gaze sharpened as it settled on his face. 'And you shouldn't feel guilty either. If you didn't stop them, they would kill you, kill servicemen and women on the ground. Kill innocent women and children.' She squeezed his hand, and the breath left his lungs. 'I know it's different for you. You see the faces of the pilots you're shooting down.'

He nodded, swallowing against the sudden thickness in his throat. 'And see them burst into flames, knowing those inside are burning alive.'

Her eyebrows twitched as if she were struck by sudden pain, but she didn't move her gaze from his face, nor did she take away the hand that covered his own.

It was this acceptance, this total lack of judgement that released the unseen grip on his heart. It was as though a huge weight had rolled away from his shoulders. A weight he hadn't even noticed until it was gone, leaving him feeling so light he felt he might float away.

'I'm so sorry you have to do it,' she murmured. 'But I'm grateful you do.'

He gave his head a slight shake in wonder. 'What did I do to deserve you?' He cleared his throat to dispel the slight huskiness in his voice.

Evie looked away, blushing.

This was it. This was the moment he had been waiting for. Sharing his burden of horror and experiencing nothing but compassion in return freed the words he had suppressed. 'Evie, I . . . What I said yesterday was true. I cannae offer you more than the here and now, and I don't expect anything in return from you. But I want you to know how I feel. Want you to know I love you.'

Her blush deepened, and she swallowed. 'I —' Her voice cracked, and she broke off, biting her lip.

A lurch of dismay shook him. She appeared to be on the brink of tears. 'I'm sorry. Forget I said it.'

But she shook her head and to his relief he saw she was smiling. 'How can I forget something that's made me so happy?'

He released a shaky breath. 'Happy? Really?'

She nodded her head so vigorously a lock of hair slid free from the elegant roll at her temple and into her eye. He reached out and brushed it behind her ear. She trembled as his fingers grazed her cheek, and she lowered her eyelids, the bronze lashes shadowing her blue eyes.

He couldn't resist the temptation any longer. He leaned forward and brushed his lips against hers.

Evie gasped against his lips. It was the first time she'd been kissed. Although she'd imagined kissing Alex, she'd never known what to expect. Certainly not this flood of heat, this fluttering in her chest as though a thousand butterflies were making a bid for escape. She slid her arm around his neck, ran her hand across his broad shoulders, scarcely daring to believe that this was really happening. Alex loved her! He wanted to be with her just as much as she longed to be near him. But when she slid her hand down his arm, relishing the firm muscle beneath her fingers, he flinched and drew back.

'What's wrong?' she asked, worried to see he'd turned a shade paler.

'Nothing.' But the corner of his mouth was pulled down in a grimace.

Her hand flew to her mouth when she realised. 'Your arm! I'm so sorry.'

He nodded. 'Don't worry. It's not bad, I was just . . . unprepared.'

She apologised again, feeling helpless. Then she spied the hamper, still unopened.

'Let's have a drink.' She unpacked the basket, marvelling at how Alex had managed to put together such a feast with rationing on. There were sandwiches — a swift inspection revealed labels, showing them to be a mixture of smoked salmon and ox tongue. Evie eased up the corner of a foil-covered package and found four large slabs of fruit cake that looked so moist her mouth started to water. Last but not least, two bottles of beer and two of ginger beer were packed into the corners, wedged with linen napkins. Glasses were strapped inside the lid, so she freed them and poured them each a drink. The action gave her a moment to compose herself after the kiss. She felt as though her cheeks must be burning, and her lips felt swollen and aching. But she felt light and happy. Alex loved her. They would work out how it would affect them at the station later. For now, she wanted to revel in the knowledge that her feelings were returned. She had the momentous feeling that from now on her life would be divided into the time before this day and the time after it.

She handed Alex his glass and felt her blush grow hotter when their fingers met. She settled herself back on the blanket, taking care to sit on Alex's right side to avoid bumping his injured arm. 'Feeling better?'

He pulled her to his side. 'I feel wonderful.'

She snuggled against him and rested her head against his shoulder. Then she shot upright, remembering that in her consternation at causing Alex pain, she hadn't told him how she felt. She gasped and sat up. 'I . . . I do love you, too. That is, if you still want an idiot who punches you right over a wound.'

Before she could say any more, Alex leaned in and kissed her again.

This time it wasn't Evie's carelessness that broke the kiss, but the roar of a Merlin engine. They both pulled away to look up at the low-flying Spitfire that roared overhead, so low Evie was surprised it didn't hit the treetops. Like the Hurricane she'd seen flying over Cowley, the fuselage was riddled with bullet holes.

'Another one for the CRU,' Alex said, his expression grim.

He must be thinking the same thing as Evie. Wondering how the pilots of Amberton were faring while Evie and Alex were enjoying Oxford's cocoon of tranquillity. She felt a stab of resentment towards the unknown Spitfire pilot for shattering it. They watched the Spitfire until it had flown out of sight, heading, as Alex had deduced, in the direction of the Civilian Repair Unit at Cowley. But when the noise had died away, leaving nothing but the gentle twitter of birds and the skirling of the larks, it was clear Alex couldn't recapture their earlier peace. He drank his beer, glancing more frequently at the sky than her. Evie remembered his distraction of the previous day and her conviction that something was bothering him beyond his wound.

'I wonder how everyone is getting on at Amberton,' she said, wishing she could think of a way to get him to confide in her. 'I feel guilty being up here with nothing to do when Jess and all the other WAAFs are slaving in Ops with hardly a break.'

'You've been ill. You need time to recover or you'd crack up.'

'So do you.'

He frowned, but she pressed on, hoping this way she could break through to uncover the trouble bothering him. 'The squadron can survive a few days without you, but they'd be much worse off if you were killed because you started flying again before you were fully fit.'

'It'll be far worse for them if I don't —' He broke off, his eyes wide in alarm. He took a drink of beer. Evie was shocked to see his hand shook.

'If you don't what?' she asked. 'Alex, what's happened?'

He closed his eyes for a moment and blew out a breath. 'I didn't want to worry you.'

224

'Well, you're not doing a very good job of it.'

The corner of his mouth twitched. 'If I tell you, you must keep it to yourself. The only other people who know are Bob Law and Sergeant Rawlins, my fitter.'

A prickle of foreboding crept down the back of her neck. 'Why? What's happened? I mean, I won't tell anyone if it's that serious.'

'It is.' Evie waited impatiently while Alex took another sip of beer. He drained the glass and placed it on the blanket before sitting straight and facing her with grave eyes. 'The reason I was injured was because my Hurricane was sabotaged.'

It was as though a cloud had moved over the sun, draining the heat and colour from the day. 'What? How?' She took a sip of her own beer to moisten her mouth which had grown suddenly dry.

'Matchsticks in my gun airfeeds.'

Evie shook her head. 'What would that do?'

'Stops them from firing. My guns jammed. I had a Dornier in my sights — a sitting duck. I tried to fire, but nothing. Then a couple of 109s got on my tail and all hell broke loose.'

Evie shuddered and tried not to picture the horror of a fight with no weapons. Alex had survived, she told herself. *Don't think of what might have happened.*

'Who did it?'

Alex shook his head. 'That's the whole problem. I've no idea. It could be anyone. Whoever did it is still at large and could strike again at any moment. Might not stop at matchsticks.'

'But that's barbaric.' A horrible thought struck her. 'What if they've done it before? Only they succeeded that time, and the plane was destroyed? We would never know.'

225

'I thought of that too.' His brows drew together as though from pain. 'Josef was killed the same day.'

'Oh no.' Evie felt sick. She could picture Josef clearly, laughing at one of Jiří's jokes. It was impossible to believe he was gone. 'Was his Hurricane sabotaged?'

'No one saw him fire a shot,' Alex replied in a flat voice. They both sat in silence for a while. Evie could hardly take in the implications of Alex's news.

Finally, Alex said, 'I wanted to question the men in other squadrons who've lost pilots. See if any of their losses could have been caused by sabotage. But Bob didn't want me interfering with any investigation he set up. Said I'd only get in the way.' He radiated frustration, and Evie sympathised. Maybe being exiled from their homeland gave them a stronger link, but the bonds forged between the pilots in Brimstone squadron seemed even tighter than those of the other squadrons at Amberton. And Alex, with his Czech heritage, was welcomed whole-heartedly into the fraternity. Evie was fond of them, but she knew that was nothing compared to the weight of responsibility Alex must feel for the young men under his command. If a saboteur was responsible for Josef's death, he would resent leaving the investigation to someone else.

It struck her then that as a WAAF she was well placed to make discreet enquiries of her own. All the men enjoyed gossiping and flirting with the girls. She couldn't ask anything directly, of course. But she was sure she could manoeuvre a conversation to find out who they had seen hanging around Brimstone's dispersal pens before the fateful flights.

She glanced sideways at Alex, her stomach performing a slow swoop when their eyes met. She mustn't tell him what she had planned. He would never allow

226

it, but she was sure she could be useful. She thought of Jess and May. Maybe she'd promised not to tell anyone, but her two closest friends didn't count. If anyone could cajole an airman into revealing a secret it was Jess. And May, as driver to Peter Travis, would surely be able to worm information from him about the official investigation.

That would have to wait until she returned to Amberton, of course. 'How long are you in Oxford for?' she asked, snuggling against Alex's shoulder.

'When does your sick leave end?'

'Tuesday.' Still four days away.

'I've got to return on Wednesday, so I'm free to spend every day with you until you leave.'

Four days. They could forget about the war for four days, and she would do her best to help Alex forget his worries in that time. But when she returned to Amberton, she would do all in her power to find the saboteur threatening the lives of their pilots.

18

'There she is!'

Evie looked round as she climbed down from the carriage to see May and Jess standing at the platform entrance, waving madly. She slung her kitbag over her shoulder and hurried over to them and was greeted with enthusiastic hugs.

'I'm so glad you're back,' May said.

'Me too,' Evie said, harbouring the knowledge of Alex to her heart, looking forward to telling her friends all about him when they were together in High Chalk House. 'How did you both manage to wangle the time off to meet me?'

'I'm on duty,' May replied. 'I had to drive one of the Erks to the hospital because he broke his arm.' She took Evie's kit bag, ignoring her protest that she could manage it herself. 'My flight officer said I could collect you on the way back.'

'And I'm back on duty in an hour, so get a move on,' said Jess, taking Evie's arm and hurrying them through the ticket office towards the waiting car. 'But I've got the whole night off, so I'll catch up with you this evening.'

By the time the three girls were curled up in the armchairs in the schoolroom that night, cradling steaming cups of cocoa in their hands, Evie felt as though she had never left.

'Spit it out,' Jess said. 'Tell us what's put that dreamy glow into your face. That wasn't put there by a dose of the flu. Am I right in thinking it has more to do with a certain squadron leader?'

'What?' Heat flooded into Evie's cheeks. 'How did you know?'

Jess laughed. 'I didn't until now, but when I heard he'd taken his Hurricane to the CRU I suspected.'

'Is the whole station gossiping about me?' Evie imagined walking into the Ops Room the next day, everyone whispering behind their hands.

'Of course not.' May frowned at Jess. 'We're your friends. We suspected Alex would call on you, but we didn't breathe a word of it to anyone else.'

'We'd never talk about you behind your back,' Jess put in. 'I'm hurt you would think so.'

'I'm sorry. I didn't —'

'Nah, I'm just teasing.' Laughter danced in Jess's eyes. 'Tell us everything. Don't leave a single thing out. Seeing as you forgot all about us and didn't write.'

Evie's eyes slid out of focus, and she was back on Shotover Hill in Alex's arms. She sighed. 'It was wonderful. And I didn't forget about you. But when I tried to write, I couldn't find the words.' Several times she'd sat in her room, pen poised over paper, but had found it impossible to express her feelings on the page.

'Find them now. We're dying to know.'

Evie told them all about the day out in Oxford, and the girls hooted with laughter when she described the incident with Julia Harris.

'Good for you!' Jess said. 'I wish I could have been a fly on the wall and seen the expression on her stuck-up face when she saw you getting into that Lagonda.'

'I'll remember it for the rest of my life,' declared Evie. 'She looked like she'd bitten a lemon! She treated me like a piece of dirt all the years we were at school together. You can't believe how good it felt to show her I've made something of my life. And Alex was marvellous.'

She allowed herself a few moments of reflection to remember the satisfaction of making Julia jealous, then went on to describe the rest of her time with Alex. 'He was so lovely,' she concluded. 'I was worried he would look down on me after seeing where I lived, but he was perfect. Oh, and I took him to meet Cornelia, and she gave him the seal of approval.' Cornelia's brusque, 'He seems like a good man,' when she'd sent Alex on a spurious errand to get him out of the way had been the icing on the cake for Evie. Her mentor had then eyed her gravely and said, 'Be certain you both want the same thing from your relationship before making a lasting commitment.'

Evie still wasn't sure what Cornelia meant by that. Of course she and Alex wanted the same thing.

She shook off the memory, letting thoughts of Alex warm away the slight chill of misgiving. 'He even helped me in the garden.' She paused to take a sip of cocoa. 'It's funny. I never knew pulling weeds and harvesting vegetables could be so romantic.'

'He actually helped?' May's eyes were round with shock.

Jess snorted. 'Give me a dinner and dance any day. I can't imagine Kincaith kneeling in the dirt with his sleeves rolled up.'

'Well, he did. And without me asking, too. When he saw how worried I was about leaving Mum's garden in a state, he offered to help.'

Evie noticed that May had bowed her head, studying her cup, chewing her lower lip. She remembered what May had said about having to wait on her father and brothers. 'Not all men are like your family,' she said softly.

May looked up. 'I . . . I hope not.'

'Alex isn't. Nor is Peter.'

May gave a wistful smile, and Evie's heart twisted. She hated what May's family had done to her, but knew it was ultimately up to Peter to win her over.

'Forget about the gardening,' Jess said. 'I want to hear about everything else.'

'I've told you.'

Jess arched a perfectly shaped brow. '*Everything?* He didn't expect anything in return for all his help?'

'What do you mean?'

'I mean' — Jess glanced at the closed door and lowered her voice — 'did he try and persuade you to do anything you're not ready for?'

'No!' Evie knew her face must be flaming; it felt like she could fry eggs on it. 'He was a perfect gentleman. And even if he had, I wouldn't let him. I meant what I said about taking my work seriously. I'm in the WAAF for the duration. I'm not going to risk getting knocked up and kicked out.'

But she'd thought about it. The day he had helped her with the garden, they'd been alone, Dora being at work. She'd thought then how easy it would be to invite him up into her bedroom. How tempting.

Jess studied her face as though trying to read her thoughts. Finally, she nodded as though satisfied. 'Make sure you hold to that. It's too easy, when the men are off risking their lives, to give in to them, but never forget you could end up ruined for life, with no blame sticking to the man, no matter the circumstances.'

Evie stared at Jess in surprise. She might have expected such a lecture from her mother or even May, but never Jess. Jess, the irreverent flirt, lecturing another girl on good behaviour? But a glance at Jess showed her that Jess's mouth was pulled tight, and her eyes seemed focused on a scene far away from the cosy schoolroom. She opened her mouth, then closed it again. Jess spoke from bitter experience, she was sure, but judging from her closed expression, it was no good asking her about it.

'Trust me. I'm not going to let Alex take advantage of me, even if he tried, which I'm sure he won't. But listen. There's something else.'

She told them of the sabotage attempt.

Jess's eyes grew rounder as Evie recounted Alex's brush with death. 'What kind of bastard would do that?' Then she paled. 'Josef. Is that what happened to him?'

'Alex thinks so.'

Jess clenched her fist. 'Wait till I tell —'

'No!' Evie leaned forward so fast she slopped hot cocoa onto her knee. She ignored the scald and grasped Jess's arm. 'You mustn't breathe a word to anyone. Alex made me promise not to tell a soul.'

'Then why tell us?' May asked, looking pale.

'Because . . .' She paused. She'd been so sure Jess and May would want to help, but was it fair to ask? They were working long hours; dark smudges ringed the eyes of both girls. It didn't seem right to ask them to spend their precious free time trying to identify the saboteur. Besides, it could be dangerous.

But Jess leaned forward, her eyes shining. 'You think we can ask around, see if we can hear anything the official investigation will miss?'

'Yes, but —'

'Count me in.'

'Me too,' said May, much to Evie's surprise.

'I don't know,' Evie said. 'Maybe I'm being stupid. I was all fired up to give it a try when I first found out but now I don't know what we could do that the station commander won't have already tried.'

Jess snorted. 'He's not going to find out anything, the way he's going about it. I mean, there have been no arrests, so they can't have caught the saboteur.'

Evie dabbed at the spilled cocoa on her knee with her handkerchief while she thought. 'Have any other pilots been lost?'

'Two. Not from Brimstone,' Jess added quickly. 'Frank Pearson from Catseye and Simon Taylor from Wagtail.'

Was it wrong to feel relief that the pilots killed were ones she didn't know personally? 'Do you know what happened to them?'

Jess focused on a distant point while she answered. 'Simon Taylor was shot down when I was on watch.' She grimaced. 'His flight was bounced by 109s when they were sent to intercept a raid heading for Southampton. Miracle any of them made it back, if you ask me. But Simon was in the fight for a while before he was shot down. No reports that his guns jammed.'

Nothing to indicate sabotage there. Evie chewed her lip. 'What about Frank Pearson?' She tried to picture him. She had a vague recollection of being introduced to him at the pub one evening: a young man with an earnest expression and dark red hair that wouldn't lie flat. He'd only joined the squadron in July, not long before the German raids had started to arrive in wave after wave and Evie had been so exhausted at the end of each watch that she'd stopped going to the pub so often.

Jess shrugged. 'It only happened today, when I was off the station, meeting you. I heard about it on my last watch, but there wasn't time to ask more. Not that I knew there might be anything suspicious.'

'I could ask Peter,' May said. 'He'll get to see the combat reports.'

'But don't make it obvious you're asking questions.' Then Evie paused. 'What makes you think Peter will tell you anything?'

May flushed. 'We've been taking walks.'

Jess grinned. 'Attagirl!'

'Not like that!' May's cheeks glowed brighter. 'Just as friends. I think he likes having someone he can talk to.'

'Keep your hair on,' Jess said. 'I was only teasing. Promise to tell me when he plucks up the courage to start courting you, so I can give you the same lecture I gave Evie.'

May gave a reluctant smile.

'But this is why we can do better than the station commander and the whitecaps,' Jess said. 'We can ask questions without raising suspicion. Make it seem like innocent chat.'

'That's what I thought, but we must be careful.' Evie eyed her friends seriously. 'This isn't a game. Someone on the station is trying to kill our boys. And never forget the person you're talking to could be the traitor.'

★ ★ ★

Alex flew his mended Hurricane back to Amberton the day after Evie left Oxford. 'Give this a good look-over, Rawlins,' he said to his fitter, climbing out of the cockpit onto the wing. 'I don't trust that crowd at the CRU as well as you.'

Rawlins grinned. 'Right you are, sir.'

Alex jumped down and slung his parachute over the wing.

He was about to stride away when Rawlins called him back. 'One more thing, sir. Good news: we've finally got our gun cameras. The lads finished fitting them yesterday.'

'Good job, Rawlins. Thank you.' Alex walked away with a spring in his step. He'd requested the gun cameras weeks ago and had awaited their arrival with increasing impatience. At last he'd be able to review gun camera footage to confirm kills.

An hour later, he was heading out of the station commander's office, cleared for duty.

'Welcome back, sir. Want a lift to dispersal?' A car pulled to a halt next to him, and Alex saw Milan leaning over the passenger door, looking up at him. He was wearing his flying kit, his parachute slung on the back seat. Black streaks decorated his face like warpaint.

Alex looked him up and down as he climbed into the back. 'What happened to you?'

Milan twisted around in his seat. 'My engine overheated so I had to return early. She packed up when I reached the coast — the engine smoked like billy-o — I put her down in a field just before she caught fire.' His odd mixture of formal English, as taught by Evie and Jess, peppered with slang picked up from the Erks and British pilots, always made Alex smile.

Alex sank into his seat as the car sped towards dispersal, but then he sat up, struck by a horrible thought. An overheating engine could be pure bad luck, of course, but it could also be sabotage. 'Can anything be salvaged?'

'No. I only just got out in time. She burned to a shell.'

Which meant any evidence of tampering would be destroyed. Alex hated feeling so helpless in the face of such a deadly threat. 'Any casualties among the others?'

'Not before I had to leave. They should be back now. Karol pulled out before me. Something about a jammed gun.'

Alex sat up straighter, all senses tingling. He gave a non-committal grunt but his mind whirred. He would have to talk to Karol immediately.

When they arrived at dispersal, Milan was greeted like a hero. Alex looked around, seeking for any face among the Erks and pilots that displayed chagrin that Milan was back safely. But everyone seemed genuinely happy to see Milan safe and sound. They welcomed Alex warmly as well.

Alex exchanged greetings but retired to his office as soon as he could get free, beckoning to Karol to follow. He closed the door behind Karol and pointed him to a chair. Then he sat at his desk and leaned forward, studying Karol across the top of steepled fingers.

'Milan tells me you had to return early.'

Karol nodded. 'The guns didn't work.'

'Did they give any trouble before?'

'No. They work well until now.' Unlike most of the other Czech pilots, Karol always tried to speak

English, and it was improving as a result, even if he did make the occasional slip.

The roar of aero engines starting up split the air, drowning Karol's last words. Alex waited for the flight from Catseye to take off before speaking again, grateful for the chance to frame his next words. Bob Law hadn't wanted him to get in the way of the investigation, but he was damned if he was going to do nothing while his pilots flew into battle in machines that had been tampered with. He would have to be careful not to make it obvious he was doing anything other than making routine follow-up on a sortie, checking the readiness of his pilot and plane.

The growl rose to a crescendo. Alex glanced out of the window to see three Hurricanes rolling across the airfield, gathering speed. They lifted into the air and began to climb, the din fading to a distant drone.

'When was your last flight before this one?'

'At first light. The report should be on your desk, sir.'

Alex sifted through the reports until he found Karol's. It was understandable thanks to a young Pilot Officer from Wagtail who'd broken his leg three weeks earlier. Alex had persuaded Wagtail's squadron leader to release him to Brimstone squadron to write their combat reports for them. Although most of the Czechs now spoke reasonable English, their written English was appalling.

'I see you returned early,' he said, glancing at the report written in Pilot Officer Walsh's neat hand. 'Out of ammo.' Clearly the guns had been in working order then.

'Very well,' he said finally, unable to find a way of asking who Karol had seen hanging around his

Hurricane's dispersal pen between flights without raising suspicion. He had no choice but to continue making flights as usual. He didn't want his pilots worried about sabotage. 'Go and make your report.'

Alex followed Karol out of his office and went out to the dispersal pens. The fitters and riggers were swarming over the machines, refuelling, replacing ammunition, patching holes. It was a warm day, and those pilots who had finished their reports were lounging in deckchairs, looking incongruous with their bright yellow Mae Wests on.

In contrast to the feverish activity around most of the machines, Karol's fitter was sitting in the shade of the wing, sipping tea from a battered enamelled cup. At a quick glance, Karol's machine was in pristine condition.

'All finished, Sykes?'

The Erk sprang to his feet, banging his head on the wing. Alex had to bite his lip to stop himself from laughing when Sykes tried to salute and rub his bumped head simultaneously.

'Yes, sir.'

'What about the guns? Pilot Officer Šimek tells me they jammed.'

Still rubbing his head and wincing, Sykes said, 'I 'ad a good look, sir, but couldn't find nowt wrong.'

'Nothing?' Alex didn't know what he had expected, but it wasn't this. When Sykes shook his head, Alex said, 'Very well. But I want Rawlins to inspect it. I'm grounding it until he's passed it.'

He went to see Rawlins.

'She's as good as new, sir,' Rawlins said in greeting. 'They've done a fine job up at the CRU. Almost as good as me and the lads.'

Alex gave a nod of thanks, patting his Hurricane's wing tip. 'If you're finished here, I want you to inspect Pilot Officer Šimek's machine. The guns jammed on his last flight, but Sykes couldn't find anything wrong.' He lowered his voice, making sure than none of the other Erks could overhear. 'Check the air feeds.'

Rawlins nodded, his eyes widening. 'I've been keeping an eye on things, just as you asked, sir. I didn't see anyone near Pilot Officer Šimek's machine who shouldn't be there.' He spoke in the same low tones.

Alex looked over at the Hurricanes, most of which were now ready to be scrambled. The Erks lounged nearby, ready to spring into action and start the engines the instant they heard the bell. It was hard to see how anyone could get near one of the planes without someone noticing.

'What about the day my guns jammed? Did you find out who'd been near my machine?'

Rawlins scratched his head. 'I did my best to ask around without rousing suspicion, sir. No one can remember seeing anyone around who didn't have business being there.'

'Very well. Go and look at Karol's machine and report to me when you've finished.'

Alex returned to his office to catch up on the paperwork that had piled up in his absence. There wasn't as much as he'd feared; Milan and the temporary clerk must have seen to it between them. He tried to come up with a plan for catching the saboteur, but found his thoughts drifting to the Ops Room, where Evie must be back at work. Did he have an excuse to go there? He smiled, imagining the pleasure of seeing Evie, smart in her uniform.

He was shaken from his reverie by a knock at the

door. He looked up to see Rawlins standing in the doorway. He beckoned him in.

'I did what you asked, sir, but the air feeds are as clean as a whistle. No sign of anything.'

Alex frowned. He'd been so sure Rawlins would discover what was wrong. 'If they had been jammed, could the matchsticks have fallen out?'

Rawlins' brow wrinkled. 'I suppose they must have. Maybe they weren't jammed as tight as the ones in your guns.'

Alex sighed and dismissed Rawlins. They were no further forward. He would have to think of something else, and fast, because until he stopped the saboteur, he would never know if he was sending out pilots in unsafe machines.

The telephone shrilled in the other room and he closed his eyes briefly, dread forming an icy weight in his stomach.

Sure enough, Milan's voice called out, "A' flight, scramble!'

All Alex could do was dash to his Hurricane, praying everyone would return.

19

Evie stretched the muscles of her back and shoulders as she followed Jess up the steps and into the daylight. It had been another gruelling watch, but she was pleased to discover that she was falling back into the routine and the week off hadn't made her forget what to do. Thankfully all their pilots had returned safely from each sortie. The raids were relentless, though. Wave after wave of bandits appeared over the Channel. At times it had felt as though they were trying to stop a flood with a dish cloth, but miraculously she had seen their boys fend off the attacks again and again.

It made her all the more determined to find the saboteur; it was bad enough their pilots faced death every day from the enemy without the additional risk of their machine failing to respond. She refused to do nothing while someone on the base was trying to kill Alex. It was bad enough having to watch the plot representing his squadron, praying they wouldn't hear the report that meant he had been shot down.

'What shall we do?' Jess asked when they emerged into the sunlight.

Evie blinked while her eyes adjusted to the light. 'I don't know about you, but I'm dying for some food.'

'Lunch it is.' Jess slipped her arm through Evie's and they directed their steps to the NAAFI. 'Or is it dinner or breakfast? I've given up trying to work out which meal we're on.'

Evie glanced at her watch. Funny how even though they were constantly looking at the clock in Ops, she only paid attention to the minute hand to see which colour it indicated. 'Four o'clock. Too early for dinner, too late for lunch.'

'Don't care. My stomach feels like my throat's been cut.'

Thankfully the canteen was set up for those like the plotters who worked odd hours. Soon Evie was carrying a tray laden with a cup of strong tea, a wafer-thin slice of bread smeared with marge and a bowl of watery stew.

'More cabbage and potato than meat,' said Jess, sniffing at hers dubiously.

She went to sit at the nearest table, but Evie shook her head. 'This way. By the window.'

Jess hung back. 'Those seats are already taken.'

'I know.' Evie lowered her voice. 'They're Brimstone's ground crew. They might know something.'

Jess's eyes widened in comprehension. Then she grinned. 'Watch and learn, Evie, my girl.'

How she managed to put a wiggle in her walk while carrying a heavy tray, Evie couldn't guess, but the eyes of the men were fixed on her long before she reached their table. 'Afternoon, lads. Got room for a couple of small ones?'

The men obligingly shuffled up on their benches to make space for the girls. Evie sat opposite Jess, next to a fitter with sergeant's stripes on his sleeve. No sooner had they set down their trays than Jess went on the attack.

'Thanks for helping out. The lads over there' — Jess gave a vague wave towards the other side of the room that could have taken in any one of a number

242

of tables — 'were trying to get a bit fresh. But I saw you boys, and I knew you'd take care of us.' A lock of blonde hair had magically worked loose from her severe up do, and she twirled it around her index finger, shooting sidelong glances at the men from beneath sweeping lashes. Evie had to bite back a grin as the four men sat up straight, pulling back their shoulders and holding in their stomachs.

'Don't you worry, girls. We'll look after you,' the man beside Jess said.

Evie had to 'accidentally' knock her teaspoon to the floor, where it clattered on the scuffed lino. Bending down to retrieve it gave her a chance to compose her features. She could only hope Jess didn't expect her to flirt so outrageously, because she hadn't the first idea how to go about it.

'I'm Fletcher.' The man beside Jess had started introductions by the time Evie had regained control and sat up. He pointed to the two men at the far end of the table from Jess and Evie. 'That's Sykes and Jackson. The sergeant, here' — Fletcher pointed at the man beside Evie — 'well, we just call him Sarge unless we want a clip round the ear.'

'Are you the lasses who were teaching our pilots?' Sykes asked. Evie, who was getting better at spotting accents, guessed he was a Yorkshireman.

'That's right,' Evie replied, feeling that she should join in wherever possible.

'Makes you one of us. We're in Brimstone's ground crew,' said Jackson.

'Aye, and we take care of our own.'

'You're so kind.' Jess gave them all a beaming smile. Evie noticed the sergeant beside her surreptitiously tug at his collar as though it was too tight. For

243

a moment she envied Jess her confidence with men. Then she remembered Alex. He didn't seem to mind she was a studious bluestocking instead of a Hollywood bombshell.

'You know,' Jess continued, 'us WAAFs are often saying the ground crew should get more credit. Aren't we, Evie?'

'What? Oh . . . yes, that's right.' Evie could only follow her friend's lead and pray Jess knew where she was going.

'The pilots get all the glory, but where would they be without your expertise?' As Jess spoke, the Erks seemed to grow taller, their chests puffing out.

'In t'ground,' muttered Sykes, stubbing out his cigarette, grinding the end into the ash tray.

'The pilots know. That's all that matters to me.' The sergeant beside Evie spoke for the first time.

The Yorkshireman nodded. 'True enough, Sarge. They're a good crowd, our pilots.'

'Yeah,' Jackson said. 'Always time for a word of thanks. Not puffed up with their own self-importance like some of the others.'

'Squadron Leader Kincaith, now, he's a true gent,' the sergeant said. A glow of pleasure warmed Evie's chest to hear Alex praised. She realised this must be the same sergeant that had discovered the sabotage. She groped for his name — Rawlins. That was it. 'He's not above asking my advice when it comes to the workings of his Hurricane.'

There were nods all around, and a chorus of agreement. 'It's good to see the CO back,' Rawlins went on. 'I had a right nasty turn when —' He paused, glancing a sideways glance at the men beside him. 'Well, the less said about that, the better.'

So he had done as Alex had asked and not told anyone else about the sabotage. Evie could tell from the slightly puzzled looks that the men didn't know what he was referring to.

'They're all a good crowd, by and large,' Sykes said. 'I'll admit when I heard we were having a load of Czech pilots, I thought Fighter Command had lost their marbles, but they're good pilots and friendlier than the toffee-nosed bunch in my last posting. Some of 'em are trained mechanics, too.'

Evie pricked up her ears at that. She'd been inclined to suspect one of the ground crew; they had both the knowledge and the opportunity to interfere with the aeroplanes. Now it turned out some of the pilots also could have done it. But she quickly dismissed the idea. The Czechs had every reason to hate the Germans. She remembered only too well the tales some of them had told of having to abandon loved ones in order to escape to continue their fight.

Jess must have had similar thoughts as she gave a breathless laugh. 'I wouldn't think you'd want anyone else messing with the aircraft.'

'Gawd 'elp us, no.' Rawlins pulled a face. 'But the pilots who understand engines are better at spotting trouble before it happens.'

'Not like that Pilot Officer Šimek.'

'Who — Karol?' Jess asked.

'That's him,' Fletcher said. 'Always bringing it back early with engine trouble. I've lost count of the number of times I've stripped down that engine. Never anything wrong.'

Evie fiddled with her spoon, wondering how to turn the conversation to who'd had the opportunity to sabotage Alex's Hurricane.

Before she could think of anything, Rawlins looked at his watch. 'Break over, lads. Excuse us, ladies. Duty calls.'

'Lovely talking to you lads. We'll look out for you another time.' Jess shot them a beaming smile that had Sykes tripping over his feet.

'Any time, ladies.'

The men hastily drained their mugs then clambered over the benches and filed out with cheery waves.

Evie stabbed at a lump of potato in her stew. 'Well, that got us nowhere.'

'Give us a chance, Evie. I couldn't exactly shine a light in their eyes and ask them where they were between two and four o'clock last Monday.'

'I know. I was so fired up to help that I didn't consider the practicalities. We didn't learn anything useful from those men.'

'I wouldn't say that. We achieved one thing.'

'What, a reputation for being flirts?'

Jess grinned. 'I already had that. And if you think what you were doing is flirting, you've got a lot to learn. No. I mean we're now friends with those men. They'd have been suspicious if we'd jumped in, firing questions. But they'll be falling over themselves to talk to us again, and now we're friends it will be easier to find out what we want.'

'You're right. Thanks for your help, Jess.' Evie ate a few mouthfuls of her now cold stew before saying, 'I know I'm being impatient. I can't help worrying the saboteur will strike again.' And terrified Alex would be the target.

Jess patted her hand. 'You never know. We might have learned more than we think. My experience of detecting has taught me that any detail can be important, even if it doesn't seem important at the time.'

Evie had to swallow her mouthful quickly to stop herself spitting it out. 'Your experience of detecting? When?'

Jess coloured. 'I once did a three-month run playing a chambermaid in a play about a murder at a house party.'

Evie laughed so hard tears came to her eyes.

'What's so funny?' Jess asked indignantly. 'My character held a vital clue that helped the detective solve the crime.'

'Jess, you're a godsend. I'd have gone insane long ago if it hadn't been for you and May.'

* * *

May hummed softly to herself as she wiped the dipstick on a rag and plunged it into the oil tank of the car she was to drive today. She was scheduled to collect Peter from the station later and she wanted the engine to be running perfectly.

'Lidford!'

May straightened, nearly hitting her head on the bonnet. 'Yes, Sarge?'

Sergeant Norris approached, holding a clipboard. Her uniform was pristine, and her tiny, neat build always made May feel like a clumsy giant in comparison. 'Got a pilot who needs driving to the station to catch the five-fifteen. I said you'd do it. You can wait there for the six-ten bringing in Squadron Leader Travis.'

'Yes, Sarge.' May looked at her oily hands in dismay. Now she only had half an hour to change out of her overalls and clean herself up. Not for the first time, she envied Evie and Jess, whose duties never left them looking like they'd spent the day rolling in a muddy puddle. She quickly finished her oil check, then left for the ablutions at a trot.

When she returned, hands clean, hair brushed free of dust and re-pinned, it was to find one of the Czech officers waiting beside her car. He looked like he was heading for a night in London — his hair was slicked back with Brylcreem, his shoes polished to a high gloss. May recognised him from the pub. She remembered wanting to giggle when she'd been introduced to him because he had a girl's name. Karol, that was it.

'Good afternoon, sir. I'm driving you to the station, is that right?'

'That's right. I've got a forty-eight-hour pass.'

May moved to open the rear door for him, but he'd already climbed into the passenger seat before she could get there, putting his case on the floor by his feet.

'Would you like me to put the case in the boot, sir?'

'It's fine here.' He put his hand on the case in an oddly protective gesture.

May gave a mental shrug and climbed into the driver's seat. If he wanted to spend the journey with what looked like a heavy case squashing his feet, that was his choice.

Some of her passengers liked to sit in silence while May drove, others preferred to hold conversation. Karol was one of the latter and he started as soon as May had driven them through the gates. She usually let them talk, only half-listening as she navigated the winding lanes with their high banks and hedgerows, adding a few comments here and there when appropriate. Now, however, she remembered the request Evie had made on her return three days ago. Her duties required her to be off the station for much of her time, so she'd not had much chance to help, but here was an opportunity to talk to someone who must have been nearby when Alex Kincaith's Hurricane was sabotaged.

'I can't believe I've got two whole days off,' Karol was saying.

'Where are you going? I mean, have you got anywhere to stay?' The Czechs didn't usually go far afield when they had time off because they didn't know the country and had no one to visit.

'London. I have money saved up. I'll find a hotel and spend the evenings at a club. It will be like being at home again.'

'Where did you live?'

'Prague. It's a beautiful city. There was a club there — the Dvě Vrány — I went every weekend.'

'Funny name. What does it mean?'

'The Two Crows. On Kampa Island, beneath the Charles Bridge.' He seemed to drift into reverie as he described the delights of the club that seemed to serve the best beer, play the best music and be frequented by the loveliest girls. 'I went there on my last night in Prague, to say goodbye to the place, when I knew I would have to escape.'

May braked to negotiate a narrow humpbacked bridge and pondered how to turn the conversation to the goings-on of his squadron without making her interest too obvious.

As it turned out, Karol himself gave her the opening she was looking for. 'I hate to leave my squadron a man short, though.'

'You seemed to manage when your CO was injured.'

'That's true. I was a great help to Flight Lieutenant Mašek while he was in charge.'

'That's . . . good.' May tried to remember which one was Flight Lieutenant Mašek. Wasn't that the man Jess had danced with at the midsummer dance? Milan. That was the name. It seemed like centuries ago but was only a few weeks in reality. Come to think of it, she'd seen Jess in his company a few times since then. Odd that she'd never said anything about it. Evie talked about Alex all the time, and May had seen how Evie and Jess smiled when she found herself mentioning Peter's name at the slightest prompting, but she couldn't seem to stop.

'I worry about leaving now. They depend on me, and bad things are happening.'

May was jolted from pleasant thoughts of Peter. 'Bad things? What kind of bad things?'

Karol leaned closer to May. As though there was any chance of this conversation being overheard, May thought in amusement. 'I heard a rumour that our CO's injury was no accident. They say his guns were jammed deliberately.'

May gripped the steering wheel tightly. Evie had been adamant no one but Alex, his fitter and the station commander knew of the sabotage. How on earth had Karol heard about it? 'What? Who would do such a thing?'

Karol shrugged. 'There are always rumours of traitors or infiltrators. Perhaps there's one at Amberton.'

'I haven't heard any rumours.' She didn't believe what Evie had told her was a rumour, so didn't feel she was telling a lie.

'Maybe not. I didn't believe it at first. But two days

250

ago, my guns jammed. It was a miracle I wasn't shot down.'

'Did you report it?'

'Yes, but I don't think anyone believed me. The fitter swore he couldn't find anything wrong. Of course, he wouldn't if he was the one who had caused it in the first place.'

May's heart pounded. Wait until she told Evie and Jess the progress she had made! Evie had been rather down since she'd not been able to uncover anything new. With luck, this should cheer her up. She finished the drive to the railway station wondering when she'd be able to see Evie to tell her the news.

The London train puffed into the station mere moments after they'd arrived, so Karol grabbed his suitcase, dashed onto the platform and disappeared into a carriage. Evie glanced at her watch and saw she still had nearly an hour before Peter's train was due to arrive. She straightened her hair and wandered into the little café opposite the station, sitting at a round table beside the window. When the waitress came over, she ordered a cup of tea and a Chelsea bun, then watched the station entrance for Peter's arrival. Her mouth watered when the delicious treat arrived, together with a cup of good, strong tea. She had discovered soon after arriving at Amberton that this café served the best Chelsea buns she'd ever had. She didn't like to enquire too closely where they got the ingredients for baking, since most were rationed. Cutting off a corner, she popped it into her mouth, closing her eyes in bliss as the mingled taste of cinnamon and sugar flooded her mouth.

'May I join you, or do you two want to be alone?'

May gave a start, dropping the teaspoon in the

saucer with a clatter. She hastily rose and saluted when she saw Peter standing by her chair, a crooked smile tilting one corner of his mouth. 'Peter! I mean, sir. I thought you were arriving on the six-ten.'

Peter waved her back into her seat. 'Peter,' he said firmly, sitting in the opposite chair. 'I've already told you I don't hold with all this saluting business off-station.'

'But the regulations —'

'I won't report you, if you won't.'

A reluctant smile tugged at her lips.

Peter leaned back and gave a satisfied nod. 'That's better.' He signalled to the waitress to bring the same as May was having. 'I want to see if the buns are as good as you make them look.'

When the waitress left, Peter cut his bun into neat quarters and tasted it. 'It is good,' he said, after savouring it carefully, 'but it's more fun watching you eat yours.'

May felt her cheeks flame. The others at Amberton thought Peter was always deadly serious, but that was because they only saw him on duty. May knew that deep down lay a wicked sense of humour and he enjoyed teasing her. Not in a cruel way, but a gentle banter that May secretly enjoyed despite the way it made her blush.

'Why are you early?' She blurted the first thing that came into her head to cover her embarrassment.

'The business I had didn't take as long as I'd imagined.'

'Oh.'

'Aren't you going to ask what my business was?'

'It's nothing to do with me.'

'I think it is.' And his gaze burned into her.

252

Suddenly her chest felt so tight it was a struggle to draw breath. 'Why?'

20

Evie trudged up the stairs to the schoolroom on heavy legs. The only light was a dim bulb on the landing and its position cast more shadows than light across the stairs. She stumbled twice, unable to lift her feet high enough. It was times like this she wished the Waafery was next door to the Ops Room rather than over a mile away down dark lanes. It didn't take long to get there on her bike, but when she only had a two-hour break between watches, every extra minute of travel was a minute less of sleep before she had to drag herself back out again. Night watches hadn't been so bad in June and July, but now they were at the end of August, the nights were noticeably drawing in. By October she knew she would have to do what Jess had chosen to do tonight and spend the hours between watches on one of the narrow camp beds in the room next to Ops. But she shuddered to think of spending the whole night in The Hole; it was so stuffy down there, and she was always aware of the weight of earth over her head. At least by coming back to High Chalk House between watches she got a chance to breathe fresh air.

She managed to climb the last steps without tripping again and pushed open the schoolroom door. May would already be fast asleep in her bed, so she tiptoed across the room, avoiding the floorboards that creaked. She had just put her hand on the nursery doorknob when she heard a sniff coming from somewhere in the schoolroom. She froze. There it was again.

'May, is that you?'

'Yes.' The word ended on a wail.

'What's happened? Hang on, I can't see a thing.' Evie felt her way to the window to check the blackout, then groped her way along the wall until her fingers found the light switch. Yellow light flooded the room, making her blink. When her eyes adjusted to the light, she looked for May.

May was huddled in one of the armchairs, wrapped in a blanket, her eyes red and swollen. All Evie's exhaustion fell away.

'What's wrong? Are you ill?' Evie hastened to crouch by May's chair and pressed a hand to her forehead. It wasn't over-warm.

'Not ill,' May said, drawing shuddering breaths. 'Just . . . Oh, Evie, Peter is joining another squadron.'

'What? How do you know?'

'He told me.'

'Oh, May, I'm sorry.' Evie's knees were threatening to give way, so she drew one of the dining chairs next to May and sat down, wrapping an arm around May's shaking shoulders. She wished Jess was there. Jess was always much better at finding the right words to say. Evie would have been far more comfortable had May asked for help solving a mathematical equation. She sought for words of consolation. 'We all know we could be transferred at any time. We should be prepared to move wherever the RAF or WAAF send us.'

May's sobs only increased. Great. Now Evie had reminded her that their tight friendship group could be broken up. 'At least you know he's on the ground. As safe as anyone can be these days.'

255

'No! You've got it all wrong.' May scrubbed at her eyes while Evie stared at her, startled by the anger in May's voice. 'He isn't being transferred against his will, and he won't be safe on the ground.'

'What—?'

'He requested the transfer.' May had got her voice under more control, but it throbbed with an undercurrent of distress.

'Why would he do that?' Evie gazed at May, feeling helpless. She'd been glad for May's budding romance with Peter. From what May had told her about her family, she couldn't blame her for being wary of men, but she'd been sure Peter Travis's determination and undeniable good heart would win May round in the end.

'He's going to fly fighters.'

Evie felt a jolt of shock. 'Can he do that?'

May nodded. 'If Douglas Bader can fly with two legs missing, Peter should have no problem with just one.'

'*Should?* It isn't definite? I mean, he hasn't actually —'

'He passed his medical board today. That's why he was in London.' May gave a laugh with absolutely no humour. 'I'm the first person he told. He'll have to pass flight training again, but I'm sure he will.'

'I don't understand him. It's not as if he's sitting at home doing nothing.'

May hugged her knees to her chest. 'He feels he's not pulling his weight. Wants to do something that makes a difference.'

Evie groped for words of comfort, but couldn't find any. She knew all too well the burden of dread that came from having a loved one in danger, and noth-

256

ing could ease it until the war ended or . . . No. She wouldn't think of that.

'He makes a difference in Ops,' she said. 'There are plenty of people alive today who wouldn't be if he hadn't sent out fighters at the right time.'

'I know. I tried to tell him.' May glanced down and fiddled with the corner of her blanket. 'I keep thinking . . . maybe if I'd given him some encouragement, showed him I returned his feelings.'

'No!' Evie grasped May's hand, closing around it and the blanket and willing her to believe what she said. 'Peter's a decent man. I'm sure he can see you love him, even if you can't bring yourself to say so. This is entirely his decision. Nothing to do with you.' Evie sighed. 'He's a pilot too, remember, even if he can't fly. It can't be easy, sending men out day after day, knowing some won't return.' She didn't say so, but also suspected Peter might feel ashamed that his injury had been caused in a peacetime accident rather than while defending his country. Evie couldn't see it made any difference — he had been wounded in service of his country even though it hadn't happened during the war. But then she found men alien creatures. She resolved to talk to Alex about it. He and Peter were good friends and he would never let Peter put himself at risk for the wrong reasons.

May sobbed with gratitude when Evie told her.

'Alex won't be able to stop Peter leaving,' Evie warned her. 'Not if Peter's made up his mind. Anyway, it sounds like Fighter Command have already approved the transfer.'

'I know. But I would feel better if Peter left knowing how valued he is.'

'I think there's only one person he wants to hear

257

that from.'

May blushed and hung her head. 'I know. I just . . . I can't.'

Evie set her jaw. If she met May's father and brothers right now, she swore she would wring their necks. 'Give it time. You'll get there.'

May sniffed. 'If he's still alive by that time.'

And there was nothing Evie could say to that. They'd both seen how quickly death could strike. No one liked to talk about it too much, but everyone was aware that each day could be their last.

After a while, Evie rose, easing the stiffness from her back. 'How about a cup of cocoa? I've got to go back in about an hour, but I could do with a drink and a bite to eat first.'

May flung the blanket aside and rose with a cry of dismay. 'I'm sorry, Evie. I shouldn't have kept you up. And you working all hours.'

'You come first, May. What else are friends for?'

May gave a shaky smile. 'You're a brick, Evie. Come on, I'll help you make the drinks.'

Once the drinks were made, they sat at the kitchen table, nibbling squares of carrot cake that Evie had brought from home and sipping their cocoa. They could hear a low murmur of voices from the Rose Room, but thankfully no one disturbed them in the kitchen. Evie and May sat in silence for a while, listening to an owl hooting in the trees behind the house.

May blew the steam from her cup. 'It's amazing how cocoa can make everything feel better. I am sorry I kept you from sleep, though.'

Evie, feeling revived by the sweet cake, waved away May's apologies. 'You would do the same for me. Besides, there's nothing like a midnight snack to perk me up. I've got the night off tomorrow, so I can catch up then.' And she'd be able to snatch a couple of hours between watches. 'What would really brighten my day would be news that the saboteur has been caught. You can't believe how scared I've been, knowing Alex and the others are up in the air, praying no one's meddled with their machines.'

May gave a small gasp. 'I quite forgot. I heard something from one of Brimstone's pilots today.'

Evie's heart rate increased as she listened to May relate the conversation she'd had with Karol. 'Alex swore it was only he, the station commander and Sergeant Rawlins who knew about the sabotage. How on earth does Karol know?'

'Maybe Sergeant Rawlins said something.'

'Perhaps.' But that didn't sit quite right with Evie. Rawlins had struck her as a man who took his orders seriously, and he seemed to have great respect for Alex. She couldn't see him casually breaking Alex's order to keep quiet. 'Ah, well. We can't do anything about it now. I'll tell Alex when I see him tomorrow.'

A flutter of excitement thrilled in her chest. They'd arranged to meet at the pub. It wouldn't be a romantic *tête-à-tête*, not in the crowded snug, but it would be a chance to talk, reassure herself he was well. It was more time together than many couples got these days, and she was grateful.

* * *

Alex taxied his Hurricane towards the waiting Erks. A glance at his watch showed him it was nearly seven o'clock. Time always seemed to pass in a strange way when he was in the air. It felt like he had been up

259

there for only a few minutes but now he could see it had been over an hour.

'How did it go, sir?' Sergeant Rawlins asked, helping him out of his parachute.

'Not bad. Think we bagged a couple of 109s between us. How many are back?' He could never relax until he knew all his pilots had returned safely.

'All bar two, sir.' Rawlins paused and shaded his eyes, gazing into the sky. 'Looks like they're coming in now.'

Alex followed where he was pointing and saw two Hurricanes making their approach. He held his breath until he saw the markings, only relaxing when he saw they did indeed belong to the two remaining members of Brimstone. All back safely to live another day. And to cap it all, he was meeting Evie soon. Days like this were bright spots that made the war seem almost bearable.

Milan ran up, looking worried. 'You've got visitors. In your office.'

The lads were laughing and chatting in the dispersal hut as they removed their Mae Wests, rescued personal possessions from their lockers and made their way to the door. They cast sidelong glances at Alex when he walked across the room to his office. He saw why when he went in. Bob Law was waiting for him with another officer and a sergeant. Alex didn't need to see the red and black armbands and the sergeant's white cap to know these were members of the RAF Police. The officer's dark hair was so slicked with Brylcreem, Alex dreaded to think how oily the inside of his cap must be.

'We need to talk about the rumours flying around the station about the saboteur,' Bob said after

260

introducing Flying Officer Dawson and Sergeant Phipps.

'What rumours? I haven't breathed a word and I can vouch for Rawlins.' A moment later he realised that wasn't true. He'd told Evie. But Evie wouldn't tell anyone, and he didn't want to get her into trouble.

'Then explain why I've just had James Fitzpatrick pacing up and down my office, demanding to know what I'm doing about the station saboteur.'

Alex went cold. If Fitz — Catseye squadron's CO — knew about it, the secret must be well and truly out. 'I can't, sir.' Oh, God, please don't let it be Evie who had talked. He'd have put his last fiver on her being trustworthy, but weren't there posters all over the place warning about just this situation? Had she played him for a fool? Surely not. He trusted her. He would talk to her about it this evening to put his mind at rest, but he knew she wouldn't have talked.

But that only left Rawlins, and the thought of him breaking orders was almost as bad as Evie letting him down.

'Fitz also said it was general knowledge that Aircraftman Sykes was the culprit.'

'Sykes?' Alex could picture the young Yorkshireman clearly. He was eager to please, hard-working and honest through and through. 'I don't believe it. Not him.'

'Nevertheless, we need to question him.' It was Dawson who spoke, and Alex took an immediate dislike to his officious manner. 'According to our information, one of your pilots' guns jammed but Sykes found nothing wrong when he examined them.' Dawson consulted a small notebook. 'The pilot concerned was named as Pilot Officer Karol Šimek, one of the Czechs.' He scrunched up his nose as he spoke as though detecting a bad smell. 'I suppose as an officer we can consider him trustworthy, even if he is a foreigner.'

'The Czechs have just as much reason to want to fight the Nazis as we do. More.' Alex glared at Dawson. 'Or are you going to investigate me, too? My grandmother was Czech.'

'Then you won't have any objection to us questioning Aircraftman Sykes.'

Alex cursed inwardly. It seemed he could defend Karol or Sykes but not both. He sighed. 'You can question him, but I don't believe he's the man you're after.'

'In that case, he'll have nothing to fear.'

With a heavy heart, Alex led Dawson and Phipps to the dispersal pens, where Sykes was feeding ammunition into a Hurricane.

Phipps strode up to the unsuspecting fitter. 'Aircraftman Sykes, you are under arrest on suspicion of sabotage and treason.'

The blood drained from Sykes' face; he shot a desperate glance between the RAF Police and Alex. 'What? No, I —'

The two men seized Sykes between them. Alex marched up to them and tried to place himself between the police and the quaking Sykes. 'Stop! I said you could question him, not arrest him.'

Bob Law pulled him away, freeing Dawson and Phipps to march Sykes to the waiting car. 'Steady, old boy. Can't get between the RAF Police and their investigation. If Sykes is innocent, he'll be released.'

But Alex couldn't help feeling that the pressure would be on the investigating team to secure a conviction and lay to rest any rumours that could upset the running of the station. He gave Bob a curt nod and strode up to the car. 'I know you didn't do it,' he said to Sykes. Sykes was pale and trembling and was barely able to stutter a reply. Alex went on. 'I'll make sure you're cleared.'

Once the car had driven off, Bob Law going with them, Alex went to find Milan. Most of the men had already drifted, all doubtless heading to the pub, but Milan was still there with Pilot Officer Walsh, finishing off his combat report.

'What's happening?' Milan asked, gesturing out to where the altercation had happened.

'I'll tell you later. Where's Karol?'

'London. On a forty-eight-hour pass. He will be back tomorrow evening.'

Alex slapped his forehead. 'Damn. I forgot.'

'Can I help?'

Alex considered Milan for a moment, but then shook his head. Best not to involve anyone else. Not until he'd worked out how word had got out. And the first person he needed to see was Evie. He glanced at his watch. It was nearly time to meet her. She'd arranged to go there with her two friends straight after her last watch of the day.

'Coming to the pub?' he asked. Milan nodded with a grin. He scrawled his signature on the bottom of the combat report and sprang to his feet.

Evie hadn't arrived when he put his head round the door of the snug, so he asked Milan to bag them a table then paced outside, listening to unseen mice scrabbling in the thatch and the squeak of the pub's sign dangling from its bracket above the heavy oak door. The sun hung low on the horizon, casting long shadows of trees and hedges. A horse clopped past, harnessed to a cart brimming with potatoes, chalky earth still clinging to them. A black Labrador with a shaggy coat regarded the world from its perch beside the driver, tongue lolling. It was a homely sight, one that had been seen on these lanes for generations. Alex wondered if he would ever get used to the incongruity of fighting for his life and dealing death in the skies all day long, only to return to a cosy scene such as this every evening.

The sound of bicycle bells and girlish laughter drifted to his ears from further up the lane, then three cycles bearing WAAFs whizzed around the corner. They rode side by side, red, blonde and brunette hair streaming behind them. Alex gazed at Evie and his stomach tightened. He wanted to snuggle up to her in a corner seat, breathe in her soapy scent and talk about anything except the war. The last thing he wanted was to tackle her about the rumours flying around the base, but he owed it to Sykes to get to the truth.

Evie, Jess and May climbed off their bikes and propped them against the wall. Then Evie ran to him, her face flushed from the exercise, tilting her face to his for a kiss. Jess and May diplomatically drifted into the snug.

Alex put his arms around her and kissed her, stretching out the moment for as long as possible. 'I've missed you,' he murmured into her hair when he finally broke the kiss and she rested her head in the crook of his neck.

'I've missed you, too.' Her breath feathered the side of his neck, making him shiver.

There was only so long he could delay the inevitable. He drew back with a sigh, put his hands on her shoulders and gazed down at her. 'There's something

I need to ask.'

She raised her eyebrows. 'What?'

'Apparently the whole station is talking about the saboteur.'

'I know. May —'

'Did *you* tell anyone what I told you?'

Evie's gaze slid from his face to a point behind his left shoulder. The spots of red forming on her cheeks gave him his answer. 'I only told May and Jess.'

'And they only told half the station between them,' he finished for her, a bitter twist in his gut.

She shook her head. 'No. They wouldn't.'

'*Someone's* talked. One of my best fitters is under arrest because of a rumour. If it's not Jess or May —'

'Oh, so it has to be one of them?'

He dropped his hands from her shoulders. 'But why tell them in the first place?' Then he paused, struck by a sense of growing alarm. 'Please tell me you're not trying to investigate.'

Evie evaded his gaze. 'I can help, I know I can. People tell us things they wouldn't —'

'No! Good God, Evie, it's too dangerous.'

'Of course it's dangerous. This is war. If I'd wanted to avoid danger, I wouldn't have joined the WAAF.'

A shard of ice pierced his heart. 'We're talking about a cold-blooded killer on the station.' It was as though the pain and loss of a lifetime coalesced into a single leaden ball of dread. 'Stay out of it, Evie. I forbid you to investigate.'

* * *

'You *forbid* me?' Evie swallowed to clear the sudden tightness in her throat. Of course, she should obey an officer without question, but she got the impression he'd spoken not as an officer, but as the man she was walking out with. Cornelia's words came back to her: *Be certain you both want the same thing from your relationship.* Did Alex think she should obey him without question in all matters? 'But, Alex, we can help. We can ask questions in a way that won't alert the saboteur.'

Alex set his jaw. 'It's too dangerous. Leave it to the authorities.'

'Because everyone's falling over themselves to talk to them.' Evie was shocked at the bitterness in her voice, but she couldn't help it. It was one thing for Alex to want her to be safe, but if this was an indication that Alex always expected her unquestioning obedience then they had a problem.

'Oh, and you've discovered something they haven't?'

'As a matter of fact, we have.' She related what May had said about Karol. 'It proves May didn't spread any rumours. She was as puzzled as I was to hear about them.'

Alex raked his fingers through his hair. 'But don't you see that firing questions around could be starting more rumours? There's already one innocent man under arrest; I don't want more.'

'Who was it?'

'Sykes.'

'Sykes! I know him.' Evie pictured the cheerful Yorkshireman she and Jess had spoken to in the NAAFI. 'No one in their right mind could accuse him. There's no way he would have done it.'

Alex gave a ghost of a smile. 'Then we're agreed on something.'

266

But Evie couldn't forget they strongly disagreed on important matters. She went with Alex into the pub, but she couldn't clear Cornelia's words from her mind. *Be certain you both want the same thing from your relationship.*

21

'I can't believe Alex thinks one of you spread rumours.' Evie sat cross-legged in one of the school-room armchairs. Unable to put on a false smile for Alex, she'd pleaded tiredness and left early. She had changed into her pyjamas but was too het up to sleep. Thinking it might calm her, she had curled up in the armchair with one of her textbooks, a dog-eared notebook and a pencil stub to work through some exercises. It hadn't really worked. She hadn't been able to silence the voice in her head whispering that Alex didn't rate her judgement as highly as his. Desperate for something to take her mind off him, she persuaded Jess and May to join her for a chat when they returned from the Horse and Groom. It might have been a better distraction if she hadn't immediately repeated her conversation with Alex. Most of it, anyway.

'You didn't argue with him, did you?' May asked. She looked a little pale; Evie hoped she wasn't going down with something.

'I wouldn't blame you if you did,' Jess said. 'He should have trusted you.'

'Well, I did tell the two of you even though I'd promised to keep it secret.' Funny how she could criticise Alex herself but hated to hear it from others. But a heavy weight remained lodged in her chest. The trouble was, her irritation was more to do with Alex's apparent belief that he had the right to forbid her to do something, but she didn't want to tell her friends about that. She could already imagine what they'd say. May would look anxious and remind her that you could never tell if you'd ended up with a bad husband until it was too late. Jess would laugh and tell her to forget Alex as there were plenty more fish in the sea.

But Evie didn't want to forget Alex. She couldn't imagine being with anyone else.

Do you truly want to spend your life with a man who doesn't consider you his equal? The annoying, nagging voice was back. Evie did her best to ignore it by changing the subject and asking Jess for the latest gossip. Jess obliged by plunging into a story about a WAAF from the Orderly Room, who had returned from leave engaged to a naval officer.

'They only met on the train at the start of her leave,' Jess said. 'Imagine that!'

Evie shifted in her seat. Had she and Alex moved too fast? She might have known him for longer than a week, but if you added the actual hours they had spent together it probably wouldn't come to much more than that. What did she really know about him? She only listened to the rest of Jess's tale with half her mind; the rest was occupied with the chilling possibility that she had seen a glimpse of the real Alex tonight.

She was only drawn back to the present when Jess gave a huge yawn and clapped her hand across her mouth. 'Sorry, girls, I'm pooped. If I don't turn in now, I'll be good for nothing tomorrow.'

Feeling numb, Evie gathered up the books and pencil from the floor, and they retired to their rooms. When Evie returned from the bathroom, she found May already in bed, curled on her side with her back to the room. She lay so still, Evie thought she was

269

already asleep. But then she heard a distinct sniffle, and May's shoulders shook.

Evie crouched beside May's bed. 'What's wrong?' She placed a gentle hand on May's shoulder. 'Is it Peter?'

May stiffened, then turned over, scrubbing at reddened eyes. She nodded. 'I saw him in the pub.' Her chin wobbled, and fresh tears welled in her eyes. 'Oh, Evie, he's had his posting. He leaves tomorrow for flight training.'

Evie hugged her wordlessly. Nothing she could say would ease May's fears. They'd both witnessed too many losses for that. 'Why didn't you say?' she asked at last.

'I didn't want to bother you. Not when you were upset about Alex.'

Evie's heart twisted. 'Now listen here, May Lidford, you're my friend. I care about you. It would bother me more to know you were upset and hadn't confided in me.' That gave her a twinge of guilt, considering she'd held back the greater part of her worries over Alex.

May pulled out a handkerchief and dabbed at her eyes. 'Thanks, Evie.' Then, after a pause, she said, 'I do feel a bit better now. Not so alone. You're the best friend a girl could have.'

That made Evie feel a complete hypocrite. 'Well, actually . . .' She took a deep breath and confided her true fears. 'What do you think, May?' she finished. 'Is it silly of me to expect him to treat me as an equal?'

'No! You're the most intelligent person I know, and if he doesn't see that, he's a fool.'

Evie squeezed May's arm, grateful for the encouragement. 'What should I do?'

270

May tucked her knees under her chin, her brow furrowed. 'What you have to decide is if Alex genuinely believes his word is law in your relationship or if he had another reason for what he said.'

'Like what?'

'Hasn't it occurred to you he's trying to protect you?'

Evie hadn't thought of that. 'Even if that's true, he has to respect my decisions.'

'Do you really expect him to sit back and watch you put yourself in harm's way?'

Put like that, Evie couldn't come up with a satisfactory answer.

They were silent for a while, both lost in their own thoughts. In the distance a fox yelped, a lonely sound.

'I do have a suggestion,' May said eventually. 'But I don't think you're going to like it.'

'Go on.' Whatever it was, it had to be better than lying awake all night, agonising about it.

'You should apply for a transfer. No, wait,' May said when Evie gave an exclamation of disbelief. 'Hear me out.'

Evie gave a wary nod and sat on the edge of her bed, waiting.

'Well,' said May, 'although I'm really going to miss Peter, I've started to think time apart will be good for me. You know . . .' May started picking at the blanket around her knees. 'You know I've had trouble making the commitment he wants.'

Evie nodded but remained silent.

'I'm going to miss him horribly,' May went on, 'but I think I need time to work out what I really want. If I can ever give Peter the love he deserves.'

'Maybe you've got a point,' Evie replied. 'I find it

271

so hard to think straight when Alex is around.'

'Exactly. It's the same with Peter. But this is a serious decision, and I've seen what a bad marriage looks like. Trust me, you don't want to end up like my mum.'

Or mine, Evie thought.

She lay awake for hours after May fell asleep, thinking over May's idea. Then she remembered Alex suggesting she applied for officer training. Her pulse sped up. Dare she try? Then it occurred to her there was someone she could ask for advice. Creeping out of bed, she groped on her bedside table for paper and pen and tiptoed back into the schoolroom. Cornelia had given her excellent advice over the years; she would surely have an opinion. She set her problem out on the page as plainly as she dared, considering her letter would be read by the censor. Then, her mind finally at ease, she went to bed and fell into a deep sleep.

She handed the letter in for posting first thing the next morning, leaving the envelope open for the censor. Then she went down to Ops with a lighter heart, confident Cornelia would reply at the earliest opportunity. She hadn't been in Ops long when Brimstone squadron was scrambled to intercept a large group of hostile aircraft. Her stomach knotted, and she breathed a silent prayer for his protection as she watched the plots approach each other on the table. She couldn't decide what was worse: not knowing what Alex was doing or knowing exactly how much danger he was in and watching it close on him inch by stomach-churning inch.

The detached voice in her headset gave the details of another wave of bandits. Evie picked up a new

272

block and slotted the numbers in place; another thirty or more enemies trying to break their defences. She put it on the table and slid it across to the given co-ordinates.

There was a stir among the observers.

'Where did that come from?' Flying Officer George Parry — the officer acting as controller — asked. 'Damn it. We're spread thinly enough as it is.'

He gazed at the board showing the readiness of all the squadrons on the station, the furrows on his brow deepening. Evie didn't need to look. She knew all available Hurricanes were in the air.

'How soon before Wagtail 'A' flight lands?' Parry asked the assistant controller.

'Any minute now,' came the reply. Almost at the same moment the observer reported six Hurricanes coming in to land. ''B' flight are ten minutes behind.'

'Get them refuelled and rearmed on the double. I want them ready to get into the air in fifteen minutes. Same with 'B' flight when they land.'

The assistant controller picked up his telephone receiver and relayed the orders.

Evie heard the girl standing next to her take a sharply indrawn breath. Lucie Watkins had recently become engaged to one of the pilots in Wagtail, Evie remembered. She had attended the celebrations in the pub just before she'd been taken ill. She leaned across and patted Lucie's arm awkwardly. 'My fellow's up there too. Brimstone.'

There was no time to say any more, because she received another position for the first hostile plot she'd been tracking and moments later an update on the new plot. She busied herself moving the blocks and placing arrows, needing to double-check the clock to be certain she had the right colour.

She was aware of everyone around her craning their necks to see the new positions. Despite the stuffiness of the room, Evie felt as though she'd been doused with icy water. The two hostile plots were converging right over Amberton.

'They're coming here again,' Parry snapped. There was a flurry of activity as he called Group Command to request support from other squadrons and others alerted the air raid wardens and the squadrons in the air.

'I'm glad I'm down here this time,' Jess muttered under cover of the raised voices. 'Safest place in the station, I reckon.'

'What about May?'

Jess paled. 'Safely out of the way, I 'ope.' She put a hand to her ear, a gesture Evie often saw her make when instructions were coming through her headset. Then with hands that trembled, she picked up a new block from the shelf below the table and slotted in the numbers representing yet another hostile plot. An Arctic air seemed to fill the room after Jess put it in position. Until the next position came through there was no way of telling direction or speed, but Evie didn't doubt it, too, was converging on Amberton.

Within a few minutes, her fear was confirmed. The new plot, just like the other two, trailed a wake of blue and red arrows. Evie knew enough about vectors and navigation to know that taking the wind direction into account, Amberton was their most likely destination.

Her heart leapt when Alex's voice cracked over the R/T. 'Belfry, this is Brimstone Red Leader. We're in

274

position at Angels two-zero.'

Peter stood and surveyed the situation map. 'Belfry to Brimstone Red Leader. You should be right on top of them.'

There was a long pause that stretched out until Evie wanted to scream to break the tension. She thought the whole Ops Room must be able to hear her heart thundering in her chest. The telephone shrilled, and her rake slipped in her damp hand. She had to clutch it to stop it clattering to the lino tiles.

'That was Group, sir,' the assistant controller said. 'They're sending two flights from Tangmere and another two from Kenley. ETA ten minutes.'

The speakers crackled; Evie tensed, but it was only the observer up on the ground reporting the six Hurricanes of Wagtail's 'A' flight taking off.

Then Alex's voice came through, sounding fainter this time. It was only to be expected as R/T communications often broke down, but she prayed the signal would get through this time. Now more than ever, they needed on-the-moment information. 'Brimstone Red Leader to Belfry. I see them. The sky's thick with them. About fifty at one o'clock . . .' The R/T faded then through the hiss of white noise, Evie could make out: '. . . and Dorniers . . . Tally ho!'

Parry snapped out: 'Brimstone Red Leader, this is Belfry. Target the bombers. Repeat, target bombers. Acknowledge.' But he got no reply but the hiss of static.

Evie could do nothing but gaze at the numbers on Brimstone's plot, praying there would still be twelve Hurricanes returning. All around her was a hive of activity, with the plotters moving the blocks representing Wagtail and the other hostile plots. Up on the ground she knew the air raid siren would be sounding, and men and women would either be running to gun emplacements or to the shelters. But Evie's focus was all on the map in front of her. What could twelve machines do against fifty? It seemed hopeless, and more hostiles were on their way. She jumped when another report came through her headset, and she hurried to move the second hostile plot closer to their target. They would miss the battle Alex was engaged in by some miles. It was a relief in one way — she doubted Brimstone could tackle any more machines than they were already fighting, if indeed they could hold out against those. But it made it more likely that some of the bombers would break through to their target.

The minutes that followed were agony. She worked mechanically. It was as though a part of her brain became separated from the rest of her, responding to the information fed though her headset while the conscious part was fixated on Alex and whether he was still alive or if he was plummeting tens of thousands of feet to a watery grave. She vaguely heard the voices around her as the controller relayed instructions to the two flights from Wagtail squadron, then his muted, 'We're in for it now,' when reports came through from the coastal observer stations reporting that one of the hostile groups had crossed the coastline. If they were targeting Amberton, they would most likely strike before there was time for any more observers to report in.

Sure enough, mere minutes later, the ground shook, rattling the blocks on the table. A moment later, the observer up on the ground reported Messerschmitt Bf 110s and Dorniers.

Then Alex's voice came through the speakers. 'Brimstone Red Leader to Belfry, are you receiving me?'

Evie's legs gave way in relief. It was a good thing her chair was right behind her, or she would have fallen backwards onto the floor.

'Brimstone Red Leader, this is Belfry. Report.' The controller's voice was calm, despite the chaos that must be going on overhead. His matter-of-factness helped Evie snap out of her numbed state and focus on her task again. But she was able to listen in to Alex's report as she did so.

'Five Dorniers shot down,' Alex was saying. 'Most fled back to France but I think some got past us in the confusion.'

'Understood, Red Leader. Land at Tangmere and await instructions. We've got a spot of bother here. Belfry out.'

Glancing at the readiness board behind her, Evie immediately saw why the controller had directed Brimstone to Tangmere. They wouldn't have enough fuel to engage any enemy aircraft. That meant they were out of the fight. Alex was safe. For now. But the day's events had shown her that she was not cut out for the daily terror of knowing exactly what danger Alex was in. That, together with Cornelia's voice nagging at her, asking if she was sure they wanted the same thing, made up her mind. As soon as she was able, she would speak to her flight officer to see if she could arrange a transfer.

If only it wouldn't mean leaving Jess and May.

May. Her stomach knotted. May was out there, somewhere. Evie could only pray she was safe.

★ ★ ★

277

May gripped the steering wheel so hard, her knuckles turned white. She had to struggle to keep her composure, not let Peter see her distress. After today there would be no more drives, no more meeting at the pub after a busy day. Instead she would spend every day with the same weight of worry Evie had for Alex. And she only had herself to blame. If she could love any man, it was Peter. If she had given him even a word of encouragement, maybe he wouldn't have requested to return to flying.

She had just driven onto the bridge crossing the River Arun when a screaming roar overhead made her blood go cold. Throwing a glance over her shoulder, she saw an aeroplane in a steep dive. It was aiming straight at them.

Peter grabbed her arm. 'Get off the bridge. Quick!'

She stamped the accelerator pedal to the floor, flinging her and Peter against the backs of their seats. She could see immediately why being on the bridge was a bad idea: there was nowhere to take cover, and she couldn't even swerve to spoil to pilot's aim. The howl of the aero engine grew louder until the whole car seemed to vibrate with it. They were over the bridge, but high walls on either side of the narrow road meant they still weren't safe. Then suddenly the wall stopped, replaced by a hedge. She pulled the car off the road, the tyres screeching as she braked hard. It had barely stopped before she flung open her door. From the corner of her eye she could see Peter do likewise. Then a hail of bullets hit the road, spraying dirt and chips of tar into the air. There was no time to think. Flinging her arms across her face, she threw herself into the hedge, heedless of getting scratched. Then she was through, tumbling into the

278

ditch beyond. She tried to sit up, but a heavy weight pressed her down into the dry mud.

'Keep your head down.' It was Peter.

She opened her mouth to answer, but before she could say anything the ground heaved beneath her. A moment later there came a huge crash that seemed to split her eardrums. The ground shook again and there was another deafening blast. She could feel Peter's arms around her, knew he was covering her with his body, protecting her. It was the only thing she knew, beside the wail of the aero engine and the ringing in her ears.

She couldn't tell how long they lay there, but finally the roar of the engine faded into the distance. The weight lifted from her back and she pushed herself into a sitting position. Her ears still buzzed and now she became aware of the sting of the many scratches and stings she'd received while burrowing through the hedge. Peter was in a similar state. He had a graze on his left cheekbone and a trickle of blood ran down from a cut above his eye.

'Are you hurt?' he said urgently.

She shook her head. 'No. I don't think so.' She pointed at the trail of blood that had now nearly reached his chin. 'Your face.' She was too dazed to put together a more coherent sentence.

Peter pulled a handkerchief from his pocket and dabbed at his brow, winced, and looked at the blood on the white cotton with an expression of surprise. 'Just a scratch, I think. Come on; let's get back to the car.' He gave a crooked smile that made her heart flutter. 'We'll use the gate this time.' He hauled himself to his feet then held out a hand to May.

May hesitated, then took it. He pulled her to her feet

as though she were a fragile, dainty creature instead of a gangling giant who was the same height as him. She had seen enough Hollywood films to know that men always fell for women whose head came no higher than their chin. All the better to shelter them in the curve of their arms and nestle them in the crook of their necks. Just as she'd seen Alex hold Evie at the village dance. The only way Peter would be able to hold her like that was if he stood on a stool. Or if she hunched over in a most unattractive fashion. She couldn't understand what Peter saw in her.

She realised she was standing so close to Peter their noses were nearly touching. She still held his hand and a wonderful, caressing heat enveloped her flesh. For a moment she stood, transfixed, gazing into his chocolate brown eyes. From this distance she could see his irises were flecked with gold. It was as though the air had been sucked out of her lungs and a tight band prevented her from drawing more. A mad impulse to lean in and kiss him seized her. Just one kiss to remember him by. She saw his gaze drop to her mouth, and knew he was thinking the same thing, and his breathing quickened as though he were affected by the same lack of oxygen that afflicted her. His hand tightened over hers.

No. It was the nearness of their escape. It was relief that set her heart pounding like a piston and weighed in her limbs with a delicious heaviness.

Making a supreme effort, she tore her hand from his and took a step back, forced her lungs to draw air. Nothing had changed. She still had no wish to end up in the cage of servitude that the WAAF had freed her from. She dragged her gaze from his face and scanned the hedgerow. 'There,' she said, pointing to a gap in the hedge. Only her trembling hand belied the cheery brightness she strove to inject into her tones. 'I think that must be a gate.'

'Anything's better than diving through the hedge again.' Peter sounded jovial, but there was something forced in his voice. May knew she had hurt him again by pulling away, but it was better this way. She'd meant it when she'd told Evie being away from Peter would give her time to think, but now she doubted she'd ever be able to surrender to her feelings. If Peter had any sense, he would find someone else at his new posting and forget her. She would do her best not to hate the girl he eventually fell for.

They clambered out of the ditch and made their way to the gate. A group of cows were running at the far end of the field, heads thrown back, bellowing their distress. May could only hope they stayed up at that end of the field and didn't stampede. She quickened her pace, but the ground was uneven, and Peter was struggling to cover the distance at speed. He seemed to be having difficulty with his prosthetic leg.

'Are you hurt?' she asked, pausing to allow him to catch up, while keeping a wary eye on the cattle. When he caught up she offered him her arm as support, tensing, doing all she could to ignore the thrill of feeling at the press of his fingers through her sleeve.

Peter shook his head. 'Took a knock to the leg. I'll —' His voice died away when they reached the gate. May followed his gaze and froze in shock. Billows of dust rose up from the road. May could just make out a huge crater blocking the road ahead of the bridge. Worst of all, smoke poured from the car's engine. The car itself was riddled with bullet holes.

281

May found her voice. 'If we hadn't got out of the car . . .' She started to shiver and found she couldn't stop.

'Don't think that way. Just be grateful we're still here.' Peter hobbled to the car. 'We'll walk to the nearest house,' he said. 'I just hope they have a telephone.' He lifted one bag from the back seat and eyed the rest of his luggage doubtfully. 'We'll have to leave everything else here and hope it's still there by the time we've found transport.'

In the event, they found a farmhouse little more than a quarter of a mile away. The farmer's wife, Mrs Bowes, let them in, exclaiming that she'd heard the attack. She gasped with dismay when she heard the road had been destroyed. 'Half our fields are the other side of the river,' she said. 'It'll take forever to get there now.' She ushered them through the house. 'You're welcome to use the telephone.' She directed Peter into the narrow hallway where the telephone stood upon a shelf. 'I'll make us some tea.'

May followed Peter into the passageway. It suddenly occurred to her that even if the car hadn't been irreparably damaged, she wouldn't have been able to drive past the crater. She would have to telephone the station to report the damage, although how anyone was going to get out to her was anyone's guess. The only road access to Amberton was gone. If anyone needed to get in or out in an emergency, they were going to have trouble.

Peter picked up the receiver and breathed a sigh of relief. 'I was afraid the lines would be down.' He spoke to the operator, asking to be put through to RAF Amberton. May looked at him in surprise, having expected him to call his Operational Training Unit.

As if reading her mind, he put his hand over the receiver and said, 'I'll get someone at Amberton to ring through to Aston Down for me. Bob Law needs to know the road is out.'

Mrs Bowes came out from the kitchen and caught Peter's attention. 'My husband says he can give you a lift to the station on his tractor when he's finished the milking.' She turned to May. 'He'll get you across to Amberton somehow.'

Peter gave Mrs Bowes a wave of thanks and relayed the information to whoever he was speaking to. Then he replaced the receiver and smiled at May. 'That's settled, then. We won't be stranded, and the powers that be at Aston Down know I'm going to be late.'

They went through to the kitchen, where they sat at a large oak table, opposite a row of gleaming copper pans hanging upon the wall. A huge, cast iron range behind them pumped out heat, and while Mrs Bowes bustled around them, the warmth seeped through to May's chilled bones and her shivering eased.

Mrs Bowes presented them with cups of tea and slices of ginger cake. 'I made it for the WRVS fund-raiser, but after what you two have been through, I think your need is greater.'

It was only when May took a bite that she realised how hungry she was. She smiled as its sweet spiciness made her tongue tingle. This was far better than any-thing she could have got from the NAAFI. Together with the tea, it chased away the last effects of shock.

'There, now,' Mrs Bowes said, smiling in return. 'That'll do you good. Now I must leave you while I —' She broke off with a cry of alarm and pointed at Peter's leg.

Peter dropped the piece of cake he was holding

and looked down. Following Mrs Bowes' gaze, May looked too, and saw a small hole in his trouser leg just below the knee, with a matching hole on the other side.

Peter's expression cleared. 'That explains what knocked it off kilter.' He grinned up at Mrs Bowes and rapped his leg so she could hear the hollow knock. 'Four years too late to do any lasting damage.' He rolled up his trouser leg and examined where the bullet had drilled clean through the prosthetic limb. 'A nice souvenir of the day.'

'Bless my soul,' said Mrs Bowes. She bustled out, her hand pressed to her chest.

But May couldn't take it as lightly as Peter. The bullet hole wasn't an amusing souvenir, but a sign of how close Peter had come to losing his life. Her hands started to shake again. Tea slopped over the rim of her cup, forcing her to place it back on the saucer instead of taking the drink she craved.

'May!' Peter gave an exclamation and covered her cold, trembling hand with his warm, strong one. 'There's no harm done.'

'Not this time.' She jerked her hand away and balled both fists in her lap. 'But what about tomorrow and the day after that? And every day you're out there in your Hurricane? Can you promise me the bullets will miss you every time?' The words poured out like a torrent. All the fear she'd held back wouldn't be denied.

Much to her annoyance, Peter gave a slow smile. 'So you do care.'

'I —' But she couldn't deny it, any more than she could voice her true feelings for him. Her throat closed. Why did life have to be so complicated? She'd

284

joined the WAAF in search of independence. Instead her heart had become hopelessly bound. 'Be serious. Please,' was all she could say.

Peter propped his elbows on the table and leaned forward, his smile fading. 'I'm always serious about my feelings for you,' he said. May's heart gave a little swoop. She opened her mouth, but Peter held up his hand to stop her. 'You don't have to say anything. I understand you better than you think. You're holding back because you're not ready. You've been little more than a slave to your father and brothers, and now you want to stretch your wings and discover who you are. And you should. It's too soon for you to tie yourself to another man. I do understand. Just know that I'll be waiting when you're ready.'

May took a hasty sip from her cup to hide the tears that sprang to her eyes. For so long her own feelings and thoughts had been ignored, it was almost too much to find someone who understood her so well. It gave her the courage to say what she'd only been able to say to Evie and Jess. 'Are you leaving because of me?'

Peter shook his head. 'No. You must believe me. I was thinking of this long before I first met you. This is something I have to do. For years, flying was the only thing that meant a damn to me. When I had the accident, I thought I'd never be able to fly again. I tried to be satisfied working in Ops, but when I learned that there were other pilots who had learnt to fly again after terrible injuries, it gave me hope. I want to play my part, and right now we need pilots more than we need controllers. I wouldn't sleep easy if I stayed safely behind a desk while others were out there facing danger in my place.'

Some of the weight of guilt lifted. 'Promise you'll be careful. I . . . I *do* care about you.' It was the best she could manage.

'I won't do anything reckless. You have my word.' He studied his cup for a moment then raised his eyes to meet hers. 'I'll write to you. Will you write back?'

Her heart lifted. 'Yes. I'd like that.' She would treasure every word of his, and maybe she would be able to include in her letters the words she was unable to say.

Peter's face lit up, his eyes creasing. 'Thank you. Remember, I haven't given up on you, May Lidford, so don't give up on yourself.'

22

Evie's head was swimming by the end of her watch. The attack hadn't lasted long, but after the observers reported the departure of the last of the Messerschmitt Bf 110s, the Ops Room had been abuzz with reports of the damage. Evie could picture the scene above ground, as people rushed to mark the positions of unexploded shells and to fill in the craters left by the bombs that had exploded. The last hour of her watch was spent waiting tensely for news of a fresh wave of attack, but as the minutes stretched out and no further hostile plots were announced, she allowed herself to relax. Her limbs felt heavy as though she had personally fought every battle instead of merely plotting them.

Jess tapped her arm as soon as they were relieved. 'Come on. I want to find May.'

May! Evie's weariness fell away. No reports of deaths had filtered down to them, but there had been several injuries caused by shrapnel. Evie couldn't relax until she knew May was safe and unhurt. They raced up the steps.

To Evie's relief, the damage wasn't as extensive as she'd feared. She could see that a hangar had been flattened, and the ground crew were busy filling in holes on the airfield, but the main buildings were untouched. May would still be on duty, so Evie and Jess directed their walk towards the Transport section. May could usually be found tinkering with an

287

engine or polishing the cars, but there was no sign of her.

A WAAF with sergeant's stripes was directing a couple of newly arrived WAAFs. After she had finished and turned to her own vehicle, Evie and Jess hurried up to her.

'We're looking for May Lidford,' Evie said. 'She wasn't hurt, was she?'

The sergeant gave a grim smile. 'She's fine. I've just heard the road's been bombed, though. She's stuck on the other side of the river.'

Evie tried to picture the geography of the area. If May couldn't cross the river by road, she'd have to get back on foot, through woods and over hills. 'How is she going to get back?'

'Apparently a local farmer can take her across the next bridge then get her across the fields in his tractor.' The sergeant turned away, clearly impatient to get on with her work.

'Come on,' Jess said to Evie. 'Let's go and find some food. I could eat now we know May is safe.'

They were halfway to the canteen when Evie caught a glimpse of Flight Officer Ellerby, who was consulting a clipboard and directing a group of WAAFs who seemed to be setting up a makeshift first-aid point. 'Save me a seat,' she said to Jess. 'There's something I have to do first.'

She dashed up to Ellerby and saluted.

'What do you want, Bishop? As you can see, I'm very busy.'

Jean Ellerby might have got over her initial dislike of Evie, but this was hardly the most encouraging start. Nevertheless, Evie plucked up her courage. 'I'd like to speak to you when it's convenient, ma'am.'

'What about?'

Evie bit her lip. She'd hoped to delay that until she'd had a chance to frame her request. But it was too late to back down now. She drew a deep breath and said, 'I've been thinking about officer training, ma'am. I wanted to find out what opportunities there are and whether you would recommend me.'

There was a long pause while Jean Ellerby regarded her steadily. Evie felt a flare of resentment that a woman not much older than her could make her feel like a naughty schoolgirl being hauled up in front of the headmistress. She straightened her back and thrust out her chin. She would show Flight Officer Ellerby she wasn't intimidated by her any longer.

Finally, the section officer gave a curt nod. 'As I recall, you're off duty at eighteen hundred hours. Come and see me then.' She strode away without waiting for a reply.

Evie sagged with relief then dashed to catch up with Jess. Someone as blunt as Jean Ellerby would have told her on the spot if she didn't think Evie was officer material. She must think Evie stood a good chance of being accepted if she had agreed to a meeting.

'What was all that about?' Jess asked when Evie caught up with her at the entrance to the NAAFI.

'Nothing much, I'll tell you later,' Evie replied. There was no point in saying anything until she'd heard what Ellerby had to say.

Thankfully their next watch was quieter. The Germans must have given up trying to destroy their station because no hostile aircraft came close. They dispatched a couple of flights to intercept bandits detected off the coast but each time the German aircraft fled for the French coast after a brief engagement.

289

'Ending a watch when none of our pilots were injured is the best feeling,' Jess said as they emerged from The Hole.

Evie was about to answer when an extraordinary sight caught her eye: a tractor spattered in mud was trundling through the gates. Perched on the seat beside the driver was none other than May. She caught sight of Jess and Evie and waved madly. The tractor jerked to a halt outside the Admin block, and May climbed down.

'What a day I've had,' May exclaimed when the girls ran up to greet her. 'We had to go miles out of our way to get here.'

'Are you all right?' Jess asked, looking May up and down. 'You look like you've been dragged through a hedge backwards.'

'Actually, it was headfirst.' May gave a brief account of her adventures. 'I know I must look a fright, but I'd love a lager and lime right now. Are you two off duty?' She turned to the driver. 'Will you join us, Mr Bowes? I owe you a drink after all your help.'

'I can manage a quick one,' Mr Bowes replied. 'Only a quick one, mind. The missus will have my head on a pitchfork if I'm home too late.' He gestured to the tractor. 'Hop aboard if you're coming. You can arrive in style.'

'I'm game.' Jess hitched up her skirt and climbed aboard. 'Coming, Evie? We deserve a break after the day we've had.'

'I'll meet you there. There's something I've got to do first.' It was time for her chat with Flight Officer Ellerby and being late would hardly be the way to convince her that Evie was officer material.

When she got to Ellerby's office, Evie paused to

straighten her uniform then knocked at the door.

'Come in.'

Evie pushed open the door and saluted smartly. It took a supreme effort to keep her back straight after spending most of the day hunched over the plotting table. At Ellerby's invitation, she took a seat and mentally rehearsed her request. She'd gone over it in her head ever since the flight officer had agreed to see her, but she couldn't for the life of her remember what she had decided to say.

'Tell me what this is about, Bishop. Make it brief. It's been a difficult day.'

'This won't take long, ma'am.' Evie groped for the right words. 'I . . . I've been wondering for some time about the opportunity to do officer training,' she stammered finally.

Jean leaned forward, regarding Evie with a thoughtful gaze. 'And what decided you to ask?'

'I . . .' *I'll go mad if I spend every day gazing at a block of wood on a map that shows exactly how much danger Alex is in.* But that wouldn't go down well. She summoned up the Evie who had impressed the interview panel at Somerville. Straightening her shoulders fractionally, she said, 'I've learnt a lot as a plotter, and from comments I've had from some officers, I think I've contributed a lot, too. But now I feel I've reached the limit of what I can achieve, and I want to stretch myself.'

'In other words, you feel your intelligence is wasted as a plotter.'

'Oh, no, I didn't mean —' Evie could feel her cheeks burning.

'As a matter of fact, I agree.'

'I . . . What?' Evie was so shocked, she completely

291

forgot she was addressing an officer.

The corners of Ellerby's mouth twitched in what could almost be described as a smile. 'I agree. You have talents that could be put to far better use elsewhere.'

'Oh. Thank you.' Evie blew out a shaky breath, knowing full well that if she'd spoken to Jean Ellerby like that a few months ago, she'd have been scrubbing out the latrines for a week, special duties or not.

But Jean wasn't finished. 'Never apologise for possessing intelligence, Bishop. For as long as you continue in the WAAF, and in your chosen field of study, you'll be faced with men with less intelligence than you who, unaccountably, always seem to get the accolades.' There was something in her eyes that made Evie think the flight officer spoke from bitter experience. It occurred to her then that she had never stopped to wonder what had turned Jean Ellerby into the strict, friendless officer she had so loathed on her arrival. 'Men never hide their intelligence, never apologise for it. Nor should you.'

For a moment Evie was reminded of Cornelia. It struck her then how lucky she was to have had such women in her life to guide her. 'Thank you. I'll remember that.'

'See that you do.' Jean glanced at a file on her desk. 'Now, I see no reason why you shouldn't succeed at officer training. Not only has your performance in Ops been exemplary, you've also been invaluable with teaching English to the Czech pilots.'

Evie glowed with pride. She had only been doing her duty, but it felt good to know her hard work was appreciated.

'I'm going to recommend you for Filterer Officer

292

training. Your work as a plotter and your mathematical abilities make you eminently suitable.'

'Thank you.' From her initial training as a plotter, Evie knew that Filterer Officers worked in the Filter Rooms of each Group HQ. Their work was to process all the information fed to them from the Chain Home stations and present them as plots which were then passed to their Group's Operations Room and on to the Operations Rooms of each sector station. It was a hugely responsible and complicated task.

But you can do it. Believe in yourself, Evie Bishop. It was as though she could hear Cornelia saying those words to her.

'Very well.' Jean Ellerby rose. Evie, too, got to her feet. 'I'll process the forms and you'll be notified when you have a place on the training course. If you pass that — which I have no doubt you will — you'll then need to go through standard officer training.'

Evie saluted and turned to leave, but Jean called her back. 'One other thing, Bishop. You might want to encourage those two friends of yours to see me for similar conversations.'

Evie was unable to stop the huge grin splitting her face. 'I will, ma'am. Thank you.'

She floated from the office as light as air. The one thing that had worried her about going for promotion was leaving Jess and May behind. Being an officer while her two closest friends were mere aircraftwomen wouldn't be easy. She wouldn't feel so bad about being posted elsewhere if her friends would also be moving on.

She glanced at her watch. Plenty of time to celebrate at the Horse and Groom before she had to be back for her next watch. She hurried to find her bike.

★ ★ ★

The farmer who had brought May back to Amberton drained his glass and rose. 'It's been lovely meeting you girls, but I must be off. Take care, both of you.'

Jess watched him leave, then did what she'd been dying to do ever since she'd seen May arrive. She scrabbled in her gas mask case for her comb and compact and pressed them into May's hands. 'For goodness' sake, go and tidy yourself up. I didn't spend months teaching you how to make the most of your looks only for you to sit here looking like a scarecrow.'

May left without a protest. She hadn't been out of the snug long when the outer door opened, and Evie appeared, accompanied by three pilots from Brimstone squadron. Jess's heart gave a little flutter when she saw Milan stroll in and catch her eye. He pointed at her empty glass then at the bar and raised his eyebrows in a question. Jess gave him a nod, and Milan went to the bar.

Evie dashed over, her face flushed.

'You're looking happy, yet no sign of Alex,' Jess said with a grin.

'Milan says he's catching up with his paperwork,' Evie replied. 'But that doesn't matter. I have news.' She looked around. 'Where's May?'

'Gone to comb out the twigs from her hair. Nearly getting bombed to bits is no excuse to go around looking as though half the crows in the world have nested in your hair.'

At that point May emerged from the cloakroom looking far more like the elegant young woman she'd become in recent weeks.

Evie beckoned May over with a frantic gesture.

Jess looked at her in surprise. What could have happened in the short time since Evie had mysteriously disappeared at the station? 'Hurry up and sit down. I've got something to tell you, and I don't want the others to hear yet.'

May took her seat, but Evie, maddeningly, didn't speak. She studied her fingernails, a small frown puckered between her brows.

'Come on, then. Spit it out.' Jess half wanted to hear Evie's news and was half afraid. Had Alex asked her to marry him? Whatever her reservations, Evie would have said yes. Women didn't turn down a man like Alex Kincaith. Then everything would change. Evie would drift away from their close friendship. Jess only had two friends: Evie and May. She couldn't bear to lose either of them.

'I've just been to see Flight Officer Ellerby,' Evie began in a low voice.

Relief made Jess vocal. 'What did you want with that dried-up old bat?'

Evie laughed. 'Hardly old. She can't be more than her late twenties. And she's not so bad once you get to know her.'

Jess snorted. 'I admit she wasn't so bad when we got bombed, but that was only because she was out cold.'

Evie's lips twitched. 'Maybe it would be more accurate to say she's improved.'

'But why did you see her?' May leaned forward, her elbow dangerously close to a puddle of beer. Jess deftly whipped out her handkerchief and mopped up the spill before May could ruin her tunic.

Evie blew out a breath. 'Don't go mad until you've heard me out. I asked her about officer training.'

'You're going to be an officer?' May's eyes opened wide.

For once, Jess was at a loss for words. She swallowed against the sudden tightness in her throat. If Evie went for officer training, she would be transferred elsewhere. Their tight-knit group would break up. The kind of friendship she had yearned for all her life would be gone almost before she'd known it.

'I don't know yet. That's why I don't want anyone else to hear. They'd be bound to tell Alex, and I don't want him to know yet.'

'Why not?' Jess forced the words through lips frozen in what she hoped looked like a genuine smile.

'I want him to hear it from me. Only when it's definite I'm leaving.' Evie fiddled with a beer mat, lining it exactly against the corner of the table. She addressed her next words to the mat. 'I love him. I know I do. But . . .' She shot a glance at May then tilted her head to the side as though choosing her words. 'I need to be sure about him. In Oxford, he swept me off my feet. It was like being in a Hollywood picture. But this is real life, and if things are going to work between us, I need to know he respects my opinion. Considers me an equal. I need to know if he'll support my studies and career after the war, not expect me to stay at home and be a housewife.'

Jess swallowed. She felt a heel, resenting Evie moving on. No one deserved success and happiness more than her. She squeezed Evie's hand. 'So this is a test. A first step. Will he encourage you or resent you furthering your career?'

'Exactly.' Evie's eyes shone. 'Ellerby is putting me forward for Filterer Officer training. It's exactly what I want to do — it's more mathematical, so it will keep

296

my brain sharp for going to Oxford if this damn war ever ends.'

'Filterer Officer.' Jess tried to hide the dismay in her voice. 'That means you'd end up in one of the Group HQs.'

Evie's smile faded, along with the glow in her eyes. 'I know. That's the one thing that's made me hesitate. I don't want to leave the two of you.'

'You'll be leaving Alex too,' Jess reminded her.

'That was actually another reason to go. You can't imagine how awful it's been, knowing exactly where he is all the time, knowing how many German fighters he's facing. I don't think I can do it much longer without going mad.'

There was a pause while they all processed this. May chewed her lip, and Jess knew she was thinking of Peter. She was about to ask her how she was faring now Peter had left, but Evie broke across her.

'There's something else. Ellerby told me you should both think about officer training.'

'Us?' Jess couldn't believe Jean Ellerby might consider her worthy of promotion.

'Yes. Both of you. She's changed her tune about you ever since you were stuck in that bomb shelter.'

'We would never get posted together,' May said.

'No, but you know what life is like in the WAAF. They're constantly moving people around. Even if none of us applied for promotion, the chances are, we'd be split up before much longer.'

That made sense to Jess. The likelihood was they would each be transferred at some point so even if none of them applied for officer training, they were unlikely to spend the duration of the war together. 'If we were all officers, it would be easier to socialise

297

when we did see each other. You know how stuffy some people can be about officers not mixing with the rest of us.'

'What do you mean, officers can't mix with you?' Milan arrived and placed the four glasses he'd been skilfully holding upon the table.

'We weren't talking about you, of course.' Jess shifted to give Milan room and changed the subject. But even as she asked May for more details about her narrow escape, the thought of promotion buzzed around her head. Hellerby thought she was a suitable candidate! No one ever thought she was good at anything. Until now. After all those failed auditions, being grateful for every walk-on part and place in a chorus line, she'd never expected to find success in the WAAF. An escape, yes, but not a fulfilling career. But did she really want to leave Amberton? She shot a sideways glance at Milan. There was something about the handsome Czech pilot that had got under her skin and she would miss him if she was posted elsewhere. Having said that, Evie was right: sooner or later they would be moved anyway. Wasn't it best to go on her own terms?

There was no harm in seeing Hellerby. She could always decline if she decided against it in the end. But wherever she ended up, she promised herself she would keep in touch with May and Evie.

'What do you think, Jess?' Evie's voice roused Jess from her thoughts. She started and looked round to see all eyes on her.

'I'm sorry. I was miles away.'

Evie grinned. 'We could see that. We were discussing whether Milan should buy a car.'

'Best wait until the road's repaired.'

298

Milan shrugged. 'It won't take long. Then I can take you all to the seaside.' He sighed. 'We don't have a coast in Czechoslovakia. It's a shame I can only see your coast in the wartime, when all the beaches are covered with wire.'

He looked so wistful Jess felt a twist of pity. She covered his hand with her own. 'You're on. Next time we can arrange a day's pass at the same time, we'll go to the sea.'

'I would like that.' Milan's fingers were warm beneath hers, long and strong. His gaze met hers and the noise of the pub seemed to fade away.

'I . . .' Her brain had suddenly turned to mush. What had she been about to say? Say something. Anything. 'Er . . . where do you go on holiday if you can't go to the sea?' Her voice sounded breathless. Milan's thumb stroked the side of her palm. She snatched her hand away.

'Lakes or mountains.'

Jess had to think for a moment to remember what she had asked him in the first place. 'Are they near your home?'

Milan shook his head. 'I live in Prague.' His face changed. It was like a cloud moving across the sun as the light disappeared from his eyes. 'Or I did, before the Germans came.'

May leaned forward. 'Karol was telling me about Prague the other day. He said it was very beautiful.' Good old May, trying to cheer Milan up. Jess was grateful to her intervention, because she could think of little else save the lingering warmth in the hand that had touched Milan's.

Milan snatched at the offered comfort. 'It is. More beautiful than any other city in the world.' His accent became more obvious as he spoke, his eyes focused on a point a thousand miles away.

'Did you know Karol before the war? He said he used to go to a club . . .' A pucker formed between May's brows. 'A funny name. Dovey Vrahn. Or something.'

Milan's face creased in a smile, the sun dawning again. 'Dvě Vrány?'

'That was it. Do you know it?'

'I did. It was very popular. It closed down some years ago.'

May shook her head. 'You must be thinking of a different club. Karol said he went there the last night he was in Prague, to say goodbye. What else did he say?' She tapped the side of her glass, frowning into her drink before looking up. 'I know. He said it was on an island. Something to do with tents.'

'Tents?' Then Milan's face cleared. 'Kampa Island?'

May giggled. 'I knew it was something to do with tents.'

'But that's the club I thought you meant. Dvě Vrány.' Milan shrugged. 'It's on Kampa Island. Or was. Like I said, it closed years ago, in about 1935. Karol can't have been there last year.'

Evie glanced between May and Milan, frowning. 'Why would he lie?'

Milan shrugged. 'Who knows?' Then he grinned. 'Perhaps he really comes from Moravia and is too ashamed to say.'

Another Czech pilot happened to pass the table, and Milan hailed him. 'Hey, Jiří. We think Karol is really a *křupan* from Moravia.'

Jiří paused. 'You may be right. The other day, I asked where in Prague he lived, and he said Vyšehrad.

I asked which street because he might know my uncle. He changed the subject.' He grinned. 'Imagine if he's really a farmer from Moravia!' Jess had learned a little of the rivalry between Bohemia and Moravia while teaching English to the pilots. The Bohemians considered themselves superior to the Moravians, more educated and cultured. The Moravians thought the Bohemians were snobbish and unfriendly.

Milan glanced around. 'Where is he, anyway? He's supposed to be back today.'

'He left a message. Couldn't get past the bridge. He's going to try going the long way around across the fields tomorrow.'

'May managed it,' said Jess indignantly. 'He should have made more effort.'

Jiří shrugged. 'It will save on ammo.'

'What's that supposed to mean?'

Jiří opened his mouth to answer, but Milan spoke to him sharply in Czech. Jiří looked chastened and walked away.

'What was that about?'

'I warned him not to spread rumours.'

'What rumours?' An idea was forming in Jess's mind. From the sudden lift of Evie's eyebrows, she could tell Evie was thinking the same thing.

'I shouldn't say,' Milan replied, shifting in his seat as though unable to get comfortable.

Evie leaned across the table. 'Milan, I promise we won't speak of this to anyone else, but this might be important. What did Jiří mean about saving ammo?'

Milan chewed his lower lip and glanced around at the three girls. 'Promise me this won't go any further?' When the girls all nodded, he said, 'Karol often runs out of ammo before the rest of us, which means he breaks off an attack early. Some of the pilots think he's afraid to fight, that he fires his guns over the sea to empty them before he returns to the station.'

'Does Alex know?' Evie asked.

Milan nodded. 'He's had a word with Karol already about wasting ammo. I think he's reluctant to take it further. The RAF doesn't approve of cowardice.'

Jess nodded. She'd heard tales of pilots accused of 'lacking moral fibre'. In some cases, they'd been transferred to the ground crew on remote stations, treated like lepers.

'I think he wants to give Karol a chance,' Milan continued. 'Some of the lads are running out of patience, though. They say he's a danger to the rest of us.'

Jess would have asked more, but Evie glanced at her watch. 'Goodness,' she said, 'Jess, we're back on watch in half an hour.'

Jess sprang to her feet. If she was going to pursue promotion, she mustn't have any black marks against her name.

Milan rose as well. 'I'll walk you back.'

'That's very kind, but it's still light.' Evie shot Jess a look, which Jess interpreted as a plea for her to agree.

'We'll be fine, Milan. Anyway, I wanted to ask Evie's advice on how I should cut my hair. You'd find our conversation terribly dull.'

May must also have interpreted Evie's stare, for she rose. 'I'll come back with you. I could use a bath and an early night after the day I've had.'

'Very well.' Before Jess knew what he'd planned, Milan lifted her hand to his lips and kissed it. '*Na shledanou.*'

The back of her hand burned long after she'd left the pub.

Evie waited until they were out of earshot of those sitting at tables outside, enjoying the warmth of the evening. She collected her bike and pushed it alongside Jess and May. Her heart pounded with excitement at what she'd just heard, but she managed to contain herself until she knew they couldn't be overheard.

'Spit it out, Evie,' Jess said finally. 'We both know you're dying to say something. We could have had another quarter of an hour at the pub.'

Evie wondered if Jess had wanted to spend more time with Milan. Milan certainly had seemed keen. She wondered why Jess, who flirted with all the men, was always more reserved when with the handsome Czech pilot. Then she pushed the thought from her head. What she had to say couldn't wait. 'What if Karol is the saboteur? Don't you find it suspicious that he says he comes from Prague, but didn't know a well-known club had closed down?'

'I wondered that,' May said, 'but he's Czech. I thought the Czechs hated the Nazis even more than us.'

'What if he's not Czech? What if he's a German spy?' Then Evie remembered something else. 'That reminds me. I met him in the woods once, and I thought there was something odd going on.' She explained about the metallic tapping noise she'd heard. 'I didn't think much of it at the time, but it could have been a Morse key.'

May came to a sudden stop, nearly tripping Evie, who'd been walking slightly behind. 'I drove him to the railway station the other day. He wouldn't let go of his suitcase the whole way there.'

Evie felt the hairs rise on the nape of her neck. 'This is it,' she said. 'It's him. It has to be.'

'But what can we do?' Jess asked. 'All we have is rumour. No actual evidence. I'll admit Karol's a bit too oily for my liking, but that's no grounds to accuse him of spying.'

Evie walked on in silence for a while. The only sound was the rattle of her bicycle chain. 'I'll talk to Alex,' she said eventually. 'He'll know what to do.' She paused again, then said, 'I hope to God he takes me seriously this time.'

23

Evie got her chance to speak to Alex late the next morning during her first two-hour break of the day. Brimstone squadron had returned from Tangmere the previous evening, but several pilots had suffered flesh wounds and most of their Hurricanes needed repairs. The station commander had taken the decision to stand the squadron down for two days to give everyone a chance to recover and get their Hurricanes back to working order. That left Alex free to meet Evie after her watch; Evie, wanting some peace after a frantic morning, elected to go for a walk.

They left the station together and strolled up the lane, heading for the wooded hillside behind the station. As soon as they were outside the gate, Alex tucked her arm inside his, and Evie leaned against his shoulder, enjoying this rare moment of closeness. The worry of yesterday still lingered in her mind, and she observed him sidelong, looking for any sign of injury. It was a great comfort to discover him whole and well. She breathed in the faint scent of soap and cigarette smoke that always seemed to linger about his person. The roar of aero engines filled the air as six Hurricanes from one of the other squadrons took off. She watched them climb until they disappeared into the clouds. It was easier to admire their graceful flight when she knew Alex was safe on the ground.

She hated to break this moment of peace, but her news was too urgent to delay. When they reached the stile that gave access to the woodland path, she paused. 'Alex, I heard something yesterday that got me thinking. Please hear me out before you say anything.'

To his credit, Alex didn't interrupt while Evie outlined her reasons for suspecting Karol. When she finished, he leant against a fence post and fingered one of the stems of cow parsley that nearly hid the stile from view. 'Who else have you told?'

'Only Jess and May, and they know better than to gossip.' Evie still stung at Alex's refusal to believe neither of her friends had spread the tale of the sabotage.

'Make sure that they don't.' Alex let go of Evie's arm and raked his fingers through his hair. 'Do you have any idea what you're suggesting? You think a member of my own squadron is a spy?'

'I know they're like a family to you but think about it. How well do you really know them?'

Alex opened his mouth but then seemed to change his mind and looked back at the cow parsley, shaking his head. 'We have to rely on one another. If I let suspicion into the ranks, the squadron will fall apart.'

There was a note of finality in his tone that made Evie grit her teeth. Was that it? Alex, her lord and master, had spoken so she was expected to accept his word as law? She couldn't let it go; the stakes were too high. 'If you have a spy in your midst, the squadron's in far greater danger.'

Alex gazed at her for a moment, the corners of his mouth pulled down. A tight knot formed in Evie's stomach; she hated being at odds with him when their time together was so precious. 'Alex, you must —'

Alex tore away his gaze and snapped off the head of cow parsley with unnecessary force. 'Give me a

306

moment to think. Not only have you just announced a member of my squadron is a spy, you've also clearly been asking around when I told you not to.'

He reached for her hand, but she jerked it away. 'That's so unfair. Believe it or not, the whole thing about Karol came out in conversation with Milan. I wasn't even thinking about the saboteur at the time but pardon me for realising it might help you find him.' Alex's eyes widened in shock, but she couldn't seem to stop the words pouring from her mouth. 'Next time I learn something that might save lives I'll keep it to myself, shall I?'

She glared at him, daring him to snap back at her. For the space of several seconds, counted out by the painful pounding of her heart against her ribs, Alex said nothing. Then he closed his eyes and sank onto the stile with a groan. He reached up and pulled her down to sit beside him. This time she didn't resist.

'God, Evie, I'm sorry. I don't know what I'm saying. I just' — he swallowed and clasped her hand more tightly — 'I cannae bear to think of anything happening to you.'

The broadening of his accent was a sure sign he was upset; the fight drained out of her as she remembered May's opinion that Alex was trying to protect her. 'I worry about you, too, but I don't try and stop you from flying. I know it's something you have to do and something you love. The flying, not the fighting.' She was starting to babble. She gathered her thoughts and tried again. 'What I'm trying to say is you need to let me do my duty, do the things I love and . . .' She fumbled for the right words then abandoned the attempt. 'Oh, I can't explain myself. I'm a mathematician, remember. I'm better with numbers than words.' She was relieved to see the beginnings of a smile tug at the corners of Alex's mouth.

'I think you explained yourself better than you think,' he said. He rose, tugging her to her feet. 'Let's not spoil our walk.' He put his foot upon the stile then paused and looked back at her. 'I promise I'll think about what you said. I do value your opinion. I hope you realise that.'

Some of the tightness in her gut eased. 'Thank you.'

Once over the stile, they walked into the woods. Now September had arrived, the first signs of autumn were appearing. The brambles were weighed down with ripe blackberries, and wasps and hoverflies hummed around the heavy, purple fruit. The edges of the beech leaves were tinged with the faintest signs of gold. Here and there Evie could see horse chestnut trees, their branches bowing under the weight of spiky green conkers.

They strolled on, their footfalls muffled by the crumbled remains of last year's fallen leaves. Eventually Alex spoke again. 'If you had firm evidence, I could investigate, but I won't ruin a man's chances because of hearsay and supposition. There are logical explanations for all your suspicions. If you'd seen him use a transmitter that would have been different.'

Evie sighed, not having an answer. The trouble was, now she came to relate her suspicions, they did sound feeble. As Milan had pointed out at the pub, just because Karol didn't come from Prague when he'd said he did, it didn't make him a spy. He could simply be ashamed of his origins. She wished more than ever that she'd seen what he was doing in the woods.

'I'm sorry,' she said. 'I didn't mean to heap more worry on your head.'

Alex spoke again. 'I'll keep an eye on him. I can promise you that, at least.'

She knew she should be satisfied with that, but she couldn't let go of the worry that Karol would cause more harm unless he was stopped. If Alex couldn't, or wouldn't, investigate, she would have to keep watch on him herself.

It was just one more thing to keep from Alex. She wondered if she should tell him about her decision to go for officer training. In the end she decided against it. She still didn't know if she'd be accepted on the course, and she didn't want to break it to Alex that she would be leaving Amberton until she knew for certain.

★ ★ ★

After parting company with Evie by the entrance to Ops, Alex wandered aimlessly for a while. Try as he might, he couldn't shake Evie's argument from his mind. Was she right? Had he been harbouring a spy and a saboteur all this time? No. He pushed aside the thought with an effort. Surely he would have noticed something wrong by now if it were true.

You've already had to speak to him about wasting ammo. The thought prodded at him, but he did his best to ignore it. He turned his face to the sky, determined to enjoy the sun on a rare day of freedom.

It felt strange being in the midst of a hive of activity with nothing particular to do. Teams of men clustered around bomb craters, filling them in, while others repaired shattered windows. By tomorrow, Amberton

309

would look like it had never suffered an attack.

The drone of approaching aircraft made him look up in time to see two Hurricanes skimming the hedge at the far end of the airfield. Black smoke poured from the engine of one; Alex held his breath as it touched down. An ambulance and a fire engine tore down the field towards it, bells ringing.

'Open the canopy,' Alex muttered. 'Don't get trapped.'

He watched, dry-mouthed, as the Hurricane taxied to a halt well away from the dispersal pens. The ground crew flung down their tools and raced towards it, shouting, probably screaming at the pilot to get out, but Alex couldn't hear from this distance. Flames were licking around the fuselage by this time, but the canopy was still closed; the fire crew sprayed water while two of them climbed onto the wing. But then the fuselage caught fire with a rush of flame, and the rescuers barely had time to fling themselves clear before the cockpit was consumed. Alex felt sick but couldn't tear his eyes from the scene. He was too far away to see but imagined he could see hands clawing at the canopy from inside.

It seemed to take an eternity for the fire fighters to douse the flames. By the time they were able to force the canopy open, Alex knew it would be too late. He watched as the rescuers pulled the pilot's limp form from the cockpit and lowered him to a stretcher. One of the ambulance crew draped a blanket over the pilot, then they loaded the stretcher into the ambulance and slammed the doors. It drove away slowly. No bell ringing. No dash to save a life.

The stricken Hurricane had belonged to Catseye squadron. Alex found his feet directing him to their dispersal hut. As he walked his mind returned yet again to what Evie had told him about Karol. No matter how it pained him to consider one of his men might be a spy, he couldn't seem to shake off the suspicion.

James Fitzpatrick, Catseye's squadron leader, leant against the rear wall of Catseye's dispersal hut, smoke spiralling from a cigarette in his hand. As Alex approached, he raised it to his lips with a shaking hand and took a long draw then blew out a stream of smoke in a shuddering exhale.

'Ghastly way to go.' Fitz jerked his head in the direction of the still smouldering Hurricane. 'That's two men bought it today.'

'Who?'

'Walker and Parsons.'

Alex bowed his head, studying the dozens of trampled cigarette butts around his feet. He didn't know Parsons, but Flight Lieutenant Rob Walker had been at Amberton longer than he had. He'd been one of the station's most experienced pilots. If he could be shot down, what chance did anyone else have?

'Was that you in the other Hurricane?'

James nodded. 'There were three of us out on a routine patrol.' He raised his cigarette to his lips again, but not quick enough to hide the way the corner of his mouth convulsed. 'It's like they knew we were going to be there,' he said, wreathed in another cloud of smoke. 'I swear those 109s were waiting to bounce us.'

Alex said nothing. What could he say? He knew the helpless feeling of unaccountably surviving when others had died, knew the relentless, exhausting cycle of self-doubt. Was there anything he could have

311

done differently? Why was he still alive when the others weren't? In the end, the only way he'd been able to function was to slam the door on his inner voice and focus on getting through each day one step at a time. Or that's how he'd operated until Evie had come along. Now he found himself getting painful glimpses of a possible future with her, a bittersweet longing for a life he would probably never have. It was growing harder and harder to take each day as it came.

James finished his cigarette, flung it down and ground it beneath his heel. 'Better get back. Letters to write. God knows what I'm going to say to Parsons' mother. He was only here a week.'

He moved to walk away but Alex stopped him. 'Wait. I'm trying to track down some of my pilots.' What was he saying? He didn't suspect Karol. But James's words were going through his mind: *it's like they knew we were going to be there.* 'Have any of my lads been hanging around here today?'

'That Karol was here earlier. Not here now, though.'

Alex heard the last few words through a dull roar in his ears. Somehow, he managed to force out the words, 'Send him to me if he turns up again.' Then he was walking away, towards Brimstone's dispersal hut, on legs that didn't seem quite connected to his body.

His pilots might be stood down, but the dispersal pens were swarming with ground crew patching holes, mending instrument panels and servicing the engines. Thankfully Sergeant Rawlins was out of earshot of the others, whistling cheerfully as he adjusted the gun sights of Alex's Hurricane. Without giving himself a chance to reconsider, Alex strode up to the sergeant and said, 'I want to see the gun camera footage from Pilot Officer Šimek's machine.'

24

24

The sun had already set when Evie and Jess trudged out of The Hole after their last watch of the day.

Jess yawned. 'Thank goodness we've got the night off.'

A kind sergeant with a blackout torch helped to direct them to their bikes. He insisted upon checking the shielding on their front lights before letting them ride off.

'If this watch system carries on much longer, I'll definitely be applying for officer training,' Jess remarked as she pushed off and climbed into her saddle.

'I won't miss the to and fro in the dark,' Evie agreed. 'But I'll miss everything else.' Alex and her friends most of all. She half dreaded getting confirmation of a place on the Filterer Officers' training course. She found herself hoping her orders would arrive after the present crisis was over. The general feeling was that if they could hold out until October, the Germans would be forced to delay their planned invasion.

The girls didn't speak much during their ride. They needed all their concentration to navigate the twists and turns of the lane in the darkness. Now the nights were drawing in, more and more of their rides would be in darkness. Evie still considered it worth it for the privilege of living in High Chalk House. Wherever she ended up, she doubted she'd ever have a billet as good as the one she had here. Her late-night cocoa and gossip sessions with Jess and May in the cosy schoolroom would soon be a thing of the past.

Before long, Evie sensed rather than saw the patch of deeper darkness that indicated they had reached the gateway. They turned into the drive, their tyres crunching on the gravel, and steered for the back of the house. After propping their bikes against the wall, they went in through the scullery door, which was always left unlocked to accommodate the girls working odd hours.

Up in the schoolroom, Evie was delighted to find a letter waiting for her on the mantelpiece addressed in Cornelia's elegant copperplate handwriting. May must have brought it back, knowing Evie would be too tired to check for post at the end of an exhausting day. She snatched it up and curled up in an armchair, kicking off her shoes, while Jess, yawning, retired to her room.

The opening paragraphs contained news of a paper Cornelia was writing on the applications of lambda calculus. Evie skimmed them, promising herself she would read it properly tomorrow. What she wanted to know was the answer to her question about Alex and officer training. She found it in the fourth paragraph.

My dear, you must seize this new opportunity with both hands. You don't know how long this war will last, so do the job that plays to your strengths and where you can find the most fulfilment. Assuming the war does end soon, and you decide to take up your studies again, having worked in a mathematical field will stand you in good stead.

I was delighted you introduced me to Alex Kincaith while you were in Oxford. I found him a most thoughtful, steady young man. However, on the question of your relationship I can only give general advice. Matters of the heart are not as easily resolved as mathematical equations. What I can say with certainty is that you must consider very carefully if your young man loves you for who you are or who he wants you to be. If the latter, you'll never be truly happy with him. When I was an undergraduate at Oxford I met and fell in love with a charming man. I even agreed to marry him. I thought because he knew I was reading maths that he would understand I wanted to pursue an academic career. It turned out that he assumed I would abandon my career and be happy to be his unpaid housekeeper while he pursued his own career. Ending our engagement was the hardest thing I've ever done, but I've never regretted it. He would never have accepted me as I am. If your young man does love you for who you are, if he encourages you to become the best version of yourself, then you've found a rare treasure.

Evie read Cornelia's words through several times, her heart full. She'd never pictured Cornelia as a young woman in love before. It was funny to think of the tweedy academic as a late Victorian girl complete with sweeping gown and full bustle. But her words resonated with Evie. *If he encourages you to become the best version of yourself.* Yes, that was what she needed from a relationship. It was why she had found such good friends in Jess and Evie: they brought out the best in each other. Was that what she and Alex did? He certainly seemed impressed by her mathematical abilities. But was that as an Ops Room WAAF or a potential wife?

She folded up the letter and switched off the light, overcome by a sudden urge to gaze out at the night sky, as if she would somehow be able to read her destiny in the stars. She groped her way to the window and pulled the blackout curtains aside, but clouds must have rolled in, for there was nothing but pitch darkness outside.

Then a light caught her eye, a faint pinprick wavering alongside the hedge, at the far end of the airfield. Was it a routine patrol? But Evie had never noticed anyone patrol that section of the airfield before. Then the light disappeared, and Evie thought she must have imagined it. That was until the light suddenly reappeared on the other side of the hedge, in the garden of High Chalk House.

Evie's heart hammered. Should she fetch one of the officers? Then the light briefly caught the arm of the stranger, revealing a sleeve in air force blue. She was fairly certain she caught a glimpse of a band near the cuff denoting an officer. Relief washed over her. She was aware some of the WAAFs had secret assignations with men from the station but hadn't realised any dared do so in the Waafery under the noses of the officers. Whoever it was had better be careful with that light or they'd get the wrath of the ARP warden on them as well as getting the girl in question dismissed in disgrace if she was found out. As a candidate officer, Evie knew she should probably report it, but she didn't want to get one of her sister WAAFs in trouble.

She had to admit to curiosity over the man's identity. Straining her eyes, she could just about make out a shadowy figure brushing himself down. He was certainly keen. There was a chain-link fence alongside the hedge, so he must have cut through that first before forcing his way through the bushes. From her strolls in the garden, Evie knew how dense the hedge was. He'd probably had to cut several branches away before he could get through.

The dim light was barely more than a pale glow on the ground, but Evie had no trouble tracking it through the darkness. The figure moved up the garden to the path. To Evie's surprise the light didn't follow the path towards the door but went in the direction of the driveway. She was still trying to work out what to make of this when the crescent moon appeared briefly from behind the clouds, illuminating the officer's face in silvery light. Evie gripped the windowsill in shock. There was no mistaking him. It was Karol.

She backed away from the window, tripping over a small table in her haste. Rubbing her bruised shin, she stumbled to Jess's door and knocked. 'Jess, are you awake?'

The last word had hardly left Evie's mouth when the door opened, spilling lamplight into the dark schoolroom. Jess stood in the doorway holding a blue enamelled hairbrush. She'd removed her tunic and was in shirtsleeves; her golden hair hung loose over her shoulders. 'What's going on?'

Evie reached behind Jess, shut the door to block the light, then grabbed Jess by the arm and dragged her to the window. 'Look!' she hissed, stabbing her index finger towards the indistinct figure now nearly at the corner of the house.

Jess pressed her face to the window. 'Who is it?'

'Karol.'

'What are you doing?' May's voice came from the

nursery doorway.

Evie spun around from the window to see May's shadowy outline approach. Fortunately, she hadn't turned on the light in their shared bedroom, or it would have flooded out of the uncovered window, alerting Karol. She beckoned May to join them then described what she had seen.

'What's he up to?' May asked.

'No idea, but it's suspicious.'

Another shaft of moonlight lanced from the clouds. Craning her neck, Evie could just see Karol making his way down the driveway. There seemed to be something lumpy on his back.

'A satchel,' Evie cried. 'He's carrying a satchel, just like that time I saw him in the woods.' She thought quickly. 'I bet he's got a transmitter.'

She strode to the chair and sat down, pulling on her shoes. 'I'm going to follow him.'

'Not alone,' Jess said. She tied her hair into a knot at the back of her head. 'I'm coming with you.'

'Shouldn't we tell one of the officers?' May asked.

'There's no time. If we don't go now, we'll lose him in the dark.' Evie paused in the act of tying her laces. She'd feel happier knowing backup was on the way. It was no good phoning the police because the road to Amberton was still out and phoning the station at this time of night wouldn't connect them to anyone who could help. She doubted anyone would wake Alex on the say so of a lowly WAAF. 'I know. May, get dressed, then go and wake up Ellerby. She knows you well enough to understand you'd only disturb her in a genuine emergency. She'll know what to do.'

May nodded. 'Be careful.'

'Don't worry. We won't let him see us. I just want

to keep him in view so we can see what he's up to.'

May darted back into the nursery while Evie and Jess crept out of the schoolroom and down the stairs. Months of working irregular hours meant they knew all the creaky steps and floorboards to avoid, so they made it down to the kitchen without disturbing anyone. Evie opened the back door and peered out but there was no sign of Karol. The two girls slipped outside and jogged to the front of the house. They were careful to keep off the gravelled path, so the crunch didn't alert Karol. When they reached the driveway, they were rewarded by the sight of the dim glow of Karol's torch bobbing up and down at the other end of the drive. A moment later it turned right.

'He must be heading for the track,' Evie breathed. 'Come on.'

Running as fast as she dared, she led the way to the entrance. Concealing herself behind one of the pillars, she glanced out into the lane. Sure enough, even though the torch light was no longer visible, she saw shadowy movement on the track leading into the fields.

* * *

Alex couldn't sleep. He couldn't stop seeing the images from Karol's gun camera: streams of tracer fire aimed at empty sky. Evie had been right about that. Was she right about everything else? It was one thing to suspect a pilot of cowardice, or 'lacking moral fibre' as the RAF liked to term it; it was quite another to suspect him of spying and sabotage. It made him feel sick to suspect one of his own pilots. Even worse was the knowledge that there could have been a spy

320

in his squadron all this time, and he hadn't noticed.

He owed it to the rest of the squadron, not to mention the unfortunate Aircraftman Sykes, to find out for sure. First thing tomorrow he would lay the whole matter before the station commander and the RAF police. They were best placed to handle it. He just hoped they didn't end up needing reinforcements if Karol turned out to be guilty and tried to make a run for it. It would be difficult for anyone to get here with the road impassable.

The road is out! Alex sat bolt upright, eyes wide, staring into the darkness. What if that wasn't a coincidence? What if the attack had been a deliberate ploy to block access to Amberton? That would mean . . . God help them all, it would mean an attack was imminent, taking advantage of Amberton being cut off from help.

He swung his legs out of bed and pulled on his clothes. Karol shared a room with Jiří on the floor below. The first thing to do was check if he was there. If he was, Alex had some questions for him. If he wasn't . . . Well, he'd cross that bridge when he came to it. He bounded down the stairs two at a time and knocked at Karol and Jiří's door. There was a mumbled reply, and Alex pushed open the door and looked inside.

Jiří raised his head from his pillow and frowned at him as though trying to focus. 'Is it time to get up?'

Alex glanced at the other bed. It was empty. The sheets smooth and neatly tucked in. He felt no surprise, just a dull resignation. He glared at Jiří. 'Where's Karol?'

Jiří yawned and rubbed his eyes, then his head dropped back to his pillow, and he looked as though he were on the point of falling back to sleep.

Alex snapped on the light switch, then in two strides he was by Jiří's bed. He shook him by the shoulder. '*Kde je Karol?*'

Jiří sat up again with painful slowness, squinting his eyes against the harsh light of the bare light bulb. Then he looked across at Karol's bed and grinned. 'He said he was seeing a WAAF.'

'When did he leave?'

Jiří shrugged. 'Around midnight, I think.'

Alex glanced at his watch. It was only half past twelve now. Plenty of time to catch Karol if only he knew where to look. 'Where did he go?' Then another thought struck him. 'How did he get past the gates?' If Karol was up to no good, he wouldn't want to risk being seen and questioned.

Jiří seemed to be more awake now. He tapped the side of his nose. 'I think he's found another way.'

Alex drew himself up to his full height. He'd never found it necessary to pull rank or intimidate his junior officers, but now he had no time to lose. 'Tell me right now, before I put you under close arrest for disobeying a senior officer.'

The barked command must have got through for Jiří straightened his shoulders as though he were on parade. The effect was slightly spoiled by the fact he was wearing stripy pyjamas and his hair stood up in clumps. 'Yes, sir. I think he has a tool for cutting through the hedge.' He mimed using wire cutters. 'I saw him putting them in his rucksack when he thought I wasn't looking.'

'Hell's bells. So there's nothing to stop him cutting through to the Waafery.' And from there he had easy access to the fields, where he could signal to the attackers. There wasn't a moment to waste.

He wasn't such a fool he would go charging off without any backup. 'This is serious, Jiří. I have every reason to believe Karol is a spy. I have to go after him, but I need you to alert the station commander.'

He barely waited for Jiří's stammered, 'Yes, sir,' before he dashed out of the room. He was about to go down the stairs to ground level when a hand grasped his shoulder. He spun round to see Milan, hair tousled, and tunic buttoned askew.

'What's happening?' Milan asked.

Alex explained in as few words as possible. Milan nodded. 'I'll come with you.'

There was no time to protest, and he could do with the help if things turned nasty. 'Come on then.'

They ran outside. Alex released a shaky breath when he saw bicycles propped against the outside wall. It was a good mile to the far end of the airfield; farther, if they went around the perimeter track. He and Karol grabbed a bike each and began to pedal furiously.

'You didn't seem surprised about Karol,' Alex called to Milan.

Milan seemed to have a bike with higher gears, for he kept up with remarkable ease, seeming to pedal only once for every three of Alex's. 'Something Jiří said at the pub got me thinking.' Milan swept back a lock of hair from his eyes. 'He joked that Karol might be trying to hide the fact he came from Moravia, which was why he'd got some facts wrong about Prague. But he doesn't sound like a Moravian. Then it hit me he might be from the Sudetenland. And everything fell into place.'

Alex's foot slipped off the pedal and his foot flailed

in the air before it found the pedal again. He was only vaguely aware of the differences between the various peoples of Czechoslovakia: Moravians, Bohemians, Slovaks and Silesians, but he knew about the Sudeten. land. It formed the borderland between Czechoslovakia and Germany. Although part of Czechoslovakia, a high proportion of Germans lived there. Everyone in Europe must know about the Sudetenland: it had been ceded to Germany as part of the Munich Agreement. They'd then used it as a foothold into the rest of Czechoslovakia.

'He's from a German family,' Alex said more to himself than to Milan.

As Milan had said: everything fell into place once you considered Karol as German. Alex had refused to believe a Czech would sabotage aircraft intended to fight Germans, because the Czechs had good reason to hate the Nazis. But how easy for an ethnic German pilot from the Sudetenland to 'escape' across Europe to England, to join the ranks of Czechs and Poles doing likewise. Alex wondered with a sick knot in the pit of his stomach whether Karol had been recruited by the Germans or if he had volunteered.

The track turned to follow the line of the fence and hedge. Alex inspected it as they cycled past, looking for an area that had been disturbed, praying it would be obvious in the dark. If not, he would have to trust his instincts and head straight for the boundary with High Chalk House.

In the end, his worry was needless. When they got to the section of hedgerow between the airfield and the Waafery, there was enough moonlight to glint on the section of fence that had been cut and pulled aside. Alex swung out of his saddle and flung the bike down. 'Give me your lighter,' Alex said to Milan, who was crouching next to him.

Milan handed him a heavy silver lighter, warm from being in his pocket. Doing his best to shield the light from above, Alex snapped it open and examined the hedge by the light of the flickering blue flame. It was immediately obvious that Jiří had been right: not only had the fence been cut, but several of the lower branches of the hedge had been cut away, leaving a gap just large enough for a man to squeeze through. Alex wasted no time in wriggling through the gap, doing his best to shield his eyes from the dangling branches that slapped at his face. He staggered to his feet once through and heard the rustle and snapping of twigs that told him Milan was following.

'Stop right there!' a woman's voice snapped.

Before Alex could respond, a tall figure loomed in the darkness. Then whoever it was stumbled, emitting a distinctly feminine squeak. She grabbed Alex's arm, pulling him off balance, and they both tumbled to the ground. He struggled to disentangle himself, then blinked when a light shone in his face for a brief instant.

'Squadron Leader Kincaith!' the voice gasped.

Staggering to his feet, he found himself face to face with a tall WAAF. 'May?' he said, rubbing his bruised arm.

Rustling from the hedge told him Milan was forcing his way into the garden. 'Where were you when I was being attacked by an Amazon?' he asked, when Milan emerged, leaves tangled in his hair.

Another figure materialised from the gloom. 'Apologies for the reception, sir.' Alex recognised Flight Officer Ellerby's voice. 'Lidford came to me with an unbelievable story of spies cutting through the hedge, so I asked her to show me.'

'It might be incredible, but I have a horrible feeling it's true.' Alex turned to May. 'Did you see where he went?'

'Up into the fields. Evie and Jess followed him.'

Alex felt as though he'd been stabbed through the chest. 'Evie?' he gasped. At the same moment, Milan said, 'Jess?'

Alex turned on the flight officer. 'What possessed you to send them?'

'I didn't. They had already gone by the time Lidford woke me.'

It was almost impossible to think when his whole mind was screaming that Evie was in danger. Alex had never known such terror, even when bullets were smashing through his cockpit. 'I'm going after them.' It was the only thing to do. Gradually his frozen mind started to work again, switching into the detached state it usually went into when he was in combat. He turned to Ellerby. 'I've sent one of my pilots to report to the station commander, but I'm worried he won't be believed.'

'I'll telephone him myself,' Ellerby said.

'Tell him we need armed men up here on the double. As many as he can muster.'

He didn't wait for anything more but set off at a run, Milan on his heels.

'What do you think Karol's going to do?' Milan panted as they passed the dim outline of the stone lions flanking the entrance and turned onto the lane.

'Only one thing I can think of.' He'd considered all angles as they'd cycled around the airfield, and only one scenario explained why Karol would need to go up into the open fields, why the road had been bombed, isolating them from outside help. 'Para-chutists.' It was impossible to say more when he was running so fast the blood roared and pulsed in his ears.

And if they didn't find Evie and Jess before they arrived, the two girls wouldn't be up against just one man, but many, maybe dozens. All armed and trained to kill.

As if summoned by his fears, the dull, ominous drone of aero engines swelled, barely perceptible above his own heartbeat at first but growing louder all the time.

25

Evie wriggled to find a more comfortable position as she peered out from between the broad leaves of the hazel thicket she and Jess were hiding in, lying prone to avoid being seen. It was impossible to find a spot on the ground that wasn't a mass of twisted roots. She shifted to edge away from a knotted lump digging into her left hip, only to find another root sticking into her stomach. Fallen hazelnuts crunched under her hands.

'What's he doing?' Jess's voice was little more than a breath, timed to coincide with the stir of the breeze rustling the leaves.

Evie looked across again at the field, straining her eyes against the darkness. The cloud was clearing now, revealing patches of star-studded sky. The light was just enough to allow her to see Karol's dark shape, motionless, maybe a hundred yards from the hedgerow. Evie could hear rather than see the sway of ripe barley in the field, the faint hiss of the breeze caressing the stems, the barely perceptible rattle of heavy seed heads knocking against each other.

'No idea,' she replied. 'He's just standing there.'

It was a complete mystery. If he was going to transmit information, why had he come all the way up here? There were plenty of places where he could conceal himself that were far closer to the station than this large field. Frustration welled up inside her. She had hoped to see evidence of Karol's treachery, but what did she have to report? She could just see herself going to Alex and saying, 'I watched him stand in a field for half an hour.' If they were caught out alone when they should be in the Waafery, they could wave goodbye to any chance of promotion.

Then she heard a sound. A distant rumble. It faded in and out of her perception for a while. Each time it disappeared, she strained to hear, wondering if she had imagined it, then the sound would swell again, a little louder than before. Only when it was an unremitting drone did it finally dawn on her what she was hearing.

'Aeroplanes!' she said to Jess.

Jess had her head cocked to the sky. 'Just one, I think. More than one engine. Why haven't our lot picked it up?'

'It must have flown low enough to avoid detection,' she whispered back. But why hadn't their observers reported it? Then she remembered Karol, always strolling around the station when he wasn't flying, conversing with anyone and everyone. 'Oh, my goodness. What if Karol's found out where all the observers are based? He could have signalled their position so a single aircraft could slip past unnoticed.' A large group of hostile aircraft would be less likely to go undetected, but one . . . If the pilot knew the locations to avoid, it might be possible.

She kept her eyes fixed on Karol as she spoke, and gripped Jess's arm when she saw him lower his satchel to the ground and pull something out. 'What's he got?'

A split second later, a beam of light emanated from Karol's hand and stabbed the sky. It flashed rapidly on and off four times, then a pause, then another four flashes. It continued in that pattern until a shadow blotted out the stars and the drone roared to a crescendo.

Evie gripped Jess's arm even harder. 'He's signalling to a bomber!' But even as she said it, she knew it didn't make sense. If the Germans had come to bomb Amberton, Karol would send his signal from the airfield, not up in this empty field. She had never felt so helpless. Whatever Karol was planning, there was nothing she and Jess could do to stop him. All they could do was watch, hoping Karol wouldn't see them, and pray May had got the message through to Alex and the others at Amberton that they needed help up here.

The aircraft appeared to be directly overhead now, and Evie tensed, waiting for the whistle of a bomb. But nothing happened. The drone of aero engines faded and rose to a crescendo as though circling, then it faded into the distance, heading south, and didn't return.

Evie heard Jess release a shaky breath beside her. 'What just happened?'

Various scenarios poured through Evie's mind, but none of them made sense. Then before she could answer, a dark shape drifted past her eyes from above and struck the ground with a thud. She had to bite her lips to prevent a cry of shock giving away their presence. Beside her, she heard Jess's sharp indrawn breath. Suddenly everything was clear.

She pulled Jess close and whispered, 'Parachutists.'

She felt rather than saw Jess's answering nod. She kept her eyes fixed on the patch of ground, no more than fifty feet in front of her, where she had seen the shape hit the ground. Her heart hammered against her ribs; the blood sang in her ears. She could only

330

pray the parachutist didn't hear their shaky breaths, because try as she might, she couldn't control her breathing. Her lungs felt as though they were starved of oxygen, and she couldn't prevent herself from drawing great gulping breaths in a desperate attempt to drag more air into her body.

The object on the ground didn't move. The more she stared, the more convinced she became that it was the wrong shape for a man. Unless he was lying with his arms and legs drawn up. Evie's eyes ached from the effort of trying to pierce the darkness. Still there was no movement. A mad impulse seized her to scream, do anything to release the unbearable tension coiled in her chest.

'Why isn't he moving?' Jess whispered.

In fact, there was movement on the ground, some distance from the object. It looked like the ground itself was rising and falling slightly with each breath of a breeze. A flood of calm swept over her as it dawned on Evie what she was seeing: a parachute canopy. Gradually she was able to get her breathing under control, and she realised she was clutching Jess's arm so tight her fingers were digging into the bone. She blew out a shaky breath and relaxed her grip.

'It's not a man,' she replied, doing her best to time her words with the breeze stirring the hedgerow. 'It's a package. Must be equipment for whoever else arrived.' She knew what they had to do. She crawled on hands and knees out of the shelter of the branches and paused on the edge of the field, listening for any sign of movement nearby. When she was satisfied no one was close, she hissed at Jess, 'Come on. Quick. We need to grab that package and hide it.'

Jess crawled out beside her and rose to her feet,

331

but Evie grabbed her arm and pulled her down. 'Stay low. They might see your silhouette.'

Crouched almost double, they made their way towards the object. Evie continually darted glances around, aware that Karol and, presumably, the other parachutists must be seeking this package. Just as she reached it, a high-pitched yelp sounded in the distance. Evie nearly jumped out of her skin, her heart pounding like a piston. She went limp with relief when she realised it was a fox.

The parcel was firmly bound in some kind of tarpaulin. It was roughly cubic, about the length of her arm. Groping her way around it, Evie's hands met the parachute lines, still attached to the bundle. 'Help me drag it over to the hedge,' she whispered to Jess.

Whatever the bundle contained, it wasn't light, but working together they were able to drag it back towards the hedgerow where they'd been concealed. The crunch and rustle of it dragging through the tall barley filled the air. Surely whoever else was here must hear and would be homing in upon them. Evie's hands grew damp with perspiration; the thin cords slipped through her fingers, burning her palms. If the enemy found them, Evie had no doubt they would be brutally silenced. Jess, too, seemed to be fully aware of their danger. Evie could see her throwing looks over her shoulder as they heaved the heavy weight, her breaths rapid and shaky.

'Nearly there,' Evie whispered, as much to reassure herself as Jess, after she felt the barley give way behind her and she staggered backwards onto the narrow path at the edge of the field.

Panting, they gave one last heave and pulled the bundle into the hedgerow. Evie wanted to scream with each crack of the twigs. If they could only get the package out of sight before anyone came to investigate, it would buy them enough time to fetch help while the parachutists were searching for their supplies. The hedgerow consisted of a line of hazel bushes interspersed with elders and blackthorn. As luck would have it, they reached the edge of the field beside a patch of blackthorn thicket. Investigating, Evie discovered the gnarled stems formed a structure almost like a tunnel, making a natural cave in the centre of the bushes.

'In here!' As they pushed, Evie caught sight of two figures striding towards them. With one last shove, she pushed the bundle deep into the thicket, then grabbed Jess's arm and pulled her deeper into the hedge. Her throat was so tight she couldn't have made a sound even had she wanted to, but the pressure of a scream was building up in her chest.

Then her foot caught in a root and she plunged to the ground, dragging Jess down with her. She scrambled to her knees instantly, but too late. The two men must have heard them, and they plunged into the hedgerow. A hand grabbed her collar and yanked her to her feet. Beside her she could see the other man grasp Jess by the arm and pull her up.

Then the man holding Evie spoke. 'Evie. Thank God. Are you all right?'

There was no mistaking the soft Scottish burr. Evie sagged, clutching Alex's arm, grateful for his strength. 'I'm fine.' Those were all the words she could manage at first. She gulped for breath, waiting for her heartbeat to ease. Behind her she heard Alex's companion talk to Jess and recognised Milan. But there was no time to lose. She fought to get the words out. 'Karol's out there. Signalling parachutists.'

'I know.' Alex's voice was grim. 'What in the blazes are you playing at? You could have been killed.'

Something inside Evie snapped, and nothing could hold back her frustration, not even the presence of enemies. 'Maybe if you'd listened to me earlier, I wouldn't have to be here.'

Alex released a long breath, and she could make out enough of his outline to see him rub the back of his neck. 'We don't have time for this. How many are out there?'

No apology, then. She shoved the thought aside for later and shook her head. 'We couldn't see. But we did find a bundle.' In a low voice she described what she and Jess had seen and done. Time enough to explain herself to Alex once they'd found Karol and the parachutists.

* * *

Alex did his best to control a wave of fear while he listened to Evie blithely describe how she and Jess had marched into the barley field without a thought of the danger they were in. Later he would drum some sense of personal safety into her. For now, he had to stop Karol before they all got killed.

'Where's Karol now?'

But before Evie had a chance to do more than draw a breath to answer, a series of four brief flashes flickered somewhere near the centre of the field.

'That's him,' Evie hissed. 'It's the same code he used when the plane came overhead.'

He must be signalling to the parachutists, to bring them together from their scattered locations. Alex

334

knew enough about parachuting in a group to know it was almost impossible to land together. They could be hundreds of yards away. An idea struck.

'You and Jess wait here. Don't move! Milan, you're with me.'

There was no time to explain his plan, so he could only hope Evie would do as she was told. With Milan at his shoulder, he moved through the barley, praying that if Karol heard them, he would assume they were the parachutists. He headed in the direction of the flashes, hoping he didn't drift off course in the dark.

Then Alex saw him — a shape slightly darker than the deep blue of the night sky. He grabbed Milan's arm and pulled him close so he could whisper. 'See him?'

Milan nodded.

'We need him alive,' he breathed. 'Without a noise.'

'Leave him to me.'

Before Alex could protest, Milan sprang ahead so silently he seemed to be hovering above the field. The next moment there was a gasp quickly muffled then a soft rustle and thud.

Heart pounding, Alex dashed towards the sound and found Milan pinning Karol to the ground, one knee on Karol's back and a hand clamped around his mouth.

'One move and I'll snap your puny neck.' Milan spoke in Czech, his voice a low growl.

Alex pulled off his scarf and crouched to tie it securely around Karol's mouth. Karol bit his finger, and it took all of Alex's willpower not to yell when he felt the crunch of teeth against the bone. There was a brief struggle which ended when Milan twisted Karol's arm up beneath his shoulder blade. Karol gasped, releasing Alex's finger, freeing him to finish tying the gag. Once it was done, Milan jerked him to his feet. Alex put his hand to the ground to push himself up when his hand touched hard, smooth metal. It must be the torch Karol had been using. He put it in his pocket then rose and grabbed Karol, who was struggling to free himself from Milan's brutal grip. Held securely between them, Alex and Milan marched him back to the hedgerow.

'Evie, Jess, open that package,' he snapped when they got there. 'We need to know how many parachutists are out there.'

Milan handed something to Jess. Alex caught a glint of reflected moonlight, but he couldn't look more closely because Karol started to struggle again. Milan twisted his arm again; Alex heard a pop, and Karol gave a muffled cry. 'Try that again and I'll use my knife,' Milan said.

Behind them Alex heard something heavy being dragged through the undergrowth, then a tearing sound.

'It's a box,' Evie whispered. 'Nailed shut.'

Then came a wrenching sound of splintering wood. Jess must be using Milan's knife to lever open the lid.

'I can't see anything,' Evie said.

'Here.' With his free hand he pulled Karol's torch from his pocket and held it out. 'Take this. I can't throw it — we'll lose it in the dark.'

He heard footsteps as Evie made her way towards him, then her hand patting his arm. It moved down to his hand and the torch. He had to fight his instinct to release Karol and clutch her to him, to protect her from whatever harm was coming her way. It cost him almost physical pain to release the torch to her and let her move away.

Then a beam of light illuminated Evie and Jess's faces as they peered into the opened crate. Jess gave a soft exclamation. 'Well, knock me down with a feather.'

'What is it?'

Evie answered, a tremor in her voice. 'Guns. Dynamite.'

Equipment for a campaign of disruption that could render Amberton completely ineffective. If Amberton was lost, it would give the Germans a foothold onto the Sussex coast. They had to be stopped. He glanced across the field again. Time was running out. By now the parachutists would have hidden their parachutes and be watching for Karol's signal. Where were the reinforcements from Amberton? A horrible thought struck him. What if May was unable to convince them it was a genuine emergency? After all, they had only seen a light. He had to assume they were on their own.

A thought struck him. 'Any fuse wire?'

'Is this what you mean?' Evie produced a bundle of thin cable.

'Thank God. Hand it here.'

There was more than enough to truss Karol and tie him to a stout hazel stem. Karol wriggled as Alex and Milan worked, but couldn't free himself. The moment Alex was able to release his grip, he strode to the crate and rummaged through the contents. He pulled out the handguns — Browning Hi-Power pistols — and several ammunition clips.

'Four guns.' He looked back at Karol. 'Is he armed?'

Milan searched him. 'Only a knife.' He tucked the knife into his own pocket.

'Then one of these guns must be meant for him, so there must be three parachutists. Two against three. We should be able to handle that with the advantage of arms.'

'*Four* against three. Don't forget me and Jess.'

Alex took his time loading two of the pistols and handing one to Milan before he answered. 'How many times have you fired a gun?'

'Never, but if you think we're going to stand by helplessly while you and Milan try to take on three Germans you can think again.'

'But Evie, I —'

Evie snatched the gun he held. 'We're wasting time. They could be here any moment. Either we're armed and ready or they find us arguing over whether two members of the team should be allowed to defend themselves.'

Put like that, Alex knew they had no choice. He loaded another gun for Jess and then took the last gun for himself. 'For God's sake leave the safety on. I don't want one of you blowing off my head by accident.' He showed both girls the location of the safety catch. 'If you need to shoot, hold it in both hands with your arms straight.' He could only pray they didn't need to fire, because in the dark the bullets were likely to go wild.

Then he crept to the edge of the field and looked out. Was that movement over by the far boundary? It was too dark to be certain, but his heart pounded in his chest. All his instincts screamed that the parachutists were getting close. And there was still no sign of help from Amberton coming up the track.

'It would help if we knew what signal Karol had agreed upon.'

338

'He used four flashes to signal to the plane.' Alex jumped. He hadn't noticed Evie creep up beside him.

He grabbed her arm. 'Get back under cover.' He snatched the torch. 'Are you sure about the signal?'

'Positive.'

'Okay, listen up. It's no good our blundering around in the dark. I'm going to give the signal to lure them here. Milan, get ready to overpower them. Do what you must to stop them warning the others. Girls, stay under cover. These men will be trained killers.'

★ ★ ★

Evie gripped the hilt of her pistol, her heart in her mouth while Alex stepped out of concealment and flashed four times with the torch. After a pause he gave another four flashes. She strained her eyes into the darkness, looking for any sign of movement. Please, God, let them come one at a time. Despite her insistence on being armed, she desperately hoped neither she nor Jess would be needed in the fight. Her studies had prepared her for many possible careers, but nothing involving guns or combat. Come to think of it, she wasn't sure how prepared a fighter pilot would be for hand-to-hand combat, either.

Jess gripped her arm and whispered, 'We'll be fine, Evie. Milan's been itching to crack a few Nazi skulls. He won't let anyone through.'

Evie could feel Jess's hand trembling though and knew her friend was as terrified as her.

Then she caught a brief flash from the left edge of the field. Evie felt as though her stomach was trying to crawl out of her throat. She tightened her grip on the pistol. It could only be a signal from one of the

339

parachutists. Another flash came from the far end of the field. That was two accounted for — where was the third? She glanced to left and right but couldn't see any other signals.

Then there wasn't time to look, because the first man was close. She could hear the rustle of barley, the sound of rapid breathing. About thirty seconds later, she saw a man's outline no more than ten paces away. Then he stopped and for an agonising few seconds Evie could hear nothing but the roar of blood in her ears.

'*Der Seelöwe kommt*,' the man said in a low voice.

She heard Karol give a muffled cry through his gag, and the parachutist turned sharply in his direction. Milan cursed under his breath and sprang forward. There was a blur of movement, then Evie heard a dull thud as Milan brought the hilt of his gun down on the German's head. The man crumpled to the ground.

Alex dashed out and hissed, 'Quick. Get him under cover before anyone else sees him.'

Between them they dragged him into the undergrowth.

'Evie, Jess, tie him up.'

Dazed at the speed with which everything had happened, Evie tucked her gun in her pocket then grabbed the cord and tied the man's hands while Jess bound his feet. She glanced up several times as she worked, and saw Alex and Milan gazing intently across the field. They had to be watching the other man approach. All the while, she wondered where the third man was, assuming there really were three of them.

Alex signalled the second man again, and Evie saw his dark shape approach at a run. Milan slipped

340

along the hedgerow then froze, fading into invisibility as soon as he stopped moving. As soon as the second parachutist passed him, Milan stepped out behind him and dealt him a swift blow. After a breathless few minutes, the second man lay beside the other German, also securely bound.

'That was easy,' Alex muttered. 'Now all we've got to do is —'

Evie had stepped back slightly as Alex spoke. She had a sudden sense of movement behind her and the hairs on the back of her neck rose. But before she could turn, solid arms grabbed her. She opened her mouth to cry out, but a hand clamped over her mouth, silencing her. She was pulled back savagely against a hard body, and she struggled, twisting in a frantic effort to free herself. Then cold steel pressed against her throat and she froze.

26

'Release them, or the woman dies.' The voice was as cold as the knife against Evie's flesh. The man spoke English, but his accent was German.

Evie swallowed, the pressure increasing on her throat as she did so. Pale light suddenly illuminated the scene: Alex had switched on the torch, keeping it angled down. Evie could just make him out by its light, with Jess and Milan behind him. For a moment, all three were rooted to the ground in a tableau of shock.

Then Alex took a pace forward. 'Let her go,' he said. 'You can't win. If you make a move to harm her, I'll shoot.'

'She'll die before you can fire. You don't have the stomach for that.'

Evie's pulse hammered in her ears, making the voices sound far away. She could see Milan, pointing his gun at the German's head. Oh, God, please don't let him try it in the dark. If his aim was off by only a little way, he would hit Evie instead. Or miss them both and the German would be sure to cut her throat in retribution.

The man took a step back, dragging Evie with him, her hands clutching at his arms. The movement bashed her side against a tree trunk, and she felt hard metal press against her ribs. The gun! She'd forgotten all about it, and the German clearly hadn't expected her to be armed. She let her hands drop to her sides, giving a sob as she did so, praying he would think she had given up the fight. Holding her breath, she edged her right hand towards her pocket, doing her best not to let her movements give her away.

'Don't be a fool,' Alex said, his voice waxing and waning in a peculiar fashion through the roar in her ears. 'There are more men on the way. You can't hope to escape. Give up before you make it worse for yourself.'

Evie's fingers edged inside her pocket, hit the smooth, polished hand grip. The safety catch was still on. Feeling sick with frustration she realised that with only one hand she couldn't hold the pistol and release the safety catch. She would have to do it while it was still in her pocket. She swallowed bile as she edged her fingers down the gun, groping for the catch. There! A fingernail snagged on the hard ridge. She screwed her eyes shut, straining to find enough purchase to release the catch.

The man gave a harsh laugh. 'How can I make it worse for myself? I'd rather die than face capture.'

'That can be arranged,' Milan said.

The safety catch released with a tiny click. Evie tensed. Surely the German must have heard? Ten heartbeats bruised her ribs as she paused, not daring to breathe. But the man's concentration was focused on Milan and Alex, and he gave no sign of noticing. The ability to move returned. Slowly, inch by inch, she worked her fingers around the grip and edged the gun from her pocket. Her heart pounded so hard she was worried the man would feel it through her back and sense she was trying to escape. She made a show of tugging at the hand gripping the knife with her other hand to distract him. It was a good thing she wasn't really trying to pull away his arm because it was as strong as a band of iron.

'Stand still, *Fräulein*.'

While he was glancing down at her other hand, she freed the gun from her pocket. But now she was stuck. She couldn't get the angle to aim at his chest or head, but if she didn't disable him instantly he would cut her throat.

She glanced up at Alex, saw his eyes widen for an instant as they fell on her gun. Then he raised his gaze to the German's face.

He aimed his gun at the man's head. 'Get down on your knees,' he said, putting an odd emphasis on 'knees'.

'Why should I do anything you ask?' the man replied. 'Untie my comrades.'

But in a flash, Evie knew Alex's comment had been aimed at her. She couldn't aim at his head or chest, but she could get an angle to point at his knee. Alex had told her to use both hands if she had to shoot, but she could only use one. Praying it would be enough, she angled the gun, pressing the barrel to the German's knee, squeezing the trigger. It was stiffer than she'd expected, but then the gun fired with a report that made her ears ring. The recoil jerked the gun from her hand. Simultaneously the man gave a howl of anguish. He dropped his knife and collapsed to the ground, whimpering as he clutched his knee.

Alex kicked the knife aside, then grabbed the man and bound his hands with Milan's help. He glanced up at Evie. 'Are you all right? Evie?'

But Evie couldn't answer. She backed against a tree trunk, wracked with icy chills. For a horrible moment she thought she would be sick. Grey dots swirled in

344

front of her eyes.

'Evie!' Arms wrapped around her shoulders, easing her down to sit cradled by the tree roots. But it was Jess who held her, murmuring words of comfort. 'You were so brave, Evie. Everything's going to be all right now.' Jess stroked her hair, and Evie rested her face against her shoulder, waiting for the shaking to subside. She longed for Alex to hold her, tell her she was safe, but he stood, watching her with an unreadable expression.

Then the sound of several running feet reached her.

'Kincaith!' The station commander's voice rang out in the night air. 'I heard a shot. What the blazes is going on?'

* * *

'Come in, Bishop.' Flight Officer Jean Ellerby glanced up from the report she was reading when Evie tapped the open door.

Evie stepped over the threshold, her stomach in knots. Her nerves weren't helped by Ellerby's stern expression. Was she going to be reprimanded? Told her application for officer training was now out of the question? Everything had become a blur last night after she'd shot the German. She'd been questioned first by Jean Ellerby, then by Bob Law until her head ached. Jess, too, was on the receiving end of rapid-fire questions. When had she realised Karol was a spy? Why hadn't she waited for help before going after him? Was she sure they had captured all the parachutists? She hardly knew what answers she had stammered. Her overriding thoughts had been to avoid getting

Jess, May, Alex and Milan into any trouble.

Finally, Jean Ellerby had cut in when Bob Law had seemed to be on the verge of asking yet another question. 'My girls are exhausted, sir. This can wait until tomorrow.' The only thing she remembered clearly after that was Karol, glaring over his shoulder at Alex as he was dragged away with cuffed hands. 'You know why we targeted your squadron?' he spat. 'Because you'd lost so many men already, no one would think to question any more losses. Did you never wonder why they could only find Czech pilots to make up the losses?'

Alex's haunted expression had stayed with her on the long walk back to High Chalk House on pounding feet. She'd been desperate to talk to him, but he'd avoided her, or so it seemed to her, accompanying the station commander instead, and not even acknowledging her when they'd reached the gateway to the Waafery and Ellerby separated Jess and Evie from the group and led them up the drive. Evie scarcely knew how she had climbed the stairs to the schoolroom. May had been waiting, her face wreathed with concern, but Jean Ellerby had insisted they go straight to bed. Evie had been too tired to remove her clothes but had fallen into bed fully clothed, and sleep had claimed her almost immediately. But Alex's stricken expression had followed her even into her dreams.

Now, as she sat in the chair Jean Ellerby indicated, she searched the flight officer's face for any clue to what judgement she was about to pronounce.

'Did you sleep well, Bishop?'

'Yes, ma'am.'

'I didn't. Your little escapade left me with a major headache.'

The knot in Evie's stomach tightened. 'Sorry, ma'am.'

Jean Ellerby scowled down at the report on her desk. 'Now I've got to decide what punishment to dole out to you, Halloway and Lidford.'

Evie gripped the arms of her chair, every ridge of the carved wood digging into her palms. Here it came: the end of her officer's career before it had even begun. 'Please, ma'am, you shouldn't punish Halloway or Lidford. I'm the one who insisted we follow Karol.'

'I'll decide who to punish.'

Her heart sank. 'Yes, ma'am.'

Jean's face softened. 'As it turns out, I've decided not to punish any of you. You all showed initiative and courage.'

Evie opened her mouth, then closed it, unable to produce any coherent words.

Ellerby continued. 'You had to make a difficult choice, but you made the right one. As a result, you've undoubtedly saved many lives. In short, you acted like an officer.'

'I . . . I don't know what to say.' Evie's head swam. She'd come prepared to defend Jess and May, certain she was about to be slung out of the WAAF. She had no idea how to respond to praise instead.

The ghost of a smile tugged at Jean's lips. 'I'm giving the three of you the day off to recover from the night's excitement. That should give you ample time to work something out. In the meantime, you might be interested in what arrived this morning.' She indicated the papers on her desk. 'Your orders to report for Filterer Officer training at Bawdsey in two weeks.'

Evie's heart gave a swoop, and she was hard pressed

to decide if it was pleasure or dismay. 'I . . . Thank you.' It was a chance to make something of her life. Become an officer. Save enough money to fund her degree should they win the war. Yes, it was definitely pleasure, not dismay that she would be leaving Alex.

'Don't thank me yet,' Ellerby said with a smile. 'You'll have to work hard if you want to pass.'

She would. Without Alex as a distraction, she would spend all her free time studying. Use work to forget how much she loved him. Because he was going to end their relationship, she was sure, and that was a good thing. She had been becoming too dependent upon him. If they had continued courting, she'd have fallen into the same trap as her mother and become so used to deferring to him that she'd lose her ability to support herself. She wanted a career, independence. Alex was holding her back. It was best she left.

Despite her resolution, once Ellerby dismissed her and Evie went to look for Jess and May, she found her mind wandering to Karol's odd comment. Or, rather, it wasn't so much Karol's words she couldn't get out of her head, but Alex's stricken expression. Karol had lashed out in his desperation, and it was clear his words had struck their mark.

Jess and May were waiting for their own summons outside the Admin block.

'Well?' Jess asked, her eyes pinned to Evie's face. 'Oh no, it's bad news, isn't it? We're going to get thrown out. And just when I'd decided I'd found something I was good at and was going to try for promotion.'

'No, it's good news.'

'Why? What did she say?' Jess's eyes were wide and eager. Then she frowned. 'Why the long face?'

Evie bit her lip. 'Alex,' she said. Then, recollecting

herself, she said, 'May, she wants to see you next. Don't look so scared — we're getting a commendation.'

Once May had dashed off, still looking terrified, Jess took Evie's arm and led her out into the sunshine. They sat on a bench by the vegetable patch to wait for May's return. 'Alex won't stay angry with you forever; he'll come to his senses. It's this blasted war. It's got everything turned upside-down.'

A ladybird landed on Evie's sleeve. She studied its shiny red back and counted seven dots before blowing it in the air and turning to Jess. 'Maybe he's already seen sense. Maybe we're not right together.' But still the memory of his stricken face haunted her.

Making up her mind, she sprang to her feet. 'I have to talk to him. Do you know where he is?'

Jess shook her head. 'I heard he's been stood down for the day, same as Milan, but I haven't seen him.'

'I need to find him.'

She took a step away, but Jess clutched her arm. 'Aren't you going to wait for me and May to finish with Ellerby?'

'I have to see him now.' Evie shook off Jess's hold. 'Meet me back at the schoolroom.'

Without waiting for Jess's reply, Evie strode towards the gates. She was certain she knew where to find him. She would tell him she would be leaving, relieve him of the task of ending their relationship. More importantly, she needed to set him right over the guilt she'd read in his eyes after Karol's poisonous remark. She had no idea what had caused his pain, but she couldn't leave without doing her best to ease it.

She found him, as she'd guessed, up in the woods. He was perched on a fallen tree trunk where the trees gave way to fields, gazing down at the Hurricanes taking off from the airfield below. As she approached, dried leaves swished underfoot; Alex glanced her way.

'What are you doing here?' He lowered his gaze as though the sight of her hurt his eyes. 'You're better off without me.'

Her rehearsed speech flew from her mind. She'd expected to have to defend herself. Faced with a dull resignation that was so unlike Alex, she blurted the first words that came into her head. 'That's not true.'

'You wouldnae say that if you knew what happened in France.'

She took a step closer, aching to touch him, to sit side by side with him, feel his arm around her again. 'If this is about what Karol said . . . it was just spite. No one blames you for any losses under your command.'

'I do.' His mouth was pulled tight as though from pain.

'You shouldn't. Fighter Command would never have kept you on as squadron leader if they didn't think you were the right man for the job.'

He faced her again, his eyes dull. 'Why do you think they had me working in Ops for so long? After what happened in France, they didn't want me leading an operational squadron again. It was only when they needed someone who could speak Czech that they were forced to resort to me because there wasn't anyone else.'

This was the first time he had so much as alluded to his experiences in France. If he could only explain what had happened, it would be his first step towards freeing himself of the stain it had left on his soul, but she had no idea how to coax the truth from him.

Seconds ticked by; the sighing of the trees and soft birdsong faded beneath the roar of blood in Evie's ears. She sought the right words, afraid to move or speak in case she shattered the moment. In the end she knew she had to speak before the opportunity passed. 'They wouldn't have put you in charge if you weren't suitable. Don't let Karol win by allowing his poison into your head.'

'You weren't there. You don't know what happened.'

'Then explain.'

Alex's response was to turn away, and it felt like a dismissal. Evie hovered behind him in an agony of indecision, unwilling to leave him but out of ideas how to persuade him to confide in her. Then a wave of anger at Karol overtook her. Maybe she and Alex were better apart, but it didn't stop her loving him. She refused to leave him bowed beneath a guilt she was sure was unjustified. It would be like giving up on a mathematical proof before she'd completed it. She went and sat next to him, careful to leave enough space between them to avoid accidentally brushing against him. 'I'm not going until you tell me.'

Alex blew out a breath. 'I suppose it doesn't matter. You're leaving soon.'

Evie closed her eyes briefly. 'How did you know?'

'Bob Law told me this morning.' He gave a strained smile. 'Congratulations. You deserve it.'

'I'm sorry. I wanted you to hear it from me first.' She made a helpless gesture. 'It's not important right now. Tell me what happened in France.'

He answered without looking at her, his attention fixed on the Hurricanes now climbing steadily as they flew towards the coast. 'I had only just been

351

promoted to squadron leader when I was sent to France to take command of Brimstone.' His mouth twisted in a bitter parody of a smile. 'I was so sure I would lead the squadron to glory.' He picked up a twig and stabbed a clump of moss with it. Evie waited more patiently this time, confident that now he had started he would complete the tale.

The twig snapped, and Alex threw away the broken end, drawing a shuddering breath. 'We didn't find glory, of course. Only disaster. After two weeks of routine patrols along the German frontier, we hadn't brought down a single enemy plane.' He grimaced. 'I got impatient. Desperate for a victory. When we got intelligence of a planned attack on Bouzonville, I was too eager to shoot down some Germans to listen to the warnings that the source couldn't be wholly trusted. I insisted upon acting on the intelligence, of setting up what I thought would be a trap.'

Evie's blood went cold, dreading to hear what Alex would say next.

'It was a German trap, of course. They knew we would be there, were waiting for us. One moment the sky was empty, the next it was black with Messerschmitts. Only a handful of us escaped unhurt. All my fault.'

* * *

For a while, Alex forgot Evie was there. Instead of the woods around him and the airfield below, all he could see was the angry swarm of Messerschmitts spitting fire, the billowing black spirals of smoke as his men were shot down. Instead of the twitter of birdsong and the sigh of the gentle breeze in the leaves, all he could hear were the frantic cries of his fellow pilots screaming warnings to one another and his own voice yelling at pilots of stricken Hurricanes to bail out.

Then a touch on his arm made him jump, and Evie's anxious face cut through the nightmare.

'I'm so sorry,' she said. 'It must have been terrible.'

Where was the condemnation, the disgust he'd been sure he'd spy in her eyes the moment she knew? He hadn't made himself clear. He cleared his throat, which felt so tight it was hard to force out the words. 'Only six of us made it out unscathed. The rest of the squadron were killed or injured so badly they'll never fly again.'

'I'm so sorry you had to go through that.'

Alex gazed at Evie in incomprehension. 'They're dead or disabled because of me,' he said, in case she hadn't grasped the obvious fact.

Evie didn't look away, but a pucker formed between her brows. 'They were killed or injured because of the German attack. You didn't do it.'

He spoke to her slowly as though to a child. 'But I led them into the ambush. It was my fault.'

Evie bit her lip and shook her head slowly as though trying to solve a puzzle. 'I've worked in Ops long enough to know that squadrons only go where they are sent. The orders to fly on that mission must have come from higher up.' Her voice softened. 'I'm not trying to shift the blame onto anyone other than the Germans, but you certainly can't be blamed for following orders.'

'You don't understand. I wanted to go. I urged my wing commander to send us.'

'Did he always go along with your recommendations?'

'Not all the time.'

'Did he ever give orders you felt unwise?'

'Aye, but —'

'Then he clearly had a mind of his own and had examined the evidence for himself before ordering your squadron on the mission.'

Alex scowled. 'It's not that simple.'

'Why not?'

Alex stared at her helplessly. How could he sum up the complex web of loyalties and responsibility that bound a squadron leader to his pilots in a few simple words? The loss of his pilots was his fault. He could have done more . . . should have done more. Should have been paying more attention to the skies . . . checked to see if there were planes lurking against the sun.

A wave of weariness struck. He couldn't bear to think about it any more. He rose and brushed dried leaves and moss from his uniform with shaking hands. It should be obvious to Evie that he'd come here to be alone. Why couldn't she take the hint and leave? He tried not to think he'd never see her sweet face again, never hold her close. Most of all he'd miss her directness, the way she could cut to the heart of a problem in a few brief words. No. He mustn't remember how good it felt to be with her. She was safer without him, so he had to send her away.

'Thank you for coming to say goodbye. I don't suppose I'll see you before you go but I'm sure you'll do well.' After all they had been through together, it was cold, almost brutal. Evie flinched as though he had struck her. It took all his willpower not to take her in his arms and beg her forgiveness. But it was better this way.

She stood up. 'Very well. Don't listen. Push everyone away and go through life blaming yourself. But if you ask me, your guilt is just an excuse to avoid getting close to anyone. Because if you stopped to think, you'd see no one else believes you're at fault.'

'I'd ask the old members of my squadron, but they're dead or too injured to fly again.'

'Not all of them. Did any of the pilots who survived ask to be transferred? Of course not. Don't you think they would if they'd lost trust in you?' She shook her head as though struggling to comprehend. 'You're just too scared to face the pain of losing anyone else you love, so you're grasping at any excuse to push people away. I —' Her voice cracked, and she pressed her quivering lips into a tight line.

For a moment, Alex was unable to frame a coherent reply. How dare she accuse him of being scared? 'I'm not the one who's leaving. I couldnae believe it when I heard you'd applied for officer training. When were you planning on telling me? I thought I meant something to you. But no, you planned this without once considering my feelings.'

Where had that come from? He wished he could take back the words as soon as they were out of his mouth, but it was too late. She gazed at him with wounded eyes, then spun round and fled down the path. Alex considered calling her back, but what was the point? He had achieved what he had meant to do: sent her away, where she would be safe from the doom that always struck those who got too close to him. She would soon realise she was better off without him and find another man.

Suddenly he didn't want to sit up here and watch the airfield from a distance. If he did, he would be

wondering where Evie was, if she was one of the tiny dots he could see moving around the station. He wanted to push all thought of her from his mind for a few hours. If only he'd had the sense to get the train up to London the moment he'd been told he had the day off, spend the day in a place that didn't hold memories of Evie in every corner.

But trying to forget about Evie only made him dwell upon the incident in France. Maybe it was the constant roar of Merlin engines down on the station, but he couldn't get the images out of his head: the helplessness of seeing one after another of his pilots shot out of the sky. It was easy for Evie to say it wasn't his fault; she hadn't been there, hadn't heard the screams over the R/T of a man trapped in his burning fuselage. But he heard them night after night in his dreams, knew he would hear them until his dying day. How dare she accuse him of using his guilt as an excuse? She might be right about most things, but she was wrong about this.

He stomped down the path, scarcely registering where his feet were carrying him. He wasn't pushing her away. She was the one being posted elsewhere, at her request, no less. What did that say about her feelings for him?

He tried to ignore the stab through the heart that came with the prospect of never seeing her again.

Anyway, she would be better off without him. What was the likelihood of him surviving the war in one piece? He didn't want to tie her to him and end up being a burden or a grief to her.

He hesitated in his stride. He could almost see her expression, hear her say, 'Isn't that my choice to make?' Evie was an intelligent girl and knew her

own mind.

Then he shook his head and walked on. Whatever she might think, he was guilty and didn't want to taint her by association. He should concentrate on doing his job to the best of his ability. See his remaining pilots safely through the war.

Again, Evie's face came into his mind, a glint of triumph in her eyes. So, he believed himself capable of safely guiding his men now? What had changed since France? What made him think he was capable of being a good squadron leader now?

Something Evie had said had barely registered at the time, but now her words rang as sharp and clear as the scramble bell: *did any of the pilots who survived ask to be transferred?* No. They had shown unwavering support.

He had dwelt so much on the pilots killed or wounded, he hadn't considered those, like him, who had been relatively unscathed. If they had lost faith in him, they could have requested a transfer to another squadron, but all had returned to Brimstone. He was ashamed to admit he'd been so wrapped up in the business of leading a squadron during the endless battles of the summer and helping the Czech pilots settle in, he'd left the old hands to their own devices. It was only after the loss of Flight Lieutenant Harper that he'd spent any time with them, drinking to Harper's honour in the pub that night. Even so, they'd been nothing but loyal. They didn't blame him for their losses, then or now.

Could it be that Evie was right? He leaned against a stout tree limb as reality sank in. If she was, maybe she was also right about him pushing her away.

Evie was leaving, taking the better part of his heart,

357

and he hadn't even said goodbye.

But what could he do? Should he do anything, or should he simply let Evie go? Did he want to let her go?

He didn't have any good answers; every atom of his being seemed to be waging a war between protecting Evie and leaving her free to make her own choice. Because that was the true battle. Did he love her enough to send her away with his blessing, trusting that she would always come back to him? He might still lose her, but if he tried to hem her in, he would lose her for sure.

27

'Anyone would think you were on your way to a library job instead of about to become an officer.' Jess wrinkled her nose as she sorted through the pile of books Evie was trying to cram into her kit bag. 'Do you really need all these maths books?'

Evie snatched her log tables from Jess's hands. 'Yes.' Now, more than ever, she was determined to continue her studies in the hope of getting a place at Oxford after the war. She bit her lip as she was struck by a cold, hollow feeling in the pit of her stomach. In the fortnight since she'd said goodbye to Alex, her dreams of Oxford had lost their allure.

She crammed the log tables into the bag. 'And I might not become an officer. I might fail the course.'

'Likely story,' Jess scoffed.

'You'll pass with flying colours,' May assured her from her perch on her bed.

Evie managed a weak smile. 'I hope you're right.' She made a conscious effort to straighten her shoulders. May *was* right. She was good enough. Ellerby had recommended her for this promotion, and she was hard to please. This was what she wanted: another step towards being a successful officer and, hopefully, the means to persuade the admissions officers at Oxford that she deserved a scholarship when she left the WAAF.

'I know what's got you looking like a wet weekend,' Jess said with a scowl. 'It's that bloody Kincaith, isn't it? Well, you're worth twenty of him, so I say forget him.'

Evie glanced sideways at Jess. It was on the tip of her tongue to retort that Jess should sort out her feelings for Milan before doling out advice about her love life, but she refrained. Jess's attitude to men was a mystery to her and she wasn't going to stir up trouble just when she was about to leave. It was a shame, because she thought Milan was good for Jess: secure enough not to get jealous of the interest other men took in her and appreciative of her bold personality when other, weaker men might strive to tame her. But it wasn't up to Evie to interfere. She could only hope Jess would come to see Milan's merits for herself.

'I've already put him out of my mind,' she replied, wishing it were true. But the rigours of her Filterer Officer's course would surely help drive away all thoughts of Alex.

May bounded to her feet. 'I think it's time for our presents,' she said.

Jess snapped her fingers. 'Yes! Wait here.' She leapt to her feet and darted out of the room, reappearing a few moments later bearing a small package wrapped in brown paper. She handed it to Evie. 'Open it!'

Evie took it. 'I wasn't expecting —'

'I know, but I wanted to. Come on, open it!'

Evie unwrapped the parcel to reveal a beautiful compact case, with an enamelled 'E' in deep turquoise upon the lid. 'Oh, it's lovely. Thank you.' She wasn't normally given to shows of affection, but she kissed Jess on the cheek, overwhelmed with love for her friends.

'And I got you this.' May handed her a small oblong box.

360

Tears sprang into Evie's eyes when she pulled off the lid to reveal a fountain pen. May must have spent a significant part of her savings to buy her this. For a moment she was too choked to speak.

'It's so you can write to us.' May looked suddenly hesitant. 'You will write, won't you?'

Evie hugged May, standing on tiptoe to reach May's shoulders. 'Of course I will.' She had to pull away from May to wipe her eyes before she dripped tears on May's shoulder. 'Thank you for the pen. It's perfect.' She gave both her friends a watery smile. 'I'm going to miss you so much. I wish you could come with me.'

'We'll see you again,' Jess said with a confidence Evie wished she felt. 'Ellerby's been at us both to apply for officer training so who knows? Maybe we'll end up being posted close to each other again.'

'Oh, you must. You'll both make wonderful officers.' Evie gave a wistful glance around the nursery and the schoolroom that could be seen through the open door. 'Although I doubt we'll ever find ourselves billeted in a place as good as this again.'

May gave a sad smile. 'It has been marvellous, hasn't it? It won't be the same without you.'

'You mean it won't be the same without Peter.' Evie hadn't missed how May had become more withdrawn after Peter had left, but she didn't have any words of comfort. She knew all too well how it felt knowing the man she loved was in danger, waiting anxiously for news that Alex had returned safe from his last sortie of the day. 'You need to occupy your mind.'

May flushed. 'I try, but it's all too easy to daydream while I'm driving.'

'Then you'll have to take the plunge and go for

officer training. That will keep you busy.'

'Perhaps.'

Evie was on the point of resuming the argument she'd had with May for the last fortnight when there came a knock on the open door. She glanced up to see a shy WAAF hovering, one hand on the door-knob. She was regarding the three girls with the same awe many of the newer WAAFs had started to display ever since news of their exploits of a fortnight ago had rippled across the base. 'Please, miss.'

'Call me Evie,' she said, biting back a laugh. 'I'm just a plain aircraftwoman, the same as you.'

The girl's eyes widened. 'Thank you, m — ah . . . Evie. There's an officer come to see you. In the Rose Room.'

Evie glanced at Jess and May once the girl had scurried away. 'Probably Ellerby, come to give me some last-minute instructions.' The girls laughed. Ellerby had taken Evie aside several times, giving advice on how to comport herself at the course. She evidently believed Evie's performance would directly reflect on her.

However, when she strode into the Rose Room a few moments later, it wasn't Ellerby sitting in a comfy armchair, but Alex.

Evie exhaled sharply, feeling as though she'd just received a blow to the stomach. 'Alex. W-what are you doing here?'

Alex had risen as soon as he saw her. Now he gazed at her, looking uncharacteristically nervous. He held a parcel and he tugged at the string bound around it, pulling the knot so tight she hoped he wouldn't need to undo it in a hurry.

'I . . .' With an awkward movement, he thrust the

362

parcel into her hands. 'I got you this.'

She looked at it blankly.

Alex winced, screwing up his eyes, and muttered something under his breath she couldn't quite catch. It sounded like, '*Idiot.*'

He recovered himself. 'I'm doing this all wrong,' he said in a more normal voice. 'I got you a present to wish you well on your course, and . . .' He hesitated and looked down at his feet briefly. Then he looked at her square in the eyes and drew a breath. 'And apologise. I've done a lot of thinking in the last fortnight, and realised I've been a total fool. You were right. I was using my fear as an excuse to push you away.' A ghost of a smile tugged at the corner of his mouth. 'And I should have known you are always right.'

Evie felt a fluttering in her chest, and in a voice that sounded oddly breathless said, 'Why did you wait a whole fortnight?'

'Because I wanted to be prepared.' He gestured at the parcel. 'Open it.'

For the third time in an hour, she found herself opening a parcel. The contents were very different from Jess and May's presents, though. Inside were two items. One was a slim, black leather case, about the same size as a paperback book, with the initials 'EB' embossed in gold in one corner. A gold zip ran along three of the edges. The other item was a long, slender oblong box made from ebony, polished to a glossy sheen. It, too, had her initials engraved. 'What are they?'

'Open them and see.'

She pulled the lid off the ebony box first. Inside was a slide rule. Evie pressed her fingers to her lips to stop them quivering.

363

Alex was watching her, frowning. 'Is it not the right kind? I explained to the man in the shop it was for degree-level mathematics but . . .' He hesitated. 'I'm no good at this. Everyone says women prefer jewellery, but —'

Evie looked up at him through a haze of tears. 'It's perfect.' She could barely manage more than a hoarse whisper through her lips that had become suddenly dry. 'I'd rather have this than all the jewels in Buckingham Palace.' It meant so much to know Alex encouraged her aspiration to study maths. Even though they were no longer courting, she would treasure the memory of their time together. She did her best to repress the wave of misery at the thought she might not see him again.

Alex gave a relieved smile. 'You haven't opened the other one yet.'

She unzipped the case and saw a beautiful geometry set containing compasses, dividers, ruler, protractor and set squares.

'You'll find it useful on your course,' Alex told her.

'I don't know what to say. Thank you.' For a wild moment she'd thought it might be a piece of jewellery, that Alex was asking to court her again. Now she hated herself for the stab of disappointment she felt.

Alex picked up one of the propelling pencils that was part of the set and twirled it between his fingers. 'I hope you'll think of me when you use them,' he murmured. 'I don't know if you can forgive me, but . . .' He paused, and Evie's heart hammered against her ribs.

'Yes,' Evie whispered. 'I forgive you. If you'll forgive me for letting you go without a fight.'

Alex fumbled the pencil and dropped it on the

rug. It rolled beneath the sofa; Evie knew it would be a nightmare to retrieve, but she didn't care. All she cared about was that Alex's gaze was fixed on her face, his eyes blazing. 'Evie, I never blamed you. Do you mean . . .' He swallowed and there was another agonising pause, but Evie couldn't form the words that were in her heart. Alex took a deep breath. 'I still love you. I've never stopped loving you. I just stopped listening to my heart and listened to my fears instead.'

Evie's throat swelled, stemming the words she ached to utter. All she could do was return his gaze, every inch of her aching to be in his arms, but unable to quite believe Alex wanted her.

'As I said, I've done a lot of thinking these past days,' Alex said. 'I realised I'd lost so many loved ones when I was young: my parents; my grandmother; even my friends, when my paternal grandparents took me away from my grandmother's home. I'd grown to expect loss. You were right when you said I was using my guilt as an excuse to push people away. I didn't see what I was doing, but now I see I couldn't bear the pain of losing the one I loved above all — you. So I tried to send you away before I lost you like all the others.'

He paused. The corner of his mouth twisted in a wry smile, sending delightful shivers down Evie's spine as she imagined pressing her lips to his. 'How come you understood me so much better than I understood myself? Are you sure you shouldn't read psychology instead of maths?'

It was a feeble joke, but enough to burst the bubble of pressure building up in her throat. She gave a breathy laugh and said, 'I'll save it for my PhD.'

Alex's eyes remained grave. 'I don't want to tie you

down to any promises. Not when we've no idea how long we're going to be apart.'

Evie couldn't stop herself from smiling, a smile so wide her cheeks ached. 'I still love you, Alex. I'll wait for you, however long.'

Alex relieved her of the gifts and flung them on the sofa then took Evie's hands in his. Evie squeezed his hands back, joy surging through her veins. 'Then, Evie Bishop, we don't know what the war holds for us, but if I come through the war in one piece, will you consent to be my wife?' He smiled into her eyes, making her stomach swoop. 'I think Oxford would make the perfect home. Maybe I should study for a degree, too.'

'Too? You mean you'd support me through a degree?'

'I want you to follow your heart's desire. The war has already put an end to too many dreams. If we survive, I'll do all in my power to make your dreams come true.'

'Oh, Alex.' Evie flung her arms around him. She had the answer to Cornelia's question. She had found the man who would encourage her to become the best version of herself. 'Yes. I will marry you. The moment we're both released from duty and not a day later.'

Then Alex kissed her. As she clung to him, relishing the feel of his strong arms around her, she prayed he would be kept safe through whatever the war might throw at them.

By the time they broke the kiss, her hair was thoroughly mussed, and her uniform needed straightening. Alex smiled at her with a shade of pain in his expression. 'Now go and dazzle everyone at Bawdsey the same way you dazzled us all here. Do us proud.'

28

'There's the train!' May pointed at the puff of steam that billowed some way up the track. Both May and Jess had mysteriously found themselves off duty all morning — Evie suspected Jean Ellerby's intervention — which meant they'd been able to accompany Evie to the station to wave her off on her next big adventure.

Evie swallowed and picked up her kit bag and gas mask, blinking back the tears as she looked at her two friends and seeing tears shimmer in their eyes too. She gave each of them an awkward hug. 'I don't know what I'll do without the two of you. Promise you'll write often.'

'So often we'll both be cautioned for wasting paper,' Jess said. For once she seemed uncaring that the tears trickling down her cheeks were smudging her otherwise immaculate make-up. 'Just don't you go forgetting us.'

'Never. You're the best friends a girl could hope for. Anyway, I'm determined that we'll all end up posted close together again, once you've both come to your senses and applied for officer training yourselves. Nothing can keep us apart for long. Not even the war.'

May gave her one last hug. 'You're right. We're WAAF girls through and through. We'll always find a way.'

Their last frantic goodbyes were drowned by the

train screeching to a standstill. Hefting her bags, she scrambled into a carriage. As the train rolled out of the station, Evie leaned out of the window and waved and waved until her friends disappeared into the haze of smoke. The train puffed out into open fields, and Evie looked at the road that wound out of the small town and led back to Amberton. She swallowed against the lump that rose in her throat. She felt she had come of age at Amberton. She'd proved she could do a demanding job, had faced difficulty and danger and won through. Most importantly she had found love and friendship. Whatever happened in the next stage of her career as a WAAF, she doubted anything could compare to her time here. She breathed a soft but heartfelt prayer for protection over May, Jess and Alex.

Just as she was about to sink into her seat, movement in the sky caught her eye. Three Hurricanes were flying in a V formation, heading for Amberton. It had just crossed her mind that one of them might be Alex when the lead machine broke formation and swooped low over the train. It performed a barrel roll before zooming back towards Amberton. Evie sat down, unable to hold back a broad smile. It had been Alex, she was sure. Letting her know he'd returned safely yet again. It gave her hope for the future, and she hugged that hope to her. Yes, she had hope for the future, but for now she was happy with the WAAF. She couldn't wait to see what adventures lay ahead.

We do hope that you have enjoyed
reading this large print book.

Did you know that all of our titles
are available for purchase?

We publish a wide range of high
quality large print books including:
Romances, Mysteries, Classics
General Fiction
Non Fiction and Westerns

Special interest titles available in
large print are:
The Little Oxford Dictionary
Music Book, Song Book
Hymn Book, Service Book

Also available from us courtesy of
Oxford University Press:
Young Readers' Dictionary
(large print edition)
Young Readers' Thesaurus
(large print edition)

For further information or a free
brochure, please contact us at:
Ulverscroft Large Print Books Ltd.,
The Green, Bradgate Road, Anstey,
Leicester, LE7 7FU, England.
Tel: (00 44) 0116 236 4325
Fax: (00 44) 0116 234 0205

THE DOVER CAFÉ UNDER FIRE

Ginny Bell

1940. As firebombs fall on Dover, Edie Castle's life is thrown into turmoil when the garage where she lives and works as a mechanic is damaged, and her beloved boss Mr Pearson is arrested.

With no job and nowhere else to go, Edie returns to Castle's Café and her formidable mother Nellie. Living with her parent is never easy, but tensions reach boiling point when an old friend of Nellie's arrives looking for a place to stay.

Desperate to clear her boss's name, but struggling with demons of her own, Edie turns to Mr Pearson's nephew Bill for help. But a shocking tragedy brings long-buried memories to the surface, and as the café is engulfed in scandal, Edie realises that she can't trust anyone — even her own mother . . .